D1429551

This book should b ... ned
Lanc... ty

.20

THE LITTLE COFFEE SHOP
OF KABUL

THE LITTLE COFFEE SHOP OF KABUL

Deborah Rodriguez

WINDSOR
PARAGON

First published 2012
as ebook by Sphere
This Large Print edition published 2013
by AudioGO Ltd
by arrangement with
Little, Brown Book Group

Hardcover   ISBN: 978 1 4713 4970 6
Softcover   ISBN: 978 1 4713 4971 3

British Library Cataloguing in Publication Data available

11824332

Printed and bound in Great Britain by
TJ International Ltd

This book is dedicated with love to the three most important people in my life. My mother, Loie Turner, is a woman who encompasses grace, beauty, and compassion. I owe you so much. Even when we are far apart in miles, you are always close to my heart. And to my sons, Noah and Zachary Lentz, whose journeys are just beginning. Our road was not always a smooth one, but I know it has made us stronger. I hope you will take wisdom from Eleanor Roosevelt, who told us that we must do the things we think we cannot do. You have both become amazing men. I am a very lucky mom.

Women are like tea bags; you never know how strong they are until they're put in hot water.
—ELEANOR ROOSEVELT

CHAPTER ONE

It was a vibrant blue-skied Afghan morning, the kind that made Yazmina stop to loosen her scarf and tilt her face to the sun. She and her younger sister, Layla, were returning from the well, their calloused feet accustomed to repeated treks on the ancient dirt. The tiny cowrie shells that decorated Yazmina's long black dress clacked with every step. She looked toward the snow-capped peaks to the north and prayed that this winter, *Inshallah,* God willing, would not be as bad as the last. It was so cold, so unforgiving, killing the goats, freezing the earth, destroying any chance of a good wheat crop. Another winter like that would surely make the threat of starvation real.

Her secret, the one she carried in her belly, the one she could hide for only another month or two, flooded her with nausea. She tripped on a rock, her body not as sure and strong as it had been working only for one. She almost spilled the water from the *kuza,* the clay pot that she carried on her shoulder.

'Yazmina, be careful! You're walking like a donkey with three legs,' Layla said, even as she struggled with her own *kuza.* It was almost bigger than she was. Layla had been in high spirits all morning. She was too young to be covered in a *chaderi* like the one Yazmina was wearing, and her dark hair shone in the sunlight.

When they arrived at their uncle's compound, they carefully placed the *kuza* in the cooking room and headed back to the main house. An unfamiliar black SUV with tinted windows was parked outside,

1

and Layla ran toward it, letting out a squeal of delight.

'Look, Yazmina! Look at the *landawar*!' Layla called. 'It's bigger than our house!'

But Yazmina knew that since no one in Nuristan could afford a car like this, it must've come from the city, and nothing good ever came from the city. A car like this brought a warlord or a drug lord. When cars like this had arrived before, girls had gone missing.

Yazmina tried to laugh with Layla, but her heart sank. Heavy beads of perspiration formed on her brow and nausea overcame her again, though this time it had more to do with her fears than with the baby growing inside her. She stood by the door of the main salon where her uncle was talking to an older man with brown teeth wearing a tan-colored *shalwaar kameez*. Her uncle looked panicked. He pulled a small cloth purse of money from his pocket and offered it to the man.

'This is baksheesh,' money fit for a beggar, the man said with a sneer, and struck her uncle's hand, making the purse drop to the floor.

She couldn't hear what else was being said, but she could hear her own heartbeat and over it she imagined her uncle pleading for mercy. She leaned heavily against the wall, letting out the breath she'd been holding. She couldn't blame him for what he'd done. After last year's harsh winter, he could barely afford to feed them all. But when Yazmina's husband was killed three months before, the one she'd known since she was a child and married when she was fifteen, she and Layla had nowhere else to go. It was tradition that forced her uncle to take them in and borrow money from these thieves.

2

She knew what was coming. He would not be able to protect her since he could not repay his debt.

'Take my goats!' her uncle cried. 'Take my house,' he begged as he dropped to his knees. 'But do not take Yazmina. It is as if I am selling her. Would you sell your eyes? Would you sell your heart?' He stopped for a moment to catch his breath, to think. 'Besides,' he continued, looking up into the cold eyes of the man looming over him, 'my goats are worth more in the market than she is. She has already been married.'

'Yes, she is not a girl anymore,' the man answered. 'What I should take is your little one.' He turned to Layla, who was now by Yazmina's side, his black eyes boring a hole through her.

Yazmina's uncle pleaded with him. 'No, Haji,' he said, using the common name for such men. 'I beg you. She is too young yet. She is still a child.'

Yazmina felt her sister take her hand and hold it tightly.

'If I cannot get the money you owe me from this one, I'll be back for the little one after the snows have melted. Now come,' he commanded Yazmina.

Her uncle stood, and as he looked from the man to Yazmina, his strong jaw worked hard to keep his mouth closed against the curses he was struggling not to utter. He brushed the dust from his knees and escorted her to the car. He told her not to worry, but his face revealed what Yazmina already knew in her heart. She would be driven from her home in Nuristan, southwest on rubble-lined, pockmarked roads, to Kabul, and sold to the highest bidder, to be his third, perhaps even fourth wife, or worse, a slave, or worse yet—she would be forced to be a prostitute.

3

A young man, unusually tall for an Afghan, with a black beard and deep-set eyes, was at the car's heavy back door, holding it open for Yazmina. Another was sitting in the driver's seat.

Yazmina wanted to fight, to kick and scream and run, but she knew that to resist meant they'd take Layla. So she asked, 'May I get my things? Can I bring a change of clothes?'

'Get in the car!' the man yelled at her, pushing her shoulder roughly.

She started to climb in, then turned to her uncle and hugged him. He whispered in her ear the poem that her own mother had recited to Yazmina when she was only a baby:

The moon is made round by the right hand of God.
The moon is made crescent by his left.
But it is God's heart that
Makes my love for you forever.

She recited the last line along with him with much difficulty, choked, as she was, by the fullness in her throat. Then Yazmina gave Layla three kisses, each saltier than the last from the tears on her cheeks. 'You'll have a blessed life, little one. Now show me that smile of yours, for that'll be my parting gift,' she said. But the younger girl had started to cry herself, afraid she'd never see Yazmina again, knowing she could be next. From her pocket she pulled her prayer beads and put them into Yazmina's hand, clasping it tightly with her two little hands, not wanting to ever let go.

'Enough good-byes,' said the man with the brown teeth. 'Get in the car.'

Yazmina quickly put the beads into her own

4

pocket, gathered her long dress, and sat inside, pulling her legs in after her.

Layla ran away, back to the cooking room. 'Wait, wait for me!' she called. Yazmina knew she was getting water to throw at the car, a tradition to ensure that the person leaving would return one day. But Yazmina knew she would never be back, so she squared her shoulders, forced her eyes straight ahead, and sat tall as the old man got into the front seat with the driver and the young one got in next to her and closed the door. The SUV pulled away in a cloud of dust.

By the time Layla got back with the water to throw at the car, it was already gone, a black speck on the road leading far down the hill.

*   *   *

The coffee shop was jammed with regulars— misfits, missionaries and mercenaries, Afghans and foreigners—and Sunny, as usual, was at the counter. She surveyed her domain, pleased with the business, the buzz, the *life* that pulsated in the room. This was her very own place, here, in the middle of a war zone, in one of the most dangerous locations on earth. After a lifetime of hard luck and bad choices, finally, at the age of thirty-eight, she'd found a home. Sunny was the center of the café, and she planned never to leave.

Kabul was the perfect place for her. Since nothing here was on solid ground, anything was possible, and anything could happen. Five men had just walked in, dressed in black, Foster Grants hiding their eyes, machine guns slung over their shoulders, sidearms hanging from their waists. She

5

hadn't seen such beautiful men in a long, long time. In another country they'd mean trouble. But here, she knew they were five tall lattes and a plate of biscotti.

'Hey guys,' she said with the slight Southern lilt that she couldn't shake loose after all these years. 'If you want a menu, you need to give me your guns, like the sign says.' She nodded toward the door where a placard read: PLEASE CHECK YOUR WEAPONS AT THE DOOR.

With a thick Eastern European accent, one of the men started to argue, and all eyes in the café turned toward them. Sunny flashed her biggest smile and assured him their guns would be safe. 'And besides,' she said, 'with guns, no menu. You want to eat? You give them up.'

They reluctantly handed their firearms to Sunny, who then handed them to her barista and right-hand man, Bashir Hadi, who put them in the back room, where weapons were stored along with mops and brooms. They took off their leather jackets and scarves and Sunny hung them in the front closet.

She met Bashir Hadi back at the counter. 'I have some errands. I'll be back as soon as I can,' she said, taking off her apron.

'I'll go with you,' he said, as he always did.

'I'm fine,' she replied, in their daily tradition. She knew what was coming next.

'Make sure that you lock your doors. Keep your windows up. Promise me you will not drive with the top down, for goodness' sake! Avoid the roadblocks. Don't stop unless you have to. Don't take the side roads, or the alleys.'

'I've already asked Ahmet to get the car from the

6

alley and bring it around to the front.'

'And I know I don't have to remind you—'

'But you will.' Sunny smiled.

'You should not be driving and you should not be alone. Call me when you get there.'

'I always do.' She reflexively clasped the cellphone that hung from her neck on a woven red cord. She'd lost too many setting them down on the counter.

Today Sunny had a mission to bring flowers to the newly elected head of the Women's Ministry. Though they'd met before at the café, a formal visit would secure an important relationship, necessary for a woman in Kabul running a business. Sunny put on a coat and took a chador from a hook behind the counter and covered her long, wavy brown hair, carefully wrapping the silky fabric around her neck and shoulders, pretending it was a luxurious, chic stole that she wore out of choice.

'*Salaam alaikum,*' she said to Ahmet, the café's *chokidor,* its guard, as she passed through the front door, which he held open for her. 'Keep an eye on that bunch inside, okay?'

'*Wa alaikum as-salaam,*' Ahmet replied. He was small, like most Afghan men; the machine gun he carried over his shoulder probably outweighed him, making him look like a toy soldier, especially with his hair slicked back like a helmet on his head.

Sunny smiled, understanding now where the gel she kept in the café's bathroom had gone. She rattled off in Dari the usual niceties: How are you, Ahmet? And how is your sister in Germany? And every other living relative? Then she inquired about their states of health. In Kabul, it would be rude to do otherwise. Ahmet was a serious traditionalist,

7

and following the rules—both unspoken and in the Koran—was important to him. He had earned her respect. He'd kept her and her customers safe more times than she could count.

He asked her the same questions and a few minutes later she was free to leave. She looked up and down the pedestrian-filled street and in front of every other business was a man dressed just like Ahmet, with dark glasses, black shirt, and black pants. Some had even bigger guns, bigger knives. She laughed to herself. These *chokidor* are competing with one another, she thought, like the schoolgirls back home with their cellphones, handbags, and jewelry. The difference was that in Kabul the accessories were Jacky clubs, guns, and daggers.

Sunny navigated the narrow, tumultuous city streets in her big brown diesel-powered Mercedes with more confidence than she ever had driving her trusty little Toyota in her hometown of Jonesboro, Arkansas. Passing the carts of figs and fruits, goat heads, fat-tailed sheep, and cardamom, and the stalls selling grain, apples, watermelon, and honeydew from the north, or colorful, hand-woven cloths from India and Pakistan, Sunny noticed clusters of men with heads bent together in discussion, and other men walking proudly, followed by women in sky blue burqas. The disparity between men's and women's lives here was something she'd never get used to. She rolled down her window to hear the hollering of children running after her car, one shouting, 'Hey, mister, need a bodyguard?' The smells of dung and sweat and spices and diesel exhaust fumes merged into a heady mix that reminded Sunny why she loved

Kabul and why she had chosen to stay.

She parked near Chicken Street. Here stall after stall of Afghan souvenirs—handmade carpets, woven pashmina, turbans, clothing, jewelry, boxes, and belts of the extraordinary native blue lapis, and the hand-carved dark wood furniture from Nuristan that she loved—extended two full blocks. Today it was unusually quiet. The shop owners raised their heads and smiled eagerly as Sunny walked by, hoping for a sale. She was one of the few foreigners not afraid to shop there since business had been beaten down by recent suicide bombings. Everyone in Kabul was affected by the blasts, including Sunny. But shopping made her feel that her life had some normalcy. She could choose, barter, and trade coins for products, as if she were a regular person and Kabul a regular place.

At the juncture of Chicken and Flower streets, East met West, with imports of cameras and electronics from Pakistan and China, juices (most had expired in 1989) from Uzbekistan, pirated videos, postcards, potato chips, Italian bottled water, cheese from Austria. Here, too, was Behzad, the one and only English-language bookstore in the country, where she and her friends bought books that they discussed as if experts on *Oprah,* and the store next door where they got their DVDs.

On Flower Street itself, her breath caught in her throat. Amid the rubble and pale beige stone, and sitting next to an open sewer, there were the roses. In pink and peach, in red and white and yellow, roses everywhere, in every stall in every shop, the pride of Kabul, glorious and life affirming. Hope grew in Sunny with each bucket of flowers she passed. Some buckets held cheap plastic flowers from Taiwan that the Afghans used to brighten their homes, as if the real roses weren't good enough simply because they were Afghan. Sunny picked two bunches of fresh pale peach roses and carried them away nestled in the crook of her arm.

She took a step in the direction of her car, back the way she'd come. But she stopped. She felt the brisk air, with its hints of winter, and could see the hospital down the road ahead. The Women's Ministry was adjacent to it. But she could hear Bashir Hadi's warnings about the dangers of a woman walking alone in Kabul. Three years ago, it was safe to walk, but today, as the Taliban and fundamentalist thinking were finding ground again in Kabul, it was not. She was courting kidnappers, Bashir Hadi had told her again and again, and was at risk of being shot. Take the car, he'd told her, and if she had to walk, she must keep her head down, not speak unless spoken to, never take the same route twice, do this and that and never this and always that, and it made her sick. She respected the ways of this country—she knew, for example, to always cover her head and her arms—but she also respected herself, and sometimes, she simply had to walk.

And so she did. She arrived at the ministry safely, and with her roses in hand. The gray-walled, somber building reminded her of the hospital where her mother had died, except for the layer of earthen dust that covered everything in Kabul. When she reached the minister's waiting room, she found a young woman shrouded in a dark blue veil sitting behind a dilapidated metal desk. The minute she saw Sunny, she clicked off her computer screen. Sunny knew from the look in her eyes that

10

she'd been on the Internet, probably chatting with someone, the only way a boy and girl could talk to each other freely in Kabul. The woman told her to sit, and from the cheap velour chair Sunny could easily see into the minister's office, a lavish space covered in deep red rugs and lined with couches. Standing in the center of the room, a young woman wearing the clothes of her native tribe pleaded with what looked to be an assistant of the minister, while the minister herself sat at her desk and talked on the phone. Sunny couldn't help but listen. Though her Dari was halting at best, she understood enough to pick up the gist of the girl's story.

*   *   *

Yazmina had stared straight ahead, afraid to fall asleep on the long drive, afraid to look out the car's window at the land passing by, afraid of what the man next to her might do even before she arrived in Kabul. She'd lost track of time. Had it been two days? Or three? Her fate was not her own. First her parents, murdered by the Taliban years before. Then her husband, killed three months ago by a land mine while walking with his goats in the field. Now what would happen when her 'owner' found out about the life inside her? She knew the answer: He would beat her, or worse. It would be impossible to pretend that her new husband was the father. Her stomach was already round; she could rely only so long on the heavy drape of her dress to save her from showing.

The man next to her suddenly moved, making her jump. He laughed and put his arm around her. She knew what he was thinking: She was no longer

11

a girl and he could take her sexually without her new owner ever finding out. She pulled away, her heart pounding against her chest, and realized then that they must've entered the outskirts of Kabul. The wall along the road was mottled with bullet holes, and there were posters for Coca-Cola and for campaigns for Parliament. The man put his hand on her leg. She screamed, and he put his other hand over her mouth. She continued to look away and noticed the blue of the sky as he moved a hand to her breast then down her belly toward her legs. He stopped.

'What is this?' he yelled. 'What have you done, you bitch whore?' His face was so close that Yazmina could feel his hot breath.

Yazmina saw the driver's eyes on her in the rearview mirror.

'What is it?' he barked.

'This mother of a whore is pregnant,' the younger man said with disgust, not taking his eyes from Yazmina. He spit at her, and then slapped her hard across her face.

Yazmina looked down, tears streaming, her face swelling, her nose bleeding. She put a protective hand across her belly.

The car stopped short, sending dirt and dust past the windows.

'She is worth nothing,' the old man said. 'Get rid of her.'

The man next to Yazmina pulled a knife from the sheath on his belt, but the old man said, 'No, no blood in the car. Get her out.' He turned to Yazmina. 'You stupid bitch. I should cut your uncle's throat for stealing from me. And then take your little sister. Now that tight little virgin would be worth something.'

Yazmina struggled to open her door to get away, but she felt a heavy punch in her back that sent her sprawling to the ground. She could taste the blood in her mouth, feel the dirt sting her eyes. She felt the kick in her side, something hard and heavy hitting her head, her face pushed into the ground, then she heard the car speed away as everything went black.

*　　　*　　　*

The woman's name was Yazmina, she told the minister's assistant, and she was from Nuristan, which Sunny knew was an area in the north that bordered the western edge of Pakistan. It was said that the people there were among the most beautiful in all Afghanistan and direct descendants of Alexander the Great. Jack had worked up there for a time, and Sunny remembered him telling her that the area was originally called Kafiristan—*kafir* meaning 'unbeliever' or 'infidel,' and *stan* meaning 'land of.' A hundred years ago the people were forced by the Muslims to convert to Islam, and the name of the area was changed to Nuristan, the land of light. In her coffeehouse, Sunny had more than once heard one Afghan insulting another by calling him a *kafir*.

She listened to Yazmina explaining how an old beggar woman had helped her up and walked with her from the far edges of Kabul to the police station. They struggled with what to do with the young woman whose blood was dripping down her face, staining her *chaderi*. Should they take her to the hospital and risk being blamed for her

13

condition? She was too ashamed to tell them what had happened, and they were, in turn, uncomfortable with her tears, embarrassed. Matters of women were handled within the family, not out on a busy street. So they dropped her off at the Women's Ministry, where someone would attend to her.

Her eyes ran with grateful tears as the assistant glanced over her shoulder to the minister, who seemed to be winding up her phone call, and whispered to Yazmina that she could sleep in the old Kabul Beauty School, now a dorm, until they were able to find a family to take her in, perhaps as a cleaning lady.

Another woman might've responded by putting her hand on her chest, or clasping her hands together, in both worry and gratitude. But this young woman responded reflexively, impulsively, Sunny thought, and gave herself away. She put an open hand on her belly, and Sunny understood what she was protecting there: She was pregnant. So that was why she'd been thrown out of the car. She'd omitted this detail when she told her story, and if the minister's assistant had figured it out, she didn't let on.

The minister hung up the phone and rose from her chair, walked around her desk, and said, 'Only one or two nights, Alayah. Not until she finds a family. There are rules. We are not running a hotel for runaways.'

'But,' Alayah said, 'she has nowhere to go. You know what will happen.'

Sunny understood what was not being said: that if Yazmina was sent back to her family, it would mean death, and that if she wasn't, she'd probably

14

end up as a beggar or prostitute. And Sunny knew that once her pregnancy had become too obvious to conceal, the baby would surely die, and she would probably be killed, too.

'There are rules,' the minister said haughtily. 'Besides, who knows if what she's saying is the truth.' She looked at Yazmina with disdain, probably thinking what everyone thought of girls like this in Kabul—that it was their fault they'd been kicked out of their homes, that they'd taken a lover or had refused sex with their husbands or had done something else to deserve this treatment. 'Two nights. That's it. And be sure to do the paperwork, Alayah.'

The injured woman thanked the minister, kissing her left cheek, then right, and then left again, three times in the customary fashion.

'Come, I'll show you the way,' said Alayah.

As Yazmina was escorted out, she glanced at Sunny but quickly looked away. In that moment, Sunny was struck by the defiance in her stunning green eyes, that even after all that had befallen her, this woman was still proud.

Sunny paid her respects to the minister as best she could. She would've told the minister where she could shove her bureaucratic attitude, but her mind was on the desperate woman and her haunting eyes.

That night, alone in her bed, Sunny couldn't sleep. She couldn't shake the image of that woman locked in the car with those thugs. She couldn't bear the thought of what would happen to her and her baby once it was born. *Shit,* she thought, the last thing she needed, the last thing the café and her customers would tolerate, was an annoying newborn crying all the time. But early the next

15

morning, she returned to the Women's Ministry to inquire about the young woman. When she found her in the dorms, Sunny offered her a room in her home and work in the coffeehouse. Only then did the young woman raise her eyes from the floor and look straight at Sunny to say in Dari, 'Thank you, may God light your way,' as she placed her open hand on her belly.

CHAPTER TWO

Yazmina woke to find the sun streaming through her small window, washing her yellow walls white. She rose from her *toshak,* the soft mat she used for sleeping at night, and that, with the many pillows Sunny had provided, she used for resting during the day. Outside, a soft veil of snow covered every surface, including the thin, frail branches of the young pomegranate tree, making them glisten in the morning sun. Winter had begun, but in Kabul, which sat near the heavens, nestled in the valley of the tall mountains, the snow was light. She closed her eyes and imagined herself back with Layla come spring, walking to get water from the well, the goats braying on the far hill. Even through the window the sun felt warm, though her worries for her sister sent shivers through her. If Layla was still safe at home and not yet stolen by the men who had taken Yazmina, the snows would already be deep in the mountains, preventing anyone from getting in or out until the spring. The snow, which cut them off from traders every winter, for which they had to prepare long in advance and pray they had enough

16

food, water, and wood to get them and their animals through, now would provide protection. Yazmina prayed for a particularly harsh winter, so that she had time to make a plan to reach Layla once the sun was warm and the banks of the Alingar River overflowed.

She knew by the light that she had slept through the sunrise *adhaan,* the call to prayer, and wondered if the muezzins had lost their voices. For the call came so loudly that every time she heard it, five times a day since she had been in Kabul, she almost jumped out of her skin. She was not attuned to the magnified voices that rose from the highest minaret in every mosque and filled the air. Their song was staggered, not sung as a chorus, voices in the sky competing like the hawks that dipped and swooped over the goat herds back home. She raised her eyebrows and sighed. Perhaps, in time, she would become more comfortable here. Or as comfortable as could be expected given that she was so far from home and had never been in such a foreign place.

She washed her face in the bowl sitting on the cabinet for her clothes. She'd been invited to use the bathroom down the hall, but she couldn't bring herself to do it, not knowing whom she'd run into and when. Indoor plumbing seemed unnecessary anyway. Getting water from the well and using the outdoor toilet was easy enough. But that shower, now that was a thing of beauty!

She took the brush from the cabinet and let loose her single braid, as thick and long as the grasses that stood by the river back home. She shook her head so that her black hair fell loose, then brushed it, slowly and carefully, treating it as if every inch

17

held a story. One stroke and then another, until it was smooth and silky, like the pajamas she slept in. They were different from the ones she wore at home, which she had made for herself. The stitching was too regular, too perfect to have been made by a young woman's hand. Obviously, they were made by machine, like everything in Kabul.

When Sunny had presented the room to her, she had been particularly proud of the full-length mirror that was framed in a shiny dark wood and sat on its own four legs. But Yazmina thought of it as vanity and had turned it away once Sunny had departed. Today, though, she turned it to face her. She put her hands on her stomach, where the life inside was growing with each new day, and looked at herself. She pulled the sleeping gown over her head, removed her undergarments, and there was her body, which she was seeing naked, in full, for the first time in her life. She was slim, her legs long and lean, her right leg still red and scraped from knee to thigh where she had fallen on the pebbled road when she was pushed out of the car. Her arms were slender but muscled from daily chores, still bruised by the rough grip of strong hands. She looked at her breasts, which were larger than usual because of her condition, but nothing like the long, low ones of Halajan, the old busybody who lived next door to the café and had an opinion about everything. Yazmina thought that woman had been sent by God himself to test her patience. No, Yazmina's breasts were still 'as glowing and round as the midnight moon,' as Najam used to tell her. She saddened at the memory of her husband's face, his kisses and his touch. She would never feel such sweetness again.

18

But she was with his baby. She turned to the side to look at her belly and stroked it with her two hands. She took a deep breath as if the air would give her all she and her baby needed to thrive. This will be *my* baby, she thought, my Najam, or if a girl, *Inshallah,* God willing, Najama (for Yazmina was convinced it was a girl, perhaps because it was Najam's wish to have many children—a son or two, of course, but also a daughter who had the same light in her eyes as Yazmina). Not only would the baby be named after her father, but she would be a star lighting up the night sky, as the name meant. Najam's seed was part of her, and she would cherish it and die trying to protect it. Now, with everything that had happened since, only God could be sure the baby lived and would be born healthy.

But she had to be very careful to keep the baby hidden from all eyes until she could hide it no longer. What if Miss Sunny found out? She would be thrown from the coffeehouse onto the streets. If that *chokidor,* Ahmet, suspected that she might be with child, those stern brown eyes of his would grow black with disgust and anger. Even Bashir Hadi, the kindest man she had ever known besides her own Najam, would be shamed by her state. For, according to the rigid, unspoken rules, if no husband was present, then the father's identity was uncertain and anyone was suspect. She had to do whatever was necessary to keep her growing body covered. Maybe by the time the baby came into the world, some miracle would happen to allow her to raise her child without danger to either of them.

The sun had moved a little higher and Yazmina knew that it was time to get to the café. The morning people would be sitting down already, with their newspapers and computers, talking in Dari and English, French and Arabic, about many things. Some words she recognized no matter what the language, like *President Karzai,* and some Bashir Hadi explained to her, like *Christmas,* a holiday that was coming soon. The kitchen would be busy, the café noisy, and she would be needed to set the tables, clear the tables, wash the dishes, and sweep the floors. She got dressed quickly, first putting on thin white pants with lace on the bottom, and then the long skirt and top, all of which Sunny had bought her. The fabric scratched as if it had been woven from the hair of a horse. She slipped her feet into pink plastic shoes that were decorated with blue and yellow flowers, and covered her head and face below the eyes with the lovely lavender *chaderi* that the assistant at the Women's Ministry had given her.

Before she left her room, she went to the low little table next to her *toshak.* It was intricately carved in the dark wood of Nuristan, her home. It had a lovely woven piece of brightly colored cloth on top to protect it. And on top of that sat a little tin box that Sunny had provided for precious things that Yazmina might collect along the way, as if Sunny had known what was in Yazmina's pocket.

She opened the box, took out Layla's prayer beads, carved wood and gold on red string, and she kissed them, then cupped them in her hands and whispered the poem of her mother's, 'But it is God's heart, Layla, that makes my love for you forever.'

CHAPTER THREE

Men dressed in Western clothes—suits with ties and jeans with jackets—as well as *shalwaar kameeze*s and turbans, stood at the café's door waiting, while others leaned against the counter, sipping espresso from colorful demitasse cups. The tables were filled; their dark wooden chairs held men talking, reading the newspaper, and eating eggs with home-fried potatoes. Bashir Hadi was behind the counter making his famous coffees while Halajan flipped pancakes on the grill and Yazmina filled syrup bottles and cleaned tables. The hubbub, the smell of coffee and grease, of bacon and bread, the brightly painted walls, the fabrics draping each table, the warmth and color of the café, all conspired to fill Sunny with longing. What should have provided her the greatest satisfaction—that this place was hers and hers alone, that she had seen to every detail from the walls of ochre, orange, green, and mauve to the shiny copper espresso machine, from her prized generators that kept the electricity flowing even when Kabul's shut down to the *bokhari* that kept the place warm on a cold day like this—also made her miss the one thing she wanted most.

One day soon, when she least expected it, she imagined Tommy would walk right through her door. She'd be standing just the way she stood now, leaning against the counter, yakking with Bashir Hadi, something about the crazy customers or when the meat delivery would arrive, and she'd hear the door open and see Bashir glance over her shoulder and then back at her, and then she'd hear the door slam, and she'd get a feeling. She'd just know. She'd turn around, and there he'd be, with that megawatt smile of his.

She let out a snort, hoping nobody heard it over the fray. Of course he wouldn't walk in anytime soon, because he'd been gone only two months. His assignments took three, sometimes four months, and then he'd come home for as many weeks, at most. Tommy, you fool, she wanted to rail at him when her longing was especially fierce. How could you stay away from me for so long? For what? For adventure? The thrill? The money? They'd come to Kabul together five years before, to find themselves and a life together away from their hick town of Nowheresville, America. There they were white trash. Here they were royalty. But then Tommy found contract work in the south, first doing security for an NGO—a nongovernmental organization—then training the Afghan military, and finally becoming a sniper. He was paid more than he'd ever imagined making in a lifetime, so he would be gone for long stretches at a time. Sometimes he'd call telling her he had a weekend off and they'd both fly to Dubai, which was surprisingly easy and worth every penny, for furtive lovemaking in a fancy, high-rise hotel. But mostly it was long stretches of waiting, trying to live her life, pretending she was independent and strong when she was just a woman spending her life waiting. For a man. So, who was the real fool, she asked herself with disgust, wiping her hands on her apron. *You, Sunny Tedder, you.*

She put both palms on the counter and straightened her arms, locking her elbows. Enough feeling sorry for herself. She was lucky to have found love, to have experienced love at all. She could even have a fling if she felt like it. (Tommy and she had an unspoken pact: Do what you want with whom you want on your own time, just don't talk about it, and never ever get emotionally involved.) She was lucky to have the coffeehouse and be living in this extraordinary place.

Tommy's earnings, which they'd shared in the beginning, had enabled her to pay the first six months' rent for the café, but her ingenuity and hard work had made it the success it was. She'd known that his money had been earned by killing, that he'd become a shooter, a paid mercenary fighting the Taliban in the south. But she'd figured that it was for a good cause. He was killing the bad guys.

Sometimes she felt that life in Kabul was like the Wild West, where bad guys were bad and the good guys were good, where the rule of law was as ephemeral as peace. She let out a sigh, took the clip out of her apron pocket, and wrapped her hair up into a bun. Life should be as easy as it was back then, as easy as putting your hair up, she thought. You love, you die, and in between you live as best you can.

'Daydreaming again, Miss Sunny?' asked Halajan. 'Meanwhile the wolves eat your goats.'

Halajan was full of ancient Afghan wisdom. Whether Sunny wanted it or not.

Sunny looked at the old woman who owned the building and was the mother of Ahmet, with her long, low breasts that hung at her waist, unsupported by a bra, her clothes that looked like rags, and her open face. She answered, 'I don't have any goats.'

23

'Then they eat *you*,' Halajan said, as she came out from behind the counter and walked toward the back door. 'I'm taking a break now.'

'Enjoy your smoke,' said Sunny.

Halajan turned and smiled at her. 'You bet your ass,' she said in English.

Sunny laughed. Halajan was the only Afghan woman Sunny knew who spoke like that, who drank and smoked, a vestige of her life from the pre-Taliban days. How she must feel now, hearing the rumors of their return, Sunny could only guess.

A table of regulars called Sunny over, but they were pains in the butt, so she deliberately walked slowly to take their order. One wanted his eggs over easy, but not so easy. Another wanted his hash browns extra crispy but not burned like the last time. And another was upset that the bread hadn't arrived yet. Sunny rolled her eyes and thought *It's going to be a long day.*

She took the order to Bashir Hadi. 'Crispy but not too crispy, okay? And watch those eggs.'

He smiled and said, 'The customer is always right. Isn't that the great American wisdom?'

Sunny smirked and took the cappuccino on the counter to the table where it belonged. There, a Western man wearing a traditional *shalwaar kameez* was reading the morning Kabul newspaper in Dari.

'And what about you, mister? You going to eat or just take up space?'

The man raised his face from his newspaper and looked at her with steel blue eyes. He was striking, his face lined with the wreckage of a hard life, his hair starting to gray and recede with age, his neck and waist thick with a few too many pounds, and yet his strong hands were almost graceful the way he

24

folded his paper, laid it on the table. He reminded Sunny of movie stars from the forties, rugged types, not too handsome but handsome enough, with something special going on under the skin.

'Are we having a bad morning, ma'am?'

He talked like a man from the forties, too.

'How about it? You going to order?' Sunny replied.

'So, this is how it's going to be, is it? All business?'

'And please don't call me "ma'am." Ma'am is for old ladies. I left America because of ma'am.'

'Hmm, really?' He put on his reading glasses, perused the menu, and continued, 'I heard you had to. They were on to you,' he said teasingly.

Sunny ignored him.

'I'll have a three-egg omelet with cheese—not too runny—with hash browns, and can you be sure they're cooked this time? I like 'em crispy. And some of that good French bread of yours.' He stopped to think. 'And, correct me if I'm wrong, but I do believe I smell bacon. How'd you get your hands on bacon?'

'I have my ways. But there's no French bread. The good old flat Afghan bread is what we're offering this morning.'

He deliberated long and hard.

Sunny waited, one hand on her hip, a slight smile forming at the edges of her mouth.

'No French bread, huh?' he said, 'Okay, I'll forgo the bread, but since I'm eating alone and won't offend one of my Afghan friends, I'll have some bacon. And some mango. I like how you serve the mango.'

'Anything else, sir?' She shifted her weight from

25

one foot to the other.

'Another cappuccino.' He took a last slug from his cup and wiped the froth from his top lip with the back of his hand.

'We have things called "napkins" for that very purpose,' Sunny said.

'But then I wouldn't piss you off, would I?' he replied, his blue eyes crinkling at the corners. He took his napkin from his lap and dabbed his mouth delicately, a bemused look on his craggy face.

Sunny couldn't stop herself from grinning as she turned back to the counter. 'Jack wants the regular,' she called to Bashir Hadi.

'Watch out, you, 'cuz I'll be back,' she said to Jack as he picked up his newspaper.

She was surprised at how much his presence instantly brightened her mood. He'd been gone for more than a month. His work, as a consultant for rural development, often took him to remote parts of the country where he worked with engineers and contractors to bring irrigation, paved roads, and electricity to impoverished, backward areas. Or something like that. Sunny learned long ago that 'consultant' was the label in Kabul for anybody doing something they couldn't talk about. Jack didn't speak much about the NGOs that hired him or the specifics of his job. All Sunny knew for sure was that he was married, had a kid in high school back home, and liked his eggs cooked through. And that he was funny and made her laugh. What he was doing here, with his family over there, she wasn't sure. Except maybe it was for the same reason 99.9 percent of the other foreigners were here: to make money. In Afghanistan, a guy who made forty, fifty thousand dollars a year back home could make ten times that just for 'danger pay.' If you were willing to die, you could earn a shitload to live.

Tommy was proof of that, Sunny thought. The love of her life, her reason for coming to Kabul, left her every few weeks for more lucrative possibilities. And Sunny had adapted to life in this town alone. *Life happens,* was her motto. You adapt or you're lost.

Look at Yazmina, Sunny thought, who was cleaning a table toward the back of the coffeehouse. Only a few weeks ago Sunny had brought her here and introduced her to indoor plumbing and electricity. When she'd turned on the light in her room for the first time, Yazmina jumped.

Halajan had had to explain the use of the toilet, which made Sunny smile just remembering her crude explanation. But when Yazmina told Halajan that where she was from, you never did your dirty business in the house and that it was very primitive of them to do such business under the same roof where they ate and slept, Halajan folded over in laughter. When she'd shown Yazmina the shower, turning on first the cold and then the hot water, the young woman's face lit up and she put her hand into the warm stream, felt it against her skin, and watched it flow down her arm. She looked as if she'd seen a miracle.

Yazmina was completely covered in the lavender *chaderi* that she'd worn when she'd first arrived. It certainly wasn't as beautiful as the one Sunny had seen her in at the Women's Ministry, with its handmade embroidery. But that one had been torn and ruined by her ordeal and now was kept folded and hidden under her pillow. Sunny had seen it one morning when she'd gone to Yazmina's room

27

to give her an extra blanket for the cold nights. She'd marveled at the *chaderi*'s beautiful work, and though she would never let Yazmina know she'd seen it, she vowed to herself that one day soon, she'd take Yazmina for a handmade *shalwaar kameez* or two. Something bright and pretty to make her feel better about being here while her family was so far away. Something light and comfortable for her to grow into as her pregnancy was further along. She hadn't mentioned to Yazmina that she knew, not wanting to embarrass her. But the day was coming when she'd have to, if only to get her a doctor and to help her feel more comfortable and prepare for the day the baby would be born.

'Yazmina,' Sunny said to her. '*Sob bakhaer*. Good morning. I hope you slept well,' she said slowly, in her halting Dari. 'How are you feeling today?'

Yazmina stood there, nervously, obviously not understanding.

Sunny shook her head in frustration. Communication between them was still slow as they tried to find the Dari words they had in common.

Jack looked up from his nearby table and spoke Waigili, the language of the Nuristani people, so fluently that he might have been from Nuristan himself. 'Don't mind her. She's trying. She'd like to know how you're feeling today.'

Yazmina smiled, and answered in her language, 'Very well, thank you, *tashakur*,' then nodded and walked to the counter. As she put on an apron over her *chaderi*, Bashir Hadi was rubbing the copper coffee machine with lime juice, the best way to make it glow like the moon on a winter night, he had told her.

The morning flew by. It wasn't until the last customer had left, and Yazmina had swept the floors and left for her room to rest, that Bashir Hadi approached Sunny, who was at the counter on her laptop.

'May we speak, Miss Sunny?' asked Bashir Hadi.

Bashir was very serious, which worried her. 'Of course,' she said, closing the computer and turning to face him.

Bashir pulled a stool behind him and sat. 'I enjoy my job here and I thank you for the opportunity you have given me—'

'You're not quitting, are you?' Sunny interrupted, her heart leaping into her throat. What would she do without Bashir? She'd come to rely on him so.

'No, no, no,' he said, shaking his head. 'But I am concerned. I know it was very busy today, but it won't be busy this afternoon or tonight. Miss Sunny, we must talk about the money. The coffeehouse is falling behind, and—'

'We always make it, Bashir Hadi, don't we?'

'But Miss Sunny, we need more money to keep the café safe. And you safe and your customers. You know what I'm talking about.'

She let out a breath and looked out the window over his shoulder. Yes, the suicide bombings were on the increase and the kidnappings, too, yes, she knew. Just last month, a young man—a boy, really, from all accounts—strapped with an IED, an improvised explosive device, had blown himself up, and everything around him, two streets away. The ground shook and the front windows were shattered. Six people were killed. Everyone said it

29

was lucky there weren't more.

Bashir Hadi continued, 'We must deal with security issues. We need a safe room, a place for customers to hide, should we be attacked. We need to put up blast film on the windows so they don't shatter and become weapons of their own. We were lucky last time. But what if the bomb had been only a little closer? We need to fortify the compound in every way. We need to stop putting guns in the closet and, instead, lock them up in storage at the entrance.'

Sunny hated how that sounded like preparing for battle, but she had to face the truth. 'Yes,' she said, 'but I can't afford it.'

'I've been thinking about that. And maybe there is a way,' he said, raising his brows, a slight smile forming at the corners of his mouth.

She looked at him closely, this lovely, trustworthy man, with his large, slanted dark eyes and warm face, his narrow frame and immaculate clothing. And, of course, his hard work that had saved her and the café more times than she could remember. Besides his running the place, and besides his dealing with the damage from last month's explosion, there was the time, last winter, when the pipes burst. The time when a power surge had killed a coffee machine because they had had only one overworked generator and had relied on the city's electricity. Getting the two extra generators that cost an arm and a leg. Keeping the *bohkari*, the wood-burning stove, working throughout the winter. Or dealing with the mud that seeped in through every possible crack and crevice in the walls each spring when the snow melted.

'You going to tell me? Or am I supposed to

30

guess?' asked Sunny, teasingly.

Bashir Hadi reached into the pocket of his *kameez* and pulled out a newspaper article, neatly folded. 'Look,' he said, 'we rebuild the wall. Then we get UN compliance and the UN people will come. Then we'll be busy.'

He opened the article and spread it on the counter. Sunny skimmed it. The United Nations was encouraging restaurants, hotels, and hostels to build their walls to height and depth specifications to ensure the safety of UN employees, and then the UN would sanction their use. It could double their business.

Sunny looked out her front courtyard to the wall that sheltered the coffeehouse from the street. She could see the brightly painted turquoise gate with Ahmet's guardhouse in front. She remembered when she first came to Kabul, riding in a taxi through the streets that were walled on both sides and reminded her of the narrow roads through the dense cornfields back home. The big difference was that these walls were rife with bullet holes instead of cornhusks. They separated one home from another and every home from the street, making it difficult for people to find where they were going or to know their neighbors. They insulated the city's residents from harm but separated them from freedom. But they were usually only about seven feet high. To get UN compliance, they had to be four meters, or about thirteen feet high.

'It's like one of those, what do you call it? A cycle. You need more money to make the coffeehouse safer, so you build a better wall and then you get more people and more money.'

'There's only one problem,' said Sunny, thinking

31

about her dwindling bank account. 'We need money to build the wall higher in the first place.'

Bashir put his elbow on the counter and rested his chin in his hand. 'So we do something to get enough people to come so that we can do what is necessary to get more people to come.'

'Hmm. Maybe a party?'

'Do you mean to sell liquor? I don't like that. It's too dangerous.'

Sunny shook her head. 'And I didn't come to Kabul to be a bartender. That's the life I left back home.'

'Something else then. We'll think of it. But we need to do something quickly. Something for Christmas, maybe. Because before you know it, it'll be Easter, and the coffeehouse will move to outside. It must be safe by then.'

Her first year in Kabul, Sunny instituted a couple of new traditions in the coffeehouse. One was Christmas, when she decorated with a big plastic tree and decorations from Chicken Street, and the other was Easter, which the coffeehouse celebrated as a welcome to spring, when Sunny opened the outdoor patio and created a Shangri-la of hyacinth and fuchsia that climbed the open-walled tents she'd brought back from Dubai. Christmas was around the corner; Easter was in just a few months.

'We'll make that our goal. Safe by Easter.'

He bowed slightly, raised his head, and said, 'Until then we can pray for safety. Thanks to Muhammad for Easter.'

'Thanks to Muhammad for Easter!' Sunny concurred.

And they both smiled.

CHAPTER FOUR

Halajan walked down the back hallway to the door that led to a small courtyard behind the café, where she could have some privacy and take off her hot, itchy scarf. It was the only way a woman could do such a brazen thing in Kabul these days and not be stoned. Ach, the stupid Talib idiots, she thought as her plastic shoes click-clacked on the marble-tiled floors, one of the many improvements Sunny made to her house. What little men they are, she thought, to put women back in the burqa. She'd gotten so used to the sun that she vowed she'd die before ever hiding in the darkness again. Wearing a head scarf was one thing. She could almost understand it, if only because of tradition. But purdah—the full covering of women at all times in public— was another. The Taliban rigorously enforced it during their five-year rule. Only in the sanctuary of the household and only in front of husbands or other women could women bare their faces. This was a prison sentence for Halajan. This was death in life. Being as old as she was, almost sixty, she'd experienced life before the Taliban and life after, and now, with the renewed violence, their presence on the streets at night, and the rumors sweeping Kabul that they were plotting their comeback, the rules were growing stricter. Halajan was worried for what might come. The taste of freedom was a strong and delicious elixir that never left her mouth.

She pushed the door open and the cold air outdoors felt wonderful against her face after a busy morning in the café. She took a deep breath, sure she could feel her old bones creak as she gazed around the patio. A lone pomegranate tree poked out of a hole surrounded by concrete and the three generators hummed loudly. Ah, the beloved generators. When Sunny had wanted to move them to the rear of the coffeehouse, because they made conversation impossible on the front patio, Halajan had first said no. And she said no again and again for months, just to assert her authority, to let this annoying American newcomer know that she was the owner of the building and would make the decisions. But as she witnessed Sunny make one improvement after another, she, too, became frustrated with the complaints and inevitable empty tables, and agreed that the generators should be moved even though they took up room back here and valuable parking spots. Neighbors had become angry, but Sunny had bribed police to open up more parking areas on the street. There was no exaggerating the idiocy of those who ran Kabul.

The great thing about Sunny, Halajan thought, was not her lousy Dari, not her blue jeans, not that loud voice of hers or her big whooping laughter or her crazy hair. The great thing about Sunny was her insistence on the generators. Electricity every hour of the day and night. It was as if a miracle of Muhammad had happened here.

She looked around to be sure she was alone. Then she put a hand through her hair and smiled at her reflection in the door's small window. Though her skin was brown and wrinkled like the walnuts in the marketplace, her short hair made her feel young and powerful. She mussed it up, enjoying its boyishness. She had given herself the drastic haircut one year before, when rumors drifted through

Kabul that the Taliban were back, hiding in the hillsides of the Helmand province in the south. In a private act of defiance, her own personal statement of freedom—for she knew what would happen if the Taliban again gained control of her beloved people—she'd borrowed Sunny's scissors and cut off her braids, which were, at the time, long enough to reach her waist. She put them in a box under a small table in her sleeping room, where they remained. And now, about every three months, she borrowed the scissors and gave herself a trim, keeping her hair just long enough to hide the truth when under a scarf.

Under her brown dress, she wore an old blue-jean skirt that ended above her knees. A remnant of the pre-Russian era of the 1970s—when women were free to study, to work, to come and go as they pleased, to wear almost anything they wanted as long as it was respectful to Muhammad— the skirt had become soft and worn over time. Her skinny legs were covered in baggy pants to keep them warm, like the *salvar*s her father wore before he'd died what seemed like a hundred years ago, when his house was transferred to her, his only child, then just a young woman. She dug into a front pocket and pulled out a box of Marlboros and a purple plastic lighter. She lit up, took a deep breath in, and let it out with intense satisfaction. And it wasn't just from the nicotine. It was from the act itself—dangerous, contemptuous, and fearless. Out here, Halajan was as close as she'd ever get again, she feared, to freedom.

She looked back on her life as a time line of the regimes that had run her beloved Afghanistan—in the burqa and out of the burqa, in mini-skirts, back into long dresses—of the wars that took friends and family, of the droughts that caused famine and killed the roses and the trees of Kabul, and she realized she, like her country, had survived. The evils inflicted from the outside had been nowhere near as deadly as the poisons that had grown from within. One look into the black, cold eyes of a young Taliban warrior had taught her that.

She dug into the pocket of her dress and pulled out Rashif's most recent letter. She admired its lovely penmanship with the flourishes that surprised her on every page. She imagined him at his shop on a narrow alley in the Mondai-e waiting for her with a smile that made her body rush with warmth, her skin tingle with pleasure. She thought of him as he nodded a *'Salaam alaikum'* and then walked toward her to discreetly pass her a letter that she immediately hid in the folds of her chador. Tomorrow it would be Thursday, her market day, the beginning of the Muslim weekend that ran through Friday, and she would pass his way again. And there he'd be with another letter just as he had been every Thursday for the past six years.

She had loved Rashif since she was a little girl, growing up in her father and mother's house. He'd lived just a few houses away, and they had played after school in the empty lot that sat between their homes, exactly where the coffeehouse sat today. They often saw each other at family events and religious holidays. But as they grew up, they were more restricted by their culture, and like other teenagers throughout Kabul could no longer talk easily or even be in each other's presence without many others present. Ultimately Rashif was married off by his family to Salima, and Halajan, at

36

age fifteen, was married to Sunil, who would be her husband for the next thirty-six years.

Those years had been filled with joy and worries, the births of two children—Ahmet and his sister, Aisha (who was now studying in Germany, living with others from Kabul, something Halajan encouraged her to do, as she had encouraged Ahmet, who wouldn't go and leave his mother alone, much to her frustration)—and disagreement and compromise as all marriages are. Though she considered herself modern, there was one thing she would have never done: bring humiliation or harm to her family by choosing her own husband. So for thirty-six years, she made her marriage work. Sunil was a kind man but a simple man. He went to work, came home, prayed, studied the Koran, and maybe spoke ten words over the course of a week. He died of tuberculosis, as so many had, nine years before.

And then, a few years later, Rashif's wife died. And almost immediately the letters began. She looked forward each week to the thrill of the exchange, to the joy of seeing Rashif's smile and twinkling eyes.

She took a drag from her cigarette, folded the letter carefully, and stuck it deep in her pocket. She exhaled, watched the smoke wind its way up the house's wall, dissipating into the air as it rose.

If only she could read. Only then would she learn what he was trying to tell her.

CHAPTER FIVE

Ahmet leaned against the wall at the gate, watching the sky turn lavender over the hills that surrounded Kabul and the mountain peaks in the distance blur into the twilight. What was on the other side of those mountains? His sister knew; she'd left long ago. But he would never know because Kabul was his home and this was where he belonged. And yet, those mountains called to him like the muezzin's song at sunrise. At times like this, when his chest tugged with uneasiness, he'd readjust the rifle on his shoulder and remind himself of his duty.

Four men approached, chatting loudly in an Eastern European language. Ahmet stood straight, not taking his eyes off them. They nodded. He opened the gate. Then two more, this time Americans. 'Good afternoon,' they said in halting Dari. *'Salaam alaikum,'* he answered them. Ahmet never stopped to talk or ask questions, and he didn't use a metal detector, like the fancy restaurants. But he had what he considered the surest method for safety clearance. He never failed to look into the eyes of the customers, because they reflected deeper truths than any momentary feelings of impatience or hunger or disappointment. The eyes of a man betrayed his heart. Even with a smile, the evil man's eyes were as hard and shallow as a dry riverbed; even with a furrowed brow, the eyes of a good man were deep. In the Koran, the eyes were the gateway to the mind. 'You will see' in the Koran meant 'to know'; 'thine heart and thine eyes' referred to your feelings

38

and your thoughts, as Ahmet had been taught since he was a young boy in school.

After the busy mornings, the café quieted down until the afternoons, when people came for business meetings or just to talk politics, war, and the latest game of *buzkashi* before going home for dinner. On Fridays, the day of rest, when nobody went to work, the café was open and busy all day. No matter how hard Ahmet tried, he wasn't interested in his people's version of polo, played with a dead calf instead of a ball. Soccer was his game, or 'football,' as the Brits called it. He enjoyed watching it on the big TV that hung on the wall inside the café. Foreign men bet on the games, but he could not participate. Betting was forbidden in the Koran.

He chuckled to himself at the memory of Sunny bringing a big TV home one afternoon. It was in a huge box, sticking halfway out of the trunk of her car, the hood tied down with twine to keep the thing from falling out as the car bounced over the severe potholes and plentiful rocks in the road.

Sunny had gotten out of the car, slammed her door shut, and turned to Ahmet. She flipped her hair out of her face, put her hands on her hips, and said, 'You're going to love this, Ahmet. Wait until you see today's game.' She was referring to his favorite team—the Brazilians, who were in the finals against South Africa.

For years they'd watched the games on that big color TV, which sat on a small wobbly table in the back corner of the café. Ahmet was sure that one day its legs would go, falling to the floor under the weight of the huge TV. But it was better than what they had before—a small black-and-white one, with rabbit ears, as Sunny called them, laughing, making fun, when she first arrived.

Getting the new TV to work had been another matter. It had taken three weeks, a new satellite dish on the roof, three friends to help run the wires, countless trips to the electronics and hardware stores, and several prayers to Allah that Ahmet wouldn't miss the entire football season.

But when the TV finally worked, it was a beautiful thing! Ahmet had never seen such color. The games seemed so alive! The TV brought more customers into the café and Ahmet felt new respect for Sunny. Here was a woman unafraid of hard work, one with the perseverance of a goat that banged its head against the fence in the hopes of getting to the other side. However, here, too, was a woman like his mother and his sister, who challenged his expectations of the weaker sex and made him uneasy as well.

Two Afghan men who Ahmet knew approached the gate. He greeted them, held the gate open, and reminded them they'd need to check their weapons. Too many guns, he thought, his eyes following them as they walked through the courtyard and were welcomed by Bashir Hadi. If everybody has a gun, everybody is prepared to kill and to die.

Though today maybe half the people inside were locals, the café's customers were mostly foreigners, both men and women, who found the place so comfortable that they would sit for hours, in groups talking or alone with a book, while Bashir Hadi worked the kitchen, Sunny took orders, Halajan, his mother, bossed everybody around, and Yazmina kept the place clean and orderly.

Yazmina, now there were two eyes, Ahmet

thought, as his own followed an old man who was crossing the street in front of him surrounded by sheep. He was hitting a particularly fat sheep on its backside with the long stick he was holding.

Yazmina's eyes were like the bottomless pools of the Band-e Amir, the lakes of the northern mountain region, which he'd seen in pictures. He was convinced she had probably been a whore before Sunny brought her here and was up to no good, because her eyes were the only pair that he couldn't read.

He turned to look through the front courtyard into the coffeehouse. And there was Yazmina, wiping a tray, laying it on the counter, placing two saucers, then two cups on each. Then a basket of sweets. *Look at me,* Ahmet thought, *let me see those eyes of yours. They will tell me the truth.* As if she heard his thoughts, she did, and he immediately turned away, back to the street.

Most certainly a *fahesha,* a prostitute, he said to himself, as he lifted his rifle high on his shoulder and nodded at two foreign women approaching the gate. Their heads were covered, but they wore the pants and shoes of the West, probably with NGOs working futilely to help a people who needed no help. Such women, like his own sister, might be intelligent, with good intentions, but there were rules, and respect must be paid. His beloved country had survived various regimes in the past and it would survive whatever came its way. But if traditions were ignored, if the Koran was not read faithfully and understood literally, then his people were just as low as the snakes crawling in the brush in the desert.

And Sunny, like all the Americans—except

41

for Jack, Ahmet admitted, who showed some respect—flaunted the traditions. No wonder his mother was so comfortable in the café. Sunny and she fought like dogs but were as connected as two cats from the same litter. They'd hired Bashir Hadi, a Hazara! And then they gave him a raise and a bigger job. Now he was almost running the place. How could they give that kind of responsibility to a Hazara? And then came Yazmina, a mountain girl from Nuristan, a Kafir. Ahmet kicked at the dirt. The café was becoming a UN of its own.

Even Ahmet was changing. Yes, he still heeded the muezzin's call five times a day, praying on his own rug or at the mosque. And he kept the rules of Islam, but he could feel himself bristle at talk of the Taliban's resurgence in his country. Tradition was one thing, but cruelty and violence were another. One could argue that that wasn't what Muhammad intended at all. He frowned at the setting sun behind him to the west. Still, it was up to him to uphold the traditions of his home. *Inshallah,* he would. The world might be changing, but the word of Allah was forever, and it was Ahmet's lifework to watch over his mother's house, to keep it safe, and to keep it righteous under Allah's watchful eyes.

*   *   *

Rashif sat at a table in the back of his shop, behind the sewing machine, behind the counter and wall covered with spools of thread, behind the curtain that separated his living space from his working space. He opened the drawer at the table's base and pulled out a piece of ivory paper, the vellum he'd bought at the art supply store on Paint Street. He

42

held the corner between his thumb and index finger, and confirmed again how much he liked the feel and the weight of this paper. It was smooth enough to accept the ink of the pen, and opaque enough to prevent the writing from showing through to the other side, yet textured and light enough to make it elegant when folded. And the matching envelopes were equally fine. He opened the ballpoint pen's cap and attached it to the back of the pen.

Dearest Halajan, he wrote, in his simple penmanship. He wanted to be sure every word could be read, not because what he had to say was so important, but because writing was the only way he could say it. And he did not want Halajan to be unable to read one single word.

Today is the most beautiful day. The air is chilled but the sky is blue and it is the day before I see you. You are the sunshine of my week.
I have news. The new sewing machine I have been waiting for has been shipped from Pakistan and is making its way across mountains and deserts to my little shop in the Mondai-e. Let us pray that it's not confiscated by the warlords or destroyed by the fighters in the Khyber Pass. They say it will arrive in six weeks. What a celebration we will have!

He looked up from his paper and laughed to himself. If only, he thought, or as the American kids from the International School who bought Coca-Colas and chocolate bars at his friend Ibrahim's kiosk across the street said, 'As if.' *As if* he could celebrate with Halajan, take her face in

43

his hands and kiss her and twirl her in a midnight dance. If only!

He went back to his letter and was about to write more, when the squeak of his metal door as it opened, and the clang as it shut, announced a customer. It'll have to wait, he thought, as he stood up, brushed aside the curtain, and greeted the man with the dark suit folded neatly over his arm. My love will just have to wait.

CHAPTER SIX

The car bumped and lurched on the dirt road, throwing stones up against the windshield. Through the cloud of dust Candace Appleton could see the green of the valley ahead. Here, on the outskirts of Kabul, it was brown, dry, and bleak, just like the city itself. But right ahead was a lush, fruitful paradise. It was everything Wakil had said it would be.

He sat beside her, behind the driver of his new SUV, talking about his plans for the new roads he was having built out this way. She admired his strong profile, imagined his lovely body under his simple gray cotton tunic and pants. On his head he wore a turban made from such exquisite silk that it looked regal. She glanced once more at his meticulously trimmed beard, his dark-rimmed eyes. He was, indeed, a beautiful man. A young man, too; ten years her junior, to be precise. But it wasn't just that. Maybe it was his commitment to his country, to helping boys without fathers of their own, to building them a clinic, a school, an orphanage out here in the vast green countryside.

Or perhaps it was his attentiveness toward her and their passionate lovemaking. Or how he'd vowed to marry her when the time was right. To have a family. Or a combination of it all. Because she had fallen deeply in love with him, which made the fact that she'd left her husband for him easier to justify.

All these years she'd never done anything for herself, except, of course, the shopping, the little nips and tucks, the necessary things to keep her looking good as she grew older, which was a requisite for being married to a man who was in the public eye. Leaving Richard was the first real thing she'd done for herself in eighteen years of marriage. Eighteen years! She looked out the car's window and sighed. And still, it had been so easy to walk away since there had been no children involved. She'd wanted them, and not just one—the way she grew up, lonely and treated like an adult even as a young girl—but an entire brood! When she didn't get pregnant instantly, Richard had no desire to find out why or explore their options.

Then she met Wakil. It was at a conference her husband had attended at the U.S. consulate in Afghanistan for representatives of NGOs and local community organizers to meet and discuss priorities and funding. She sat with the other guests, in the back, behind the round tables of the participants. But she couldn't keep her eyes off Wakil even then—he was so very passionate about his work, and he spoke with such eloquence. Later, at the reception, her husband introduced them. The connection was instant.

'Your school sounds wonderful,' she had said to him.

'It's a clinic and a home to orphans as well. You

45

must come and see it,' he'd answered. 'It's in a green and lush part of my country. A place I know you will appreciate.'

She laughed. 'Because you want my support?'

'Because I noticed you—how could I not?—during the conference, listening, taking notes, and I saw a woman with not only beauty and passion but a deep power to accomplish things.' He paused, smiled as her face flushed with the effects of his charm, and then added, 'And I think you must love children as I do.'

Were these simply corny pickup lines? It didn't matter. She was hooked.

And look where it had brought her: to this rich, verdant valley with this glorious man, where she would do something with her life, for once. Wakil gave her a real reason to be. Not just designer clothes, fashionable parties, a townhouse on Beacon Hill in Boston, and volunteering for this museum or that educational institution.

He gave her life purpose. And she was, perhaps for the first time, excited to be alive.

The car headed toward the cluster of trees in the distance below. She was eager to tour the school, meet the children, and see firsthand what Wakil was talking about when he spoke so ardently about building new lives and giving the boys hope, a new direction. He hadn't been talking about her life, but he could've been.

'There,' he said in flawless English, pointing out the windshield toward her side of the car. 'Through the trees.'

'Yes,' she replied, 'I see it.' There were several buildings in the distance, a village.

He turned to her. 'My sweet Candace, my light. I

46

cannot wait to show you everything. Then you will see what we have worked so hard for, and for such a long time.' He took her hand in his and held it firmly.

She smiled. And she thought about everyone she could approach for money for Wakil's project. Her contacts would come in handy. As the wife to the U.S. Ambassador to Pakistan (and many other Middle East and Gulf countries prior to that), she had met every important businessman and entrepreneur, every significant philanthropist and activist interested in the area. But she wasn't stupid. She knew her divorce from Richard Appleton III had caused a lot of gossip and damaged her reputation. But she was confident in her own ability to persuade and attract attention. It was how she, the hick from Bumfuck, USA, had landed a Boston Brahmin in the first place.

They drove through a grove of tall trees, the geography having changed dramatically since they left Kabul. The sun sifted through the leaves and in between the black trunks that passed by in a blur.

'We're here,' said Wakil, as they parked in a clearing circled by buildings. 'The school first. Come, my love. Come see this place I've told you about for so long.'

He came around the car to open the door for her. Then they walked into the building, out of the midday sun.

Inside was one large room filled with boys sitting silently on *toshak*s on the floor, their legs folded and books on their laps. They all wore white, clean *shalwaar kameeze*s and small hats of ivory wool, and they were rocking back and forth as they recited the Koran. An older man in a white turban sat facing

47

them—their teacher, apparently.

As soon as the boys noticed Wakil's presence, they stood up, crossed their arms, holding their wrists, and put their eyes to the floor.

'You see,' whispered Wakil, 'the boys are Pashtun, Uzbek, Tajik, Hazara, Turkmen. They come from all over. Boys with no family, nothing, boys left orphaned, beggars. We give them an education. And from here, they will build lives, get jobs, be fruitful.'

He went to one of the smaller boys and rubbed his head. The boy turned and tried to kiss his hand. Politely, Wakil pulled his hand away. 'It is not me he should be thanking, it is Allah,' Wakil said to Candace. 'I only do this because it is the right thing to do.'

Candace looked out over the sea of faces, and then at Wakil's. How proud he was to offer these boys a home and a place to learn. How proud she was to be able to help—and to be so close to him.

'But we need more books, we need more room. This school has grown in size in only these few months. And what you've just seen is only a part of it. The girls come in the afternoon.'

'Girls live here, too?' How remarkable it was that he, an Afghan man, would want to educate girls, especially in a country where the girls were predominantly illiterate, raised to be subservient.

'No, they're not orphans. Just poor girls with no place to learn. Why should they grow up ignorant? How can our country prosper if its women know nothing of its history? Or if they cannot read the Koran? Here we are unafraid to teach them. Now, come, let's see the clinic, and then we shall have a tour of the boys' home.'

As they turned to leave, the boys sat down and began their chanting again. Candace was overwhelmed by Wakil's vision. Affection welled up in her like a wave and she so wanted to take Wakil's hand but knew she couldn't. So she followed him out, as was the rule. But once outside, she couldn't contain herself. She whispered to him and he followed her behind the building, behind a tree, like two teenagers. And there she kissed him hard, felt his body against hers, his strong hand on her lower back. Stealing a kiss like this, during the day, outside, was dangerous. She felt Wakil pull away.

'Careful, my love,' he whispered. 'There will be much time for this later. For you'—he hesitated, breathed into her neck—'are almost impossible to resist. But now, I want you to see the clinic.'

They walked around the next building to the front door. Inside was a line of boys, women in burqas, and old men, which snaked from the waiting room all the way down the hall to a closed door.

'We do not have enough doctors, and these few must help people for miles around,' Wakil said, his eyes full of concern. 'The people in this area have experienced such hardships, and suffer from many ailments and diseases. They try to be strong. But they only get sicker. We have already lost many . . .' His voice drifted off.

He walked over to one boy and stroked his hair. He spoke quietly to another, putting his hand on the boy's shoulder. And to another, and another. Then he returned to Candace and said, 'We need more doctors, equipment, medicines. Or our young will continue to die young.'

She looked at the little boy and wished she could

hold him, too. She fought her every impulse to pull him into her arms, stroke his head. If she could say what she really wanted, what she held deep in her heart, it would've been this: to have a child with this man standing next to her, to make a life, a family, together. Instead, she said to Wakil, 'We will help them, my dear. We will get everything you want. I promise you that.'

CHAPTER SEVEN

With the recent violence in the city, Sunny was anxious about the café's being open late. It wasn't only the latest suicide bombing that concerned her, but there were gangs of young men terrorizing foreigners and holding them for ransom—an Italian aid worker was kidnapped recently on her way home from a yoga class. Ahmet would have to guard the door and hire a friend to guard the gate. At the same time, because of the dangers, these late nights were terribly slow. People weren't going out as much. They'd lived with violence in the past, but they'd become accustomed to the peace, which made the recent occurrences particularly frightening.

But Bashir Hadi was right. They needed to make money and the longer they stayed open, the more chance they had of doing that. So she had put up signs on the front door and walls, and smaller ones on each table for the past week, announcing the late hours and entertainment. She even emailed some of her regulars.

'He gives you a gift, Bashir Hadi does,' said

Halajan. 'Life changes and you choose to flow with the river or you build a dam. In this case, flow. Let's make some money. It can be fun.'

'Forget fun. I'm just hoping people show up,' Sunny replied. Maybe she'd be lucky and Jack would stop by, as he often did late in the day.

In the meantime, some entertainment would liven things up. She had her iPod and the speakers for music. But music wasn't enough. Tonight they'd show a movie.

That afternoon, while the coffeehouse was quiet, she put on a large purple scarf and went out the back door, past her beloved generators, past Yazmina's window and the pomegranate tree, and out the back gate to the narrow alley where her car was parked.

When she got out of her car on Chicken Street, a horde of young boys wearing the standard brown pants, shirts, and vests came whooping and begging for an afghani or two, their arms outstretched, their eyes laughing to belie their hunger. She'd made the mistake once of giving a few coins to a young boy who looked desperately hungry. The minute she'd turned her back, he was attacked by a mob of boys intent on stealing the money she'd given him. She'd tried to break up the fighting and was bitten in the process. Now she gave only to children who were selling something, anything, just so she wasn't encouraging begging. It wasn't as if it was acceptable to beg in Kabul; in fact, begging on the streets was new to the city, something that appalled Halajan. But it had become a way of life for the hundreds of thousands of people with no work, the displaced, the starving, the uneducated and disenfranchised.

When she got to her favorite store, she stepped inside and greeted the owner. *'Salaam alaikum,'* she said. 'Anything new?'

'Wa alaikum as-salaam,' he answered with a small bow. 'Definitely, much new. Check out my New Arrivals wall, over there.'

Sunny was, as usual, impressed with the store. It was well lit and organized like a mini Blockbuster back home. It was critical that she find something good to show, so that people would come back. The problem was that the only videos available in Kabul were pirated. You couldn't rent one, so those for sale had to be cheap, and the legal versions were too expensive to sell. The pirated videos were secondhand versions—made illegally— sometimes impossible to hear or see, because the movies had actually been videotaped by some guy who snuck his camera into the movie theater under his jacket, or made in someone's living room, where somebody copied an already lousy copy of a TV show or movie. Recently, though, more tapes were coming in from China, and though they were not the homemade variety, they were a gamble as well. So Sunny made it a habit of buying a few at a time to be sure there was something watchable. Today she picked up the complete first season of *Grey's Anatomy* and the recent Academy Award winner *Crash.* She'd wanted *The Man Who Would Be King,* but it was so popular because it was about Afghanistan that there was a perennial waiting list. She added her name to it.

Sunny had ordered delicious sweets from the French bakery that brought her the warm, crusty bread each morning all the way from Carte Se, about a forty-five-minute drive in traffic, and

Yazmina had agreed to work late to serve coffee. The coffeehouse was inviting at night, with its soft lighting and warm colors. Who wouldn't want a place to hang out and talk and watch a great movie and drink the best coffee in Kabul?

Nobody, that's who. Or almost nobody. At seven, Sunny wondered if there'd been a bomb or a roadside blast. She tried the walkie-talkie with the UN channels, but everything seemed normal. So she told herself maybe they would still come, that there was a lot of rush-hour traffic.

At 8:00, Halajan said, 'No one's coming. And why not? Because people are afraid, and they won't go out just for a movie and some talk. You have to offer more. And then maybe even tell people about it. That would help.'

At 8:10, Sunny's cellphone rang. The landlines in Kabul were about as trustworthy as the rug dealer in the market. If the wind blew too hard, if it rained, if a little bird landed on a wire, the line went dead.

Sunny answered the call, but nobody was there. So she told Ahmet to let his friend at the gate leave. Ahmet resumed his usual place outside.

At 8:22, Jack walked in, a large canvas bag hanging from his shoulder. He looked around the room and raised his brows. He laid the bag gingerly on a table.

'Nice crowd,' he said.

Sunny couldn't stop herself from smiling. 'At least you decided to show up.'

'Honey, I wouldn't have missed it,' he said. 'Hello, Halajan,' he said, and then said something in his perfect Dari that made Halajan laugh.

Sunny didn't know precisely what he'd said, but

53

it was somewhere in the vicinity of Sunny having scared everyone off. Jack sat. And Sunny said, 'Very funny.' She joined Jack, and Yazmina served them each a Coke, then retreated behind the counter to the kitchen.

But Jack dug into his bag and pulled out a bottle of wine.

'Let's get this party started,' he said. 'Got any movies?'

'She's got them,' said Bashir Hadi from the counter. 'Miss Sunny took the car out today.'

Sunny glared at Bashir Hadi and then looked at Jack, who was shaking his head unhappily. As if she were a teenager.

'I'll deal with that,' offered Halajan. She took the bottle to the kitchen and returned with a teapot and three cups. She poured.

'Nice tea,' Jack said. 'Good vintage. Let's toast.'

'To busy nights,' Sunny said.

'To safe driving,' he answered.

At that moment, the door slammed open and two Afghan men, twenty-one, maybe twenty-two years old, walked in and, instead of waiting to be seated properly, sat themselves at a table. They were clearly Pashtun, dressed nicely, of some privilege. What was also clear is that they were high on hashish or something, which made them loud, arrogant, and demanding.

'Hey, two beers over here!' one yelled in his native language, slamming his hand on the table. The other laughed, tilting his chair back.

Sunny's hackles rose and she looked at Jack. He nodded to her in response.

'It's okay,' he whispered.

Bashir Hadi whispered something to Yazmina,

54

probably to stay behind the counter, and approached the table himself.

'We don't serve beer here.'

'Come on,' the young man said. 'Sure you do.' He looked Bashir Hadi up and down. 'This guy won't serve us beer,' he said to his friend, 'because he's Hazara and we're Afghan.'

'No—it's because—' began Bashir Hadi, but he was interrupted.

'Because why?' asked the other.

Sunny stood, looked at Jack.

'Wait,' he whispered. 'Let him handle this.'

She slowly sat down.

'We don't serve beer,' explained Bashir Hadi slowly, as if with each word he was struggling to contain himself, 'because we're a coffeehouse, not a bar. Perhaps you want some tea.'

The two men looked at each other. And then the leader looked over at Sunny, gave her an obsequious smile, and laughed out loud. That was when Jack stood. The young man also stood and faced him.

'Come on,' said his friend, worried about the fight that was brewing. 'Let's get out of here.' Then he dug into his pocket and threw some coins on the table and said to Bashir Hadi, 'Here, to feed you and your family for a week!'

'Filthy Hazara,' the other man sneered.

As they sauntered out, Jack followed behind them to the door and watched them until Ahmet closed the gate behind them. Then he turned and said, 'Bashir Hadi, my man, come have a drink with us. You handled that well, sir.'

Sunny looked at Bashir Hadi, who obviously felt the weight of Jack's compliment, but his eyes couldn't help but convey hurt and anger. He sat next to her.

'I'm sorry,' she said softly. 'The way those boys spoke—'

'I'm used to it,' he said. 'It's nothing.'

Yazmina came in then, carrying a tray with a pot of tea and cups, and served the tea to Bashir Hadi.

'Bishine,' said Sunny, asking Yazmina to sit. 'We've got no customers anyway.' When Yazmina froze, Sunny continued, *'Bya,* come sit.'

Yazmina looked to Halajan for a sign of what to do.

'It's okay,' said Halajan. 'We women are always outnumbered. Now we'll have the vote.' She nodded at Sunny, as if she'd read her thoughts. 'Two of them, three of us.'

'Here,' Sunny said, pulling out a chair. 'Join us. It's okay.'

Yazmina looked at Halajan again, who smiled and nodded, and then she sat, her hands in her lap, her eyes down. Jack filled Yazmina's teacup.

'Okay, so we're all here now? To feel sorry for me?' said Bashir Hadi.

'Nobody feels sorry for you,' said Jack. 'How could we? It's those guys—'

But Bashir Hadi interrupted, held his cup high, and said, 'Well, here's to feeding my family for a week, to being Hazara, to being Shia, to—'

'It could be worse. You could be a woman,' interrupted Halajan, as she poured from the teapot.

'And let's not forget the women!' he said, and drank.

They were joking around, but Sunny reflected that there was much truth and sadness in what they said. The Hazara people were the third largest

56

ethnic group in Afghanistan after the Pashtun (some of whom were Talib) and the Tajik. They'd descended from the Mongolians, and some even said from Genghis Khan, which was why their features had an Asian influence. Sunny had always thought that Bashir Hadi looked like the American Indians she knew as a kid—the golden skin, the heavy-lidded black eyes, and the strong, straight nose. His people had been persecuted for years by the Pashtun Sunni majority, mostly because the Hazara were Shia.

'But like women, Bashir Hadi, you should be careful,' Jack was saying, all hints of joking gone. 'The country is on the verge of changing again. And not on the side of being more tolerant, if the Taliban come back into power.'

'Let me tell you something, Mr Jack. Tolerance is overrated. I'm no more tolerant of the Pashtun Talib than they are of me. They just have bigger guns. Which brings me to the point. Making money to make this place safer. How are we going to do it?'

They talked into the night, sharing ideas, making suggestions, putting together plans, their anger over Bashir Hadi's treatment by those men turning to excitement and fueling their creative energy. Only Yazmina sat quietly, not saying one word, with her hands clenched tightly on her lap, though every now and then she looked up from the table and let the light of those green eyes shine on everyone. When she did, Sunny would nod, acknowledging her presence and letting her know she was welcome. Jack would translate for her to bring her into the conversation. But it was Halajan who kept her hand on Yazmina's the entire night so that she knew she

57

wasn't alone.

CHAPTER EIGHT

Yazmina woke even earlier than usual, eager for market day with Halajan. The old woman annoyed her, grated on her like the sharp braying of her uncle's old goat that made her skin prickle. But the Mondai-e Bazaar! It was like visiting the moon, it was so foreign to her. Every week Sunny gave them a shopping list. There was a stall that sold the best fruits and vegetables she'd ever eaten. And a meat market that had electricity and the ability to keep the meat cold and fresh. There was a fancy store on the way to the bazaar with boxes of the Frosted Flakes cereal that Sunny loved so much, stacked to the ceiling, and peanut butter that Yazmina devoured the first time she tasted it. There was chocolate, cheese, popcorn, and a drink called Mountain Dew. There were pencils and peanut butter cups, too. Everything cost so much that Yazmina blushed when Halajan paid. Her family wouldn't have spent as much in five months as Sunny spent each week.

When she and Halajan returned to the coffeehouse, Sunny would enjoy emptying the bags onto the counter before putting the items away. They would open the chocolate and finish the Mountain Dew in one sitting.

Sunny was like that. She got very excited about things, which made Yazmina feel uncomfortable. At home, she and Layla could laugh and cry, but never in the presence of their uncle. She hadn't been able to help feeling uncomfortable sitting at the table the previous night in the café with Jack and Bashir Hadi. To sit together like that was something Yazmina had never done before. And they were drinking wine! Everything in Kabul was foreign. Everything was uncomfortable and everything was wonderful—except Layla wasn't with her.

She put on her clothes and sighed deeply at the plain dress she wore. At the Mondai-e, there were clothing shops with dresses and *shalwaar kameezes* that looked like they'd fray if you sneezed on them. Nothing like the ones made by Sharifa, the woman back home who had taught Yazmina how to sew the loveliest garments by her own hand out of fabric she herself had embroidered and embellished with beads and shells and old coins. Someday, *Inshallah,* she dreamed of being able to sew like Sharifa. Someday, she thought, looking out her window to the rising sun, she would sew in the colors of that sky. A dress in a pale orange. What a sight she would be. With golden bangles on her wrist. And shoes of real leather. And her eyebrows threaded and her hair strung with beads under a scarf of the finest silk, like the ones Sunny wore.

She'd want to share it all with Layla.

*   *   *

Ahmet opened the car door and watched Yazmina climb into the backseat. She was completely hidden under the burqa, but as her hand reached out to close the car door, the sleeve slipped up her arm, revealing her narrow wrist. It was brown and slender. His mother climbed into the backseat after her, and he slammed the door with a little too much strength. He had other things to do than act as her driver, but it was going to rain and how could he be a good son and let her walk through the muddy streets? Rain or not, he felt that two women should always be accompanied on the streets of Kabul, even though his mother often felt otherwise.

He got into the driver's seat, shut and locked his door, and adjusted his rearview mirror, seeing Yazmina behind him. He turned and locked her door, too. Behind the mesh of the burqa, he could make out her stunning green eyes—or imagine them there. Where did she come from, he wondered, where was her family, why was she alone? He'd seen no signs of her entertaining customers, which confused him, for she had to be a prostitute—there was no other reason for a woman as beautiful as she to be without a husband. And if she had one, where was he? Ahmet had heard of women leaving husbands who beat them or worse, which was something he swore he'd never do, but that was the husband's prerogative, was it not? And it was the wife's duty to endure. There was only one reason she could be excused to have left him: if he was dead.

He told himself to pay attention to the crowded streets as he headed toward the Masjid-e Haji Yaqub, the mosque where he frequently prayed, not because it was more righteous than praying on his own rug in his own room, but because the mosque was so beautiful. He loved its blue tiles from Herat, and the acacia trees that framed the patios. It was the mosques of Kabul that were its proudest achievements.

As if Muhammad were laughing from above,

when he passed the mosque he would have to turn onto Butcher Street, the ugliest in all of Kabul, where animals were slaughtered right on the streets, their carcasses left to hang in the sun. He made sure the windows were up, the vents closed, so that the stink of entrails and blood wouldn't permeate the car. At the end of the street was a roundabout, and past it the wide road with the Chinese Embassy, with its high walls, where beggar children approached the car, their arms outstretched. Women sat on the edge of the road begging near the open sewers, holding their babies in their laps. Here the traffic was at a standstill as it always was, the exhaust fumes were inescapable, and makeshift shops, selling the used clothing donated to Kabul out of pushcarts and hanging on barbed-wire fences, lined the streets.

Ahmet didn't have to wait long to hear his mother's rant, the same words she said every time.

'In the days of the king, you'd never see this. Kabul is not a beggar's city. This is because of years of war and displaced people with no homes, no way to make a living. And it's because of the Talib. Their violence has created an entire city of people under the city.' She frowned. 'Afghanistan is not India! And this is not my Kabul.'

'Mother, your Kabul has been gone for a long time.' He knew she was right. But if it were him, he'd rather die of starvation than beg in a ditch on the side of the road.

Traffic was slow and dense, but eventually they could see the beginning of the Mondai-e ahead, where it began on this side of the Kabul River. But you had to cross the river, over the bridge, to really get to the center of the bazaar.

He could feel his mother getting anxious, as if she couldn't sit another minute.

'Hurry up, Ahmet! Is there no other way? I have an errand. And it's looking like the heavens might open at any minute.'

'We're almost there, Mother,' he answered as patiently as he could. But there was so much traffic that he knew they'd be sitting there for at least another ten minutes.

Then his mother said, 'We're getting out. We will be faster on foot.'

'You will wait until we get there,' he insisted. 'It isn't safe.'

'Come, Yazmina. Let's go. Ahmet, we'll meet you at the bridge.'

Ahmet threw up his hands. He could do nothing to prevent his stubborn mother from getting out of the car with Yazmina and then walking away into the crowded street.

He got through the roundabout, parked as quickly as he could, paid a teenage boy to watch the car, and ran to catch up to them, but they were already out of sight. The sky had blackened and rain was imminent.

*   *   *

Walking toward the river, Yazmina felt her heart beat faster. Her legs felt as though they'd gained length and strength with each stride. But she knew the rules even under the burqa: Keep your head down and your eyes to yourself. It was unacceptable to look at a man straight on or to laugh aloud or to smile at a small child or to gaze longingly at a dress in the market. In the country, she was freer

62

to be herself, to show her feelings, but there had been no place to go with them. All she had, after her Najam died, was her uncle's house, the hills, farm, and barn, and perhaps the local market when the traders came through. Here she had people of all colors and clothing, people from all parts of the world, an entire city of changing faces. And yet she couldn't allow herself to show her excitement.

They walked briskly, keeping their eyes to the ground, moving faster than the cars that were being stopped at the corner by police. She had seen this many times since coming to Kabul. Police in full uniform, rifles drawn, standing at intersections and bending over into car windows, searching the backseats and the fronts, and sometimes the trunks. She had no idea what they were looking for, and she hoped they didn't find it while she was there.

It had begun to rain by the time they arrived but it didn't matter. Yazmina couldn't stop herself from looking fully, head up, eyes wide, a rush of blood to her cheeks. Everything looked marvelous. But it was the dresses, the *shalwaar kameeze*s, and the *chaderi* that she was after. She checked her pocket to be sure the money that Sunny had given her was still there.

Suddenly, Halajan turned to her and said anxiously, 'I have some errands. I must hurry— the rain. Let us meet back here in ten minutes.' Yazmina was both afraid and relieved. Sunny had been very careful to tell her not to leave Halajan's side, but she wanted time to explore the clothing shops.

'Do not leave this area and do not speak to anyone,' Halajan continued.

'But Sunny gave me money for a new *shalwaar*

kameez.'

Halajan quickly gestured to a store nearby. 'That one is good. I'll meet you there.'

*   *   *

Halajan was frantic that she'd miss him. The sky grew dark, the clouds burst, and the rain was coming now, soaking her. She didn't care. She rushed down the street without caution. Though one rarely saw a woman running on the streets of Kabul, she had to get to Rashif's before he was gone. She stayed straight and fast, her heart racing to the beat of the downpour.

When she got to his stall, she immediately realized she needn't have worried. There he was, holding a large red and white Coca-Cola umbrella, his other hand in his pocket. He smiled at her and looked relieved to see her.

'*Shukur Khodia,* thank God,' he said softly as she drew near. He looked from right to left to be sure they wouldn't be seen, but the street was empty because of the rain. He handed her the letter, wrinkled and damp, from his pocket. His fingers touched hers. They were warm, and he let them linger there for a moment.

'Be safe, take care,' Halajan answered, pulling her hand back and quickly burying the letter in the folds of her *chaderi*. She smiled then, and opened her mouth to say something, anything, but her words got caught in her throat. She spun on her heel to hurry back to meet Yazmina.

But there was Ahmet, waving to her from the corner. Her heart rapped hard against her chest. *Inshallah,* he saw nothing, she thought. If he did,

64

she'd say that Sunny had asked her to go to the tailor to check on her new dress. Or maybe that he was fixing a tablecloth. But, no, Ahmet couldn't have seen much, if anything, with all the rain. She willed herself to calm down. Her stomach tugged at her for a moment, but she waved back and smiled. He was a good boy, her Ahmet, but sometimes she wished she could get him to do something— anything—more than worrying about her, more than his *chokidor* duties. Like his sister, off in Germany studying at the university. If only she could get Ahmet to loosen up a little, maybe be just a little modern instead of holding on with reddened knuckles to the old ways. Then she would have succeeded as a mother.

*   *   *

The dress shop was filled with color and light. Dresses of every color hung suspended from the ceiling, while hundreds of others, under plastic covering, lined the walls. Yazmina had never seen so many dresses. Some had mirrors, some beads, some plain, but all beautiful.

The shopkeeper came over to her and said, '*Salaam alaikum.* It's a bad day to be out. You are wet. But can I help you find a new dress perhaps?'

'Yes, please,' she said. 'I'd like pants with it, too.'

'So you want the Indian-style *shalwaar kameez.*'

'Yes,' she said, 'like in that picture.' She pointed to a brightly colored photograph of a beautiful young Indian woman wearing the gaudy, bright Bollywood style of dress. Even in her remote village, everyone was obsessed with Bollywood movies. Her uncle had a tiny generator, enough to power a small VCR. And Yazmina, Layla, and their neighbors would watch movies they got from traders, who'd gotten them on the Pakistani black market.

The old man looked at her, from ankle to neck, making her feel very uncomfortable, and then walked to a rack. 'Come, young one,' he said. 'Here are dresses in your size. They all come with pants. Did you have a color in mind?'

'Orange,' she said, 'like the sun. But I'd like it a size or two bigger than me. It's for my mother.' She had to lie, for how could she tell him that she needed room to grow?

*   *   *

'Why the tailor on such a day?' Ahmet asked his mother as they walked quickly in the rain, the muddy ground giving way beneath their feet.

'Sunny asked me to check on her curtains, but they were not ready. There is no time for talk. We must get to Yazmina before she becomes drenched.'

He looked at her but she didn't turn to look at him, and he felt foolish. He sounded suspicious and silly, but he knew of Rashif from the elders at the mosque and he didn't like him. It was a long time ago, but, as the story was told, when Rashif was younger he'd been active in a reform group that aided Afghan refugees, one of those antitraditionalist groups of so-called intellectuals that received American money, embraced Western values, and helped Afghans in only one way: to forget who they were and who they are and who, in the eyes of Muhammad, they were destined to be.

66

That tailor had the heart of a modernist, just like his own mother. Ahmet had to love and respect his mother, according to the precepts. But he didn't have to like Rashif one bit.

CHAPTER NINE

'What's with you?' Sunny asked.

Jack had come in that morning distracted and cranky. He hardly said hello, sat, gulped his coffee, and buried himself in his newspaper.

Finally, he looked up. 'You,' he said. 'That's what's with me.' And he went back to his paper.

'Excuse me?' Sunny said, putting a hand on her hip. 'When you're ready to discuss it, you know where to find me.' She turned and walked away.

But behind her she heard, 'Two things.'

So she turned around, walked back to his table, and said, 'So give me the bad news.'

'Driving that damn car around town like you did yesterday.'

He sounded as closed minded as an old Afghan man talking to his youngest wife. She knew he hated the car; he'd warned her about it and had explained why a woman shouldn't be out alone in Kabul, many times.

She sighed loudly. 'And?'

'Jesus, Sunny, it's dangerous,' he said with frustration. 'And two, Bashir Hadi gives you this great idea to build your wall higher so you can make more money and be safer and then you just sit on your ass, as nice as it is,' he said, craning his neck to look at her butt.

67

'Oh, shut up,' she said in return. 'What am I supposed to do? Nobody came.'

'Give them a reason, for God's sake. We came up with a hell of a lot of good ideas last night. I know you're not stupid. So, what is it, are you stupid?'

She scowled then, and he smiled. She sat down at his table. Picked up his fork and tasted his egg. 'Um, that's good.'

'Yes, it was.'

'Okay, so I liked the idea of getting a speaker. But who?'

'If I knew I wouldn't tell you because you'd only blow me off, Ms Stubborn Know-It-All.'

She smiled again, this time fully. He could be cute, this fat old fart, who wasn't so fat or old, and he was only sometimes a fart, not to mention handsome with his square chin and deep eyes.

'You're right. I'll think of someone.'

'But I do know of a doctor from India working here in the field. Passionate about women's health issues in Afghanistan, and I know she wants to get the word out about the dire straits these women are in. Besides, I helped her once with something. She owes me.'

Sunny's eyes widened. 'Really? You think she'll come speak here at the café?'

'Only if you beg me.'

She put her elbow on the table and rested her chin in her hand. 'Please.'

'But promise me one thing.' He paused, waiting for her response, which she took a while to provide. 'Hello?'

'Okay, I promise.'

'You get people here. Otherwise I'll be

embarrassed.'

'And we wouldn't want that,' she said.

'Come on, Sunny,' he answered with some impatience. 'Out of respect for the doctor.'

She realized, then, how serious he was. 'Don't worry. I'll get people.'

*   *   *

One week later, on a bitter cold Wednesday night, Sunny lit the candles, Halajan poured the wine into the teapots, Bashir Hadi arranged the cookies and pastries on platters, Yazmina set the tables, and the windows rattled on their hinges. Whistling drafts came through the caulked edging of their casements, and it seemed only a matter of time before the roof blew off and the house lifted up into the sky.

Jack had confirmed that Dr Ramita Malik would come and speak about her work. So Sunny had gone to the bazaar to buy poster board and tempera, and made dozens of signs that she took to the Women's Ministry, the hospital, the schools, the French House, the UN, the American Embassy, and the other guesthouses and compounds—everywhere she knew where female foreigners lived, worked, and gathered—and pleaded with people to put them up. She'd thought about emailing her women friends, but they'd all left Kabul over the past few months. Sunny had never been one to need or want more than one or two close friends at a time, and really had to know someone well before confiding in them. Her Kabul friends—Chris, the schoolteacher from South Africa; Ellen, a cousin of a cousin of an old friend

69

who had been in town studying Dari; and Suzanne, whom she'd met on her very first day in Kabul, and who ran a beauty school—had all left. Kabul was a temporary stop or a momentary adventure for all but the stalwart or foolhardy, of which Sunny realized she was the latter. Recently she'd felt a little lonely, and not only because Tommy had been away so long this time, but because she didn't have someone to talk to with the kind of shorthand that only a close friend understands. A look, a raised brow, a down-turned mouth.

It wasn't that men weren't invited to the evening talk. It was just that Kabul was such a world of men, a place where women's concerns and voices were secondary at best, so why not give women a place and a reason to come to hang out and talk and just be together? The more she thought about it, the more excited she was about the idea. Wednesday nights for women: food, drink, and something to think and talk about.

The coffeehouse was ready, and hopefully Jack would show. He wasn't a woman, but he had the heart of one. She hadn't seen him since he'd made the offer to pull in Dr Malik, and it made her realize that she too often took him for granted. He was one of those people who make others feel safe and comfortable, make them sit up a little straighter and feel good about themselves.

The front door opened with a whoosh of wind from outside. It wasn't Jack. But it was people, and Sunny was glad for that. One, surprisingly enough, was Petr, a tall, gorgeous Uzbek whom she'd met at a party last year at L'Atmosphere—or 'L'Atmo,' as the regulars called it, the French nightclub that hosted the Eurotrash, the ex-pats, the wealthy and

70

the wannabes, the drug dealers and the warlords. In short, it was a place where she didn't belong, but not because they didn't accept her. She just didn't want to associate with those types anymore. When Tommy first left, they were all she had. But then she came to realize that they were the same people she had wanted to get away from in the States, only in Arkansas they wore cowboy boots instead of Hugo Boss and carried .38s instead of Uzis.

Petr was spiffed up and decked out, all raffish charm, with a cashmere scarf around his neck and a Persian lamb jacket, carrying a Porsche man bag in one hand and talking on his cellphone with the other. With him was one of those women who could wear baggy pants loaded with pockets, scruffy hiking boots, a baggy sweater under an oversized safari jacket, and a scarf to cover her head, and still look glamorous. Her face was strikingly beautiful, with pale skin, large black eyes, and a wide mouth. As the woman took off her outer clothes, and then the baggy sweater to reveal a tight T-shirt, one couldn't help but notice how petite she was, with slim legs and a tiny waist that made her big boobs look even bigger—Petr's weakness, if Sunny remembered correctly. The woman's black hair was very short and raggedly cut, which only accentuated her large eyes and good-gene cheekbones. From one wrist dangled a two-inch-wide swath of leather bangles, but her hands were delicate. She was working hard to look tough, thought Sunny.

This woman had to be an idiot to be sleeping with Petr. Sunny knew this from firsthand experience, because she had been exactly such an idiot herself. So who was she to judge?

Ahmet had followed them in, carrying Petr's

71

shiny silver handgun, meant for close-up business, and handed it to Bashir Hadi, who put it in the back. Sunny looked at Ahmet as if she were going to say something about sticking close, and he nodded and said, 'I'm here if you need anything,' before returning to his post just outside the gate.

Immediately Petr headed to Sunny, his arms outstretched, and said in his thick Russian accent, 'Hello my dear. *Preevyet kak dyela?* How are you?'

He asked the way all of Sunny's Russian acquaintances and customers asked—like they meant it. He held her arms and kissed her on both cheeks. 'Where've you been hiding? Haven't seen you once at L'Atmo—'

'Petr, nice to see you.' All right, she told herself, try a little harder. Be nice. They kissed on both cheeks, and breathing in his scent, she experienced a rush of déjà vu.

He lingered a moment too long on the second kiss. 'This I remember,' he said in her ear, holding her arms firmly. But she pulled away and then he introduced his friend, Isabel Hughes, who was visiting from London.

'Petr's told me much about you. Apparently this coffeehouse is considered Kabul Central,' said Isabel in a thick British accent, reaching out her hand.

Sunny shook it. 'Yeah, well, it's not L'Atmo,' she said, with sarcasm. She looked at the couple before her and decided she didn't trust them for a second. Petr's story was that he was a 'consultant' working in 'counter narcotics,' as if anybody would believe that, since work of that kind didn't pay enough to buy his Gucci shoes, much less his entire lifestyle. She was fairly certain that Petr

72

was an opium dealer, and if not a dealer, then a middleman. He knew where the poppy fields were, whom to contact, and how to get what to whom. He was Russian, fluent in Turkish and Uzbek, which were helpful for the poppy trade in the north, with connections including an Uzbek warlord's son. And Sunny had no doubt he made millions from it. And Isabel? Though her clothes were cliché college student attire, she was older than that and obviously just another of his many women, who'd come to Kabul to find adventure and maybe a high-rolling boyfriend or husband in the process. But those women usually found themselves doing whatever it took to make a living. If she was with Petr, enough said.

They sat at one of the empty tables, Halajan served cappuccinos and the illegal wine in a teapot, and they chatted with some foreign aid workers and the other people who'd come in. No Jack yet, but a much better crowd than last time. And it was still early. The doctor hadn't even arrived.

'Look,' whispered Bashir Hadi. 'This place, it is rockin'!'

Sunny chuckled at his slang. 'Well, it's not bad. For our first.'

Isabel had apparently been listening. 'It's brilliant,' she said, reassuringly. 'Look at you. Look at all this. It's magnificent.'

'Bashir Hadi, I think she's lecturing me on the power of positive thinking.' Sunny smiled, but she couldn't hold back her cynicism.

'Rubbish. Relatively speaking, you seem to be doing okay.'

She was trying to be nice, Sunny thought. Give her a break. 'And what about you? Why are you in

Kabul?'

'I'm on a story.'

'You're a journalist?' She couldn't conceal her surprise. She'd thought the woman was a bimbo. Guilt by association.

'Freelance. A private foundation's hired me to do a story for the BBC on the effect of the government's plans to spray the poppy fields.'

Impressive, Sunny thought. The plan was highly controversial, and anything to do with poppies was dangerous, given the money involved in opium.

'The people are worried,' Isabel continued. 'The women for their children, for other crops. It's going to be indiscriminate aerial spraying and if the chemical kills poppies, it kills vegetables, and if it kills vegetables, it may not kill people, but it'll make them sick. Dr Malik has spoken on this subject before. Thought I could get a minute with her. People will lose their farms, their livelihood. They'll starve. Don't get me started.

'And of course it's the women who feel strongest on this issue. They're the ones who have to feed their families and watch over their children. But they have no protection and no voice. They're not allowed to protest. It's really become this insane issue, mothers siding with poppy growers, with drug lords.'

'But the story, it's good,' Sunny said, raising her brows. 'Dangerous, though. Anything involving opium. You be careful.'

'Now who's giving the lecture?' Isabel smiled.

And Sunny smiled back. This woman with the *Playboy* body, the punk haircut, and the stupid boyfriend might just be okay.

'And Petr's not my boyfriend,' Isabel said, as if

she heard Sunny's thoughts. 'He's just a friend. With friends.'

And she was smart. And the way she talked made Sunny realize this was not a regular Petr woman at all.

'Want some tea?' Sunny held up her teapot filled with wine.

'Don't mind if I do.' Isabel held up her cup. Sunny poured, and the two women toasted to being positive.

*   *   *

The doctor arrived about a half hour late, having gotten lost on her way to the coffeehouse. There were no street signs in Kabul, so the only way to find a new place was to use markers, like the herd of sheep grazing on the garbage, or the green gate under the Nokia billboard, two houses down the muddy alley, or the third gate with the blue metal door.

But the driver had missed the green gate and ended up a mile away. So he called from his cellphone and Sunny had to navigate him through the streets. By the time they arrived, there were almost twenty customers—nineteen more than the usual Wednesday night. The doctor was wearing a beautiful *punjabi,* a long dress with baggy pants, in a deep blue with gold embroidery, and a long blue scarf that she wore on her head and then wrapped over her shoulders like a shawl. Once inside, she took the scarf off to reveal beautiful long black hair that had been woven into a single thick braid.

She spoke in Hindi, which most Afghans had some familiarity with because of their obsession with anything Bollywood, with an English translator repeating what she'd said. She cited statistics most people in the room already knew: that the Afghan fertility rate was the second highest in the world, but that Afghanistan was second only to Sierra Leone for maternal mortality rates, that every twenty-eight minutes a woman died in Afghanistan during childbirth. But she spoke mostly about her recent visit to the Badakhshan province, where the maternal mortality rate was known to be the highest in the world. For every sixteen babies born, the doctor said, one woman died in labor. Clinics were too far away, and even if a woman in distress could reach one, they weren't well enough equipped to help. Besides, the doctors were men. Given the strict separation of the sexes, women would rather die than be helped by a male doctor.

She told a story about a pregnant woman in the village of Shattak who had complications during labor. The nearest hospital was thirty-seven miles away and there was no car. So what were the villagers to do? They got a ladder and laid it on the ground, then they laid the woman on the ladder and lifted it up, and twenty men took turns carrying the makeshift stretcher along the windy, rocky path, rarely used by a vehicle. The pace was slow, and the mother died on the way.

The room was silent. Sunny noticed from the other side of the room that Yazmina had stopped washing dishes and was listening with rapt attention from the kitchen. Watching Yazmina, her eyes full of concern and questions, Sunny knew she'd have to talk to her soon, even if it shamed her. For the health of the baby, if nothing else. Yazmina looked her way and Sunny smiled reassuringly.

76

Dr Malik continued, explaining the midwife-training program she had created for young women from districts throughout the province, from which she already had more than fifty graduates. She spoke passionately about the need for donations of medication and supplies, for food and shelter, for education, for volunteers. With the illiteracy rate so high and the disrespect for women so deep, women didn't have a chance to deal with their own health issues without more support. The crowd bombarded her with questions, with ideas, but she eventually prepared to leave in order to make an early morning meeting with the NATO health agency. She promised to return the following week to talk about the issues of children's health, if people agreed to give some time to her cause.

'I'll be right back. Got to meet Dr Malik before she leaves,' Isabel whispered into Sunny's ear, with Petr looking on. 'Provide her with some insights about NATO.'

Sunny watched Isabel as she pushed through the crowd, and as it slowly dispersed, she could see her deep in conversation with the doctor. Isabel was one tenacious woman.

Later that night, after the customers left, Halajan said to Sunny, 'When the doctor comes back, there will be more people. And the next time, more still. Like the saying goes, drop by drop a river becomes.'

Sunny felt as if she'd awakened from a long sleep. The night had been a success and she was invigorated. 'And we're helping the doctor. If we can get her some volunteers and make some money while doing it . . . So, how'd we do, Bashir Hadi?'

He was counting money at the coffee bar. He looked at her and smiled. 'Very well, Miss Sunny.

We did okay. But at this rate, a wall is months away. And winter's just beginning. You know how difficult it is to get people to go out at night in the cold. We'll have to work harder to get people here next week.'

'Let's plaster the coffeehouse—a sign on every table, the front door, and I'll email everyone I know in town and ask them to email everyone they know. Maybe I can get the email list from the UN.'

'Now you're talking,' Bashir Hadi said.

Sunny went to her room carrying a teapot and a cup, turned on her computer, and checked for email. There were the usual news reports (Taliban insurgents fighting in the south, Pakistani nuclear weapons suspected) and promotions from her meat distributor in Dubai and from her oil company.

Jack was trying to reach her on the instant chat. She opened it.

Tried to get there, held up in a meeting. Miss me? :)

To which Sunny replied:

Don't you smiley face me. Someday when you're the head of the CIA, I'll tell everyone that you use emoticons. That'll get their respect.

She sipped the wine and awaited the reply.

You disparage the smiley face? What am I to think of a woman who would do that? Speaking of which, did you get people tonight? Or do I have to feel ashamed?

Sunny answered:

It wasn't bad. You can hold your head high. But we'll do even better next time. The doctor is coming back. She is incredible.

She took another sip while waiting for Jack's response.

78

So . . . I'm waiting.

Sunny smiled and wrote:

Thank you. Seriously. It was a great night.

It seemed like forever before Jack responded:

So, when do you start work on the wall? Maybe then you'll smiley face me.

Sunny typed furiously:

Stop being such a nudge!!! My god, you're a pest. :) :) :)

And she laughed when Jack sent this:

Only if you stop with the exclamation points. And the smiley faces.

She responded:

Good night, you.

And then he did, too:

I have to go out of town. I'll be back in a couple weeks. I know you'll miss me. Stop crying. And go to bed.

She left her room, walked down the hall and up two flights of stairs to the roof. This was her place. There was a small table and chairs, pots for planting flowers once spring arrived, and her easel and palette. If riding in the car was where she could see, the roof was where she could breathe. In Kabul, in the coffeehouse, she was sometimes lonely, but never alone, except in the small space where she slept. And so, she made this roof her own.

It was windy and the sky was clear, black, and littered with stars, one of the wonderful perks of living here. Without electricity at night, there was little man-made light to diffuse the natural light that emanated from above. It was as if you could see into the sky, she thought, through its layers and into its core. Layers of stars, like translucent blanket upon blanket. The beauty was overwhelming. The wind blew her hair, and she willed herself to stop, to breathe, *to feel.*

It was a good night, tonight. She felt it was the beginning of something, more than just making money for the café's safety features. People had come to *her place* to learn something, to talk and listen and be moved. It felt good, it felt like she was doing something important and not just making a good cheeseburger.

She wondered what Tommy would think when he got back. She shrugged. He'd have liked the crowd. He was a people guy. But he wasn't impressed much by ideas, and he hated politics. Now, Jack, well . . . she stopped herself. No use comparing them. They were very different men. Not to mention that one was hers and one was her friend.

Finally she went downstairs to her room, wishing Tommy were waiting for her there. It was in bed where they got along best, she had to admit. And it was in bed at night when she missed him the most. Tonight, feeling the buzz from the coffeehouse, the passion of the doctor's words, all the people, the emails from Jack, she was acutely aware of feeling lonely. As she spread her favorite orange-scented lotion over her arms and then her legs, giving more attention to her elbows and her heels, she allowed herself to think that maybe Tommy would come back soon. Another month, hopefully. He never wrote, he never called, so there was no way to know. No contact from the field, he'd told her. The only times he called was to get her to Dubai to meet him for a two-day furlough.

She climbed into her bed and covered herself in the warm soft blankets of rusts, reds, and russets.

And then she turned over on her side, as she did every night. But tonight, she admitted to herself that she'd felt lonely even with Tommy the last couple of times he was home. Her mind shifted to Jack and how, if she were honest with herself, she'd like to be touching him, laughing with him, holding him against her body there in her bed under her roof, under the stars. But like Tommy, he was gone, too. And if he was thinking about anybody in his bed under the stars, it was surely his wife back home.

CHAPTER TEN

Candace looked out at the valley from her apartment in the tower that rose high above Wakil's compound, past the tops of the trees. From this vantage point, the trees appeared sparse. The Taliban had cut many of them down during the war to prevent the enemy from hiding in them, and local people had cut down many more since to burn for heat. The forest had been nearly wiped out and it occurred to her that the thick grove of trees they'd driven through to get here existed only because it had been situated along a river.

To the west, she could see the dry, dusty wasteland that led to Kabul, and to the east, the Hindu Kush that rose dramatically, their jagged peaks silhouetted against the early morning sky, their barren sides partly shadowed so that they looked like folded paper. From this vantage point, the problems of the country seemed as small as the houses far off in the distance. She felt like a queen surveying her vast kingdom.

The guards outside her door, and the female servants who would bring her breakfast and take her to Wakil's private *hammam* to help her bathe and give her a massage, added to her feeling that she was part of Wakil's royal retinue. He attended to every detail except the one that she wanted most: to spend private, intimate time with him. She felt a wave of desire, to hold him, and feel his body under her, but this was not going to happen. They hadn't made love since they'd arrived.

Wakil said it was because he was here in his home, his school, and he could not. It was impossible. He said she was his soul mate, that his heart had found its home, that making love to her was one of the great pleasures of life, and that she was almost impossible to resist. But that they should not, not here anyway. It would have to wait until after they arrived in Kabul.

They were leaving for the city today and Candace had mixed feelings about it. Though she respected all he had done for these children, and loved seeing him with them and at his work, she'd rather have Wakil the man than Wakil the prince. And yes, she had to admit that she was ready for nice restaurants, to wear pretty clothes, and to sleep with Wakil in his house. Of course, they couldn't really sleep together, and they'd have to stay on separate floors, but in the night, when everyone else was asleep, he could come to her room.

She was also eager to get back to work. It was her responsibility to raise money for Wakil's school, and she'd set up meetings with several NGOs involved with the welfare of Afghan children.

It was late morning by the time they said their

good-byes and got into the same black SUV with the same driver who'd brought them here. Sitting close to Wakil in the back, their shoulders touching, she thought back to when they'd met and how warm and gracious he was, the way most Afghan men are. He'd invited them to his home if they were ever back in Kabul, and a month later when a meeting sent Richard there, she'd contacted him. She knew that night, as they ate their elegant dinner in his home, what she wanted to happen between them, what seemed destined to happen given the strong pull toward Wakil she felt in his presence, but had no idea that she would come to see him as a leader, a man of such importance. She had no idea then of his ability to persuade her to do almost anything. Wherever he led, she would follow.

Back up through the pine trees and out into the open, dirt-brown, rock-strewn plains, the car headed toward Kabul. Past shepherds tending their goats, wood-slatted trucks carrying chickens to the city's market, transport donkeys carrying bags of produce, a convoy of army vehicles at the roadside with camouflaged soldiers, their rifles hanging from their shoulders. They passed a truck of men in white shirts and baggy pants, Pashtun vests, brown jackets, and turbans, all carrying rifles—probably Taliban. As they neared the city, they passed a dilapidated sea of tents, as far as the eye could see, set behind a high barbed-wire fence, where shoeless children played with a ball, its skin sheared partway off, so that it flopped instead of rolled, where men loitered and women crouched on the hard earth, huddled together, it seemed, to ward off the cold. There, a long line of people snaking out from under a tent. And there, several dogs pulling something

83

apart with their teeth.

Candace looked at Wakil for an explanation.

He said, 'A refugee camp.'

'Yes.' She had seen these before, had even entered their fences, when traveling the country with Richard. She'd never forget the eyes of one mother, her baby wrapped in tattered blankets, her three other children with stomachs swollen with hunger leaning against her as if she could provide them the shelter they needed. 'But so close to Kabul. Where are these people from? From Pakistan?' she asked, turning back to her window. 'How can they let people live like this? Look at the children. They have no shoes.'

'Shoes? They have no clean water. Little food. And they are Afghans. Displaced during the war, returning to nothing. Some have come back from Pakistan, where the government is shutting down their camps, forcing them to return home to nothing. Their houses gone, their land gone, no jobs, no money. The corrupt government has nothing to do with them,' he said bitterly. 'The Russians, NATO forces, the Americans, the insurgency—with every war, homes are destroyed, people flee, and then they come back to nothing. To less than nothing. Destitute, living on top of land mines, living in squalor, in their own shit. Afghans living worse than prisoners in their own country.'

'So don't you think the UN and the—'

'We must not be so naive. NATO, the UN . . . they have no power to make real change. Even the rich countries are not concerned. Afghanistan needs to rid itself of the people who only want to rape its women, enslave its children, destroy its land, its resources.' His voice spit anger. 'And keep it far from God.'

Of course she agreed with him. After witnessing his school, his clinic, and the refugee camps, she knew he was right.

His face was reddened with frustration. 'This is exactly why the Taliban are on the rise. Out of the depths of our people's misery.'

But this stopped her. 'You can't be saying that the Taliban is a better alternative!'

'I certainly *understand* their growing popularity. That is all.' He turned to her, gentler now. 'You have a good, open heart, my Candace. This,' he said, pointing to the tents, 'is exactly why we need your help.' He took her hand in his. 'You will change these people's lives. And many more.'

His tone quieted Candace, who kept her eyes on the camp as they passed. They sat in silence a long time.

As they entered Kabul's outskirts, they went from makeshift city to makeshift memorial. A forest of green flags, raised high on thin wooden poles that were stuck into the dusty earth, stood bent in the wind. Candace had seen these many times before. They marked the graves of martyrs— Afghan boys and men who died fighting in battle. There was a real cemetery for foreign fighters, the Sherpur Cemetery, but an Afghan was buried on the hillsides, on the plains, in the valleys, with only the small green piece of fabric on a wooden pole to mark his grave.

Then they reached the city walls, plastered with posters and sprayed with bullet holes and graffiti, mostly in Dari, with antigovernment slogans. These words Candace knew. Her husband had spent a lifetime trying to turn the spread of this feeling in Iraq, Pakistan, and Afghanistan, without doing the real work of raising funds to invest in schools, hospitals, and businesses. Now, after spending time with Wakil, she realized how futile and wrong-headed Richard's efforts had been.

Through the clogged streets, they finally made it to Wakil's house. The car was whisked through a double gate, guarded by two armed *chokidor*, and drove up a long U-shaped driveway paved in smooth stone. Wakil's house wasn't just large; it was a mansion. It had five floors, and the tiled mosaics covering much of the exterior reminded Candace of a mosque, but without the domes. They were greeted at the front door by a servant in a silk turban, who escorted them to an inner courtyard where a blue-tiled fountain gurgled with water into a small pool and potted trees reached up to the stained-glass skylight five stories above. The stone-pillared canopies surrounding the courtyard gave the building the feel of a palace. It was simply breathtaking, even after she had been in it many times. Another servant then rushed in and whispered something to Wakil, who turned to Candace.

'I must go. There is an emergency. I will see you at dinner, my love.'

She smiled at him, though she felt rejected. They'd come to Wakil's home precisely because he was supposed to have more time for her. Was she being a spoiled baby or had some heat diminished in their relationship?

She was shown to her room on the third floor. While she was unpacking, her cellphone rang. It was her contact at the embassy telling her that a renowned Indian doctor was speaking tonight on children's health issues at a local coffeehouse. He thought Candace would be interested in meeting the doctor given Candace's recent work on behalf of Wakil's clinic. She closed the phone and sat on the high bed that was covered in gorgeous handmade silk fabric, rich with color and texture. As she ran her hand across the luxurious bedspread, she smiled. This was a sure way to get Wakil's attention. The doctor—her skills as well as her ability to get attention for her projects—was just what his clinic needed. She knew he'd cancel any plans he might have to attend this event with her so that she might entice the doctor to help the clinic. So what that Candace wasn't the main attraction. She'd be more than happy to share the spotlight with the good doctor.

CHAPTER ELEVEN

Yazmina hadn't been feeling well all week. She was exhausted. On some mornings she found it difficult just to get out of bed. And then the chores were almost impossible to complete. But she smiled and did everything in her power to pretend she was fine. It worried her, this feeling of lethargy, and she wondered if the baby was well or whether her fall from the car, or the disinfectants she used to mop the floors, or the filthy sewage-strewn streets could have injured the baby deep inside her belly. But she couldn't risk anyone's suspicions—because that would be even worse for the life growing inside her.

And it was Wednesday again. If last week there

had been twenty people, tonight there would be double or even triple that, if the number of calls Miss Sunny received on the phone she wore around her neck like a talisman was any indication. People asked directions, confirmed the time. Already many had arrived to eat well before tonight's event began. And there had been much preparation as well— the errands, the baking, the ordering, the cooking, cleaning, and straightening. It seemed as if all week led to this day.

Yazmina was resting now on her *toshak*, her hands on her belly, dreaming that her baby was well, warm, and afloat in her womb. She hoped the baby had found her thumb to suck and that she had every limb in its rightful place. She wondered if the baby was dreaming of her.

At that moment, the nausea she'd been feeling for days swept over her like the winds over the mountains, and she barely made it to the washbowl that sat on the chest. Sweating, she vomited for what seemed like hours. Eventually, she was emptied, and she took the bowl to the toilet in the rear courtyard. On her way back, she encountered Halajan, who was leaning against a wall, smoking. Yazmina had never seen a woman smoking, and on another night, she might have been startled. But considering her own physical condition and how terrible she felt, she had no judgment left for anyone else. The sun's setting light shone on the trail of smoke as it rose into the air. But everything else was in shadows, which Yazmina was thankful for. She knew her sickened face would betray her.

'Are you all right, lost one?' Halajan asked.

'I am fine, thank you,' answered Yazmina. 'I just needed to use the toilet and clean my bowl.' She looked up. 'It will be an interesting night, won't it?'

Halajan kept her eyes on Yazmina. 'You are curious about the doctor's stories?'

Yazmina lowered her eyes. 'We all must be concerned for mothers and children.'

'Yes, we must,' Halajan said. 'But what matters is how quickly you do what your soul directs.'

Yazmina's eyes widened. 'You quote Rumi. I know this from my mother, who used to sing his poems! She loved Rumi from the time she was a young girl, when her own mother recited his poems. From generation to generation his words were beloved in my family. One day, a trader came through on his way from Kabul and he had a book of Rumi poems, and though my mother couldn't read, she had to have the book. So my husband bought it for her.' She laughed a little. 'My Najam would have bought a blind man a sewing needle if he had wanted it.'

'I suppose it must be, then. Rumi it is.' Halajan took a long puff from her cigarette and let it out with a loud breath. 'Now finish your rest because it will be a busy night.'

Yazmina noticed that the moon had risen behind a low cloud. Rumi. Mother. Layla. Perhaps it was the memory of them or her thoughts of Najam. Yazmina was surprised to be feeling better. She had but one prayer that night: that Sunny would come to need her before she learned of her secret.

*   *   *

Sunny was elated. Almost every chair, every table in the coffeehouse was taken, and people were busy eating and talking well before the doctor was to

89

begin. The crowd was mostly women, split almost equally between foreigners and Afghans. She had hired an extra *chokidor* for the night, at Ahmet's urging, but she needn't have. Women didn't stash guns in their purses, especially when they were coming to hear a renowned doctor talking about children's health issues in today's Afghanistan.

Isabel had returned to talk further with the doctor. She was sitting with Petr at a table nearby, already sipping the 'tea' that she had brought in her large saddlebag, and which Halajan had quickly dispensed into a teapot. There were two empty seats at the table, which Sunny was saving for herself, once the doctor started to talk, and for Jack, if he showed up. She hadn't heard from him since their last instant message. She didn't know whether to be worried or pissed—but above all she just wanted to share another successful night with him.

Meanwhile there was serving to do, coffees to be made, and tables to clear. Sunny imagined the wall outside bigger, the evenings profitable, and the money coming in so fast that she had to figure out what to do with it all. *Stop,* she thought. *You're getting way ahead of yourself.*

And then there was a loud crash that made everyone turn and stop talking. Yazmina had dropped a tray of cups and saucers on the floor, shattering them into tiny fragments. The poor girl looked shocked, but beyond that she looked gray and tired, too. Sunny wanted to kick herself for letting Yazmina work so hard, and was quickly at her side.

'Yazmina, *khair asti*? Are you all right?'

But she didn't answer. She went to the closet and

90

returned with a twig brush and a dustpan.

'Yazmina, I'll do that,' said Halajan.

But Yazmina was already on her knees sweeping up the shards.

'What's up with Yazmina?' whispered Halajan. 'She doesn't look good. Is she sick?'

'She's okay, I think,' said Sunny. 'I'll keep an eye on her.'

'Maybe she's just lazy. Maybe not used to this kind of work.'

'Are you kidding? She doesn't stop, and she's as strong as two men. We wouldn't survive without her on a night like this.'

Halajan smiled, put a hand on her hip. 'We survived before and we'd survive after.'

'Too much competition for you, Halajan?' Sunny teased.

'Me? You joke. Look how fast she has become important to you. Be careful not to need her too much. She won't be here always.'

'Well, I'm going to make sure she's okay,' Sunny said.

She went behind the counter to the kitchen, where Yazmina was throwing the remains of the china into the garbage.

'Sunnyjan. *Emorz,* I no good. I will work to repay the damage.'

Sunny understood that she was saying that she was very sorry and today she wasn't feeling well. 'It's just *pyala*s, a few cups. We have many more. No problem.'

Sunny saw the stunned look on Yazmina's face and realized her family probably couldn't afford even one cup like the many she had just broken. She'd have to try to be more sensitive. Right now, though, her mind was on Yazmina's health.

'Are you feeling *khub,* all right? Are you *mareez,* sick?' Sunny cocked her head to the side and tried to see into Yazmina's eyes, but they were downcast. 'Would you like to see a *daktar*?'

Yazmina looked up. 'No, no, *tashakur,* thank you, I *ba khoda,*' she said. 'As God is my witness, I promise to be more careful.'

Sunny knew she was saying she was fine, but she could see that Yazmina was flushed. Beads of perspiration formed on her brow and her eyes were glassy.

'Maybe you should go to your room and rest,' said Sunny. 'Perhaps after the *daktar* has finished speaking, she could come and—'

'No, no, please. *Besyar,* many people. How will you—' She looked afraid, as if she was certain she was about to be punished.

Sunny took the pan and broom from her and said, 'Okay, no *daktar.* But you go rest so that tomorrow, when it's very busy, you will be ready to help.' She saw the concern on Yazmina's face. 'Don't worry. You still have your job and your home here. And you will, no matter what happens. Okay? It's natural, I think, to feel nauseous when you're . . .' Sunny caught herself.

Yazmina widened her eyes and looked at her with fear.

'It's okay, it's possibly something you ate. But if you don't feel better tomorrow, we'll have to go to the *daktar.*'

'Yes, but I will be okay. I'm just a little tired,' said Yazmina.

Sunny watched her as she untied her apron and hung it on the hook next to the refrigerator.

92

Yazmina started to walk out the back door but stopped and leaned against the wall. Sunny rushed over with a chair.

'Are you all right?' she asked. 'Please, sit.'

'I'd like to stay and hear the doctor,' Yazmina said.

'Yes, of course,' Sunny answered. She put a hand on Yazmina's shoulder.

*   *   *

The door of the coffeehouse opened, and in walked a woman who was dressed like a celebrity, with knee-high boots, tight jeans, a huge, bespangled designer bag over her arm, and a tight, cropped white down jacket. Except for the shawl she wore over her head, she could've been at a ski resort. With her was an imposing, much younger Afghan man wearing traditional clothes and an elegant turban. He was very handsome, broad and tall, but also serious, with a rigid stance. It was his eyes that drew you to him, dark eyes with a stern gaze that was mesmerizing.

The woman took off her shawl to reveal long, straight, bleached platinum hair. She leaned on one foot and tapped the other, clearly used to entering a restaurant and being seated immediately.

Instead of waiting for Halajan to make her way over from the kitchen, the woman scanned the room and then she sat herself and her companion with Isabel and Petr, in the seats Sunny had been saving for herself and Jack. The two men shook hands and began to talk.

Sunny was tempted to say something snarky about waiting for a table, but she stopped herself.

This night was meant to bring in paying customers and a new wall was more important than correcting someone's sense of entitlement. So she went over to greet them.

'It's *Candace,* Candace Appleton,' the platinum blonde said, holding out her hand to be shaken, while looking Sunny up and down, and waiting for her response.

'Welcome. I'm Sunny.'

'Sunny?' She smiled. 'That's a cute nickname. What's it short for?'

Sunny narrowed her eyes. 'It's just Sunny, the name my mother gave me.'

'It sounds, well, *rural.*' She turned an ear toward Sunny. 'Like your accent. You must be from the South.'

Sunny looked at Isabel, who raised her brows and smiled, basically daring Sunny to respond. But Sunny just cocked a shoulder and put a hand on a hip, thinking, *and yours makes you sound like a stuck-up bitch.* She knew that her accent made her sound like a hick. But hell if she was going to let this woman get away with being rude. 'And what's Candace long for—*Candy?*'

Isabel barked a loud laugh and said, 'There's my girl.'

Sunny couldn't help herself. She'd met women like Candace before. They came to Kabul in the guise of wanting to help, bringing their privilege and Western expectations with them, often hooking up with a man just like the one this Candace was with, but when they were unable to deal with the bureaucracy and the corruption, the filth and the violence, they left, feeling that this place, and its people, were of no use.

94

'To be honest, yes,' answered Candace. 'And it's taken my whole life to shake it. So I thought we had something in common.' She shrugged. 'Guess I was wrong.'

Sunny felt bad. Maybe she'd judged too soon, as she so often did. Now she was curious. 'Where are you from?' Sunny asked, unable to place Candace's accent.

'Boston,' she answered. 'Beacon Hill.'

'Oh, Beacon Hill,' Isabel said pseudo-seriously, 'quite posh.'

'Funny,' Sunny said, 'you don't have much of a Bahstin accent.'

Candace hesitated, looked from Isabel to Sunny, and then said, 'I wasn't *born* there, just *from* there.'

Sunny liked her honesty. 'So where *were* you born, since we're getting personal?'

Candace hesitated again, turned to look at the man she'd arrived with, who was clearly enjoying his conversation, and said, with a deeply Southern accent, 'Darn it, you got me. Willow Springs, Mo.'

Sunny had to laugh and told herself to give the girl a break. 'Welcome, Missouri. I'm Arkansas.'

'And I'm afraid I'm London,' said Isabel. She put out her hand and introduced herself.

Candace smiled warmly and took Isabel's hand in hers, and shook it, and then took Sunny's and shook it the way they did back home: hard.

Sunny was about to ask Candace why she'd come to Kabul and, more specifically, to her coffeehouse, but one look at the handsome, charming man beside her explained it—or at least part of the story. Besides, it was time for the doctor to speak. So she walked to the makeshift podium and introduced her proudly, looking out on all the faces of those

95

who'd come to hear the doctor speak. Then she returned to the table and listened to Dr Malik report on, with the help of the English translator, what happened to babies born to women whose husbands had died. And what became of babies born to women pregnant out of wedlock, usually from rape, sometimes from a love affair without the sanction of the family. And how female babies weren't given the same care if ill, since girls were going to be given away eventually to their husband's family. She mentioned the old Indian saying 'Why water your neighbor's tree?' and everyone laughed.

The doctor paused for some questions. Sunny was distracted by Candace and her friend, who sat riveted throughout, his coal black eyes on the doctor. Periodically he'd whisper something into Candace's ear and she'd whisper back. It was clear they had a natural intimacy, making Sunny feel a twinge of jealousy. But then he whispered something to Candace, causing her to sit up in her seat and wave her hand.

'Excuse me. Excuse me!' Candace whispered loudly, holding up the palm of her hand as she tried to get Halajan's attention. 'Well, *finally,*' she said when Halajan eventually approached. 'I'd like a cappuccino. And make it decaf, please.'

Halajan raised her eyebrows and hesitated. But eventually she answered, 'Certainly, madame. Of course. And your friend,' she said, now directing herself to the man sitting next to Candace. 'Would your friend like something as well?'

'The cappuccino is for me, thank you,' he answered in Dari.

To Sunny, Halajan said under her breath, 'Afghan men who are too big to order their own coffee are too small to enjoy it.'

'Rumi?' asked Sunny.

'No, but it could've been!' And she rolled her eyes, cocked her head toward Wakil, and went to the kitchen.

The doctor finished her talk by answering dozens of questions, offering the name of a website where you could make donations, and promising to come back the following week. Then Isabel and Candace approached her. First Isabel asked to interview her about the health concerns over crop-dusting the poppy fields. Then she introduced Candace, who spoke to her for a few minutes before she brought Wakil over.

During the few moments Wakil was out of earshot, Candace seemed to relax. 'What a night! Thank you so much, Sunny. I've been spending so much time trying to get help for the children, I don't know when the last time was that I got to hang out with some regular girls. I can get very tense, I know,' she said, looking at Halajan.

Sunny took that as an apology, but from the look on Halajan's face, she wasn't sure that she did. In any case, Sunny was willing to give Candace the benefit of the doubt.

'And thanks for introducing me to Doctor Malik,' Candace said to Isabel.

'Anytime, *Candy*,' she said with a smile.

'If it weren't for that charming accent, I'd have to kill you.'

'Then, see you all next week?' Sunny asked, surprising herself that she really hoped she would.

'Definitely,' said Isabel, as she walked out with Petr.

'Yeah,' said Candace in her thick Southern

drawl. 'We'll all come back, now, ya hear?'

Sunny laughed and watched the two women leave, one following behind an Afghan, and the other arm-in-arm with a Russian.

*   *   *

If mornings made Ahmet feel restless from the pull of the mountains, then Kabul nights made him feel his self-imposed limitations as sharply as if he were lying shirtless on the rubbled roadway before him. He readjusted the rifle on his shoulder and arched his back as if to shake off the imprints of the stones. It was dark and the last guests were leaving the coffeehouse. Few cars were on the road; the streets were emptied of people. The sky was black and filled with stars; all the soot and smoke that gave the daylight sky a thick, brown haze had vanished into the night air. Those stars, which looked so close and glittered with life, only angered him. He kicked the wall with the heel of his boot. He was only twenty, but he felt eighty years old.

He blew out some air and laughed to himself. That's what standing at a gate for fourteen hours will do—make you feel old and tired. He thought of his father then, and how he'd gotten very old very quickly and didn't live past sixty. His father, whom he respected, who taught him how to use a gun, fix a roof, and install a toilet but had few words even though his heart was as kind as his mother was stubborn. He missed his father. He'd have expected Ahmet to stay at home, to not dream big or go too far. He wouldn't have been as disappointed in Ahmet as his mother seemed to be.

The woman with the straight golden hair let the

coffeehouse door slam behind her as she walked toward the gate, the tall Afghan she'd arrived with next to her. She was pretty, Ahmet thought, though much too modern for his taste, with her high boots and brightly colored clothes. She covered her head with a scarf but wore her hair loose under it, he could tell from the many strands that blew in the wind. She was much older than the man. Ahmet saw this over and over again: foreign women with local men, forging a kind of bond around money and mutual need. This was not for him. But he wanted a bond with a woman. He was waiting to be introduced to his bride the right way, the proper way: family to family, under the rules of Kabul, within the laws of Islam. Not to be moved by green eyes; never to gaze into his bride's eyes until the wedding day.

He wanted his own business. He wanted to protect his mother and at the same time to be free of his responsibility to her. He wanted this and that and everything. He wanted, he wanted, he wanted—much more than a steady good Muslim should. Much more than Muhammad would sanction. Much more than his beliefs would allow.

He swallowed, hoping his desires would go down with the bad taste in his mouth.

The man and woman walked out, and he closed the gate behind them. As the gate banged shut, the man turned back to him and looked him in the eyes. And with that one look, Ahmet summed him up, using the instinct that had served him well for the four years he'd guarded this post: no good. The tall Afghan with the flashy American woman was simply no good.

CHAPTER TWELVE

Rashif sat at his table, pen in hand, the vellum before him. His room was black like the sky out the one small window across the room except for the table that was lit by a lone bulb overhead. It was late and he was tired, but he had a letter to write before going to sleep. He looked at the blank paper and touched his pen to it.

My dearest Halajan,

Tomorrow is Thursday and you will come to the bazaar. I am dreaming of seeing your eyes and praying to Allah that you will not be wearing a burqa. I know it is safer that way, but it makes me so angry. It's as if a woman's eyes, a woman's face, are evil. We, who are old enough to have lived through one regime after another, know the burqa is about a man's fear, not about a woman's malice.

Hala, I would like to write about your eyes and what they do to me, but today I am angry. I'm sorry, I know it's not the way of Islam to waste your heart on anger, but I can't help it. Two of Karzai's soldiers entered my shop this morning. Both with rifles, one with two military coats over his arm. Winter has come, one said. We need these coats made to fit us, the other said, or we will freeze. They'd been previously worn by soldiers killed in action. Winter was upon them, the army's resources were low, and the coats were to be reused. But a tall man replaced a short one, a stout one took the place of a thin one, and tailoring them to fit was a big job.

I gave them each a coffee. And it was then I saw that they were no more than boys, maybe fifteen, sixteen. And I thought that their lives had been stolen from them.

I know you feel in your heart as I do. The Talib are returning in larger numbers than the last time, and there is nothing our military can do to stop them. There is nothing the Americans can do. Their presence here only fuels the fire of the Taliban hatred. It's as if everybody thinks that Afghans are theirs for the taking. It's as if we're not real people with hearts and minds of our own. It's as if we're animals who need humans to shape us. By Muhammad, I know that if more of us had some education and could read, we could be a mighty force. We could rule our own lives.

Don't worry, Hala—I know I'm only a tailor and not a leader. But I can dream like one!

I am afraid for you and for us and for our beloved country. As you and I both know, life can turn quickly. How recently did we walk around in jeans and sweaters? I still have my Nike shoes, but now I wear them only inside my home. Silly, I know. There I am in my pajamas and my Nikes. Am I telling you too much?

And so I am angry that we cannot be together because of foolish rules. My wife is dead, your husband is dead, and yet—if the wrong men were to read this letter, you would be stoned to death.

I know what you will say to me, if you would ever write me a letter. You would quote Rumi,

*who said, 'Patience is the key to joy.' Well, I am
sick and tired of Rumi!*

*Tomorrow, my love. Have a safe trip. One day
I will visit you at your coffeehouse. You say don't
come because of your son, but one day I will
disobey you, my love, and show up at your door.
I will smile at your son and he will be like a son
to me.*
Yours,
Rashif

CHAPTER THIRTEEN

Bashir Hadi was sitting on a stool at the counter,
and with a calculator, totaled the earnings from
the night before and posted them in the accounting
book. He looked up and said, 'Just one or two more
nights like that and we'll have our wall.' He smiled
broadly. 'And then, nothing will stop us. Here,
look.'

Sunny pulled the book toward her and leaned
over it. 'Today the wall, tomorrow the world.' She
laughed.

'Where is that girl?' Halajan asked, rushing in
from the kitchen. 'Has anyone seen Yazmina?'

Oh, great. Sunny felt like kicking herself. She
had planned to check on her this morning, but
she'd gotten distracted. Yazmina normally came
down before the first muezzin call, when the sun
appeared over the mountain peaks to the east of
Kabul. The sun was already spilling in through the
windows, leaving a blinding glare as it bounced off
the tile floors.

She stood and said, 'Not yet. I'll go and—'

'I will get her,' said Halajan as she headed toward the back.

'Halajan, wait. I'll go,' insisted Sunny, putting a hand on Halajan's arm. She felt responsible, knowing Yazmina's exhaustion had to do with her pregnancy, and she did not want Halajan to find out. Halajan was a modern woman, but she would do anything to protect her son, the café, her home. Harboring an unmarried, pregnant woman was dangerous for them all.

But Halajan said, 'I am going,' and she was already out the back door before Sunny could stop her.

*   *   *

Halajan knocked on Yazmina's door. And when there was no answer, she opened it slowly. She hadn't been in here since Sunny had fixed the room for her, and what a lovely job she had done. Even a mirror! She saw that it was turned to face the wall, and she understood, for this girl was from the mountains. Yazmina was still in her *toshak*, apparently sleeping. But Halajan couldn't tell because her face was turned away.

'Yazmina,' she whispered, as she knelt down next to the bed. 'Yazmina, it's time to get up.'

Yazmina rolled over toward her without saying a word. Her skin was a greenish gray, her eyes sunken. Her flimsy nightdress revealed a swollen belly.

Halajan's skin bristled with fear. She'd seen that look before on the faces of other women when she was a midwife many years before. And on her own face when she was pregnant with Ahmet. Twenty years ago and she could still remember the nausea. She glanced behind her to be sure the door was closed.

'Yazmina,' she whispered. 'Are you with child?'

'Of course not,' she said, pulling her blankets over her and turning back to the wall.

But Halajan pressed further. 'You must tell me, young one. Who else can help you?'

'No one. And if you try to, you will be punished just like me,' Yazmina said fearfully.

'But who is the father?'

'My husband,' she cried.

'Where is he now? Does he know?'

'He is dead. An explosion on the hillside.' She spoke as if her world had ended on that day.

Halajan hadn't asked about the circumstances that brought Yazmina to the coffeehouse, though she suspected it was something like this. For what other reason would a woman of Yazmina's beauty be alone with nowhere to go? She let out a deep breath and wiped her brow. She was perspiring even in the chilly room.

'How far along are you?'

'About halfway,' she said, panicked. In the lightweight *kameez* she wore for sleeping, she couldn't hide the roundness of her stomach. It protruded like a small melon.

'You're a silly girl not to tell Sunnyjan. We must now.'

'But how can I?' Her eyes filled with tears. 'Once she knows she will have no option but to throw me out. And then I will have nowhere to go, nothing to protect my baby. Please, Halajan, let me keep hiding it. I want this baby. It is my only connection to my Najam, who went to paradise too soon. I beg you. Do not expose me. I will lose the baby. I will lose everything. Didn't you hear the doctor's words last night? Her stories about baby boys stolen, baby girls killed? And I have lost everything already.' The tears fell down her cheeks onto her pillow.

'You underestimate Sunnyjan. She will understand. And she will find a way.' Though Halajan knew firsthand what happened to women who had babies with no husband. She didn't require a foreign doctor to tell her that often the infants were stolen to be sold as slaves, warriors, or sexual playthings, the women jailed or killed.

'There is no way. Not in Kabul, not in all of Afghanistan. A woman and her baby are only as good as the man who takes care of them.'

Halajan hesitated, looked into Yazmina's eyes, and then made a decision. 'We will have to hide it until we can hide it no longer. First, though, we must make you well. I will go to the market for some herbs. It is Thursday, after all. It is market day.'

She leaned toward Yazmina to kiss her forehead but then stopped herself, realizing this wasn't her daughter. Instead, she touched the tips of her three middle fingers to Yazmina's forehead, then brought them to her own lips and kissed them, and then touched them again to Yazmina's forehead.

Halajan whispered, 'I will tell Sunnyjan that you are with a fever and that I will get you a remedy in the market. You do not move today, understood?'

Yazmina put her hand on Halajan's hand and said, 'Thank you, Halajan. Thank you.'

Then there was a knock on the door, and Sunny entered. She closed the door softly behind her and looked at the two women's faces and knew that Yazmina's secret was out. But she was going to play it cool. She approached the bed as Halajan stood, giving her place to Sunny, who knelt on the floor next to it.

'How are you feeling, Yazmina?' asked Sunny softly.

'She has the *tab,* a fever,' interrupted Halajan.

'Is that it?' asked Sunny. 'You have the *tab*? We should get her to the doctor.'

'She just needs to rest,' said Halajan.

Sunny turned to her and said, 'Halajan, please. May I talk to Yazmina? I know my Dari isn't great, but she understands me.'

Yazmina nodded and smiled weakly.

'So, don't you think you should see a *daktar*?'

'She doesn't need a doctor!' insisted Halajan. 'She just needs to take things easy.'

Sunny stood and faced Halajan. 'But'—and now she bent forward and whispered into Halajan's ear—'she is pregnant. And she needs to see a doctor.'

Finally, Halajan was silenced. She looked at Yazmina and nodded.

Yazmina began to cry.

'You knew?' asked Halajan.

'Yes,' Sunny said quietly. 'I knew, but I was waiting for some time to pass so that Yazmina would trust me. I didn't want to frighten her, or shame her. And I wasn't sure how others would react.'

'But when did you know? How long not a word?' asked Yazmina.

'At the *wazarat-e-zanan,* the Women's Ministry, when I first saw you.'

Halajan smiled and nodded. Sunny was a good woman, very annoying, but good.

'You knew I was *hamla* and you took me to your house?'

'Of course,' said Sunny, knowing the word for *pregnant*. 'How could I not?'

Yazmina's eyes were full of tears. 'What gave me away?' she asked. 'How did you know?'

'There was one small thing. And you're doing it right now. Your hand. When the assistant to that terrible *wazir* said you could stay the night or two in the beauty school, you put your hand on your belly. Just like that. A woman like me, who's never been *hamla,* would never hold herself that way. Only a woman carrying a life would hold her belly—'

'With such love,' said Halajan.

The three women stayed quiet for a while, and then Sunny asked Halajan, 'So now what do we do?'

'Well,' answered Halajan, puffing her chest out like a rooster, 'lucky for you, and for you, Yazmina, I am a *qaabela,* a midwife. I used to help bring babies into the world. Hundreds in my life.' And then she looked at Sunny and said, 'So, until it's time, *Inshallah,* it is our secret.'

A look of relief swept across Yazmina's face.

'But no one can know,' Halajan said. 'Not another soul. This is very, very dangerous. Even a good man can turn bad in this situation. So it is agreed?'

'Not a soul,' said Sunny. 'But what happens when the baby—?'

'That is another story for another day.'

Then Sunny looked at Yazmina and saw that she was asleep. And she and Halajan tiptoed out of the room.

*   *   *

When they returned to the café, Bashir Hadi was busy preparing coffee. And, then Sunny saw him. There, at his usual table, was Jack, sipping on a cappuccino and reading a newspaper, his legs crossed to the side of the table because there wasn't the height underneath it to accommodate them. She exhaled loudly, as if she'd been holding her breath since he left, and told herself to walk right by him, to act naturally, to not be irrational. He'd been gone for two weeks, and seeing him made her want to sing. But she sure wasn't going to show it.

He ignored her, too. '*Salaam alaikum,* Halajan. Hope this beautiful morning finds you well.'

'*Wa alaikum as-salaam,*' she answered with a broad smile across her face. 'How was your trip? You're still in one piece, I see.'

Sunny grabbed a cloth, wiped the counter, put out two trays, and placed napkins, saucers, and spoons on them, stealing a glance at Jack. While she waited for Bashir Hadi to bring the cups, she noticed that Jack's skin was tan from the winter sun, the gray at his temples more evident, the creases at the corners of his eyes deeper. It was as if the two weeks had been two years.

Jack slapped his thigh. 'All here. You know me, Hala. I'm not one to use a gun. I let the young, brave guys do that.'

'No, but they can be used on you. I don't know what you do, but it's a relief when you come back.'

'For me, too, I can tell you that. And you'—he turned to Sunny—'hey, you!'

108

She finally smiled at him and he nodded toward the door. 'Come on. I have something for you outside.' He stood. 'Come on.'

'That's it? No "hello"? No "how are you"? Much less "I missed you and can't believe I stayed away so long"?'

'Shut up and come with me. I come bearing gifts. Actually, *a* gift.'

She headed for the door, but Jack grabbed her arm. She felt her chest fill and her skin tingle.

'Excited to see me, are you? Put something on. It's freezing outside.'

She grabbed her coat from the hook on the wall, and putting it on, she said, 'What's so big it has to be outside? I love gifts, but usually the very small kind that fit in a pocket.'

'Like chewing gum?' Jack's eyes twinkled.

'Only if it's diamond studded.'

'Funny, you don't seem like a diamond kind of girl.'

'Where'd you get that idea?'

'Oh, I don't know,' he said, looking her up and down. 'Maybe the hair, the jeans, maybe . . .' And with two long fingers, he gently lifted the cord holding her cellphone around her neck, and continued, 'It's the jewelry you usually wear.'

She grabbed the cord away, letting the phone fall between her breasts.

'Come on,' said Jack, 'I have something so special, it will change your life.'

'A motorbike!' She'd wanted one since she first came to Kabul. Tommy had promised to buy her one, but left before he did. Jack, of course, had told her she'd be an idiot to get one.

'Would you just come?'

She gave an exaggerated frown, crossed one side of her coat over the other, and held it closed. 'Okay, okay. But if it's not a motorbike . . . I don't know . . .'

He held the door open for her, and she felt the blast of cold air against her face. The sky was already blue, and the sun's rays were reaching out to her over the courtyard's walls. A glorious day! A present! And Jack was back! What could possibly go wrong?

First she saw Ahmet, his eyes wide with fear. In his hand was a rope. And on the other end of the rope, sitting on the ground by the front wall, was a German shepherd, all hundred and fifty pounds, four legs, four paws, and one drooling mouth of him. *A fucking dog!* He must've seen Sunny's expression because he started to bark at her. Ahmet jumped back, and then the dog turned to him and licked his hand.

Ahmet wiped his hand on his coat with disgust.

'Come, Poppy,' Jack called, and the creature loped over to him. Jack scruffed its head and scratched its ears. 'Sunny, meet Poppy.'

Sunny hated dogs. They were dirty, stupid, and demanded your love and attention, as if you had it to give to them. She turned around and headed back into the coffeehouse.

'Wait,' Jack pleaded. 'Just slow down there a minute. Let me explain.'

She sighed, then turned to him and put her hands on her hips.

'Poppy here is a trained police dog. She worked for years opium sniffing. Hence, her name. Now she's older and it's time for her to retire. But she's too young to do nothing. She'd go crazy. She needs

110

a job. And that job would be you.'

'What the hell am I going to do with a dog?'

Poppy barked several times, as if arguing for herself. Very loudly.

'A *dangerous* dog.'

'You're going to take her driving. She's going to be your driving dog. Your car canine. Your Mercedes mutt.' He laughed. 'Your protective pooch!'

'Stop, I beg you.'

'Seriously, every time you drive around town, a woman alone, in a car, in a Mercedes, for God's sake, even though it's old, you're risking your life. From now on, you take Poppy. When you take one of your walks, you take Poppy. Most Afghans, as you know, hate dogs—'

'Maybe that's why I feel such an affinity for the people.'

'—and fear dogs. I've been sick with worry every time you go out driving. Well, now—'

'So you're actually giving me this old German shepherd—I mean, it's not even cute—for *you*. So *you* won't have to worry. Typical philanthropist.' She turned back to the door and yelled, 'No thanks.'

She couldn't see that Jack had taken the leash from Ahmet, relieving him from a terrible duty.

'Come on, look, Sunny,' Jack said.

She turned back to him and Poppy came to her, her large paws prancing like a horse's hooves, her tongue flopping out of her mouth, her ears pointed straight up. She stopped at Sunny's legs and sat, looking up at her, panting, tongue out, mouth open, saliva flowing.

Sunny petted her head. Poppy licked her hand.

111

And Jack put his hands in his pockets, looking very satisfied.

'So can I get some breakfast? I'm hungry and it's cold out here.'

'First, a test run.' Sunny looked from the dog to Jack. And then she smiled. 'Let's take her for a drive.' She ran inside for a minute and came back with a ring full of keys.

Jack picked up Poppy's makeshift leash and handed it to Sunny. 'She's all yours.'

As they went out the front gate, Jack thanked Ahmet for watching her. Ahmet took a step back as they walked past him, but Poppy, apparently, had to thank him, too, so she rubbed against his leg and looked up at him with her tongue out and her tail wagging. Her love was unrequited, however, and Ahmet turned away from her.

They walked around the outside walls of the house to the narrow alley where the car was parked. Sunny sat in the driver's seat, Jack beside her, and Poppy in the rear. It was cold, but Sunny opened one of the rear windows and immediately, Poppy's paws were up on the door and her head outside breathing in the lovely sewage-smelling Kabul air. Before pulling out, Sunny checked the rearview mirror and then the side.

'Oh shit,' she said.

'What?' asked Jack.

'The mirror, it's gone. Shit, that one is, too. For crying out loud.'

Someone had stolen both side-view mirrors on the outside of the car, a nice little business in Kabul—second only to stealing cars themselves. Fortunately, Tommy had installed an uber-ignition on the car that required a jackhammer to get it

112

going without a key.

'I know how to fix this,' said Jack. 'Make a left at the next alley.'

'Where're we going?' Sunny had to do a lot of head-turning and looking over her shoulder without the mirrors there to help. The streets of Kabul were not only a maze, they were lawless. Afghans drove on the right as in America, but all the double-parking, the passing, the lack of lanes or markings on the cobbled roads made driving safely a feat.

'To get 'em back.' He smiled, as if he got a joke that nobody else in the room did.

Sunny followed his directions, her Mercedes careening through the crowded, dusty streets, with Poppy's huge head sticking out the side back window. People stepped back from the car when she stopped at a corner, kids playing ball pointed, old men crouching in their stalls shook their heads in dismay.

Jack took her to the outskirts of town, where the narrow streets gave way to wider roads with low gray houses on either side, rubble and rocks in between, goats braying and children playing, the smell of sewage that reeked in the center of the city changing to a mix of dust and animal odors and smoke from the fires burning in the homes to keep them warm.

He directed her onto a road that seemed to head straight up into the mountains, but then he had her stop a hundred feet in. 'Here,' he said. 'Let's go.'

He put Poppy on her leash, got her out of the backseat, and led her and Sunny down a dirt embankment and across a wooden plank, with no rails to hold on to, where a river or a sewer once was, to a wide plain where metal shipping

113

containers were lined up end to end. Some had Chinese writing on them, some Arabic, some Russian. On top of them were piles of old car parts, tires, and other unidentifiable paraphernalia. Everything seemed to be covered in soot, filthy. Surrounding them were old cars, with men inside, sipping tea. One old station wagon was open in the back, and three guys, wearing the tan-colored *shalwaar kameezes*, with woolen coats and gray turbans, were hanging out, sitting on old car seats, and eating something.

Sunny felt as if she were on another planet.

But Jack said, 'It's a tailgating party!'

The men looked up at the couple. They stood up when they saw the dog. Each pulled his gun from over his shoulder and pointed it at Poppy.

'Hold on a minute, guys,' Jack said to them in Dari, sounding like an Afghan himself. He showed them the car; they said they had mirrors that could work, then dug around in the pile and held up two mirrors.

'These would work,' they said. The head guy didn't take his eyes off Poppy, who was looking very serious, her policing instincts coming back to her.

Of course they would work. They were Sunny's mirrors. Jack was negotiating to buy back the very mirrors that had been stolen from her car.

'What a racket,' Jack said as he got in the car, putting the mirrors down between them. 'But ingenious. And Poppy, good girl. What an animal.'

'Oh yeah,' Sunny said sarcastically, 'the next time my mirrors get stolen and I have to buy them back, she'll be very helpful.'

They got home, Jack screwed the mirrors on, and once back in the courtyard, Sunny said, 'Okay.

114

I'll give the mangy mutt one week. But if she does anything bad—bites someone, eats something she shouldn't, does her business somewhere she shouldn't, she's gone.'

'Okay,' said Jack.

'Okay?' Sunny asked Poppy, as she held her hand under her muzzle, lifting her face to hers. 'So how about some breakfast?' she asked Jack. 'It's cold out here.'

*   *   *

When they walked into the coffeehouse Halajan screamed.

Sunny laughed. 'It's all right, Hala. This is Poppy, our new dog. You can thank Jack for this lovely gift.'

'There are no four-legged creatures in the coffeehouse! If you must keep it, keep it out back, like a goat or a horse.' Halajan was both angry and afraid. She lingered in the corner. 'You Americans—'

'What?' interrupted Sunny, teasingly. 'What about us Americans?'

'You live with dogs, you sleep with dogs! It's crazy.' She was wringing her hands, her face in a disgusted grimace. 'It's like they are the princes and you the animals. I hear that in some cities in America, the people even pick up their dog's dirt and carry it in a bag.' She shook her head. 'Is this not the truth?'

'I'm on your side,' said Sunny.

Jack laughed. 'It's the truth. But Halajan, dogs, you will find, are . . .' and then he began to speak in Dari. Sunny tried to keep up. He was telling

Halajan that dogs are clean, loyal, and protective. He told her about Poppy's background and how he got her for Sunny because of the car, but that the coffeehouse could use all the protection it could get. Then he made a joke about how if it didn't work out, she could always cook Poppy up and serve her to the plumber who overcharged her, and Halajan laughed so hard, she bent over.

Then Jack pulled out his cellphone from his pocket and said, 'Got a text.' He read it and turned to Sunny and said, 'You know what? I gotta go.' He walked to the café's door.

'Really?' she replied, following him. 'Why? What's so important on a Thursday, the day before *Juma*, the Sabbath? Huh?' She poked at his chest with her index finger. 'What is it?'

He turned serious. 'I have to call my son.'

'So call him from here. Where's your cell?'

'Nah. You know, I like to talk where it's quiet.' And then he spoke loudly, 'Away from all you nuts.'

'Uh-huh,' Sunny said. 'Keeping us a secret?'

She immediately blushed, wishing she could take the words back.

'Ach, come on,' he demurred. 'He may have heard from some colleges this week.'

'Oh, well, I'm sure he'll . . .'

'Yeah, well, he wants to go to Michigan, like his old dad.'

'Good school.'

'Yeah, and Ann Arbor is a nice place to live. But it's hard to get in. Not like when I was a boy. Hell, I got in. Proof of how easy it was.'

'Yeah, you got in.' She sounded so stupid, but this entire conversation was making her feel uneasy because it hit a nerve. She'd never gone to college

116

and she always felt embarrassed about it. Not something she liked talking about.

'It's just that his mom, well, she wants him to stay closer to home. Virginia, somewhere near D.C.'

'How, um, is his mom?'

'She's good. I think. I mean, it can't be easy. I mean, you know what I mean, being a woman alone, waiting for your husband—'

'I'm not waiting for my husband.' She sounded defensive.

'All right. Don't get your panties in a twist. You're not waiting for your husband. You're waiting for your *boyfriend*.'

'Hey, I'm not waiting. I have a life.'

'So does she. But . . .' His voice trailed off.

She waited a moment, giving him time. But when he said nothing further, she asked, 'So, why are they there and you're here?'

'Why are you here and Tommy's out there?' He nodded toward the door.

'We're not married and we don't have a kid. And we're in the same country. Your family is halfway around the world.'

Jack put his hands in his pockets and looked out the window.

'Well, answer me,' Sunny said. 'Why are you here and they're there?'

'Hey, I just got you a great old dog to protect you. You should be nice to me.'

'I didn't ask for it.'

'Yeah, well, you need it.'

'How the hell do you know what I need?'

'You need somethin', baby, and when I'm gone—'

'When you're gone? And don't call me "baby"!'

117

Jack grinned. 'What I meant was that I have to go back to the States. Not today, not tomorrow, but sometime soon.'

'Well, don't worry about me.'

'You can take care of yourself. That's what I love about you. Sunny can always take care of herself.'

'You love that about me, huh?'

'If we're being literal again, that's one thing I *like* about you. And that you're as stubborn as an ox and about as strong, too.'

'Really? What else?' She heard the words come out of her mouth but didn't believe it was really her asking them.

He looked at her for a long time, and then he said softly, 'How you pretend to be tough even though you're not. How you're stingy with nice words but have a big, open heart. I just love that about you. That's the sad damned truth and the real thing that's making me so mad.' He touched her hair with two fingers.

She pulled away out of reflex and put her hands on her hips.

'So go already,' she said softly, 'call your son.'

'I'll see you tomorrow.'

'Not if I see you first.'

'What are you, twelve?'

'Yeah, going on thirty-eight.' She grinned.

'Gee, I wouldn't have put you past thirty-seven.'

He was close to her now. She could see flecks of black in his eyes. 'Would you go already?' She said it as if it were a command.

'You be nice to Poppy.'

'Yeah. I'll treat her like a . . . dog.'

And then Jack bent toward her and before she could pull away, he kissed her on the cheek.

118

The door clanged shut behind him and she leaned against it to get her bearings. What the hell was she supposed to do with that? She touched two fingers to her cheek. She knew what to do. Nothing. Absolutely nothing.

CHAPTER FOURTEEN

Sunny was putting more than her usual maniacal effort into preparing for Christmas this season in order to distract herself from Jack. His completely innocuous kiss had seared into her cheek like a brand on the bulls back home. It was typical of her to make something big out of nothing, to obsess and worry and wonder. But this time, she knew she'd gone too far. So, she'd gotten the boxes from storage in the back closets and was opening them and beginning to organize and decorate with a frenzy. First she put a CD in the player and cranked up the volume. The Chipmunks were singing Christmas carols in their high-pitched whines.

Christmas, Christmas time is here
Time for toys and time for cheer . . .

Bashir Hadi—who was hanging the twinkling little lights that Sunny adored on the wall of the patio, outlining the outside door, the inside door, where the ceiling met the walls of the café, along the countertop, zigzagged on the walls, and of course, throughout the huge plastic tree she'd had shipped from Dubai years before—stopped what he was doing, turned to Sunny, and tried to speak loudly enough to be heard.

'Miss Sunny! Please. I don't mind your Michael Jackson, singing "Santa Claus Is Coming to Town," but I really cannot tolerate the Chipmunks. Please, I beg of you!'

Sunny laughed and told him he could put on any Christmas CD he chose. The only rule: Christmas music from now until the party on Christmas Eve, in two weeks. She knew it was silly, but her patrons had come to expect it of her. She threw the best Christmas party in Kabul—a night of roasted turkey and cranberry sauce, of gifts under the tree, of elf costumes, and this year . . . Poppy dressed as Rudolph the Red-Nosed Reindeer! No need to borrow the neighbor's goat!

It had been a tradition for five years. There weren't too many Christmas parties in Kabul, outside the embassy or the UN. Her party could accommodate forty people for dinner, and even though the price was a little steep, they'd sold out already. There was much to be done.

*   *   *

As the car wove its way toward the Mondai-e, police and military clogged the streets along with the beggars.

'What's happened to us?' asked Halajan of her son, who she noticed had trimmed his beard and was wearing a crisp new *shalwaar kameez*. 'Look at this. It's disgusting. When did we stop taking care of one another?'

'We've lost prayer, Mother. We've turned a deaf ear to the muezzin's call.'

Halajan clicked her tongue and watched a

woman in a burqa crouching in the sewer, her arm out, a baby in her lap. She thought of Yazmina, confined to the café for the duration of her pregnancy, and became angry. 'You think prayer will help her? So where is your mighty Allah? Have you prayed for these people? Either you're praying for those nice new clothes you're wearing or your prayers for these people have gone unheeded.'

She saw the hurt on Ahmet's face and realized she had spoken too harshly. They would never agree about the Koran or politics, but he was her son and she loved him. She didn't want her words to drive a thicker wedge between them than the one already there.

Finally they arrived at the river, which was dry except for a soft layer of snow from the night before. Halajan told Ahmet to wait there at the car and she'd be back in two hours.

'Be careful, Mother,' said Ahmet. 'I pray for you, but since nobody's listening, you're on your own.'

She laughed at his humor, but, if she were to be honest, this time his words hurt. Halajan hurried across the dried riverbank to the Mondai-e and navigated its alleyways with assurance. In a matter of minutes she was at Rashif's shop. She knocked on the door, and he came out wearing a coat and hat.

'Halajan,' he said, slipping her an envelope. 'Are you alone today?'

'Ahmet drove me. He waits in the car.'

'I will come to meet him!'

'You cannot. All these years and you still can't accept this world we live in? To outside eyes, my son runs my house. He makes the rules. And you don't understand the mind of that one. With your past and his present, well, as Rumi says—'

'My past? Ach,' he said with a grimace. 'Those mullahs at the mosque poison any effort they haven't conceived. Why don't they teach from the heart of the Koran instead of from their own fears?'

'As Rumi says—'

'Stop with Rumi! Tell me what's in your heart with your own words.'

She was silent for a moment. 'My son, he is of another generation. He will never accept you.'

'We will help him grow younger.'

Halajan noticed the light in Rashif's eyes. She smiled. 'Your heart is younger than his. I'm afraid for him that it's too late.'

'Our love will change him. I will talk to him. I will come to the café and—'

'I will be off to do my Christmas shopping.' She turned to leave.

'I will come to your party,' he called after her.

'If you do, I will not speak to you.' She turned to him and smiled.

'You do not write, you do not speak. I will be happy to be in the same room.'

Halajan felt her knees weaken, but she held firm. 'We're sold out. We don't have room for even one more.'

He raised his brows and sighed with undue patience. 'We'll see, my Halajan. We will see.'

'I will see you next Thursday, *Inshallah.*'

'*Inshallah,* next Thursday. If not before.' He smiled at her, his dark eyes glistening.

Halajan turned and made her way to the crowded, narrow alleyways of the market, worried that Rashif's patience would end. She loved him dearly, but she loved her son, too. Whose heart should she break? Whose anger should she rile? As she shopped—for popcorn for stringing, dried pomegranate, and red ribbon for decorating the tree, and the other supplies on her list—she tried to enjoy it, but she was burdened by her thoughts. She was careful to get exactly what Sunny had asked for, because this holiday made Sunny a little crazier than usual, and who knew how she'd react if Halajan brought home the wrong cranberry sauce. At this time of year, every year, Sunny had a fire in her, and a sadness, which Halajan understood. Halajan felt the same way. She was excited by the preparations, and the anticipation alone made her feel lightheaded and silly, making her fingers tingle and her head feel as if it could burst. But her memories of the past and fears for the future made her heart heavy. Celebrations were a complicated mix, Halajan thought as she carried her bags back to the car. There was no way Rashif could come to Christmas Eve at the café. It was already complicated enough.

CHAPTER FIFTEEN

Petr disappeared on the morning Isabel was scheduled to leave for the poppy fields. She woke up groggy and hungover from the night before to find him gone. She vaguely recalled a quick conversation they'd had, somewhere between shagging and the second (or was it the third?) glass of vodka, in which Petr said something about needing to vacate Kabul, that it had been fun and maybe they'd hook up again sometime. But he'd left no note, didn't call or say good-bye. She wasn't surprised. She'd known men like this before: He gave her what she needed in exchange for what he needed. It would sound frightfully cold if she were to try to explain it or say it out loud, but as a female journalist in a man's country she did what she had to do. Only once had her strategy backfired, but that was history and something she vowed not to replay or use for self-pity.

It had taken Petr several days to set up her trip—to get her into the poppy fields so she could talk to some people, and get her out. They'd spent those evenings at L'Atmo, getting pissed and partying, those late nights having sex, and the mornings sleeping it off. And last night was like any other, only, when she woke up, it was almost as if he'd never been there at all.

It was the eight a.m. call that woke her. The driver Petr had arranged to take her to the airport was checking in to confirm her pickup time. Her flight was at eleven and the entire trip would take several hours by plane and then car to get to the Badakshan province in the northeast, on the Tajikistan border. Mountainous and remote, Badakshan had become one of the largest areas of poppy production in Afghanistan because it contained the Wakhan Corridor, a viable trade route to Asia. Of course, the southern provinces of Helmand and Kandahar were even larger, but they were held by the Taliban and unsafe for travel even for Isabel, who had been to some of the world's most dangerous places. Badakshan was not Talib, not yet. It was ruled by the Northern Alliance, a resistance group. Since 9/11 it had been supported by America and Britain and was now straining to keep out the Taliban.

Afghanistan supplied from 92 to 95 percent of the world's illegal opium poppies for heroin production, depending on the year, the weather, and how active the United States was in its eradication. President Karzai had encouraged American projects designed to help find the farmers another way to make a living. Money poured in—to improve irrigation and roads, to build clinics, and to farm food products, like potatoes and tomatoes. But workers were tortured, others murdered, and in the end it just wasn't worth the battle with the drug lords and the other countries vested in Afghanistan's poppy exports.

And the corruption—the collusion between the government and the drug lords, the fact that politicians *were* the drug lords—was out of control. If you can think of it, they're doing it, Petr had told her.

She packed her small duffel bag with a few days' worth of clothes, extra trousers for the mud and sweaters for the cold, clothes that provided the necessary cover for her, as a woman, and necessities like toilet paper and hand sanitizer, plus a few customary gifts she'd bought in the market: scarves for the women and nice prayer beads for the men. And, of course, she carried her cross-body canvas bag containing a notebook and pens, tape recorder, mobile, her newspaper ID, passport, and camera. She picked up her bags and left the comfort of her hotel for her car, a small SUV driven by a man named Mohammad, and left Kabul.

The city was fantastic from a car, she thought. Since the driver couldn't possibly go fast, she had the opportunity to see everything: what was directly in front of her eyes, and then what was behind that and what was behind that, as if the narrower the perspective, the more there was revealed. They passed two young boys playing ball in the street, barefoot in the sewage, right next to the car. Little boys were waving a tin can filled with *spandi*, a granule burned to ward off the evil eye or clean the bad spirits away, hoping for an afghani or two. Beyond them an old man crouched on his heels under a tent in his stall, his rear low to the ground, the way she'd seen her little nieces sit back home as she'd thought at the time only children could do. And he was cutting the hair of a man who was squatting in front of him. Two women bundled against the cold air were standing over them, heads together, chatting away. And behind them was a little store that sold mobiles, its sign falling down, its door off its hinges, two men walking out, arguing.

She opened her window ever so slightly, knowing the danger of opening it fully, to experience the mingling of smells—the sewer, the diesel fumes, the grilled nuts, the animal dung. She could hear, too, the shouts of children playing, the hushed voices of the women, the shuffles of ill-fitting shoes on gravel, horns honking, men arguing over a bet, goats braying, and the muezzin singing.

Sunny was right. Walking in Kabul provided too limited a vision. You missed the full depth of the city's life.

From her vantage point, she could see past the city walls to the green valley at the foothills of the Hindu Kush, to their snow-covered peaks. Then it started to snow. The flakes were small and silvery against the deep blue of the sky, and Isabel imagined a million Tinkerbell fairies, reminding her of her mother, who had read her *Peter Pan* so long ago. Her mother, who was only a child when her family escaped Nazi Germany. Her mother, whose passion for life couldn't stop the hideous cancer that ultimately killed her before Isabel would realize how much she needed her, after the incident in Sierra Leone. The car rattled and bumped, the driver talked in Dari non stop and so quickly into his mobile that she could barely make out a word he was saying, just like the drivers back home. Soon they arrived at the airport, the snow still falling but not sticking on the tarmac.

On the flight, she fell into a fitful sleep. In those minutes of semiconsciousness, she saw what she always saw almost every sober sleep since then—the man with the knife at her throat, his face on hers, his pounding away on her body that left bruises much deeper than the physical kind. And she woke, as she always did, at the moment when he was done but before he got up and hit her with the butt of his rifle so hard it knocked her out, along with several teeth. Her breathing was fast and short, her heart racing, her anger raging, her shame for her weakness, her size, her inability to stop him. That's why L'Atmo was good for her. Besides making the connection with Petr, all the drinking and partying gave her an escape from her own memory.

She was met at the airport by a man Petr had hired to be her driver, guard, and translator. They arrived at the compound by late afternoon. To the right and to the left, in front and in back, were poppy fields, shrouded by the mountains behind them. It was off-season, so the seedpods lay fallow in the frozen earth. A tractor stood silent like a sentinel at the far side.

Inside the stone walls of the compound, a few low mud buildings appeared straight ahead, where the road ended. The car pulled up beside several other vehicles that were parked there. Isabel got out of the SUV, faced the craggy mountain ridge that rose malevolently against the sky, and stretched.

A voice behind her made her jump, and she turned to find a man in traditional clothes—white *shalwaar kameez* and sheepskin vest, wearing a *pakul,* the flat-topped hat, and sunglasses—with his hand on the automatic rifle that hung on his shoulder.

She swallowed her fear and said, *'Salaam alaikum,'* and continued in English, with her driver translating into Dari, 'I am Isabel Hughes, here to see Abdul Khan.' Petr had given her the name of the drug lord of this farm, which was the name of every drug lord who ran every poppy farm. He said he'd arranged for her to get a quick look and an interview.

The man with the rifle motioned Isabel toward the door of the nearest building and told the driver to get back into his car where he was to wait for her. The driver argued in Dari, and Isabel suspected he was saying that he had to go with her to translate. But the man with the rifle was adamant. The driver looked at Isabel and shook his head in frustration. Isabel took a deep breath, swallowing her fear, and followed the man with the rifle, leaving the driver alone at his car.

Inside was a large room, its floor covered with maroon and red rugs, filled with furniture of dark wood, gilt, and velvet. A man in a *karakul,* the hat made famous by President Karzai, sat on a thronelike chair at a huge desk with intricately carved legs. There was a laptop in front of him. At his side stood another man, perhaps his deputy.

Abdul Khan stood, greeted Isabel warmly in Dari, and then the men escorted her to a table covered with small bowls of *kish mish,* the little goodies that Afghans served in their desire to be gracious even when they carried guns: sugared almonds, green raisins, dried chickpeas with pepper, and caramels wrapped in paper. The drug lord sat across from Isabel, smiling warmly, never taking his eyes off her. She was nervous, her heart beating hard in her ears, but she smiled back in an effort to pretend she was unafraid. The right-hand man left through a side doorway and immediately returned with a man who was to be their translator. Another man appeared with a teapot. And the drug lord welcomed Isabel to his farm.

'In the spring there will be poppies as far as the eye can see,' he said with a proud, broad gesture of his arm. 'This is a very successful farm. But the spraying will destroy everything we've worked so hard to attain.'

Isabel took out her small handheld tape recorder and asked, 'Is it all right if I tape our conversation?'

'For now,' he said. Then he smiled. 'When it's not, I'll let you know.'

'Thank you,' Isabel said. 'And for your generosity, for seeing me and giving me your time.' But she knew that drug lords, like all celebrities, liked to talk, loved the limelight.

'Last year was an excellent year for us. Perfect weather and the market continued to be strong,' Abdul Khan said proudly. 'Not like when we tried tomatoes. That was a tremendous mistake. Everyone growing tomatoes at the same time, no way to get them quickly enough to market, and even if we did, too many tomatoes! Very costly, no storage facilities. That was a stupid idea—some American bureaucrat's idea of a better way to make a living. Poppies are the most viable crop. No storage issues and a guaranteed market. Everybody wins: the farmer in the field, the landowner, me'— his Cheshire-cat grin widened—'and Afghanistan, my country.' He stopped and exhaled. 'And that is the problem, in a nutshell,' he said as he picked up an almond and popped it into his mouth. 'It will all be gone come spring and the spraying, and we will have nothing. It is wrong. It is unjust punishment. The Americans say they will kill only the poppies. But it is a ploy. They will be killing everything. They will accomplish what they're after: ridding Afghanistan of the Afghans.'

'But what about *Haram*, going against the rules of Islam? Isn't the Koran specific about rules against smoking, drinking alcohol, or taking drugs?'

'It is you Westerners who misinterpret the Koran. It is *Haram* to smoke, drink, or use drugs, yes. But it is clearly written: If a man must do something to ensure his survival, it is not *Haram*. If I don't produce poppies, my family will starve. And hundreds of other families will as well.'

'Excuse me,' Isabel said, looking down as she spoke so as not to seem too provocative, 'but why not build roads? Put in irrigation systems? Improve your country and your people's lives? You're a good businessman. You could get rich doing that. And not be responsible for creating a population of addicts.'

130

'I am rich, thank you very much. And you are excused for being shortsighted. It is Americans, you British, and all the other Westerners who think they know what's right and what's wrong, who make money from the sale of heroin and opium with one hand, and yet pay mullahs to preach that growing poppies is against the Koran with the other.' He laughed. 'Hypocrites, all!'

She looked up at him then and nodded to show she understood. He had a point. The corruption when it came to any drugs in any part of the world—and she knew this from her experience reporting in Africa—was astounding. But she persevered. 'I just don't see how you can justify the addiction of workers in your fields,' she said, noticing the drug lord gesturing to his right-hand guy. 'Of women who get the sap for you and then become addicted to it themselves. You're causing . . .' She stopped herself, alarmed at how biased and unprofessional she sounded. Her job was to get the story, not show her hand.

'But what about the poisonous spray? Do you really think they can contain it? What about our fields of fruit and vegetables? What about the air our children breathe?' He was interrupted by the ring of his cellphone. It played the *William Tell Overture,* which would've made Isabel laugh had she not been angered by their conversation.

'Bali, bali,' yes, yes, he answered, then said to Isabel, 'Excuse me, please,' and got up and left the room.

Perfect timing, she thought.

And he never returned. Instead another man came in to escort her out. It was, apparently, the end of the interview and time for a tour of the

131

facilities. A superbly orchestrated PR effort—it pissed Isabel off, but how could she have expected anything else?

The man first took her to a small mud-and-brick outer building that served as a dormitory for men, lined with *toshak*s from wall to wall. Some men were napping, some were listening to a small AM/FM radio, and others were drinking tea.

Then they went through a gate to a separate compound for women and children. It was dark, lit only by a single lightbulb that hung from a cord overhead. She could hear the hum of the generator that stood in the corner, the *clack* of several looms. As her eyes adjusted to the dark, she could see women weaving rugs, using large wooden looms that took several of them to maneuver. Children helped with the yarn, which hung on ropes strung across the room to dry after being dyed. They gathered the yarn into balls, then sat on long wooden benches and worked closely with the women, presumably their mothers, while wearing woolen wraps to ward off the cold. The women's knuckles, Isabel could see even from across the room, were swollen. The children looked up at her, their black eyes dull from the painstaking work, and then turned back to their heavy skeins of yarn.

Something—a sound, a movement, she wasn't sure what—made Isabel turn to her right where an open door led to another room. While her guide was talking to one of the kids, Isabel carefully, slowly, made her way over to see what was there. The distinct smell of opium—sweet, rich, intoxicating—wafted out through the open wedge of space. She saw a woman in the corner, holding a baby wrapped in worn brown blankets. The woman

132

was smoking an opium pipe, her fingers reddened from it. And what Isabel saw next shocked even her hardened journo sensibilities. Each time the mother exhaled, she blew the smoke directly into the baby's face. The baby was silent. No crying, no screaming for a breast. The other children, too, she now realized, were eerily quiet and moved slowly as if in a daze. It dawned on her that they were stoned—opium junkies—probably from the time they were infants as well. This must be how mothers kept their babies from feeling hunger or the cold; they 'medicated' them with the same drug they were addicted to.

Isabel had to get a shot of this. She dug into her bag for her camera. She pulled it out and immediately felt a firm hand on her shoulder.

'No cameras, please,' the man said in his native language. 'Come this way,' he said, and guided her down the hall to wait while he returned to the room where the women were. Isabel heard a thud and a small cry, and she rushed to the doorway to see the opium pipe lying on the floor as the man hit the woman again right across her face with a loud *whack*. Isabel was sure that, given the force of his raised arm and the sound of his hand against her cheek, no amount of opium would prevent her from feeling it. She knew the pain of a hit like that herself.

The man turned and was shocked to see Isabel there. *'Beya!* Come!' he yelled angrily.

Isabel followed him, but not before turning for one last look into the eyes of the opium-addled mother, her mouth bloodied, her lip already swollen, and her intoxicated baby in her arms. The woman turned away, covering her face with her scarf, probably hoping, Isabel sensed, simply to disappear.

That night, after bedding down in a local house that had been arranged for her by Petr, Isabel made some notes while the events were still fresh in her mind, and determined to return the next day to check on the woman. For Isabel knew that had she not gone to the door, had she not seen her smoking, the woman would not have been hurt. It was because of her that a woman had been beaten. She paced her room, unable to sleep, horrified by her error, ashamed of herself.

What Isabel didn't understand was the real danger she'd put the woman in, simply because she'd seen the man hit her. Shame in Afghan society occurs only when something is witnessed, not when something happens behind closed doors.

The next morning she returned to the poppy field, despite her driver's warning against it. Returning could result in angering the drug lord, putting herself in danger, even risking her life.

In the end the risks and the probing were for naught; the woman and her baby had vanished into thin air.

CHAPTER SIXTEEN

Candace opened her eyes to blackness and an empty bed. Once she was able to focus, she realized from the bedside clock that it was only four-twenty in the morning and already Wakil was gone. She had a faint memory of him kissing her on her cheek and whispering that he had to return to his room.

His smell lingered in the air and her skin still tingled from their lovemaking. And yet, he was gone. This she knew, not only from his physical absence. He had left her emotionally. It hadn't happened abruptly but slowly and steadily over weeks, the way the sun makes its way across the sky from the heat of its midday height to its low burn as it settles on the horizon. The thought made her sigh audibly, for comparing the trajectory of their relationship to the sun's orbit was a desperate cliché and she wanted to kick herself. But it was pretty apt. She ran her hand over the sheet where Wakil's body should have been and it was cold.

She knew she'd never be able to go back to sleep, so she got up to take a shower. Normally one of the servants Wakil provided for her at his mansion would help her, but the hallway outside her room was empty at this hour and she was, gratefully, alone. She tiptoed to her bathroom and closed the door behind her.

A beautiful mirror, framed in intricately carved dark wood, covered the wall. She stood close and with an index finger touched the fine lines under her eyes, at the corners of her mouth. She pulled her hair off her face and checked its thinning at her temples, either from age or her regular bleaching treatments. She stood back and sucked in a deep chestful of air, as if it had the power to help her accept her age, her looks, her life.

She breathed out and knew it hadn't worked. She stepped into the shower.

She had an early breakfast meeting at the Serena Hotel, the most luxurious in Kabul, where she'd arranged to meet an American delegation of wealthy philanthropists. The Serena was Kabul's only four-star hotel, built only a few years before by Prince Amyn Aga Khan, and it obviously took great pains to maintain a facade of luxury and security. She'd prepared her presentation, and she knew exactly how to pitch to them, having lived among women just like them for the past ten years. Some may have come from wealthy families themselves, but more likely they were like her: They had wealthy husbands to rely on so they didn't have to work. Some had children, others did not, but all were bored. They searched for the right projects that would make them feel important. Feeding the hungry in their own backyards wasn't good enough. They sought prestige in Africa or the Middle East, wherever there was war and media attention. Good, Candace thought. She'd vowed to herself—and Wakil—that she wouldn't take no for an answer, nor anything less than several million.

She understood women like this. She'd been one, and she was still one. Pathetically relying on a man who seduced her, fucked her, and pretended he'd loved her—just to get what he needed from her. Not that she hadn't gotten something in return, not as if she were a total victim, but what she really wanted—a life together—didn't seem to be in the cards.

She turned off the water and wrapped herself in a large, plush towel. She went back to her room, blow-dried her hair, put on her makeup, and dressed. She certainly looked the part. In her Chanel suit she appeared stylish, wealthy, and conservative enough. Her nails had been done the day before in the Serena's salon. There was no way anybody at this breakfast would ever guess that she'd been sleeping with an Afghan.

She went to her dressing table and picked up a pearl earring, tilted her head to the side, and inserted it into her pierced ear. What had happened? she wondered. They'd been so passionate, but gradually the sex became less frequent, the touching out of bed almost nonexistent. He kept saying it was because they were back in his country, but she wasn't a complete idiot. She knew something else was going on. She put the other earring in, then looked at herself again in the mirror. She was still attractive, she *was*, she told herself. Yes, Wakil was much younger, but her body was as taut and shapely as those of most twenty-five-year-olds. She still turned heads, she knew. She let out a sigh and reapplied her lipstick. He was just distracted, that's all, he'd told her. And why shouldn't she believe him? He loved her. He'd told her that, too.

And still. She sat down on the edge of her bed and noticed the sky was already getting lighter. It wasn't his words that bothered her. Maybe he did love her, in his way. It was that she was so damn *disappointed*. Yet again. She gritted her teeth and fought back the tears. Right now she felt as lonely as she had as a child, living with her poor aunt Lucy in the outskirts of a nowhere town.

She got up and went to the window where, past the courtyard, the chaos of Kabul was laid out before her. She sure was a long way from home, if only she knew where the hell home was.

She raised her chin then, and forced her shoulders back, determined not to be a fool like so many other women she knew who sat around and waited for something—or *someone*—to make their lives worth living. Look at Sunny. Look at Isabel.

Though she'd only recently met them, they were inspirations to her. Sunny had the coffeehouse, Isabel had her career.

And she had a meeting to attend. She'd have the car take her early and she could have some coffee and prepare before the others arrived at eight. She smoothed the jacket of her suit, took one last look in the mirror, and, satisfied, she picked up her bag and walked out the door, confident in her ability to raise money. It was the Christmas season after all. She couldn't have timed this any better.

CHAPTER SEVENTEEN

Sunny stood at the door of the café, her hands in the pockets of the ridiculous Christmas apron that she'd worn every year since she'd come to Kabul, imagining she was a customer entering the coffeehouse on Christmas Eve for the first time. She'd gasp at how the room glowed with candles and thousands of tiny twinkling lights. She'd breathe in the aromas of roasted turkey, sweet potatoes, and apple pie. She'd laugh at the dog wearing the Rudolph red nose and antlers. Her eyes would widen at the size and beauty of the Christmas tree that took up a quarter of the room. And she'd hope that one of the many presents under the tree was for her. The holiday cheer in the room would remind her of the happy times of her childhood and make her miss her family and her country.

But this wasn't her first Kabul Christmas. This was her sixth. Her apron was disintegrating; green glitter littered the floor with each step she took, and the appliquéd reindeer had lost one of its black-and-white bauble eyes. The tree was plastic and getting a little thin and crinkled after so many times being squished into its plastic bag, stored for a year in the back closet, and then taken out. The dog looked pathetic. And the gifts had all been purchased by her—one for each person who had RSVP'd to the dinner at the café that night. There were scarves for the women, *pakul* hats for the men, toys for the kids, and something silly for Jack.

And yet, the huge tree reached to the ceiling and filled an entire corner of the room, leaving room for only ten tables. It didn't matter that it was plastic. It was a Christmas tree, here in Kabul, a bazillion miles from home. Sunny's childhood felt even farther away. The truth was, hers had never been as warm and wonderful as they were in books or at other people's homes. She was often lonely, maybe just her mother and her, with only a utilitarian gift of needed clothes or shoes, and always marked by her father's absence or drunkenness, and she wasn't sure which she preferred. Perhaps that's why doing Christmas right had become so important to her as an adult. Back home, her best friend, Karen, had called Sunny the Hallmark Christmas Queen because of her bordering-on-obsessive commitment to Christmas—cards, gifts, bows, and the right wrapping, ornaments, decor, lights, music, and even clothing. The whole damn yuletide thing.

In Kabul, Sunny asked every café regular to pick up an ornament if they happened to see one on their travels, to take advantage of post-holiday sales if they were in the States, and to bring back Christmas paraphernalia. Border crossings were particularly hilarious for them. Instead of packing drugs or weapons, her friends had to explain the plastic crèche or the glittery star or the crystal dog with the green hat.

Each table had a centerpiece created by a shop on Flower Street. Sunny would bring them her boxes filled with Christmas knickknacks that she bought from the dollar store on Chicken Street and the shop would add flowers and make festive, if sometimes hilarious, designs. Flowers and plastic Santas, little reindeer and rubber snowflakes. Sunny loved them.

Bashir Hadi was bent over the open oven, his Santa hat flopping in the wave of heat, basting the turkeys. Thank God for all the people she knew going to and coming from the States, who got her the canned pumpkin and stuffing mix. The ones who were able to go home for the holidays felt especially guilty and would bring back a suitcase full of food for the following year. But the turkeys, now, they required special ops and the talents of Tommy's friend, her military black-market connection, Buddy Donaldson, with his fat cigar and mirrored aviators, who seemed to know how to get anything for anybody for the right money. Finding four of them was, apparently, difficult, and they'd cost her an arm and a leg. But Sunny didn't care. It was Christmas.

Finding red wine was another matter. Kabul was quickly becoming dry, yet another impact of the return of the Taliban. There was only one place in all of Kabul where Sunny knew she could find it. And that was in the Chinese brothels. On a cold day two weeks before, she'd taken the car, with Poppy as her escort, and driven across town, where she went door to door until she had accumulated two dozen or so bottles. It wasn't enough, but everyone coming from the French or Italian embassy knew they wouldn't be admitted without a bottle of wine.

Behind her the door opened and clanged shut. She turned, and a group of NGO workers from New York said hello and began to take off their coats. All of a sudden Halajan was at her side to show them to their table. Sunny checked their names off her list, and Yazmina, who looked so pretty tonight, wearing a new orange scarf and dress, offered them each a menu.

When the door opened and closed again, there was Jack. He was dressed in a handsome new *shalwaar kameez*. He was holding roses. He smiled.

And when he smiled, Sunny smiled. It just happened that way. Maybe it was his eyes, or the way his mouth turned up at the corners. Maybe it just was.

'I like the apron,' he said, 'and the earrings.' He lifted one of Sunny's dangling Christmas tree earrings with his index finger.

'You see, I do like diamonds,' Sunny said, referring to the fake ones that dotted her earring trees.

'But Poppy looks a little under the weather. Look at her.' Poppy loped over to Jack and he squatted to scratch her ears. 'Poppy, my girl, look what they've done to you. My sweet, poor girl.'

'She looks cute.'

He stood and looked deeply and seriously into Sunny's eyes and said, 'Never, ever, put clothes on a dog. It's the number one rule of dog ownership. It's abuse, grounds for arrest.'

She ignored him but took his flowers. 'For me?'

'Well, now they are.'

'I'd say "you shouldn't have" but then I'd be lying!' The urge to kiss him, to say what she was really feeling, was so strong that she turned away from him and headed to the closet for a vase.

*   *   *

Halajan, wearing an elf hat over her scarf, sat Jack at a table and poured him some wine from a teapot. She was nervous. What if Rashif were to come here tonight as he said he would? Ahmet was working inside; his friend Khalid was at the gate. Ahmet would surely recognize Rashif as not only the tailor from the market but as his opposite—the young man representing the old Afghanistan, the old man representing the new. How could she conceal her feelings for Rashif? It would be impossible. And according to tradition, which her proud son took so seriously, feelings had no place when it came to a man and a woman. All that mattered were correct introductions and managed courtships, under the unspoken social rules that squeezed the life out of life.

She tried to squelch her bitterness and ignore her worries. There was so much to attend to anyway. Four courses of dinner, the wine, the water. Serving and clearing.

But it was a beautiful room and Sunny had never looked so happy. She was sitting with Jack and the affection in her eyes was obvious to everyone but her.

And then Halajan felt a tap on her shoulder. She turned and there he was—Rashif, still in his coat and scarf, his hat over his brow, a huge smile on his face. She immediately looked over his shoulder to be sure Ahmet was out of earshot.

'I am here! Merry Christmas, Halajan!'

She couldn't help but smile in return. What was it about some men? You had to smile back. But this was a very risky thing to do, for him to come here to talk to her face-to-face, a man to a woman. Luckily there were no Afghans in the room at the moment. On the other hand, that's exactly what made Rashif stand out.

'I knew you'd be happy to see me,' he said.

'I am not.'

'You look happy,' he said.

'I pretend so as not to hurt your feelings.'

'Well, thank you. It's working.'

'How did you get in, past the guard at the gate? And then past Ahmet at the door?'

'I have a delivery—see?' He lifted his arm, which had a garment in a bag hanging over it. 'For you, the new dress you bought for tonight. It needed altering, remember?'

'My new dress?'

'I had to think of something!'

'Well, thank you, good-bye.'

Rashif laughed. 'Don't worry. I'm not staying. I have dinner with my family tonight. My cousins, whom I so want you to meet.'

'Good, because I am busy. This is too much. Even I am afraid.'

'Then I will leave,' Rashif said, quickly glancing over his shoulder to check for Ahmet, who was hanging up a guest's coat. 'But first'—he dug into his pocket and pulled out a letter—'this is for you.' He handed it to her.

Instinctively, Halajan glanced toward Ahmet, who had come out of the closet but was busy with a group of UN workers who'd just arrived.

She took the letter as quickly as possible and put it in the pocket of her apron. 'Now go,' she said.

Rashif took two steps toward the front door, but then turned back to her and handed her the garment bag. 'I almost forgot. This is my Christmas gift to you. Wear it tonight, for me.'

Halajan gasped. She looked at the wonderful man before her, wanting to put her hand on his cheek. But then she looked at Ahmet, who stood alone and stoic by the door, his eyes surveying the room while it filled with laughter and sounds of clinking glasses. For a moment, their eyes connected, but he quickly turned away from her. Was he pretending not to see? Was this his Christmas gift to her?

'You, my Hala, have a beautiful night. I will say hello to Ahmet on my way out. That is him by the door, I know. I have seen him waiting for you in the market. And besides, he looks like you.'

Halajan lost her breath. She had never felt so overwhelmed by love and by fear. People in Kabul disappeared for smaller social infractions than this. An Afghan man and woman, who were not married, talking in public? In front of a traditional son? In front of others? Thankfully, the only other Afghans in the café were Yazmina, who would close her eyes to this, and Bashir Hadi, who was deep in his kitchen, preparing the meal.

'You must not,' she begged. 'Please.'

And then he was gone, stopping at the door to greet Ahmet. The older man was warm and offered his hand; the younger did not take it but instead stood like a tree—straight, tall, and unbendable.

Halajan figured she had about three minutes to

rush to the back and put on her new dress before her absence would be noticed. A new dress! After all these years. She would wear it as if it were crafted of Rashif's letters themselves—with his words touching her from her skin through to her heart.

*　　　*　　　*

Isabel took off her coat and scarf, feeling pretty in her dress and long gold-beaded Indian earrings that she'd bought on Chicken Street. It had been a long time since she'd gotten dressed up, and she wished there was someone she wanted to notice. She handed her things to the guard at the front door, who asked her to wait for his mother to come and seat her. Over the heads of others, she could see the old woman talking to an elderly Afghan gentleman. She smoothed her dress and adjusted her shoulders, as if shaking off her usual garb of safari pants and baggy V-neck sweater.

She smiled at the door guard as he closed the closet door behind him. He simply stood, his hands clasped behind his back, his feet shoulder distance apart, as if he were a soldier. *What a terribly serious boy,* she thought. He reminded her of the aristocratic boys in London, the snooty ones who felt obligated to uphold their high-class legacy. *Stuck up* is what she used to call them.

Finally the old woman greeted her, nervously.

'Sorry to keep you waiting,' she said.

'No worries,' answered Isabel.

'He was just making a delivery. Sit here,' she said, with a plastic garment bag draped over her arm.

145

Isabel hadn't asked, but clearly the old woman felt the need to explain. Isabel was seated with Jack and Sunny, and leaned toward them and said over Frank Sinatra singing 'The Little Drummer Boy,' 'Looks like the old lady has a boyfriend.'

'Halajan? Interesting.' Sunny frowned. 'Ahmet would shit.'

'Who's Ahmet?'

'The stiff one, over there,' Sunny said, nodding to the front door. 'He's her son. He guards the place.'

'Why would he care? Especially if his mother is happy?'

'Even today, it's not allowed,' explained Sunny.

'Because according to the Afghan ways,' said Jack, 'a woman like Halajan, whose husband has died leaving her with a son, can only remarry if the son not only accepted it but arranged it.'

'I tell you, I've witnessed firsthand in the past few days how women are treated here. It's not new to me, and it exists all over the world, but it's still shocking each and every time. But let's not discuss it tonight. It's a holiday!'

'Tell us,' Sunny said, sympathetically. 'Go on.'

Isabel was hesitant, knowing how she could always be relied on to bring a party down. But she continued. 'At the poppy fields, I saw a woman hit by a guard, and I was seen witnessing it. By the time I returned the following day, the woman was gone. Along with her baby.' She stopped, sipped some wine to mask the emotion welling up in her.

'They disappear all the time,' said Jack. 'Wasn't directly because of you.'

Isabel was stricken. She breathed out. She swigged back her wine. 'Please, can we discuss something, anything, else?'

146

'Well, we had been talking about love,' said Jack. 'And how it just ain't for everyone.'

'Well, that's rubbish!' said Isabel, putting on a smile.

Sunny laughed. 'It is!' And then in a fake British accent, she said, 'Blimey rubbish!'

'Making fun, are we?' asked Isabel.

Now Jack looked directly at Sunny. 'Trust me, love isn't for everyone.'

What a sweet man, Isabel thought, aware of his eyes on Sunny. *Why, he's in love with her!*

Sunny looked back at him silently, uneasily, and then sat up straight in her chair. 'What are you talking about?'

It was so obvious, Isabel thought, how she felt about him. She remembered feeling that way, too, a long time ago. Once. Maybe. And though she'd known Sunny for only a short time, she knew Sunny hadn't a clue how she felt, or if she did, she wasn't ready to face it.

'I just know how it is, that's all,' Jack said. 'It's tough to wait for someone to come around.'

Sunny looked like the silly dog on her Christmas apron, her hackles standing straight up. 'Do you mean Tommy? You think I'm pining away for Tommy?'

Jack looked at Sunny as if his seat was uncomfortable, as if he couldn't stand it one moment longer. 'I wasn't even thinking . . . Tommy! *Are* you? Is that what you're saying?'

'No! I'm not saying anything. You were the one who brought this up.'

Then Jack put his hand on Sunny's. Isabel took a breath. Their conversation had escalated so quickly in the way conversations like that did between two

147

people whose feelings for each other had gone unspoken. They were ignoring Isabel completely, as if she weren't even there. But she was noticing every detail, every unspoken word.

'I'm just saying,' Jack said in a hushed voice, 'you know what I mean. This country is hard on people.'

Isabel thought of excusing herself, to give the bloke a chance to say more, but she couldn't move. This was just too good!

Sunny looked at Jack. And Isabel wondered if she saw in Jack what Isabel did: that this man, who looked like a tough old codger, was warm and sweet and somebody you could get used to cuddling with. If you were one to cuddle with anybody. She looked down at Jack's strong hand on Sunny's and wished someone held her hand that way. Then Sunny pulled her hand away and got up from the table.

She was flustered. 'I have to help Halajan,' she said, and walked off toward the kitchen.

Isabel used the moment to speak to Jack. 'I know it's none of my business, but she's very special, isn't she?'

Jack looked at her and smiled. 'If it weren't Christmas Eve, I'd tell you that you're right: It *is* none of your business. But, tonight, I'll just say this: You're one hell of an observer. I just don't want to read about it in tomorrow's paper.'

Sunny appeared with a tray but she didn't look at Jack. 'This is for you.' She placed several plates of delicious-looking hors d'oeuvres on the table. 'Enjoy.'

Isabel picked up a fork and said, 'And to all a good night!'

*   *   *

148

Rashif the tailor! In his café! Had that man been talking to his mother in the open? Ahmet would've stopped him at the door, but the café was filling up, there were people to greet, coats to check, and guns to store, and he was quickly distracted. And besides, there were no other Afghans in the room at the time except Yazmina and Bashir Hadi, who were busy working, so he was less concerned about his mother's reputation.

Only when Rashif offered his hand to him and wished him a Merry Christmas did Ahmet have the opportunity to say something. He'd wanted to say, 'Stay away from my mother.' But what he said was, '*Inshallah*, Muhammad is watching over you.'

Now, as he looked over to discover that his mother had put on a new dress, the very one that Rashif had carried over his arm, and he saw how it was tailored to fit her perfectly, he vowed then and there never to allow his mother to see Rashif again.

*   *   *

Yazmina wore her new scarf tonight, shedding the *chaderi*. She wore her new dress, too, but under it wore another, so that her stomach wouldn't show. But she wanted to be a part of the celebration and show Sunny respect for her holiday. The coffeehouse was wonderful—warm and welcoming on this cold, cold night. She loved the music that was playing and couldn't wait to try some of Bashir Hadi's potatoes and that very red compote of cranberries.

Layla, she thought, *if only you could see this. Such a room you have never seen! Layla, the days go by, but I will find some way to bring you to safety before it is too late.*

At the counter, she put four bowls on a tray and filled them with the squash soup that Bashir Hadi had made. It smelled of cinnamon and cardamom. She dotted each soup with a spoon of the whipped cream, exactly as he'd instructed. Then she carried the tray to a table by the front door, near where Ahmet was standing.

She could feel his eyes on her. She dared not look at him.

She served the soup to the two men and two women at the table. They were American. They were young and dressed nicely, the women with long hair that they wore without anything on their heads, the men handsome and slim. She wondered why they were here, so far from home. But their laughter and intense conversation showed they were enjoying themselves, even across the world from their families.

She glanced then at Ahmet, without thinking. His eyes were on her. She looked away and then willed herself to look back. He nodded. Now there, she thought, is a man who could benefit from getting away from his mother and acting like his own man. What held him here? she wondered.

But she was glad he was. He was so handsome, and the rare times he did smile, it was as if he did so only for her. She smiled, then, at him. He nodded, looked away.

She turned to walk toward the kitchen, but something made her glance back over her shoulder. This time, he was smiling at her! She shivered, feeling as if cool water had washed over her.

Then Halajan appeared in a beautiful new dress,

150

the joy on her face as bright as the beads that decorated it. She wondered when Halajan bought it and who had made it, for it fit her so perfectly that it was clear it had been made with love and care.

*　　　*　　　*

All of a sudden, it seemed, even with the Jackson Five singing 'Santa Claus Is Coming to Town,' and the smell of turkey and sweet potatoes, the air changed in the Christmas coffeehouse. Candace had come through the door, with that electric-charged energy of hers. She whisked off her coat, handed it to Ahmet with a brusque 'Treat it nicely, please,' and waited for Halajan to show her to her table.

Sunny, busy serving and schmoozing (her word for Christmas Eve chatting up the customers), watched The Candace Show from the kitchen counter. She was wearing an emerald green one-shouldered silk dress, very fitted, with silver very-high-heeled sandals (her driver must've had to carry her from her car to the door), with long, fake (they had to be, right?) jeweled chandelier earrings. Her makeup was impeccable, her hair a cascade of blond. Only a woman like Candace would know *the* salon in Kabul. She walked to the table as if all eyes were on her—which they were. Candace was impossible to ignore. You envied her, you wanted to be her, and you wanted to kill her. She had the energy of a leader, but she didn't seem to know what to do with it.

Sunny went to greet her, but on the way she passed Halajan, who was wearing a colorful new dress.

151

'Halajan, you look beautiful tonight!' said Sunny.

'Yes, my new dress. It was time, and for this occasion, I agreed. As Rumi says, "The flower that—"'

But she was interrupted by Candace, who'd walked up to them.

'Sunny, it looks gorgeous in here!' she said. Then she added to Halajan, 'You look very nice, too. May I sit? May I get something to drink, please? What a week I've had, you cannot imagine. Isabel! How are you?'

Sunny glanced at Isabel, who smiled back at her with a little smirk. Not a word needed to be spoken. Because here was Candace, assuming that hers trumped anybody else's bad week, as usual. They'd hung out together at the coffeehouse only a few times, but in Kabul people get close quickly, bound together by experience, fear, and loneliness. Time is compressed, relationships move fast, and the normal patterns of waiting before you talk intimately are forgone.

Sunny said, 'Try us,' as the women sat, joining Isabel at her table.

Candace proceeded to bring them up-to-date about her fund-raising efforts for Wakil's projects. She must've talked for an hour—they'd eaten two courses, Sunny had gotten up several times to work, serve and clear and pour 'tea'—allowing for only a comment here, a response there. Candace seemed lonely, as if they were the only people she had spoken to in days.

As she drank more and more wine, her voice grew louder; she threw her head back to laugh. Candace was getting a little plastered, and her talk turned from fund-raising to something more

152

personal.

Sunny noticed Halajan hovering near the table, listening. She couldn't invite her to sit with customers, and Halajan would never join them if Sunny did. It just wasn't done.

'And we haven't made love in a month,' Candace said softly. 'I don't know what's happened. He's always in the valley, he barely calls me because he has no cellphone reception out there, and when we do see each other it's for me to hand over the checks.' She paused. Everyone at the table was silent. Then she shrieked, 'I feel like a neglected wife! And I should know. I was one!'

'You know, Candace, maybe he's married,' Jack said.

Interesting, thought Sunny, *coming from him.*

That got Candace's attention, but she laughed it off. 'Then I'd be his lover, and we'd be fucking, right?'

'Or maybe he's not into people of the female persuasion,' Isabel said.

'You mean, maybe he's gay?' Now she wasn't the only one laughing. The teasing, the wine, getting under Candace's skin, made them all giggle like kids.

'Honey, they're all gay,' said Sunny, referring to the commonly held belief that Talib men had a habit of 'enjoying' boys.

'Oh, come on, that's an old wives' tale,' said Jack. 'Not all Afghan men or even Talib men—'

'He's not gay,' insisted Candace.

Bashir Hadi had come to the table, and Sunny became nervous about him overhearing this conversation. She tried to alert Isabel that he was standing behind her.

153

'Come on there, Jack,' said Isabel. 'It's common knowledge that Talib men enjoy their boys terribly young—and as often as they can. All that repressed sexuality. It's like your American priests.'

'And your British ones,' said Candace.

'Not all Afghan men,' Jack said again, more emphatically, glancing at Bashir Hadi, as he poured another round of wine.

'I mean, perhaps he's a Talib,' said Isabel, raising her brows, ribbing Sunny with her elbow.

'Yes, that's it, precisely,' said Sunny. 'Maybe he's training boys to become martyrs for the seventy-two virgins they'll find in heaven.'

'Now that's funny. My lover, Osama bin Laden.' Candace downed another teacup of wine, threw her head back in laughter, and then nodded to Bashir Hadi to pour her another cup.

It was her laugh that made Sunny's heart go out to her. It wasn't because of Wakil—nobody seriously thought he was anything but a guy who was all ego—but she knew that Candace did, indeed, see the ridiculousness of her situation, that she actually had a sense of humor. And given that she'd come a long way from Willow Springs, Missouri, perhaps she was just insecure. Somewhere deep down, so deep it wasn't easy to fathom, Candace was okay. Sunny had known girls like her back home—all blustery and sexy and confident, and all of it covering the truth. She felt as if she had known Candace all her life. Maybe it was because they came from the same white trash neighborhood, a very particular location that made you want to get out but also made you feel like you didn't deserve to.

'Whatever it is, I miss him,' Candace said. 'He

154

gave me something to, um . . .'

'To *do,* perhaps, on a cold wintry night?' Isabel asked. 'I can definitely get behind that.'

'Oh, and he did!' said Candace, with a little wiggle. 'Again and again!'

'So there you have it,' said Isabel.

Sunny glanced at Jack, whose eyes were on her. He was smiling. 'So this is how women talk about us when we're not around. But you forget—I'm around! Sitting right here!'

'But you're one of us,' said Isabel.

'Yes, you are,' said Sunny.

'Now I don't know if I should laugh or cry,' said Jack.

'Nobody do anything,' said Sunny as she got up from her chair and walked to the tree. Poppy was lying near it, on her bed, looking humiliated in her antlers and red nose. Sunny scratched her ear and whispered, 'Hey, girl. Forgive me for the getup.'

Then she piled several gifts in her arms and returned to the table. 'Time for presents!' She handed gifts to Isabel, Candace, and Jack. And as she did, she felt truly happy. These new people were her people. So what that she'd only recently met these women. In their hearts they were all the same: women yearning for rich lives, someone to love and to love them in return, friends to laugh with, drink with, and cry with. She had so much in common with Candace it was crazy, and she saw the world through the same eyes as Isabel. And, of course, Jack got under her skin. *So there you have it,* Sunny thought.

Candace opened her gift and found a lovely scarf. It was similar to the one Isabel received, but hers was the perfect blue for her complexion, and

Isabel's was a deep red. Sunny got Jack a toy for Poppy so that they could play together, which made Jack laugh out loud and made Candace look at him as if she was about to jump his bones.

'I'm sorry I didn't bring you a gift,' Candace said to Sunny.

'I didn't either,' said Isabel. 'Not just rude, quite sad, really!'

'I did,' said Jack. 'Me! You lucky girl.'

Sunny ignored him. 'That's okay,' said Sunny. 'This is my party. Let's just hope we can do it again next year.'

'What do you mean?'

'We're still struggling and may not have enough money to make it through. We're trying to get UN compliance so we can get more customers, but it's expensive. Anybody got any ideas for raising more money? We had the doctor, but we need something more.'

'I have an idea,' Candace said, getting up from her chair. 'Bashir, Bashir Hadi, come here, please. What do you think of this—?'

And she whispered something to Bashir Hadi that made him clap his hands and yell, 'Impossible! You cannot do it. That would be something, all right.'

'But I can,' she said. And then she turned to the table, her eyes wide with excitement.

Bashir Hadi was breathless, waiting for her announcement.

'My ex,' she said, 'knew everybody. And he introduced me to many, many people, mostly boring old bureaucrats. But he also introduced me to Malalai Joya. And that girl owes me one. She sure as shit owes me.'

156

*   *   *

Even over the music and the hubbub, Ahmet heard Candace almost scream the name 'Malalai Joya,' and he wondered what this café was becoming—a center of revolution? A place of angry women and old reformers? Everyone in Afghanistan knew of Malalai, the member of parliament who spoke out against injustice, who wasn't afraid to accuse the politicians of being partners with the drug lords and the warlords, probably the bravest woman in the country. Probably, the bravest person.

Ahmet admired her. How could you not? But here? At the coffeehouse? It would be dangerous and require many men to protect it. Malalai had so many enemies that he wondered how she went out each day knowing she could die at any minute. Of course his mother would surely enjoy having her here.

He breathed in deeply, his chest filling with the rich scents of the room, and felt two things: proud that maybe this brave woman warrior would come to his coffeehouse, and angry that her visit would put his mother, Sunny, and especially Yazmina in danger.

Yazmina, he thought, *look at her tonight*. She is like the sun in that dazzling dress, with her hair showing under her scarf. He wanted to kick himself for smiling at her earlier, but he didn't even know he was until it was too late. Controlling his impulses was something important to him. And what about the very rules he insisted on for his mother? But every single day Yazmina challenged these things in him. She brought out the child in him, made him forget his duty, and made him to want run and play in the streets. And especially on this night, this silly annual tradition of Sunny's that he secretly enjoyed and looked forward to—even Muhammad liked a good party!

Yazmina made him want to hold her, protect her, and love her. *Yazmina,* he thought, watching her serve, talk to customers, clear plates, pour water. *Yazmina.*

*   *   *

Before the night was over, Sunny turned off the music and stood by the counter. She clinked her glass several times with a spoon to quiet everyone down. Of course, Jack was watching her the entire time, so he stood up to help. 'Hey, everybody! The lady has something to say!' he roared with his deep voice and his contagious smile. He waited until the room was silent before he sat back down.

Then Sunny did what she did every Christmas, and only on Christmas, since she'd run this café in Kabul: She gave a short speech. She began by thanking everyone for coming, for making the evening perfect. She said she hoped they enjoyed the food (at which everyone whooped and hollered) and brought out Bashir Hadi to thank him for his delicious meal. He gave a slight bow and the room rumbled with applause. She introduced Halajan as the owner of the building and therefore the big boss and responsible for the place. She thanked Yazmina, who blushed, and Ahmet, who stood proud as she thanked him for his service all year. She gave each a beautifully wrapped gift and the café patrons applauded warmly. She thanked her

158

turkey smuggler and the people who brought her Christmas baubles from afar.

And then Sunny's voice grew quieter, and she raised her glass and said, 'I could never run this place without the help of these wonderful people. This far away from my home and my family, I have found a home and a family that means the world to me. And this season always does me in. There's something about Christmas, no matter where you are, it's a time we put aside our differences and . . .' Her voice trailed off. She swallowed and blinked back tears. 'I sound like a fucking Hallmark card!' she screamed, and everyone laughed and applauded. She quickly looked at Jack, who was watching her intently, his brows furrowed, worried for her, smiling, happy for her. She looked at Isabel and Candace, and the room full of customers and acquaintances. Her heart was so full it expanded to fill her chest, her throat, making it necessary to breathe out and in again. 'I know I'm about as corny as they come, but on this night sappy is okay, right?' There was a resounding response. And then Sunny raised her glass and said, looking at her table of cohorts, 'Here's to friends. Merry Christmas, everybody!' Everyone yelled back, 'Merry Christmas!' and then Sunny added, 'And don't leave without a gift!'

As Sunny stood by the door to say good night to everyone, she handed everybody a present and kissed their cheeks. Only her friends and family remained: Jack, Isabel and Candace, Halajan, Bashir Hadi, Yazmina, and Ahmet. She wasn't sure who were family and who were friends, and maybe they all were both, and maybe it didn't matter one bit.

The night was all she'd hoped it would be. The music, the food, the wine and laughter, and not one argument—that made it different from her family back home.

There was no Tommy, and his absence had always weighed on her. But tonight she felt lighter than she had in ages. And, there was one last thing to do.

She took Jack by the arm, saying, 'Come with me,' and pulled him out the back doorway of the coffeehouse to the hallway leading to her own rooms. She could hear Candace shout behind her, 'Where the hell are you two going?'

There, hanging from a light fixture, was a bunch of plastic mistletoe.

And there, she kissed him.

CHAPTER EIGHTEEN

It took only three Wednesday nights in January to make enough money to build the wall, because Candace had come through with her promise. Malalai Joya agreed to speak. She was accompanied by a group of UN security forces, which she dared not travel without. Ahmet, who'd tried to persuade his mother to dissuade Sunny from allowing her to come, eventually accepted his duty and hired several experienced *chokidor,* men who were licensed to use guns, not just carry them, to ensure the café's safety from the *muhajideen* Joya often criticized for the deaths of thousands of Afghans. The café was standing room only, with people jammed together, shoulder to shoulder, sharing chairs, sitting on the floor, lined up against the walls. But there were no incidents. Only an evening that was thrilling.

In everything Sunny had read and heard about Malalai, nobody spoke about her beauty. That was probably because when she spoke, you didn't see her anymore, only heard the passionate words of a staunch defender of human rights. You even forgot she was a woman when she bravely called for warlords to stop using the cloak of democracy to control Afghanistan. She also criticized America and its intentions in her country. Afghanistan had for so long been a place to wage war, fight for power, and harvest poppies, that the people were left uneducated, illiterate, impoverished, completely disenfranchised with no voice of their own.

Malalai stood in the front of the room, her black hair covered with a black scarf, her dark eyes fierce with commitment and determination. *You can speak for me anytime,* Sunny thought as Malalai gave her speech.

'Warlords are responsible for our country's situation,' she said. 'They oppress women and have ruined our country. They might be forgiven by the Afghan people, but not by history.'

Some women, Sunny thought, are meant for greatness. Some, like her, she supposed, were meant for providing a place to spread that greatness around a little. She found pride in that and wanted to hug Bashir Hadi and kiss him and thank him for forcing her to get off her butt and make more money. Without his pushing her, none of this would've happened.

*   *   *

The next week, Sunny researched the height requirements, Bashir Hadi hired the team of workers, and construction began. It wasn't a difficult job. All they had to do was build another four feet onto the existing wall that encircled the building. They'd need to lay red clay bricks for the basic structure, side the wall with cement, and then add a fresh coat of paint so that the new section would blend seamlessly with the old.

As the wall went up, rising so high that the acacia tree in the courtyard of the house next door was barely visible, and the mountains to the east were completely obliterated, Sunny watched from her windows, standing with her hands on her hips. The wall was meant to protect, but it made her feel walled *in*. It was a perfect visual metaphor for the sad state of her beloved Kabul and the changes that had occurred in the years since she'd first arrived. When Sunny first came to Kabul, the Taliban had been 'ousted,' which really meant they'd gone undercover, shaving their beards and cutting their hair when the Americans had invaded only a year before. Within a few short years, Hamid Karzai, a Pashtun from Kandahar, was elected president in the country's first democratic presidential election. Then America turned to Iraq, leaving the drug lords, the various mafias, all the bad guys, to raise money, get strong, and carve up their fiefdoms. Now the Taliban were back out in the open in force, broader and bigger, having used the time wisely to recruit and wage another rigorous insurgency that was feeling more palpable by the day.

So the wall represented more than mere protection. It was also about keeping things out,

162

being separated from life on the streets, being fully aware that there were dangers encroaching on her home. The wall, in a word, sucked.

But on a bright, brisk afternoon in February, it was completed. All it needed was to be painted, and Sunny was taking color suggestions.

Halajan wanted a peacock blue. Bashir Hadi liked the pale orange that had been there, was used to it, argued that customers were used to it, too, and besides, he said, their gate was blue, and the walls should be different. When Sunny asked Yazmina her opinion, she was hesitant to answer but ultimately voted for orange, as did Jack and Ahmet.

'In the spirit of democracy, orange it is,' Sunny said.

She took her car and Poppy to Paint Street to buy the supplies, her spirits high. It had been a long time since she'd bought paints. Her favorite shop was one about halfway down the street. She parked in front and left Poppy inside to guard the car.

The shop was tiny, with brushes and supplies hanging from hooks on the walls and from the ceiling. Two walls were lined with displays from various American brands that had shallow shelves of little cards with a sample square of the color, the number, and the name, like #54 Florida Orange, or #208 Soft Mango, just like at the hardware stores back home.

Sunny took her time gathering the oranges that appealed to her, comparing them, trying to see them large and imagine what would happen to their color in the sunlight, and then, slowly, deliberately, narrowing them down to three. She took the little color cards to the shopkeeper, who sat on a stool

163

at a counter, reading the newspaper and drinking from a can of Coke.

'*Salaam alaikum,*' she said in greeting, and continued in Dari. 'I'm considering these colors for the wall around my house. What do you think?'

He looked carefully at the samples, and said, 'Very, very nice. Joyful! Orange is one of my favorites.' Then he pointed to one and said, 'But I don't have that one in stock.'

'Well, that narrows it down,' said Sunny cheerfully. 'Do you have a preference between these two?'

He thought long and hard and then said, 'This one. It's brighter. It will distinguish your house.'

'That's exactly what I want it to do. Okay, so let's go with that one.' Then she told him the height and length of her walls, and they discussed how much paint she would need, calculating enough for two coats.

The shopkeeper went to the back, while Sunny looked around the shop, waiting. But he returned quickly, shaking his head.

'I'm out of that color,' he said.

'That's too bad. Well, then, let's go with the—'

'I think I'm out of that one, too, but I will check.'

Sunny felt her impatience rise as she waited while he disappeared into his stockroom.

'As I thought, none of that color either!' he yelled from the back.

Sunny had to laugh. 'Do you have *any* orange paint in stock?'

'No, not as such at this time. *Inshallah,* tomorrow. I'm sure that a shipment will have arrived.'

Sunny knew that 'tomorrow' could mean a week

164

or two or maybe never. 'I don't have that kind of time. What colors do you have in stock? Maybe a pale green? There was one that I liked—'

He looked down at the floor. 'Sadly, not enough of any one color for your wall. I do have some Federal Blue, number 67, and some Colonial Yellow, number 317, which might look very nice together. Very stately. Oh, and some Designer White, and Bright White, but surely you don't want to paint your wall white! That would be silly.'

She had to smile. His lack of paint didn't stop him from being charming. 'So that's it? Of all these colors?' She gestured toward the displays with their hundreds of offerings.

'Perhaps I can order from Dubai.'

'Never mind,' she said in frustration, and then quickly added, 'but thank you.'

She left the store thinking she'd try another paint store, but she knew it would be fruitless. If one didn't have paint, none would have paint. She went back to her car, where Poppy was sitting in the front seat right behind the wheel, looking like a doggie driver.

'Let's go home, girl,' Sunny said as the dog leapt to the shotgun seat. 'We'll figure something out.'

When they got back to the coffeehouse, Poppy went to her special place at the back of the café, where she followed her tail around and around several times before lying down in a ball on her *toshak*. And Sunny went to the courtyard to look at the wall.

It was now late afternoon. The sun was low in the sky and it lit up the wall as it settled into the west. The part of the wall that was unpainted seemed to sparkle as it caught the light; the fragments of glass and stone in the cement glittered. It reminded Sunny of the wall she'd painted in high school that got her suspended, sent to court, and sentenced to two weeks of so-called community service, which in actuality was picking up litter from the side of the highway.

'Community service, my ass,' she said aloud.

Everyone hated Jonesboro High, especially the building itself with its gothic balustrades and small windows and its four-story height. It loomed over the edge of town like a fortress. They called it the Pink Prison. And so, Sunny had decided to beautify it. She knew she could draw, and her notebooks covered with doodles and more elaborate drawings that filled the margins proved it. But she'd never painted. So she went to the hardware store and, using the money she made working as a cashier at the corner market after school and weekends, bought paint and brushes and thinner and flashlights, and got some friends to meet her behind the school at midnight that Saturday. They were to hold the flashlights as she painted. And paint she did, as they all drank beer and smoked weed. Had she had more time, it would've been better, but by six the next morning it was done.

She remembered the sun rising over the flatness of Jonesboro, its light reflecting in the windows of the small, nondescript houses that lined the streets. The sky was purple, a lighter yellow and orange at the horizon. As the sun rose, it shone right onto her painting. She hadn't planned it that way, but there you are. Sometimes the things unplanned are the things that make magic. Some said they could see it from miles away. Some said that the way the rays of the morning sun hit the yellows and golds

166

of her painting that morning created a glare so intense that you needed sunglasses even that early. (Of course nobody was up and out that early on a Sunday morning, but it became the stuff of legend, nevertheless.)

She remembered standing back, paintbrush in one hand and the other hand on her hip, trying to look at her work objectively. And all she could think was that if only she'd had a better blue, it might have been something. As it was, with the sun's rays on it, the nude figure lying in the forest literally shimmered. Surrounding the figure were large palms and flowers and animals very simply wrought like folk art, primitive, an outsider's view of paradise. Her friends stood, openmouthed, awestruck, at the painting. It was beautiful. It was lush and vibrant. And it was going to get her into one heck of a mess.

You just don't paint your principal in the nude.

For that's exactly who the naked woman was. It was Mrs McQueen's face on a completely nude body, still wearing her horn-rims but without her shoulder-padded suits and sensible shoes. It was Mrs McQueen looking very postcoital, reclining on her side, up on her elbow, head in her hand, her other hand covering her crotch.

Standing in her courtyard now, thousands of miles and worlds away from her small town, Sunny decided she'd paint her wall herself. But not with Colonial Blue or American Mustard, or whatever the hell those colors were. She'd paint it with her own oils. A mural. Her heart caught in her throat with excitement, and she ran inside to begin sketching. She would paint the street side of the wall with something bold and simple so that it would be easy to identify the coffeehouse, and she would paint the wall facing the windows with an elaborate scene, so that when she looked out she could pretend, if only for one moment, that the wall didn't exist.

*   *   *

It was the same late afternoon and Yazmina stood before her mirror. She was glowing. This baby, now that she was over the sick period, was making her hair shine, her cheeks rich with color, and her smile broad. And yet, the same baby was making her terribly worried, though nobody looking at her would've ever known. Her dark, heavy dresses and her long *chaderi* hid her pregnant stomach, but soon the day would come when the baby would want to show itself. And then what? Her smile faded. She never understood before the shame that pregnant women felt, but she understood it now. Why would anyone believe this was her husband's baby? She would bring shame to everyone, especially Bashir Hadi and Ahmet. Everyone would think she was a prostitute. If she was not killed for being pregnant, she would certainly die in childbirth as so many women did. But, perhaps, *Inshallah,* Muhammad would watch over her and see to their safety. And in Muhammad's absence, since he had many more important things to do, she had Halajan, who could move mountains almost as well.

And what about her sister, Layla? Was she still at home with their uncle? Had the snows been enough to block the roads and prevent anyone from going out or coming in? Or had the sun been stronger this winter and allowed the drug lord to come for her,

168

too? Not a day went by that she didn't pray to Allah for Layla's well-being as much as that of her own baby. She had to find a way to ask Sunny to talk to her friend Mr Jack. He would know people. He would be able to reach Layla before the spring. But Sunny was already keeping one secret for her. To ask her for another deed? It was too much.

And then Halajan was at her door as if her thoughts had conjured her.

She was frantic. 'Yazmina, the pipes! We are flooding! Ahmet is at prayer. I need your help. Come!'

Yazmina grabbed a scarf to cover her head, and then followed Halajan to the bathroom down the hall, opened the door, and found herself standing in two inches of cold water. The toilet was running nonstop, pumping water out of its tank and onto the floor. Halajan opened the back and pulled a lever and it stopped pumping. Then she let the lever go and it began pumping water again, this time spraying water onto her.

'Here,' she said, 'you hold this to stop the water, and I'll be right back. And here, you're getting soaked. Put this on.'

She slipped her apron over her head and put it over Yazmina's and tied it for her. Then she left. And Yazmina was left alone standing in the icy water, with one hand holding the toilet lever. The other she put in the apron pocket for warmth. There was something there. She pulled it out. It was a folded piece of paper. It was wet from the spray of water, so she put it under the apron, in the pocket of her own dress, for safekeeping.

Soon Halajan reappeared with Ahmet, who went to work without a smile or a word.

He fixed the toilet, replacing a plastic part that had broken, and Yazmina was amazed at how resourceful he was. Yazmina mopped up the water and cleaned the bathroom. She was soaked after the ordeal, her pants and dress wet from her ankles to her knees.

'This will need more work to prevent it from happening again,' said Ahmet, 'so there will be no trip to the Mondai-e today.'

'We will take a bus,' said Halajan.

'You will, please, not go without me,' he answered sternly. 'It just isn't safe any longer, for two women alone. And besides—'

'Besides what?'

'It isn't right. And he's—'

Yazmina wasn't sure what they were talking about, but she could feel their anger.

'He is what, Ahmet?'

'Just promise me that you will not go again to the market without me to accompany you.'

Halajan said nothing, but shook her head, her jaw clenched and her eyes as tight as the slits of the lizards that sat on the rocks by the river back home.

And Ahmet said, 'She is wet, Mother.'

'Yes, you don't want to catch a cold,' said Halajan, finally looking at Yazmina.

'I have nothing to change into. My other *shalwaar kameez* is drying, too. I washed it last night.'

'Ach, you need more than two changes of clothes. We will go to Chicken Street for more, perhaps tomorrow,' she said, eyeing Ahmet. 'Right now, come with me.'

Yazmina followed Halajan to her house, which was directly adjacent to the coffeehouse and within the compound, so they didn't have to leave the gate.

'Please come in,' said Halajan. 'Let's get you something to wear and then some *chai* and *badan,*' referring to the sweet tea and almonds. She took off her head scarf and her own wet *kameez*, allowing her arms to be exposed to Yazmina, comfortable the way women were in Kabul when they were with each other in the privacy of their own homes. She wore a white T-shirt with a large red heart and some English words in black letters.

What are the words on that T-shirt? thought Yazmina. *And look, her hair is short! Had she cut it herself?*

'I like it this way. Much easier to keep clean,' said Halajan as if she were reading Yazmina's mind. She ran a hand through her hair. 'Please, you be comfortable, too. Give me your scarf and the apron and then I'll be back to exchange your pants and dress for dry ones.'

She took off her scarf and handed it to Halajan, revealing her long, thick braid of shiny black hair. As she took off the apron, she said, 'But no *chai*, thank you, for it makes my stomach ill.'

Halajan took the clothes and left. Now alone, Yazmina could see that Halajan's home was warm and inviting, filled with colorful pillows and fabrics, pictures on the walls, shiny draperies with gold threading, and lovely furniture. Surprising, given the tattered clothes the old woman wore to the coffeehouse each day. There were several beautiful rugs on the floor and *toshak*s lining the walls. Next to one was a low table, beautifully carved with inlaid wood, and another high chest with many drawers against the far wall.

171

Then Halajan reappeared with clothes draped over her arm. 'Come,' she said, 'take off those wet clothes and put these on.'

But Yazmina didn't want Halajan to see her belly and how it had grown since she last saw it. She turned around and started to lift her dress over her head, but then remembered the letter, stopped, and took it out of her pocket.

'This is yours. It was in your apron and I—'

'Is this what you do in my home?' asked Halajan, her voice rising as she stood up, visibly upset. 'You sneak and see things you shouldn't?' She grabbed the paper from Yazmina's hand.

'No, no. I only wanted to keep it safe. The water might've ruined it. I hope the ink has not smeared and it can still be read.'

'Besides, it isn't even mine.'

'Really? It has your name on it.'

Halajan's eyes widened. She unfolded the letter, looked at it quickly, and then put it into her own pocket.

'I've seen you at the market talking with the tailor. He seems like a very nice man,' Yazmina said.

'It's none of your business! You must promise never to mention anything to anyone about him or the letters.'

'I would never. I promise.'

'Now change your wet clothes.'

Yazmina was braver then, knowing a secret of Halajan's. Still, she turned away to take off her wet clothes and put on the *shalwaar kameez* that Halajan handed to her. It was beautiful, a lovely green, vivid and so silky that it clung to her round stomach, revealing its condition. She turned around, holding her wet clothes in front of her but not so close that they would soil the beautiful clothing she had on. She wondered why Halajan never wore clothing like this, only her brown burlap sacks.

'Yazmina, you look beautiful. Why don't you keep it and wear it?'

'Thank you, but no, I couldn't.'

'But why not? An old woman like me has no use for such a color. It is yours—'

'Why not? Here is why.' And she took the wet clothes away from in front of her body and there, for the whole world to see, was her very big stomach, looking low and close to ready to give birth.

Halajan sat, as if the wind had knocked her down. 'Of course.' She just stared, then closed her eyes and shook her head. The baby would be coming soon. She could imagine her son's words upon finding Yazmina this way; she imagined the anger on his face, his features dark and reddening, his mouth almost frothing like a tiger's in a goat field, and all that had sustained her—her desire to be herself, to be modern, to be open-minded—vanished like a specter. Finally she spoke her fears, spitting the words, without thinking of their poison. 'Don't you see what is going to happen? You will bring shame upon yourself. You will be called a whore.' She stood up. 'You will be beaten. You could be killed. Let's just hope that your child, *Inshallah,* will be born a boy. Because otherwise, life for it will be very short.'

Yazmina looked at Halajan through wide, shocked eyes. She couldn't believe the words she'd just heard. This was not the woman she'd come to know and love.

'But Hala—'

'Don't you see? I cannot protect you!' She collapsed onto her knees on the rug.

'Halajan, I don't expect you to. I will bear the shame if I have to.'

'Don't be stupid, girl. They will throw acid in your face. They will not only call you a whore, they will treat you as one. My own son, Ahmet—'

'He is a good man. He will—'

'He will feel betrayed and ashamed, and he will turn on us both. Didn't you hear him just now? Forbidding me to go to the market without him? Because he doesn't like Rashif? He has a good spirit but a mind like stone. He cannot shed the old ways.'

'Then you and Sunny will—'

'Stop and listen! I am nothing. And Sunny can protect you for only so long. She can't stay in Afghanistan forever. Don't you see? It doesn't matter what I think, or what you think. It doesn't matter that women deserve to be treated better than dogs. Kabul, this country, is too big for you, for me, for a baby. The only way . . .'

'Yes,' Yazmina pleaded, 'what is it?' She clasped her hands, almost in prayer, in front of her chest.

'Is to let me take it after it is born, when it is strong enough, to the hospital, and give it to them. Tell them I found it, and let them do with it what they want.'

'I cannot believe my ears!' Yazmina cried. 'You have cared for me as your own.'

'That is exactly why the baby must go. To protect you. To save you. If anything ever happened to you . . . My own son, my dear Ahmet, he will not allow—'

Yazmina dropped her head, and her heart dropped, too. Somehow, since she'd come to Sunny's coffeehouse, she'd begun to feel that good things were possible. But she herself was aware of the shame her condition would bring.

Halajan said, 'When the baby is born, I will get rid of it.'

'You cannot do that! I have already lost one . . .'

'What do you mean? You had a baby before this?'

Yazmina shook her head. 'No, my little sister, Layla, who is now twelve years old. By the time the snows have melted, the men who took me will come for her. I cannot lose two.'

Halajan nodded. 'This I will tell Miss Sunny. Maybe Jack can help you. But the baby you carry, she is already gone.'

Yazmina began to sob—for the baby that was doomed before it was born, and for Halajan and how, as independent as she was, she could not move mountains, after all. She wept in hope, too, that Mr Jack might help get Layla. Halajan offering to ask him was as if Allah had heard her prayers! With sadness and optimism, she wept for all the daughters of Afghanistan.

Halajan went to her and held her head in her arms and said, 'There is nothing more I can do.'

Yazmina nodded slightly and said, 'I understand.' She raised her head and looked at Halajan's aged yellow eyes, her skin like a lizard's, wrinkled from the years of sun and cigarettes. She would never let Halajan take her baby. She would leave before it was born and find Dr Malik or someone who would help her. But she owed Halajan for keeping her

175

secret.

'And in exchange for your help, perhaps there is something I can do for you,' Yazmina said.

'For me?' Halajan laughed. 'What help would I need?'

'Maybe not today, but one day.'

'"One day" is a long way off, and I am already halfway to paradise,' Halajan said as she impulsively put her hands in her pockets. She looked at Yazmina, then nervously turned away.

'What is it?' asked Yazmina.

'There is something . . .' Halajan's voice trailed off, as if bringing herself to ask was more difficult than climbing the Hindu Kush.

Yazmina waited. When Halajan said nothing, she was reminded of Layla's shyness, the reticence of a little girl who wanted something but was hesitant to ask for fear of the response.

So she implored, 'What is it, Halajan? You can ask anything of me.'

Halajan looked directly at her, let out a deep sigh, and whispered, 'You read, don't you?'

'I do. Since I was a child.'

'But how is it that you learned to read?'

Yazmina felt her color rise. People were narrow-minded when it came to judging others, especially people like her who were different from those in Kabul. 'And I write, too. Do you think because I am *jungli,* as you would say—a backward girl from the mountains—that I am ignorant, uneducated? My mother taught me to read—to appreciate poetry and good stories. I am uneducated otherwise, so you are correct.'

'I meant no judgment. It is just that you are such a young woman to be so educated.'

But Yazmina always knew when people were telling stories—like when Layla said she'd finished her chores when really she just wanted to run the goats outside on a sunny day—and she thought Halajan was telling her one now.

Slowly Halajan pulled the letter from her pocket. 'Now that I know that you can read . . .' she said, trailing off.

Was it possible? Yazmina understood now. Halajan couldn't read! And therefore how had she read Rashif's dear letters? Had she been able to ask someone to read them to her? Or had she never read even one because of the risk of shame she'd have brought to her family by acknowledging that the letters even existed.

'Yes, I could read your letters to you. And if you'd like, I can teach you to read them yourself. And help you to write him back.'

'Show me,' said Halajan. 'Read it. Go ahead, read it.'

Yazmina opened the letter and read:

Halajan my love,

This week, much has happened. I received a letter from my son in New York. He is well. His wife is with child. I am to be a grandfather! I dream of the day I will see him and his family.

Also, I finished paying my bill for the new sewing machine and the generator that will run it. So I will have more money to spend on flowers for you.

Six more were killed yesterday outside the Russian Embassy. This is only going to get worse. The struggle for Afghanistan has begun again, heightened by what's going on in Iraq. I could never side with the Taliban or al-Qaeda, but I can see how the war in Iraq has created an entire army of orphan boys eager to be part of something, to find a kind of family.

We are so lucky, you and I, my dear Halajan. We know the joys of real family. One day very soon, we will be together, you and I, and create a new one. Your Ahmet will like me. I know he will. And all the years apart will vanish like smoke in the night air.

Please write back so I will know what's in your heart. I long to hear from you. Seeing you once each week is wonderful but a letter from you would be as if Muhammad himself, peace be upon him, had written.

Yours,
Rashif

Halajan had lowered her head. She was crying, tears that she'd probably kept deep in a well for all these years.

'Halajan,' Yazmina said softly, 'I have no desire to hurt you. You've helped me more than words can say. And now, I can offer you something in return.'

'It has to be a trade,' said Halajan.

'It is a trade. You're keeping my secret.' She put her hand lovingly on her stomach and continued, 'And asking Mr Jack if maybe he can help my sister.'

'No,' said Halajan. 'Keeping your secret is a trade for keeping my secret. And asking for help to find Layla is what any good woman would do. But for the letters, something more.'

Yazmina knew that this old woman's pride was

178

stronger than her own, so she thought about it, and yes, there was something Halajan could do for her.

'Fabric,' she said. 'I'd like you to help me buy some fabric.'

'Yes.' Halajan smiled. She wasn't sure if Yazmina wanted to make her own pretty *shalwaar kameez* or a blanket for the baby to be wrapped in when they took it away, but it didn't matter. Every project a person does, she knew, gets her one step deeper into life and closer to God.

CHAPTER NINETEEN

An hour later Halajan and Yazmina were headed toward the Mondai-e. Halajan had lied to her son, who stayed behind to replace the broken toilet, telling him that they were going to Chicken Street. Instead, she and Yazmina had taken the bus, then were walking the remaining half mile with their heads bowed, their arms clenched in front of them to ward off the cold, when they heard the explosion, felt the earth move, and saw the buildings sway. They stopped where they were, ducked into a doorway, and smelled the smoke in the air. Then they saw it rise over the buildings exactly where they were headed.

'A bomb,' Halajan said, her face etched with fear. 'At the market, I think. We must hurry.'

'Wait!' Yazmina tried to call to Halajan but she was already far ahead, running directly toward the blast, along with hundreds of other people.

Yazmina knew they should return to the coffeehouse, but she couldn't let Halajan go alone,

179

so she ran as fast as she could to catch up to her, weighed down by the baby, struggling to keep her in sight, watching for her purple scarf. Halajan seemed to have acquired the legs and wind of a child. She was so fast and agile as she dodged in and out of the chaos of the streets. People were running, screaming and bleeding; sirens were blaring, trying desperately to reach the bomb site. The police were everywhere, their weapons drawn, as if they had been hiding in the shadows knowing this was going to happen. The sky turned gray with soot and ash; the air was thick and it was difficult to breathe.

Finally, Yazmina reached her, pulled her arm at her elbow, and stopped her. 'Halajan, we should go back.' She could see Halajan struggling to breathe. She was holding her chador over her mouth and nose, and her chest was heaving as if she couldn't get enough oxygen to fill it.

'No, I must get to the marketplace. I must . . . You return at once to the coffeehouse. I will follow shortly. Now go!'

'Halajan, you must come with me. It is too dangerous. I heard that there are usually two blasts: The first gets people to come, the second is for everyone who has arrived.'

'Go home and let me do what I have to.'

'If you go, I will go, too. I will not leave you alone.'

Halajan and Yazmina stood stubbornly, each waiting for the other to move. When neither did, Yazmina knew that Halajan would never return to the house without first being sure that Rashif had survived. 'Okay, but quickly.'

They walked briskly through the narrow streets

toward the river, the emergency vehicles passing them, their sirens blaring. People were running in all directions, shouting and screaming—a man carrying a wounded boy, his head falling back over the man's arm, a woman in a burqa holding the hand of a young girl who was missing a shoe and had blood running down her leg, men with rifles, men with makeshift weapons. The closer they got to the market, the darker the air became, until it was a dense fog, almost impossible to see through.

Once there, they saw the devastation. They paused, glanced quickly at each other, their eyes tearing from smoke and fear, and reached out to each other, took hands, and entered the chaotic wreckage.

*   *   *

When the first bomb exploded, there was a mild rumble, a far-off sound like thunder. But thirty seconds later, there was a second bomb, much closer. The front window shattered and the brand-new wall came down. Sunny was sitting at the counter, ordering supplies from Dubai on her laptop, when she heard the first and felt the second. Time seemed to expand; a split second became five, as if in slow motion. It was disorienting, the sight of the thick, solid wall rolling and then, finally, crumbling to the ground. She turned quickly to Bashir Hadi, whose eyes, too, were on the wall. When he turned to find her, no words were necessary. His eyes held back tears, his face etched with disappointment.

After the dust settled in their front courtyard, they assessed the damage. The front window could

181

be replaced—they had bought an extra glass pane the last time in case this happened, but the wall that faced the street needed complete rebuilding because the new section hadn't set yet and its vulnerability had brought down the rest of the wall with it.

Sunny stood, wiped her forehead with the back of her hand, shook her head, and said, 'Shit!'

Though the wall had been such an accomplishment, its destruction was nothing compared to the lives that had probably been lost in the explosion. Still, it was frustrating. Sometimes it felt as if she had taken one tiny step forward and two long steps backward in Kabul.

Bashir Hadi said, 'That was close. As long as we're all fine, this is nothing. We can rebuild. Just a few weeks to make the money—'

But Ahmet interrupted as he ran in from the back, yelling, 'The bombs! My mother! Yazmina! They went to Chicken Street and have not yet returned. Miss Sunny, I must go.'

'They went to the Mondai-e,' Sunny said immediately. 'Let me drive you.'

'Miss Sunny, I don't think you should—' said Bashir Hadi.

'The Mondai-e?' Ahmet said with a mixture of worry and anger. 'But she promised—'

'Poppy, come!' Sunny commanded the dog, who was immediately at her side. She grabbed her chador and coat, and Poppy's leash. Then the three of them were out the door.

As they got into the car, her cellphone rang. It was Jack.

'We're okay,' she said, 'but Halajan and Yazmina went to the Mondai-e. Ahmet and I are taking the car—'

'The streets will be blocked in Qal-i-Fatula and the old city. The emergency vehicles, UN soldiers, the police. Don't go. And there could be another bomb. In a car you're a sitting duck. Halajan is a smart cookie. She will find their way back.'

'Unless they were hurt.'

'I'll go on my motorbike. But you stay right where you are. Tell Ahmet that I can get there much faster.'

She didn't want to argue. 'Okay.'

He didn't respond for a moment. Didn't he trust her? 'Okay. Call me when they get back.'

'You be careful.'

'Sunny—'

'Yeah?'

'Nothing. Just take care, okay?'

'I have Poppy. But Jack, who's protecting you?'

*   *   *

The streets were filled with broken glass. Yazmina's feet were bleeding, her plastic shoes little protection from the rivers of shards. People were running toward the blast instead of away, and Halajan wanted to shout at them to go home, that running to the scene was exactly what the terrorists wanted. Emergency vehicles were speeding in both directions—to pick up the injured, the dying, and take them to the hospital and return again for more.

An entire block of shops was in smoky rubble. Yazmina's favorite dress store, the bookstore, and several others had been razed to the ground. But Rashif's store was still farther on, if it remained at all.

183

Halajan, who had never been a religious person, who felt strongly that strict beliefs were precisely what kept women imprisoned, whether behind bars or burqas, prayed now, quietly, under her breath. If there was a God, if Muhammad could, indeed, get his people to accept why the mountain hadn't come to him, then he certainly could, please, let Rashif be safe.

What kind of person kills others in this way? she cursed to herself. Animals, which were beneath the human being, without the capacity to talk, reason, and think, weren't low enough to compare to the uncivilized, ignorant, and hate-filled people who bomb busy streets.

Finally, they arrived. The shop was still standing, but the electricity had gone out so it was dark inside. The glass was blown out of the front windows and door as well, which Halajan opened carefully. As she did, more glass fell from the frame.

'Be careful,' she said sternly to Yazmina. 'You wait here. I'll be right back.'

'You cannot go in alone. Who knows what you might find. Including looters and thieves. It's dangerous.'

Halajan smiled. 'And you will protect me?'

'You would be surprised how strong I am,' Yazmina replied.

'I don't think I would.' She smiled and turned and the two women went through the door.

'Rashif!' Halajan called. 'Rashif, are you here? Hello!'

'Of course I'm here. Where else would I be?' he said as he came through a curtain in the back. 'Halajan! Am I glad to see you. I was worried

184

that—' He rushed to her, but seeing Yazmina, he stopped himself and said, 'It is not safe. You must go.'

Halajan noticed that his clothes were torn and dirty, his face blackened, and his head bleeding. 'You are hurt.'

Yazmina's presence prevented any further talk, and Rashif said it again, but more forcefully this time: 'You must go. It is dangerous. Return to your home.'

Halajan's eyes filled with tears. She couldn't understand how, even when faced with death, the old habits and rules still prevailed. Even for someone as open-minded as Rashif.

'Let us go,' she said quietly to Yazmina, and walked out.

They had taken only a few steps when they heard Rashif's voice calling for Halajan. She turned. He was waving at her. 'You left your fabric in the shop. I know how you like the scraps,' he said.

'Wait here,' Halajan said to Yazmina. 'I'll be only a moment.'

Halajan followed Rashif back into his store. He handed her a small bag filled with fabric scraps, and by the look in his eyes, his letter.

She looked outside at Yazmina, who was helping a little boy who was crying. Halajan saw Yazmina take his hand, looking around as if for his mother. She then said loudly to Rashif, 'Thank you. I will use them for patching.' And then whispering, 'And guard it with my heart.'

He smiled. 'And yet,' he said, 'you do not answer my letters. After all this time, look around you. Life is short. In a wisp, a blast, a stupid idiot's bomb, we could be gone. Why don't you answer me?'

Halajan paused, watching as a woman approached Yazmina and took the little boy in her arms. Halajan was trying to find words, a reason, something to tell him. 'Because no words can express what I feel.'

Rashif laughed. 'Are you certain that is the reason? Maybe you don't share my feelings. Maybe . . .' He turned away.

'Rashif, of course I do. How can you not think that?'

'Because our communication is very one-sided.'

'I come the distance to see you. You keep us close while we're apart.'

'I suppose that's fair, but I long for a letter from you. Any words are good. Please try to find them for me.'

'Oh,' said Halajan, 'I have them, I know where they are. It is just that my heart, well, "the most living moment comes" when we meet each other's eyes and what flows between us.'

'That's beautifully said.'

'Rumi, not me.'

'You give Rumi a beautiful voice. Look,' he said, as he went back into his store. He returned with a small package in his hand. 'This is for you.'

Halajan untied the string that held some brown paper around what felt like a book. Fear rose in her and made her forehead perspire. It was a book. She knew it had to be a collection of Rumi poems.

'So read one to me,' Rashif said. 'Just one and I will think you wrote it for me.'

'But which one? I cannot pick.' Why was he doing this today, of all days? Perhaps, she thought, it was because of the bombing that he was pushing her so.

186

'Here,' he said, and opened the book haphazardly. 'This.' He pointed to a page with few words.

Halajan took the book, pretending to read the poem to herself. Then she looked up at Rashif. 'I do not like that one.' She turned the pages again and again, pretending she was searching for just the right poem. Then she stopped and said, 'How about this one?' She prayed to Allah that she got the page right and she recited from memory:

Soul receives from soul that knowledge,
Therefore, not by book nor from tongue.
If knowledge of mysteries come after emptiness of
    mind,
That is illumination of heart.

A loud crash interrupted them, and suddenly Yazmina rushed into the shop. It wasn't a bomb but perhaps a falling building.

'We must go,' said Halajan, feeling as if she were spared from lying and being humiliated. 'Were you able to help that little boy?' she asked Yazmina.

'Yes, thank Muhammad.'

'Good-bye then,' said Rashif. 'Enjoy the fabric. Thank you for my poem.'

Halajan smiled sadly. 'Come, Yazmina, we must go.' She nodded toward the cut on his head. 'Wash that and clean it, then apply a salve.' She put the book into her bag.

Rashif answered, 'I've had cuts before.' He smiled.

Once out on the street, Yazmina instinctively covered her belly with her arm as if to protect it. 'We must get back to the house. This filthy air

187

cannot be good for anyone.'

And they headed through the decimated streets toward home, each carrying her own secret.

*   *   *

Rashif watched them go from his broken doorway and observed the tumult in the streets. It had quieted down, sirens were few, and the night had been taken over by sleep and the fears of another day.

All this time and not a letter from Halajan. At first he thought his feelings were unrequited, but when she returned to his shop week after week, he knew better. Then he rationalized that she was just shy, not wanting to share her thoughts. Eventually, he suspected that perhaps she was unable to write. And maybe, also, unable to read. Now his suspicions were confirmed. The poem Halajan had recited was certainly not the poem on that page. It was close, though. If she had flipped one more page, she would've gotten it right. But, apparently, Allah felt it was time for him to know the truth. All these years and all these letters and she had never read one. Because she couldn't. He had never wanted to humiliate her. But feeling the thunder of the bomb under his feet, seeing its destruction, knowing people had died—loved ones, mothers, sisters, children, fathers—he had to know, now, today, this moment. He would change none of his habits. He would continue to write, to pour his feelings onto the elegant paper. And he would continue to love his proud Halajan. One day soon, they would be together, and he would kiss her and teach her to read Rumi for herself.

188

*   *   *

Jack weaved through the streets, driving between cars and through the traffic, in and out of people streaming away from the bomb site. It would be almost impossible to find Yazmina and Halajan in this turmoil. When he finally reached the Massoud Circle, about halfway between the coffeehouse and the market, a third blast occurred, throwing him twenty feet from his motorbike and sending stone, debris, and glass on top of him.

What he couldn't have known as he lay there, with a terrible shooting pain in his left arm and blood trickling into his mouth, was that Yazmina and Halajan were far from the Mondai-e and almost back home when the third blast occurred. So he forced his way up from under the rubble, growing faint from the pain from a cut in his head and from his obviously broken arm, and headed toward the blast to find the two women. But he didn't make it. He fell to the ground, lost consciousness, and wouldn't wake again until he was in a hospital bed.

*   *   *

Sunny was up on her rooftop looking out over the city. The areas where the three bombs had exploded were still bright from fires that had yet to be put out, the smoke rising against the sky, which had taken on a ghostly orange cast from the reflection of fire and emergency lights. Sirens wailed through the night air, but the coffeehouse was still. Yazmina and Halajan had already returned. They had bandaged Yazmina's feet and boarded up the front window, and now everyone was asleep in their own rooms—but she hadn't heard from Jack and she wouldn't sleep until she did.

She feared that Kabul would never change, that the incessant, pervasive violence undermined any potential for its people. And now the inane bombs might have hurt someone she deeply cared about. Where was he? Why hadn't he called? Knowing Jack, he was probably helping get people out from under the rubble, but it was also possible that he was one of those people himself. Who would be helping him? The thought of losing him struck her hard and threw her. If Tommy walked through her door right now she wouldn't care the way she would've a month ago. Why does it take terrible moments in life, like this, to make you realize what's important? She stamped the floor of the roof, wishing she were the kind of woman to appreciate the sweet moments, the lovely times.

And then her cellphone rang. It was her worst nightmare—the hospital. She reeled at the news but there was no time to waste. She was out the door and in her car in two minutes flat, with Poppy in the front passenger seat.

The hospital was teeming with people, the emergency room filled with blood, cries, and anguish. Sunny didn't even try to ask at the desk. Instead she pushed through the doors and ran down the hallways, checking every room. She knew from the call that he was alive. She also knew he'd been injured, and she had no idea how badly.

And then she found him. In a room with eight beds, and as many people with a variety of cuts and casts, stitches and wraps. His face was swollen, his head bandaged, his arm in a sling. When he saw her, he tried to smile but instead let out a groan.

'Nice to see you, too,' she said, her throat aching with her efforts to hold back her tears.

'It only hurts when I laugh,' he said, his face a mess of bruises and scratches.

'You look like shit.' She put her hand on his forehead, careful not to touch the bandage that crossed the top of his head.

'Over a hundred stitches,' he said proudly. 'I'll never grow hair there again.'

She laughed. 'Nobody will notice. You had so little already.' She held his good hand firmly, blinking back tears.

'It was a close one,' he said, squeezing her hand.

She didn't have a clever response to that, and so she just stood, holding his hand until he fell asleep. Only then did she let herself cry.

CHAPTER TWENTY

Jack came to say good-bye. It was a sunny afternoon five days after the bombs had rocked the city. Two dozen people had been killed, and almost a hundred injured, which everybody felt was a miracle because there could've been so many more. In the few days since, the Mondai-e had already been cleared and repairs had begun. Sunny didn't know if this was a good or bad thing, but Kabul residents had become efficient when it came to bombings. The coffeehouse's front window glass was back in place; the pieces of the destroyed wall had been carted away. Tomorrow was Wednesday, and they were hoping for a big crowd and, once again, to begin the process of raising enough money to rebuild the wall.

Sunny was working on her laptop, now that service had finally been restored, when Jack came through the door. His arm was in a cast held by a sling, his head still in its bandage to protect the hundred stitches he'd received.

But today he looked serious. He didn't sit at his usual table or make a joke or wave at Bashir Hadi. He walked straight up to Sunny and said quietly, 'I have to talk to you. Outside.'

He took her arm and they went to the courtyard. It was cool, but the sun was bright, the sky blue. Sunny would remember this later when she thought about their conversation.

'I have to go home,' he said in his direct way. He shook his head, looked down to the ground, then straight into her eyes. 'This thing that happened, I, well, I can't die here without seeing my son again. Or without trying to make it work with Pamela.'

Sunny couldn't breathe. She tried to fight back her tears, but they filled her eyes, spilled onto her cheeks. Jesus H, she thought. This isn't about *you*. It's about him. Let him go.

'I don't know if . . . or when . . . I don't know,' he said. 'All I know is that I have to go.'

But she couldn't stop herself from saying something. 'You've been in many more dangerous situations than that stupid bomb. So you broke your arm, got a few stitches. You've had much worse. Your family knows what you're doing, how important your work is.' She hated how selfish and stupid she sounded.

'I know. But something about this . . . It's not just what happened—I know it's just a broken arm, for crying out loud! But Kabul, the entire country, is changing, and look, it's only going to get more dangerous. I can't leave my son without a father. And Sunny, you should think about leaving, too. Going back.'

Sunny knew what he was saying was true, but she couldn't think of leaving Kabul. Not yet. She wasn't finished. Something held her. And what about Tommy? He was bound to show up sooner or later . . . if he was still alive.

'Though,' Jack continued, 'without you, everything would see—m'

'Me?'

'You have to know.'

No, she thought, *don't say it, not now, when you're leaving.* 'What do you mean? Know what?'

He took a deep breath, and then again, as if there wasn't enough air in this entire country to reach his lungs. Then he pulled her by her elbow, through the front door, and seeing Bashir Hadi in the kitchen and nobody else in the room, he pulled her into the closet and closed the door. He said, 'Sunny,' and he kissed her. He kissed her like she'd never been kissed before. His lips parted and so did hers and his body pressed into hers up against the wall. They could've made love right there and then, but they knew what they were doing was disrespectful and foolish enough.

He pulled away.

'I don't know when I'll be back,' he whispered, stroking her hair. 'If I even—'

'Don't go. I know I shouldn't say that. But please, don't go.'

He held her face with his good hand and said, 'That's all I wanted to hear from you.'

193

'It makes me horrible, right? You want to go home to your family, your son, your *wife,* and I say don't.' She tried to look away from him, but his hand held her there. Her eyes were brimming with tears.

He kissed her again, softly this time, his hand now on her neck. 'I'll see you,' he said, and then he was gone.

*   *   *

Yazmina watched Jack come out of the closet and then walk out of the café. She was disappointed, because she'd thought that maybe tonight Halajan would talk to him about Layla, now that he was out of the hospital and back on his feet.

Then Sunny appeared from the closet and shut the door behind her. She smiled at Yazmina, though she looked embarrassed and upset. Still, Yazmina couldn't stop herself from asking, 'Will Mr Jack come *zut*?'

Sunny smoothed her blouse over her jeans and put a hand through her hair. She didn't look at Yazmina. But she said, 'I don't know, Yazmina, if he'll be back soon. Who the hell knows? And I don't care.'

Yazmina felt weak and took hold, with a tight grip, to the back of a chair to steady herself. If he was gone, there was no chance they'd ever get Layla by the time the snows had vanished from the mountains. She turned back to her cleaning duties and was overcome with sadness. For Sunny, for Jack, and for her beloved sister, whose destiny was written by the drug lords and now there was no way in heaven or on earth to change it.

CHAPTER TWENTY-ONE

Isabel couldn't stop thinking about what had happened to the woman and her baby at the poppy fields. She was aware of the possibilities, and there were few: She'd been beaten, perhaps hospitalized, or even killed; she'd been put in jail, where women who committed 'moral crimes,' such as adultery, marrying men of their own choosing, running away from an abusive husband, or shaming the family were often sent; she'd been committed to the insane asylum, where women were put for the same reasons; or she had died of self-immolation, the terrible decision made by an increasing number of Afghan women to commit suicide by dousing themselves with cooking oil and setting themselves on fire.

At the coffeehouse that Wednesday night, after several cups of wine, she told Sunny where she was going and what to do if she wasn't back in a week. She took out her notepad and pen, scribbled something on it, ripped out the piece of paper, and handed it to Sunny.

'Here's the number of my boss at the BBC, and my producer, too. And here's the number of my cousin in London, who I don't talk to much, but I'm hopeful the old tosser will provide some help if you need any. Thank you, Sunny. I know we haven't been friends long, but it feels good between us, wouldn't you agree? It's as if we have.'

Sunny folded the paper into a neat square, stood, and put it in the pocket of her jeans. 'Nothing's going to happen to you,' she said, putting a hand on Isabel's. And then in a futile attempt to lift her spirits she added, 'So stop with the drama queen shit.'

But Isabel didn't crack a smile.

Sunny leaned toward her and again put her hand on hers. 'Women disappear all the time in this country. Not that we shouldn't be concerned, but why is this one so important to you? It wasn't your fault. You saw her smoking. You saw her beaten. That's why you were there. To see.'

Isabel tossed back a cup of the wine she'd brought. 'That's what we journos do, all right. We see. And then we don't do bloody hell about it.'

'But you do. Without you—'

'Sorry, love, but without me, the world keeps on spinning.'

Sunny straightened and put her hands on her hips.

'What's up with you tonight, huh?'

'Me? I know a bit about violence. About women who—' Isabel shook her head to stop the tears pricking her eyes. 'Oh, bollocks.' She felt ridiculous! It was the stupid wine talking.

'What is it?' asked Sunny.

Isabel didn't answer. She just looked away.

'Come with me,' Sunny said. And she led Isabel up to the roof.

The night was balmy, spring winds drifting from the mountains in the east. The sky was dark but not yet black. The sun was setting later now and there was a dramatic streak of red and purple where sky met land. Sunny's easel was silhouetted against the low light, her paints and palette sitting on a small table.

'So, we're alone. You can talk to me,' said Sunny.

196

'Who's the painter?' Isabel asked, delaying.

'I guess that would be me.'

'I didn't know.'

Sunny looked at the easel, shook her head. 'I don't tell too many people. It's just a silly hobby. But they'll all know too soon, because I'm thinking of painting the new wall. Now, please—'

'You mean a mural? Of what?'

'I don't know. Animals, a jungle. Ridiculous, right?'

'I don't know about the jungle, really. Maybe something more—I don't know—*indigenous,* perhaps, to Kabul?'

'You have a point,' Sunny said, with a tilt of her head. She was hurt by Isabel's sarcastic tone, but she knew that something bigger was bothering her, and she was intent on finding out what.

Isabel walked to the edge of the roof and looked out over the city. She was silent for a long time.

Sunny walked up to her, put a hand on her arm, and finally said, 'You know, sometimes it's better to talk ab—'

Isabel pulled away without looking at her. 'It's not a big deal.'

'Things happen in our lives that we think nobody else could understand.'

'That's for sure.'

'But you'd be surprised.'

Isabel spun around and glared at her. 'Oh yeah? What happened to you, Sunny? Whatever could've happened to you that you couldn't talk about? Smoked too much weed? Got drunk? Had sex with the wrong guy? Come on, Sunny. There are things, and then there are things.'

'You think you have the lock on bad things

197

happening? You're the only one?' Sunny frowned and nodded. 'Makes you feel more special? Gives you a reason to be distant and aloof and very utterly British, does it?'

Isabel could feel her anger rising, her blood pumping. 'What the fuck do you know?'

'This is what I know. I know what it's like to be hit by your own dad. And I mean hit, like with a fist, like thrown across the room. I know what it's like to watch your mother beaten by her husband, and then beg him not to leave her. Until he finally does and then she spends the rest of her life living in a muumuu, depressed and chain-smoking.'

Isabel looked at her, her face softening, a small smile forming. 'That's not bad.'

'It's the truth,' Sunny said. 'Now tell me.'

'All right then,' she said softly. 'I'll tell you. I was raped. Okay?'

'Isabel,' Sunny whispered.

Isabel turned away from her.

And then she turned back, her face angry, her chest heaving. 'In Sierra Leone, last year. At knifepoint. And as if that wasn't enough, the wanker butted me in the face with his rifle when he was done and knocked out my front teeth.' She grinned crazily. 'You see? Whiter than white. Faker than fake.'

'I'm sorry. That's something to live through.'

'You could say that. It's one of those things that mark your life, as in "before the rape" and "after the rape."' She turned her head to the darkening sky and breathed in deeply, her chest lifting. 'Just look at those stars. Wherever you are—in London, in LA, in Sierra Leone, in Kabul—the sky is still the sky. At least something is certain, no matter where

198

you are in the world or whether it's before or after. But I used to be different.'

Sunny was quiet, knowing Isabel had more to say.

And she did. 'You know I'm Jewish.'

'When you spoke of your family and the Nazis, I assumed. But what does that matter?'

Isabel shook her head. 'I don't know. Having been raped. And being Jewish, my mother having survived the Holocaust, and then hiding her Judaism her entire life. Not so different from the woman smoking the opium. We Muslims and Jews, we're *like this*.' And she crossed two fingers. 'Very tight.'

Sunny laughed. 'You're my first, you know.'

Isabel raised her brows. 'Your first what?'

'You, Isabel Hughes, are my first Jew.'

'Oh my God, and I do mean that quite literally, how can that be?'

'I grew up in *Arkansas*. In a *small town*. There were no Jews there. Then, I came here. There are no Jews here. Well, there's one.'

'Thanks. Glad to have that moniker. The Only Jew of Kabul.'

'No, funny, I didn't mean you at all. There is another.'

'There's *another*? As in *one other*? Meaning, there is *only one*? How did this avoid my brilliant journo radar?'

'Seriously, his family left, everyone from his community left. But he stayed. I'm not sure why. What makes a person stay in a place that's so threatening, when he's alone?' She could have been asking that question of herself, of Isabel, of Jack, of Candace. Even of Yazmina. It struck her how they were all the Last Jews of Kabul, outcasts and loners with troubled histories in a war-torn country.

'Who knows? But we all find ways to deal, don't we. Superb at self-protection.'

'Or denial.'

'Yeah.' Isabel chuckled. 'Speaking of which . . .'

Sunny turned to face Isabel, her face now lit by the moon. It was a lovely, intelligent face. Her friend.

'The rape. It doesn't define me. At least I make a magnificent attempt not to let it. And it's not for common knowledge. Just sometimes . . .'

'I promise. Not a word to anyone. Besides, we are so much more than one thing that happens to us, you know? We're both living proof of that. You, lady, are so much more.'

'Yeah, I'm your first Jew!' She laughed, her dark hair shining under the moonlight.

Sunny laughed, too, and the two friends went back downstairs to the coffeehouse to drink wine, listen to music, and enjoy the rest of the evening. But the words 'before and after' echoed in Sunny's ears. As she surveyed her coffeehouse and looked at her friend, she thought about the experience that had changed her most. It was obvious: there was already a 'before Kabul' for her, and, should she leave, there would forever be 'after Kabul.'

CHAPTER TWENTY-TWO

It was early morning and Sunny was outside on the patio, wearing a leather jacket—happy to have shed her down coat—jeans, a scarf over her head and around her neck, sipping her coffee. She was sitting on a low stool at the wall, her knees wide apart, artist charcoal on the ground between them. It was cold, but not like the winter had been. She leaned her head back and breathed in. It even smelled different. It was warm enough that people were lighting fewer wood fires, but it was still cool enough that the open sewers didn't overpower. She closed her eyes and could see the clean air scented with pines sweeping down from the Hindu Kush across the basin and into her front yard.

The wall had been rebuilt, again. The coffeehouse was one step toward becoming UN compliant. Now all they had left to do was to get the blast film on the windows, build a safe room, and mission accomplished. The coffeehouse would be put on the list of approved places for foreigners. Jack, if he ever returned, would be pleased.

Sunny picked up a piece of the charcoal, felt its lightness in her hand. The plan was to first get her feet wet by sketching the mural in charcoal, right on the wall, and then dive in with acrylics. This was the hard part, getting the images right, and having the discipline to finish before actually painting. It was going to be a jungle scene, after all, with tall grasses and foliage and exotic flowers, animals of all kinds—toucans and tigers, monkeys and macaws, snakes and lizards. She would paint it in bright colors, not realistically but more like the kind of mural found on school walls: simple and whimsical.

She was going to use cheap acrylics because that's all that was available on Paint Street. She bought black, white, red, blue, and yellow and then would mix them on her palette to make other colors. She'd use the cheap, coarse brushes from the paint store, and save her better brushes, which she'd gotten in Dubai, for her canvas paintings.

Poppy stayed outside in the courtyard with her, sometimes chasing flies or barking at the wild dogs that often roamed the streets outside the gate, sometimes lying on her side, legs straight out in front of her, in the warmth of the sun. Sometimes Ahmet would even play catch with her. Sunny got a kick out of this new friendship and thought that maybe it was a portent of other changes going on in Ahmet. She'd noticed how he watched Yazmina, and spoke to her so tentatively, but how couldn't he? She was so beautiful. Who knows what would happen when she had her baby, given Ahmet's traditional disposition. Would he soften to the baby the way he had to Poppy? It was hard to predict; men were a proud and strange bunch, and Afghan men more complex than most.

Thank goodness she had this project or else she'd be frantic about Jack. She missed him like crazy, that last kiss still lingering on her lips, his taste still in her memory. She missed his wisecracks and friendship. She missed his being a solid, strong presence in this place that could be so chaotic. She missed how he made her laugh. She missed everything about him. And she was worried that he might never come back.

Why did the men in her life always leave? she thought as she drew the outline of a toucan's beak. Her father, so many years before, when she was still a little girl, then Tommy, and now Jack. Her mother had told her when Sunny brought home her first boyfriend, after seeing his tattoos and hearing his so-called big plans to start a used-record store, that Sunny's expectations for men were terribly low,

202

just like hers had been.

Well, Mom, she thought as she finished the toucan's body, and then drew a huge leaf that covered half of it, *I proved you wrong.* Her expectations of men weren't too low. Look at Jack. He was a wonderful pick. Apparently too wonderful for her.

She looked at what she'd drawn and did what she'd been doing every morning for a week. She picked up the damp cloth that sat at her side and erased the sketch from the wall, leaving it as she'd found it: blank, except for the dirty smear of charcoal.

*   *   *

Later that night, after all the customers had left, the coffeehouse was quiet, and Bashir Hadi had gone home, Halajan was watching an Indian soap opera, Yazmina was cleaning the floor, and Sunny was on her computer at the counter. You could smell a new wave of ammonia each time the wet and soapy mop hit the floor. Yazmina seemed distracted the way she was almost throwing the mop hard onto the floor and then back into the bucket, almost spilling it over each time. With each hit, Poppy would raise her head, look at Sunny to be sure she was okay, and then lay her head back down. The clock ticked, the mop slopped on the floor, and the day was almost done.

And then the door opened and closed with a slam.

Sunny assumed it was Ahmet, who came in every night to walk his mother safely up the outside stairs to her home, so she didn't even look up.

203

Ahmet said, 'Miss Sunny—'

And Halajan said, *'Ma khoda.'* Oh my God.

And Poppy barked and ran over to the door.

And then a man's voice said, 'Hey, babe.'

Only one man would dare call her that. Sunny was so startled that she knocked over her bottle of water. She stood and pushed her stool back so hard that it fell over with a loud bang onto the floor. She could have lit half of Kabul if her shock could've been converted to electricity.

'Miss me?' And there was that kilowatt smile that Sunny had fallen in love with so many years before.

She tried to answer but her throat was full. Her heart was beating so loudly she imagined everyone could hear it.

'Tommy' was all she could say.

*   *   *

'So you're not dead, after all,' Sunny said to him later, when everyone had gone home. She sipped from her teacup of wine. She was calming down now and starting to feel pissed off. Perhaps stage two in the Seven Stages of Reaction When a Person You Love Returns After Months of No Contact, stage one being Shock, stage two Pissed Off, and she'd know the next stage when she got to it.

'You sound disappointed.'

'It's been five months!'

'It was my *job*. I had no choice if I wanted to get paid.'

'You could've called, maybe. Sent an email, for Christ's sake. Let me know you're okay. Give me a hint about when you'd be back.'

'I'm not denying the money wasn't terrific—

unbelievable is the shit's honest truth. But it was more than that. It was important. The first time in my life. I knew you'd underst—'

'It's been five months!' She knew she'd said that already but she said it again anyway.

'But you sure look good,' he said with that smile of his. 'Younger, even, than when I left. I like your hair longer.' He reached out to touch it. But Sunny backed away.

'You didn't call, or email, or anything. What was I to think?'

'I couldn't. Orders.'

'You sound as if you were on a CIA mission or something. Get over yourself.' She was angry now.

He was, too. 'But if we had married like I'd wanted to—'

Sunny was doing everything in her power to not jump across the table and tear his eyes out. Not that it would be wrong. It would just give her feelings away, and she didn't want to give him the pleasure of that. He didn't deserve it.

'Are you telling me that if I had been your wife, you could've called? But because I was your girlfriend of a million years you couldn't? That is so much bullshit.'

'Sunny, that's the military. I couldn't tell you. Had you married me when I asked, everything would have been different.'

'But I didn't, and it's not. Besides, you're not in the military.'

'I was doing the military's dirty work, okay? But I still had to follow their fucked-up rules. Like no girlfriends. But it can be different now. I'm back. Here, for you.' He paused, looking at her. 'That is, if you still want me.'

Sunny stood up. She could hardly look at him, he was still so gorgeous. His blondish hair long over his eyes, those startling blue eyes, his skin tanned, and his body lean and long, and she had to look away. 'You think you can go away for so long, not tell me where you've gone, not communicate in any way, come back and everything will be the same?'

'Yeah. Why not? This wasn't so much longer than usual. I love you, you love me—or you did. At least I think you did.'

She turned back to him. 'You know I did. But for some reason this time it felt longer. It felt different.'

'Why? Why this time?'

She looked away.

'Oh, Jesus, is there someone else?' he asked.

'I don't know,' she said, which was the truth. And then she added, 'There's no one else,' which wasn't. She sat back down. 'But so much has happened.'

'You don't know, huh?' He looked around the coffeehouse. 'Well, it looks better in here. You've done some work, right? You're painting the wall—hey, and you made it higher, going after those UN rights, huh? You've got a new Afghan woman working. You have a dog! Come here, boy!'

Poppy didn't move from her bed.

'It's a *female.*'

'Then come here, *girl,*' he said. But Poppy stayed where she was. Tommy laughed and sat back in his chair, tilted it back on its rear legs, crossed his arms over his chest. 'I knew you'd be fine. I never had to worry about Sunny.'

He reached over and put his hand on hers. His shirt was rolled up to the elbows and his forearms looked strong, his hands beautiful. She could barely breathe.

206

But she stood again. She was not going to let this happen. 'It's late. You gotta go.'

'What do you mean, go? I live here—'

She shook her head. 'It's too much. You're here one minute. Then you're gone for three months. Then you're gone for five. Next time . . . who knows? And you don't *live* here. You've *stayed* here between going everywhere else. I think you have one shirt here. Maybe.'

Now Tommy stood up. 'But I'm here now, Sunny. I want to stay.' He went to her, held her firmly by her arms, pulled her to him, and kissed her hard and long.

She didn't even try to pull away. She had waited so long for this moment to come. They went to her room, where the Kabul moon shone through the windows. He kissed her again, he unbuttoned her shirt, he put his hands on her breasts, between her legs. It was almost as if nothing between them had changed after all this time, except for one big thing: Tommy was here with her, but her mind was somewhere else, with someone else. And so she pulled away, kissed him on the cheek, and showed him to the door.

CHAPTER TWENTY-THREE

Isabel had to let her eyes adjust to the darkness before she could make out the long corridor of small cells with blue-painted bars. In the dank Pul-e Charkhi prison, lighting was poor, the ceilings were low, the windows had no glass, there was no electricity, the food was sometimes only two pieces of flatbread a day—and yet it sat right near Chicken Street, across from shops of souvenirs, blue lapis, and leather jackets. There were at least eight women in a cell, along with their children. Isabel could hear a baby crying. She could smell urine and unwashed bodies.

She'd gotten inside Pul-e Charkhi with the help of Sunny, who'd introduced her to the women's minister and then helped her bribe the warden. Past the barbed wire and the heavily guarded front entrance, she'd been taken inside, where she was searched for guns and weapons and told to leave her bag in the front room. There were to be no pencils or pens, no cameras. She was provided with a 'guide,' a large woman with huge, sagging breasts and a gray, dull face.

It was difficult to see their faces, even those without burqas. They wore heavy, crudely woven head scarves, but the faces she could see were dirty, and they pulled their scarves low to hide them in embarrassment.

Isabel could see their eyes, boring through her like a laser. There were several women who suffered from leishmaniasis, the sores on their faces scabbing and oozing; others looked as gaunt as the concentration camp victims her mother had showed her photos of when she was a girl; one was nursing her baby, which was screaming, unable to satisfy itself with the meager milk the mother's breasts provided; and others just stared, hollow-eyed and pleading.

But among the faces, Isabel did not see the woman who was beaten at the poppy farm. She hadn't really believed she'd find her, if she were even still alive. But her journalistic training compelled her to keep searching for the story that was bigger than one woman's disappearance, certainly bigger than the story about the spraying of the poppies. So, from Kabul, she planned to fly north to Mazar-e Sharif and even to Lashkar Gah, the capital of the Taliban-controlled Helmand province, where their prisons held hundreds of women.

She felt a tug on her *kameez* and looked down. A young woman, a girl, dirty, quite thin and pale, who'd obviously been a beauty, was sitting at the bars of her cell, looking up at her, her hand stretched out. She said something inaudible. Isabel squatted to hear her.

'Please,' she whispered. 'Please help me.'

The girl knew English. But her guide and the other women did not, so she and the girl could speak freely.

'Why are you here?'

'I was sold.' She turned her face away, embarrassed.

'It's okay. You can tell me. Were you sold to be a—?'

The woman couldn't speak. But tears welled in her eyes, and then, as Isabel watched, they spilled over her black lashes onto her cheeks.

Finally the girl said, 'For men. I was sold for men.'

'Then why are you here? What happened?'

'One day I . . . I just couldn't . . . any longer, I—' She put her face in her hands.

But Isabel pressed on. 'How long have you been here?'

'Six Ramadans,' she said.

Isabel fought not to raise her voice. 'Six years?

209

You can't be more than eighteen!'

'I am nineteen now.'

'Is anyone helping you? Has anyone been here?'

The girl nodded. 'A foreign lawyer comes, but the only thing that gets you out is money. I am an orphan. I have no one.' She looked away, and then directly at Isabel, and she pleaded desperately, 'Please. We are hungry. We have no clean water. They hurt us, they do things—'

The guide then pushed Isabel's shoulder, urging her to move on.

But she turned to look back at the young woman. Her black eyes spoke centuries of pain.

'Please help me,' she said, which made Isabel's whole body shudder under the weight of responsibility and the desire to act on her behalf, right here, right now.

But again, she felt the nudge on her back and heard the guide's angry voice telling her to move.

So Isabel left the young woman with a nod and a strong clasp of her hand in hers and a whisper, 'I will try. I promise.'

In another room, there were several women with older children, one holding a three-year-old who, the mother showed her, was unable to walk. 'Look around,' the mother said in Dari.

The combination of Isabel's limited knowledge of Dari and the woman's gestures helped Isabel understand what came next.

'Do you see a place for a child to move? But what choice do I have? I have no family. I have no one.'

Isabel had heard of women who jumped into the river, drowning themselves and their children, rather than be imprisoned. Only now did she understand. It was better to live on the streets begging.

Isabel left shortly after. Knowing that trying to find her woman at another prison was bloody futile, she returned to the poppy fields where she'd first seen her and was told that she and her baby were both gone, though nobody knew where. But the look from the man who'd hit the woman told Isabel everything she needed to know: The woman was probably dead; the baby, if it was a boy, would be taken care of until it could be trained to fight for the Taliban and then die as a martyr. If it was a girl, she'd be dead already, or sold to become a sex slave within a few years.

Now Isabel had a story to write. It wasn't about poppies or spraying or the collusion of the government and drug lords, or the corruption of drug enforcement officials, or the billions of dollars made in opium production. It was about the women held for years behind bars for refusing sex, for being victims of rape or of abusive husbands, or for becoming opium addicts. It was a story about the children being raised behind bars with them. The story was summed up in one young woman's three simple words: *Please help me.*

CHAPTER TWENTY-FOUR

Sunnyjan, *besyar,* I have made something for you,' Yazmina said.

Sunny looked up from her laptop, where she was placing a new order from her meat guy in Dubai. Bashir Hadi's burgers had become famous, and it was sometimes difficult for Sunny to keep ground beef in stock. The higher wall had worked its magic and the foreigners, bored with the same old places, were happy to try a new menu and drink a real latte.

Yazmina stood on the other side of the counter, with a garment of the loveliest lavender fabric folded over her arm.

She held it out to Sunny. 'As my *tashakur* for all you have done for me.'

Sunny looked into Yazmina's eyes and knew not to argue. 'It's very beautiful,' she said as she gently touched the silky material.

'I made it myself, Sunnyjan. I made it by hand. For you. Please,' she said, holding it out again, shyly. '*Loftan,* put it on. I want to see if it fits.'

So Sunny took it and lovingly touched the handmade embroidery. It was such a personal, beautiful gift. She kissed Yazmina three times. '*Tashakur,* Yazmina. I'll go put it on now.'

'*Bali, loftan,*' Yazmina answered, lowering her eyes. Her face was flushed.

Sunny went to her room, took off her boots, jeans, and sweater, and put on the pants that were meant to be worn under the dress and then slipped the dress over her head. She looked at herself in the mirror and smiled. The dress fit her perfectly. The pants under it did as well. It was not like any other dress in all of Kabul, with its liquid folds and sculpted neckline, its beadwork and simply perfect structure. She smoothed the dress down over her hips, adjusted the collar at her neck, slipped on her dressy shoes, and returned to the café.

Yazmina was waiting for her, anxiously pacing. When she saw Sunny, she stopped and stared at her.

'What do you think?' asked Sunny.

'*Wah, wah, wah,* Sunnyjan very *beautiful,*' Yazmina whispered.

Sunny twirled and posed and the two women laughed. Yazmina pulled on the wrists to straighten the garment over Sunny's arms and checked the hem at the knee to be sure it was straight. She fussed over the unusual neckline so that it sat as she must have envisioned it.

'Yazmina, how did you learn to sew like this? To design such a dress would take much training for even an experienced seamstress.'

'My *madar* taught me how to sew a regular dress. But this, I don't know. It is something from my heart, something that Allah has given me. I have only needed someone to sew for. So I *tashakur* for giving me the opportunity.'

'I will wear it tonight and show it off to everyone who comes to the coffeehouse. What do you say to that, Yazmina?'

'*Az shuma tashakur.*' Then Yazmina turned and went back to setting the tables.

*   *   *

Later that evening, when the March winds freshened the dusty Kabul air, the coffeehouse was bubbling with talk and good smells from the kitchen. Bashir Hadi stood at the counter, lording over his domain, grinning ear to ear, proud of what he'd accomplished.

'Miss Sunny, in only another week we can buy the film for the windows and start construction on the safe room. We're cooking with gas!'

213

Sunny laughed at the expression. 'And look—we only had to rebuild the wall twice. It could've been worse.'

Then Candace walked in. She handed her coat to Ahmet, who was working inside tonight because of the crowd. His friend Khalid was once again handling the outside gate.

But when Candace asked for a 'good table, away from the front door and the kitchen—I mean, it's just so hot and loud, and I can't think,' Halajan, for whom the expression 'suffer no fools' had been coined, had absolutely no patience for Princess Candace's attitude.

'This is the only table available,' Halajan said as she leaned on the back of one of its chairs. It was right at the front door.

'Then I'll wait for another,' answered Candace, crossing her arms as she looked around the room calculating which table might be paying its check and leaving shortly.

'Wait until Jesus returns if you want,' said Halajan as she walked away.

'Trust me, for me, he'll be here before you know it.' Candace laughed, as if fully aware of her own self-centeredness.

Sunny watched this scene with much bemusement. That Candace would be treated by Halajan with the same disdain with which she treated others was perfect justice.

'Come on, Halajan,' pleaded Candace at Halajan's back.

Halajan turned to her and said, 'Listen, American woman, if you'd like a good table and good service, all you have to do is be nice. Sunny likes you. Otherwise, I'd—'

214

'She does? You think she likes me? I adore Sunny!' Candace responded, walking over to Sunny and giving her a kiss on each check. 'How are you? Have I had a week!'

Of course she has, Sunny thought. And yet, she was glad to see her.

Then Candace held Sunny's wrist, took a step back, and looked at Sunny from head to toe. Her voice rose nine decibels. 'What are you wearing? Where did you get that? Stand still. Let me see that.' Candace walked around Sunny as if she were an alabaster statue in a museum.

'It's to die for,' declared Candace.

'It is, isn't it? Made by our very own Yazmina.'

Candace looked at Yazmina, whose face had turned red with embarrassment.

Ahmet turned to look at Yazmina as well. Then he looked at Sunny's dress and back at Yazmina.

She smiled at him, then bowed her head.

He looked away.

When Candace saw Ahmet look at Yazmina and Yazmina smile, she raised her brows and said, 'Interesting. Wouldn't those two be perfect together?'

Halajan said, 'Mind your own business.'

'Well, look at them. Both are young, single, and gorgeous,' said Candace.

'They're fine. Just leave them alone,' said Halajan.

'Oh, really? Well, they don't look so fine to me,' she continued. 'Maybe they're *not* so fine. Maybe they need *you* to help them figure out a way. Why don't you help this along?'

'Candace, please stop,' Sunny intervened.

And then Isabel walked in, and after handing her

parka to Ahmet, sat at the table available by the door.

Sunny said, 'Now, take your busybody body over there and sit with Isabel and be quiet.'

So Candace did just that, and the two women kissed hello, and then Candace nodded toward Ahmet near the front door and said to her, 'Ahmet likes Yazmina.'

'And that's my business because?' Isabel answered.

'Because, we have to help! Come on, let's be matchmakers. Ahmet has no father. Yazmina has no one at all.'

'Candace, really,' Sunny said, joining them. 'Foreigners shouldn't butt in to their affairs. They will find a way.'

Bashir Hadi brought over coffees on an etched metal tray.

'What about you, Bashir Hadi? Don't you see what's going on here?' Candace said. 'I think Ahmet and Yazmina like each other.'

He looked surprised. 'You think that could be true?' He smiled, then caught himself, and said, 'Even if so, that is a very personal thing. Very private. Something we don't discuss.'

'What do you mean? This is the twenty-first century! Can't a man and a woman like each other?'

Bashir Hadi looked at Sunny and sighed. 'It is not for me to talk about.'

'Come on, Candace,' Sunny said. 'You're aware this is another culture. You're not in Kansas anymore.'

'That's for certain,' said Isabel. 'But it's bloody time this country changes.'

216

'Change is right!' said Candace. 'Come on, Bashir Hadi. Tell me you don't want your country to be more modern, more tolerant, more—'

'Of course I do,' he said, 'but from the inside out. I want Afghans to change Afghanistan.'

'Oh.' Candace laughed. 'So you're a snob! Nobody else's opinion matters.'

'Candace, please,' said Sunny.

'What? Bashir Hadi knows I'm kidding.' She laughed again.

'I'm just tired of everyone treating us as if we're like babies in our mothers' arms. We can figure this out ourselves,' he said.

'That makes sense,' said Isabel.

'Not so far,' Candace said, shaking her head.

'Candace, please,' Sunny said, putting a hand on her arm.

Bashir Hadi then put the tray down on the table. 'It's okay. Let me explain. I think you forget who I am,' he said calmly to Candace. 'I am not American, you who have no obligations to your family or to your own history or destiny. And I am not British,' he said, looking at Isabel, 'you who are so hypocritical to hold on to the worst of your past—your classes, your place in society based only on your family's history—and then, at the same time, say you're modern?' He looked away.

Everyone sat in silence, stunned by Bashir Hadi's seriousness.

He continued, 'At least I know my duty as an Afghan and a Muslim. I honor the ancient traditions and my family's wishes.'

'Don't you see,' argued Candace, 'they cannot love. They—'

'Who's "they"?' demanded Bashir Hadi. 'Who

217

do you mean by "they"?'

'You, that's who! And Wakil, and all the other men who were raised in this culture that debases women and glorifies the worst aspects of men.'

'Candace,' said Isabel softly, putting her hand on her other arm, as if Candace needed both women to hold her down.

Sunny realized that something must be wrong. This had gotten way out of line; Candace was taking all this too personally.

Bashir Hadi lowered his voice and hissed, 'Do not put me in the same classification with your Wakil and "all the other men." I am Hazara. I am hated by all those other men. But you might be right about one thing: The parents have always chosen for the children. Halajan would have to make this happen. Even now.' He stopped and finally smiled. 'But I'm certainly not going to push her. How about anybody else?'

Finally the people at the table relaxed—except Candace, who was clearly upset.

And then Isabel cut through the awkwardness in that spot-on direct way she had and said to Candace, 'What's going on with you? Are you saying that you and Wakil aren't together anymore? Is that what this is about?'

Candace looked straight at Isabel while her eyes filled with tears.

'I don't know what happened, what I did wrong.'

'You didn't do anything wrong,' said Sunny soothingly. She couldn't believe it, but seeing Candace's tears, she felt, like Isabel, sorry for her.

'I raised the money he wanted, I got commitments for supplies from an NGO, I even got Dr Malik to come. She wrote a letter of recommendation to the consulate and . . .'

Sunny looked at Isabel and they understood then and there what the relationship had been about.

'. . . and still it wasn't enough.' She shook her head.

'What happened?' Sunny asked.

'What happened?' Candace sniffed, wiped her tears. 'He dumped me! That's what happened.'

Sunny reached over and put her hand on Candace's.

'He told me he appreciated everything I had done for him and his orphanage, but that it could never work. He could never marry a woman who wasn't Muslim. But I know the truth. He never really loved me. He used me.'

'What's love got to do with it?' said Isabel. 'As the song says. In Afghanistan, love is for everybody else. Here it's a horse trade. You got what I need? Then I got something for you. Ask me sometime about my general Stewart and his swag. Met him in Africa. But he's stationed here now, if my sources are correct. He was very upright and tweed, and nothing to talk about in bed, but he could get you anything you might want or need, straightaway.'

And Sunny thought of Jack, whom she wanted nothing from—except *him*. She missed him and thought she might even be in love with him, and yet he was thousands of miles away. And she thought of Tommy, whom she used to love and now was here and she didn't think, she wasn't sure, she didn't know. She hadn't heard from Jack once since he left weeks ago. She could understand. He had his life to work out, without distraction. But it made her feel as if what happened between them— not only their kiss in the closet, but their growing

219

closeness—was a fantasy and had never actually happened at all. Sometimes, she knew from past experience, she had a great ability to believe in her own bullshit.

By then the coffeehouse had grown quiet. The people, except *her* people, were gone for the night. Tommy sauntered through the door as if he came every day, knew everyone, and maybe even owned the place. In his jeans, his white rumpled shirt, and his leather jacket, he looked excellent. This was a sexy guy, and as he talked his hair fell into his eyes and he brushed it back with his hand, a hand Sunny could imagine on her. She couldn't help it. It was always about sexual attraction with him. And, he was *here*. But she hadn't mentioned him to her friends, and now, there'd be some explaining to do.

'Hey, everybody.' He kissed each woman on the cheek as they were introduced, and when he got to Sunny, he said, 'Look at you, gorgeous.'

She smiled and twirled around like a little girl. 'Yazmina made it for me.'

'It suits her, doesn't it?' said Isabel.

'She looks like a princess, a very *sexy* princess,' Tommy said, not taking his eyes off Sunny.

'So, Sunny, where have you been keeping this one? How do you know this lovely man?' Candace said.

'She hasn't told you about me? Keeping me a secret, Sunny? So,' he said quietly as he took her two hands in his, 'how about we go away somewhere together?'

She lost her smile and said, 'What are you talking about?' She glanced at Candace and Isabel, who were listening as if they were taking notes.

'Let's take a few days. To catch up, to get to

know each other again. We can't do it here.' He looked at the table of her friends. 'Too crowded.'

'I can't. We're busy. I'm painting the wall.'

'Come on, we need some time together. Mazar-e Sharif. You're not going to believe how beautiful it is there.'

'I've been.'

'Not with me,' he said arrogantly, with a sly smile.

Sunny put her hands on her hips and said, 'I can't just drop everything to go off with you. I don't even know you anymore.'

'Sunny, if you don't go with this beautiful man, then I will,' said Candace.

Isabel nudged Candace with her elbow and said to Sunny, 'Why don't you take some time and think about it?'

'Can we talk about this alone?' asked Tommy. 'Please.'

'Outside.'

She walked out to the front courtyard, with Tommy following, and stood in the moonlight in front of her wall, with its smeared and faded outline of the tiger looking like it was going to devour Tommy. *Perfect,* Sunny thought.

He took her hands in his. 'Let's just go. I was thinking we'd go tomorrow.' He was excited, like a boy, and it was infectious.

Sunny was tempted to say yes but she shook her head. She hadn't slept with him since his return, insisting it was time she needed—time to get used to him, to *them*—but knowing that it was her ambivalence that stopped her. 'Not tomorrow. I need to, I mean, there's a lot to . . . I don't know.'

'Okay, then, it's settled. I'll pick you up in the

morning. Figure we'll be back in a few days, on Sunday.' He looked through the window at Bashir Hadi. 'He'll be fine without you.'

Sunny turned to look at Bashir Hadi, who was cleaning up for the night. Of course he'd be fine without her. She'd taken days off before, when she went to Dubai, when she went to Beirut and Morocco. This was different. This had nothing to do with the coffeehouse or Bashir Hadi or anything else. This had to do with her and what she wanted, if only she knew what that was.

She looked into Tommy's bright blue eyes, whose crow's feet and heavy lids betrayed his age and whatever violence he'd experienced this past year. And in a reckless moment, outside, under the moon, she heard herself say, 'Yes.'

*   *   *

Later that evening, after the customers had left, and after she'd answered Candace's and Isabel's questions, particularly the ones regarding why the hell she hadn't told them about Tommy, and how she felt about him versus Jack, which she had a hard time answering because she didn't know herself, Sunny left Candace and Isabel drinking at the table to go to pack. She passed a small window that looked out onto the back courtyard, and through it she saw Halajan smoking, her scarf down around her neck, her short hair shiny in the moonlight. She decided to join her. Halajan jumped when the door opened, quickly covering her head and hiding her cigarette behind her back, but when she realized it was Sunny, she relaxed and continued smoking.

'It's a beautiful night, Halajan, isn't it?' said

Sunny.

'It's the start of spring. This is what happens,' Halajan responded, taking a big drag.

Sunny smiled with a shrug. 'True. Still.'

There was a long moment of silence as the two women stood leaning against the wall. Then Sunny turned to walk back inside, but when she did, Halajan spoke.

'Please wait. I must talk with you. I am so angry at me!'

'Hala, what is it?' asked Sunny.

'I've waited too long. And now Jack is gone. I am ashamed.'

'Then it's good to talk about it now.'

'Now it could be too late! Jack may never come back. Don't you see?' She was agitated.

'Jack? What's this about?' Sunny said quietly. 'Halajan, whatever it is, whatever help you need, we can deal with it.'

'Not me. It's Yazmina who needs help,' she said desperately.

Sunny turned. 'Is it the baby? Is she okay?'

'It's her younger sister, Layla.'

'She has a sister? She's never even mentioned—'

'She's worried for her. She's so young, only twelve, but she will be taken by the same men who stole Yazmina once it's spring again in the north and the mountain roads are open. But she won't be as lucky as Yazmina. I thought that maybe Mr Jack, maybe he could go get Layla and—'

'Oh, Halajan, it's true, I think. Jack would know how to deal with something like this, given his experience with negotiating. But I don't know when or if he'll be coming back.'

'You trust in Jack and yet you're going to

Mazar-e Sharif tomorrow with Tommy,' said Halajan.

'Yes,' Sunny said, in barely a whisper. *I'm ashamed, too,* she was thinking. 'What about Tommy?'

'What do you mean?'

'To help get Layla out of there. He knows the area. He has friends in the military that can help. Maybe get a helicopter to get him up there fast. Maybe not even have to wait for the roads to open.'

'I trust Jack more.' She lit another cigarette. 'But in his absence Tommy will do.'

'My thinking exactly.'

And the two women laughed for a moment, understanding each other's meaning.

'If you would ask him, I would be so grateful.'

'I will, while we're in Mazar. How could he say no to me there? Have you ever been there, Halajan?'

'Miss Sunny, we've all been there.'

Sunny pursed her brows and cocked her head. 'I don't understand. What are you talking about, Halajan? That mystical stuff doesn't sound like you.'

'Who knows what sounds like me anymore?' Halajan took another drag from her cigarette, and as she blew out the smoke, she explained, 'There's a legend about the white doves of Mazar-e Sharif's blue mosque. It is said that all doves that go there turn white after forty days and forty nights. Then, every seventh of the white doves is given a spirit, a path to God. So you see what I mean.'

Sunny thought about it for a minute and then said, 'I'm sorry, but I don't quite get the connection—'

'Do Americans have no use for metaphor? Or is it only you who needs such a literal translation?'

Sunny laughed and said, 'I hope it's just me.'

'Well, Sunny,' Halajan continued, speaking very slowly for Sunny's benefit. 'Like the doves, for which walls, mountains, and wars are no barrier, people who live in Afghanistan are from other places—whether a thousand years ago or yesterday. But they quickly become a part of this country, and as they do, they change color and will never go back to being their old gray selves. The experience of Motherland Afghanistan makes everyone Afghan.

'But not everyone is worthy of being rewarded with a spirit. So only every seventh dove or every seventh person is blessed.' She inhaled from her cigarette. 'So now you understand?'

'I don't know, Halajan. I think so.'

'So you see, we're all white doves. But only the special ones are the seventh dove.' She dropped her cigarette on the cement patio and crushed it with her foot, then said, 'Too bad you're going with an eighth.' She covered her head with her scarf, wrapping it around her neck and throwing the rest over her shoulder.

'But you always liked Tommy.'

'I did. I hope I do still. But you should not be going with him. You should be going with someone you love. Because everything we do in life matters. One thing leads to another.'

'Love? Someone just told me that in Afghanistan love is for everybody else.'

Halajan laughed. 'Since when do you listen to such nonsense? Even I know that love is in our Afghan bones, flows through our blood. That's why I get so angry at those who try to make love a sin.

225

But don't listen to me, an old lady. Go, have fun, feed the birds.'

'Thanks, Halajan. I'll see you on Sunday, and I will do everything I can to get Tommy to help bring Layla here.'

* * *

Sunny rushed back to the café, sat with Isabel and Candace, and said,

'Yazmina has a twelve-year-old sister.'

The two women just looked at her, waiting for more.

'And we have to get her out. She was left with her uncle and she'll be taken just the way Yazmina was, only she may not be as lucky,' she said breathlessly.

The two women looked at each other and then back at Sunny.

'She has a sister?' asked Isabel.

'She was taken? By who? Is that how she got here?' Candace asked.

'Please, we have to try to find her sister,' said Sunny impatiently.

'Okay, slow down, everyone. Sunny, tell us the whole story,' Isabel said, 'from the beginning.'

Sunny took a deep breath and told them everything—almost everything. She'd promised to keep Yazmina's pregnancy a secret, and she would. But she told them how she'd met Yazmina at the Women's Ministry, how her uncle had been forced to give her away to repay a debt, how Yazmina had escaped from the men before they could sell her, and now, of the threat that the men would return for her younger sister, who'd been left behind.

That, once the snow melted and the mountain roads were clear, Yazmina feared Layla would be in danger.

'There must be *something* we can do to help her,' Isabel said.

'We have to,' said Candace.

'And, shit. She's just a baby. Jack knows the area and the delicate relationships of the people up there. I know he'd be willing to do whatever he could. But he's not here and God knows when or if he'll be back.' Sunny paused and sighed. 'I can ask Tommy, though. He doesn't have Jack's smarts, but he's got the brute strength to get Layla out. But . . .' She hesitated.

'It's so fucking barbaric,' said Isabel. 'I've seen it a hundred times and never get used to it. Women being bartered or sold to the highest bloody bidder for their bodies. I was just telling Candace about Pul-e Charkhi, the conditions, the waste of women's lives. For nothing! For being women, for saying no!'

'You want to do something?' Candace demanded impatiently. 'So stop talking and do something!' She pounded her fist on the table. 'And you, Sunny, what's the problem? Get your men up to the mountains to save the girl. You gave Yazmina her life back, but now her little sister needs you.'

Sunny and Isabel exchanged looks. Candace was right. And given all she'd done for Wakil's clinic and school, and her proven fund-raising skills, Sunny suspected she could use something to sink her teeth into now that Wakil had hurt her.

'So help Sunny bring Layla here,' Isabel said to Candace. 'Help *me*.'

'It's not so hard,' answered Candace. 'Just get off that little butt of yours.'

'I could use your involvement.'

'Of course you could,' she said, sarcastically. 'Everybody could. That's my reason for living, apparently.' But then Candace leaned forward in her chair, put her elbows on the table, and said, 'Okay, tell me the details. We can do this. There ain't three more formidable women in all of Kabul.' Then she paused and said, 'Except for Halajan.'

And Isabel said, 'Okay, but listen.'

'What're you thinking?'

And for the next hour Isabel talked about the possibilities, the complications, how difficult it would be, but with Candace's social connections, and Isabel's media and political ones, they might just be able to pull off something brilliant that would save women's lives. And change their own in the process.

And then they turned their attention to Layla. Sunny knew Yazmina could never be happy if Layla wasn't brought safely to her side. The best plan would be for Sunny to persuade Jack and Tommy to work together to get up there and get her out at the first sign of spring. If Jack didn't return from wherever the hell he was in time, she'd have to resort to Plan B: relying on Tommy alone. But that wouldn't do it. They knew that without Jack, there had to be a leader to organize the helicopters, the extra men, the arms for protection from the inevitable violence. There was only one person among them strong enough, wily enough, and committed enough once she began something to see it through to every minute detail—and that was Candace.

She heartily agreed. 'So, it's a plan,' Sunny said. 'Simple, right?' Isabel asked. Sunny let out a nervous laugh. Nothing in Afghanistan was simple.

*   *   *

In her room that night, it was impossible to fall asleep. Sunny didn't know what the hell she was doing. Mazar-e Sharif with Tommy. A week ago she thought he'd been gone so long that she might never see him again. And tonight, her mind exploded with the realization that, as the cliché goes, life changes in an instant, that right when you think you know what's next, how your life will be, something can happen to change it dramatically. The very reason to live and keep on living.

Not that she knew exactly how her life would go, since she'd thought, before Tommy returned, that she was at the beginning of something, maybe, possibly, with Jack. And she knew she couldn't stay in Kabul forever. So, really, she hadn't a clue what was going to happen to her.

She just hadn't considered Tommy in the picture at all, though to be honest she'd have to admit she'd hoped that one day this very thing would happen. Another cliché: *Be careful what you wish for.*

She got up and brought her laptop from the table to the *toshak,* resting it on her crossed legs.

There was an email from Jack. Weeks since he'd been gone, and now, tonight, an email. She laughed out loud. Somebody up there was joking around with her.

She opened it. It read:

Dear Sunny,
    Sorry I've been out of touch but had to figure this all out. The good news: My son is doing

229

great. We've spent important time together. The bad news: There really is no bad news except how things change. More good news: I'm on my way back to Kabul.
See you soon.
Jack

What the hell? How cryptic was that? *These men,* she thought. They can't communicate, or choose not to. And then they expect you to drop everything for them.

Well, tomorrow she was going to Mazar-e Sharif and that was that. With Tommy, her eighth dove. Jack. Tommy. Jack. Tommy. *Shit.*

CHAPTER TWENTY-FIVE

Yazmina and Halajan sat in Halajan's main room on *toshak*s with Rashif's letters piled on the floor. Halajan had created her own cataloging system, tying the letters together with ponytail holders that she'd found at Tamila's Beauty Shop on Shar-e Naw Street. For winter, she used white, for spring, green, for summer, yellow, and for fall, red. Even the illiterate in Afghanistan knew how to read and write numbers, which they'd learned from money, so she'd used numbers to mark the years, from one and on. She had about three hundred letters that had never been read, so Yazmina started at the best place she could think of, the beginning.

It was shortly after Rashif's wife died. Times had been different then, and the letters told the story of how life in Kabul had changed since the Soviets left and the Americans invaded and took control, until Karzai was elected in Kabul's first democratic election (which Rashif cynically joked about, as if, he said, with the Americans still in force, there was any real democracy going on—making Halajan laugh out loud), his involvement with the refugee aid group, for which he helped to make and distribute clothing, until the present, when the Taliban's encroaching presence could be felt in every aspect of life. The letters weren't long, but they were full of details of Rashif's family life, his business as a tailor, the books he read, the movies he saw, the music he listened to and was moved by, and his dreams of a life, every waking day, in the open, with Halajan.

The letters were vital, funny, and smart, and with each one Halajan felt her heart grow big against her chest, her yearning for Rashif beating like the wings of the birds in the tree outside her room. Here was a man full of interests, full of zest and humor and observations that could make even a serious cow like Ahmet laugh. How Rashif kept writing to her each and every week, with no response, was a thing of wonder. Was his love for her so big that he needed nothing in return? Or, and this was even more surprising, did he know her secret?

Yazmina read with feeling.

My dearest Halajan,
Today I write with anger and sadness. Our Talib compatriots have destroyed the Buddhas of Bamyan. They've stood massive and strong, watching over the valley from their sandstone cliff niches since the sixth century, and now, all these hundreds of years later, these Talib animals

231

think they are the judges of great art? They cannot create a thing. They can only destroy.

I wonder about men who hate so much. I worry for our country, I worry for our people. I worry for us, my Halajan. I worry for us . . .

Halajan was moved by this and other, more personal, sad events (like the stillbirth of a granddaughter) and by happy ones (finally a birth of a healthy grandson). Yazmina looked up from her reading from time to time to see how Halajan was responding to the words in the letters. Halajan wondered if Yazmina noticed how her eyes were unfocused while she listened, looking out into some distant place where she might've spent all those years with Rashif, living in happiness together. She wondered if Yazmina could read her mind the way she read the words on the page. Because then she would know how Halajan dreamed of spending many more years with Rashif in the future.

*   *   *

The Masjid-e Haji Yaqub mosque was unusually crowded today. This always happened after a bombing, as if the men felt guilty about the deaths, as if, had they only prayed more frequently, more fervently, nobody would have been killed. Though the midday prayers were over, the men milled about talking in small groups, trying to delay the inevitable return to work.

Ahmet was greeted by his friend Khalid.

'*Salaam alaikum,*' he said.

'*Wa alaikum as-salaam,*' Ahmet answered.

'Busy here today.'

'Lots of praying going on,' Ahmet answered.

Khalid laughed. 'You'd think Allah would hear us already and make our world a little easier.'

Ahmet nodded. '*Inshallah,* one day he will.'

Khalid raised his brows doubtfully. 'So, Ahmet,' he said, 'come to the field with us. A few of us thought we'd catch a game of football, and then watch *buzkashi,* have a *chai.* Take the day off.'

Ahmet hesitated. He was tempted, but work was mandatory. 'Not today. There is work to do.'

'We all have work to do. Come on, taking one afternoon off won't hurt anyone. Come with us.'

'Sorry, next time.'

'You're too serious, my friend. We all need time to do nothing, have some fun, stretch our legs.'

Ahmet wanted to stretch his legs, so to speak, more than anything. He couldn't remember the last time he did nothing and felt no remorse about it. But he said his good-byes and returned to the coffeehouse and used the afternoon to clean his guardhouse, polish his guns, and oil the gate, which had recently begun to squeak in an intolerably annoying fashion.

Yazmina and his mother were at his mother's house. He was pleased that they had bonded and were spending so much time together these days. Every afternoon they talked, sewed, watched the Indian soaps, or did whatever it was that women did when they were alone together.

But did they, he wondered, ever talk about him? Did his mother tell Yazmina stories about him as a child? Or as a student? Or why he became the *chokidor* instead of going to school or even to Germany, like his sister had?

He could feel his stomach clench with the

thought that his mother might reveal things about him that no one should know, particularly Yazmina. There was so much about her that was special, from her beauty, her green eyes and slender wrists, to how she covered so thoroughly when she went out, out of respect to tradition, and how she covered indoors but a little less so the longer she was here, as if the shelter of the coffeehouse was cover enough. And her artistry as a seamstress! Who knew that behind that beauty was talent and intelligence?

There was nothing about Yazmina he didn't like. He put on his coat, draped the rifle's strap over his shoulder, and returned to his post at the gate to greet the mail truck that had just pulled up.

*   *   *

Yazmina was reading about a time when Rashif had been hired to alter the clothes of an American army colonel who'd gotten so fat that his pants had to be let out several centimeters, and the buttons on his jacket had to be moved.

> *. . . and then he said to me, this big fat American, that he had no idea why his pants were so small around his waist. He said he didn't eat much and he was active and he couldn't understand what had happened, except that maybe his pants had shrunk.*
>
> *Halajan, my dear, you probably felt the walls shake from the laughter that I did everything to hold inside. This is what I wanted to say to him: Stop eating the Afghan bread! Stop eating the kish mish and the sweets. Take a walk now and*

then. But I held my tongue . . .

But she wasn't thinking about the words she was reading. She was considering whether to bring up with Halajan her growing fears for Layla. It was almost spring in Kabul, which meant there wasn't much time before the snows would melt in the northern passages and the men could make their way to her uncle's and take her sister. With Jack gone, what could be done? She wondered if Tommy would help, but he didn't seem to be the sort of man who went out of his way for others. She planned to bring up the subject when she was finished with this letter. But just as she read, *With love, Your Rashif*, there was a knock on the door.

They could see the outline of Ahmet through the gauzy curtain. Hurriedly they gathered the letters and hid them under a *toshak,* shouting to him, '*Yak dahka,* one minute, while we prepare ourselves.' They quickly covered themselves fully, Yazmina putting on the heavy dark *chaderi* to cover her belly and head, and Halajan putting on a head scarf to hide her short hair and because Ahmet would expect her to respect tradition.

'*Salaam alaikum,*' he said, with a little bow, and his right hand over his heart. 'A package for you, Yazmina, from Candace's driver.' He handed her a box, looking directly into her eyes, which were wide and excited, the only thing on her face he could see because of her *chaderi*.

Her eyes caught his, and he shyly looked away.

'What could that be?' asked Halajan.

The box had been shipped from Dubai, according to the customs stamps and writing on it. Yazmina had never received anything like it before, and she excitedly tore the box open, pulling the strip at its end, having seen Sunny open such boxes many times. She lifted out a package wrapped in brown tissue paper tied with twine. There was a note written in Dari. She opened it and read aloud, 'Dear Yazmina, Please use this fabric to make a dress for me like the one you made for Sunny. Your friend, Candace.'

'Did she tell you this was coming?' asked Halajan.

'No, not a word.'

'Typical of her, to order instead of making a request, as if you're her worker.' Halajan shook her head, looking down, thinking of the way that woman thought she ruled the world and that everyone was there to serve her. That's when she saw it: one of Rashif's letters still on the floor, not quite hidden by the *toshak*. She quickly looked up at Ahmet to see if he had noticed it, but his eyes were on Yazmina. She exhaled in relief.

Yazmina's thoughts were on the beautiful fabric she pulled out of the paper. It was gold like the sun with sparkly beads hand sewn with purple thread in an intricate design. This was for the scarf. There were two other pieces, a purple silk and a gold with blues and purples, for the pants and dress. All three fabrics woven by hand, with love and an eye for beauty. Where was it from? she wondered. The vibrant colors, the artistry of their weave and beadwork, told her these were from India, perhaps. This was fabric unlike any she had ever seen, and she rubbed her palm over it and then took it between two fingers, feeling its softness and its texture. Her chest rose with excitement. She would make Candace the most beautiful dress she had

236

ever seen.

*　　*　　*

Ahmet watched Yazmina's eyes as she opened
the box and felt the fabric, and all he wanted to
do was take off that heavy *chaderi* and touch her
hair, which he imagined to be long and black and
silkier than any fabric that could ever be sewn. But
it was her hands on the fabric, her slim fingers, that
moved him. She had such grace, to accept the work
order as if it were a gift, and then to appreciate
the materials—he had no doubt that had it been a
hammer to build a house, she would've reacted the
same way. It proved to him, again, that she was a
woman of virtue.

What troubled him was the folded note he saw
on the floor with his mother's name written on
it—he was certain that, yes, it was her name, or at
least the first three letters that he could make out—
and how the women ignored it completely as if it
weren't there or they hadn't seen it or didn't want
to bring attention to it. Who would write a note
to his mother? Why was it there, partially hidden,
when both women were in the room? He knew his
mother couldn't read. Was Yazmina reading it to
her?

And then he remembered that day in the market,
when he saw the tailor, the small, dark man with the
big smile, hand his mother something, she putting it
in the folds of her *chaderi,* a few whispered words
before she walked quickly away. He thought of
Christmas Eve, and how the tailor had come to
deliver a package but handed her something else as
well, which she'd put in her apron. Ahmet looked at

237

the folded paper on the floor again and wondered what it could be.

It was probably a statement of his tailoring services. What else could it be? He could not imagine. Anything else would bring shame to her, to the family, to *him*.

He couldn't stand the thought. He knew he was jumping to conclusions. But he could feel his heart beating and his anger rising, so he said a quick good-bye to the women and walked out, considering what he was going to do, what had to be done. What made him so suspicious was the look on his mother's face when she saw the tailor in the café the night before Christmas. It was a look he'd never seen her give to his own father, her husband, in all their years together.

*   *   *

'He saw it, I'm certain he did,' said Halajan.

'I'm not so sure,' replied Yazmina. 'I hope not. But you are the mother, the elder. Certainly he would respect—'

'I am the elder, yes,' Halajan interrupted. 'But it doesn't matter in this country where men rule. To think that I gave birth to this baby who can now run my life as if I am a stupid donkey! I love my country and hate it at the same time. My rules, my way of life—they are all meaningless when it comes to the tradition of men. My son is Afghanistan. He holds on to the old ways even when the new ones are right in front of his face to pluck and taste and enjoy. He could've changed his life, gone to Germany with my daughter, gone to university, become something bigger, but he chose to be a

238

chokidor. And do you know why? To protect me, to take care of me, because he feels a responsibility to his family, an obligation to his heritage. It is my fault that he didn't have the same opportunities as his sister—because he would never leave me.

'But'—and she walked to the window, opened the curtain, and looked out beyond the wall to the city beyond—'it's also about his obligation to himself, and his desire for acceptance that has imprisoned me, always watching to be sure I follow the old rules, at least outside where others will see. It's a very weak, very hypocritical way to live. He knows what goes on in the coffeehouse, and he earns a good living from it, but he hates it and needs to limit it to the confines of its walls, not allowing it to run wild into the street.'

Yazmina was silent, trying to understand how a mother could speak this way about her son and how a son could be as rigid as Ahmet with a mother like this.

'We must be more careful when we read. We must do it by flashlight after Ahmet is asleep. His apartment is right next door.'

'He would never hurt you.'

'Shame does something to a man. It makes him forget those he loves. It makes a good man do bad things.'

Yazmina joined Halajan at the window and thought of Ahmet, his large dark eyes, his broad shoulders, and his warm face that was etched with something else. She'd always thought it was anger, but now she understood. It was the face of a man torn between love and duty, the face of bitter confusion.

CHAPTER TWENTY-SIX

Mazar-e Sharif was a good eight-hour drive from Kabul but only a forty-five-minute ride on the military plane that Tommy had arranged to transport him and Sunny. It was a bright, blue-skied morning, and the plane first flew past the mountains that looked so close that Sunny thought she could grab the snow right off their peaks. It then flew low over the Salang Valley, beautiful with oases of green lining the rivers and surrounding the lakes and framed by the dusty brown plains that marked Afghanistan's outer regions. Sunny chose the window seat, and the view was literally breathtaking. Tommy leaned in close to her to see out the window, so close she could smell him, reminding her of what felt now like ages ago—lying naked with him, making love to him, laughing with him into the morning hours.

He got up and asked the pilot to fly over Lake Band-e Amir to the west, so they cut back and lowered their altitude so Sunny could take in the lakes, truly one of the wonders of the world, she thought. Their deep, lapis blue waters looked as if they cut away the sand-colored mountains like glass, their edges at a ninety-degree angle, their cliffs frighteningly high above. The incongruous relationship of crystal clear water and dry, barren cliffs gave the area an eerie beauty, unlike anything Sunny had ever seen. Just east of where they circled was Bamiyan, the Hindu sacred site where the Taliban had destroyed the giant thirteen-century-old Buddhas only months before al-Qaeda did the same thing to the Twin Towers in New York.

Then they headed north up to the province of Balkh, where the fourth largest city of Afghanistan, Mazar, as Tommy casually referred to it, was located. Its name translated to Noble Shrine, which referred to the shrine of Hazrat Ali, a spectacular blue-tiled mosque in the center of the city, a tourist destination for millions of visitors every year. According to most Afghan Muslims, this was where Ali ibn Abi Talib, the cousin and son-in-law of Muhammad, was buried.

As the plane circled over the city, Tommy took Sunny's hand, which felt awkward and made her shift in her seat. She let him hold it for a minute or two, careful not to be too abrupt when she casually slid it out of his clasp.

They landed at the airport, where a driver was waiting in a minivan and took them into the city, to the Royal Oak Hotel, not particularly luxurious but modern, clean, and nice enough. When they checked in, they were issued one key, as if it were assumed that they were staying together in one room. Tommy must have told the receptionist they were married, because it was illegal for an unmarried couple to stay together.

Sunny pulled Tommy away from earshot of the desk and asked, 'And is there a key for me?'

'I'm sure I can get a duplicate.' He turned back to the receptionist.

'No, I mean, for my room.' When she saw his quizzical look she whispered, 'Did you think we were staying together?'

'That's exactly what I thought.'

'I don't think so. I'm here, I agreed to come, but I need some . . . time.'

241

'But that's why we're here, isn't it? To get to know each other again?' he said, smiling, as he put his hands on her waist. 'Come on, babe—'

But she pulled away, embarrassed by his inappropriate public display of affection, and said, 'Please don't "babe" me, but I need to see if there's still something between us, besides the, you know.' The sex would always be there, but what about the emotional relationship? Did they even have one? Besides, he could very easily disappear again and leave her with her heart in her hand.

'All right, but you know there is, and I know there is.' He turned back to the reception desk to get another room.

*   *   *

Jack walked into the coffeehouse that night carrying a beautiful bouquet of peach-colored roses wrapped in newspaper. He greeted Bashir Hadi warmly, they exchanged pleasantries about Bashir Hadi's family and Jack's flight, and then Jack asked him, 'So where's Sunny? She in the back?'

Bashir Hadi paused for a moment, considering what he should say. 'No, um, Miss Sunny is away right now.' He turned around quickly and went back to work, not wanting to be the one to tell him.

Jack looked at his watch, frowning. 'So when do you expect her?'

'She'll be gone for a few days.'

'What do you mean?' The hand holding the roses dropped to his side, the bouquet pointed to the floor. To say he was disappointed was an understatement. He'd counted the days since he left, then the hours on his return flight, then the

242

minutes as he was driven from the airport to the coffeehouse, and then, finally, he was here. 'She go to Dubai? Picking up supplies?'

'Yes, exactly, she went to Dubai,' Bashir Hadi said as he walked into the back pantry and disappeared from sight.

Jack raised his brows. He scanned the room and saw Halajan in the rear cleaning a table. He passed her on his way to the back to get water and something to put the roses in.

'Hello, Halajan.'

'Welcome back, and hope your family is well.' She turned away from him and went back to work.

'They are, thank you. It was a good trip. So, Halajan, where is Sunny? I brought these for her,' Jack said, holding out his flowers.

She stopped, looked at him, and with her hands on her hips, she said rapidly in Dari, 'Where is she, you ask? Not with you, because you weren't here.'

'What do you mean? What's going on? Both you and Bashir—'

'What's going on? What are you, a stupid donkey? You did this to yourself. Like the saying goes—'

'Halajan!' Jack interrupted. 'Tell me now.'

'Guess who's back?'

He felt his stomach clench. It couldn't be him. Could it? 'Halajan! Please just tell me for God's sake!'

And as quickly as she could speak, Halajan told him, without taking a breath.

'Tommy,' Jack whispered.

Halajan breathed deeply and then with unveiled anger, said, 'And so he and Sunny went to Mazar-e Sharif for a few days and will be back on Sunday.

243

She is there with him, and you are here alone. This is all because of you!' she railed.

Jack looked stunned, drew in a deep breath, and looked away.

'She went with him, they went *together*, to Mazar-e Sharif?'

Halajan nodded and went back to work.

'It's a romantic place,' Jack said, 'if you're into stupid clichés.' He threw the flowers onto the table. 'Good move,' he said sarcastically as he headed out.

'You don't have to worry, Jack,' Bashir Hadi called after him. 'It would take much more than a fancy mosque to steal her heart.'

'Let's hope so,' said Jack, walking out. He's away for a few weeks and she's gone for good? What had he been doing in America but freeing himself for her? For crying out loud! He slammed the coffeehouse door behind him.

*   *   *

The doves were what did it for Sunny, the thousands of white doves of Mazar-e Sharif. The mosque itself was a wonder in dark blue, turquoise, gold, and earth-colored tiles, intricately patterned, completely covering every inch of the huge shrine except for the domed rooftops. But the doves gave the place life. She was alone, having arranged to meet Tommy here after he explored the old museum in the mosque. She wasn't sure if it was the mosque that made Sunny feel claustrophobic or being with Tommy. All she knew was that she needed to breathe.

Spread out over a section of the plaza were millions of doves. They were a bubbling froth, their

244

warble a low boil. What added to the magic were the groups of women in white burqas feeding the birds wheat they'd bought from the small metal cart of a nearby vendor. Without apparent hair or face or distinguishing characteristics of any kind, they looked like large doves themselves.

But there was one woman in a sky blue burqa who stood and turned to Sunny, and though Sunny couldn't see her eyes through the mesh fabric, she felt the woman's gaze on her. Then the woman gestured to Sunny, subtly but distinctly, and Sunny went to her, not knowing why. Normally, she would've ignored her, thinking she was a beggar. Up closer, Sunny could see the woman's dark eyes through the mesh, and she imagined that the woman was smiling at her.

The woman took Sunny's hand in her own, kissed it, and placed it on her forehead. She whispered something to Sunny in Dari and turned Sunny's hand over and poured wheat into it.

'Tashakur,' thank you, Sunny said with a small bow of her head. Then she dug into her bag for some change to give her, but when she looked up, the woman in blue had vanished, leaving only those in white. Sunny turned around in every direction searching for her on the plaza. It seemed impossible for her to have disappeared so quickly, but she was gone. Maybe, just possibly, the magic of this place had transformed the woman's blue burqa to white, just like the doves in the legend. And if so, she was, indeed, a seventh dove, one with a link to God.

She stooped to feed the doves with the wheat the woman had given her. When she stood, tears began to flow down her cheeks. She didn't know

245

what it was nor did she expect it, but she was embarrassed and put on her sunglasses. Something powerful had touched her. Even though she was not Muslim or very good at any sort of religion, she was overwhelmed with the spirit of the place. She breathed in deeply and felt that God or whatever it was that gave people strength was with her now. It was as if the woman with the wheat and the white doves, the holiness of the place itself, put her in touch with something powerful and made her feel more at peace than she'd felt in a long time.

She met Tommy at the prearranged time and place, where he'd told their driver to pick them up and take them to the village of Balkh, the birthplace of the prophet Zoroaster, where Alexander the Great headquartered for two years after his invasion and where he'd taken his wife, and which was destroyed by Genghis Khan, more than a thousand years after that. This tiny village, now big on carpet weaving and tourism, was a microcosm of Afghanistan itself: rich in history, devastated by plunder, the people decimated by a frequent changing of the guard, and then exploited by a government in cahoots with one set of foreigners or another. Like Balkh, Afghanistan was owned by everybody but Afghans.

In the car on the way back, Sunny said to Tommy, 'I need your help with something.'

'Oh, really,' he said, with a dopey grin. 'And in exchange—'

'Yazmina was stolen from her home in Nuristan to pay off a debt of her uncle's. She got away. So now she fears the men who took her will return for her sister, who's only twelve. When the snows melt and roads open—'

'And?' he asked, putting a hand on her leg and leaning over to nuzzle her neck.

She picked up his hand and put it on the car seat. 'And, I need your help. We need to try to get Layla out of there before the men come back.'

'You're kidding, right?' He leaned back and looked at her.

'No, I'm not kidding! I'm deadly serious, Tommy! Come on, you could get a small plane. You know a million people. You can do it. Please.'

'You're serious!' He laughed. 'You're fucking kidding me! I don't think you understand: It's easy to get her. It's what happens *after* we get her. We're talking blood oaths. The uncle owes money, but he can't pay, so he pays with the girl. He doesn't pay and . . . this is how wars get started. I am not risking my life and the life of my "millions of people" to save—or maybe save—the life of one little girl. It ain't happening.'

'You're an asshole.'

'Yes, but a practical asshole.'

Afterward they went back to the hotel, where they each went to their own rooms, and then met for a late dinner. It was nice, the food was good, and Tommy would've looked delicious if she wasn't so pissed off. But she couldn't stomach the idea of sleeping with him. As attracted to him as she was, as invigorated as she felt to be out of Kabul, she was angry. Her experience at the mosque today told her to be at peace with herself, to follow her heart. Oh, she was at peace. Tommy was a selfish jerk who had no soul or empathy. He was a coward.

So for the second time in her life she did something that surprised her: She didn't sleep with the cute guy when he asked, she simply went home.

She'd rather be alone than alone with someone she no longer had feelings for, except for anger and the distant memory of once having loved him.

* * *

Two days earlier than expected, on a quiet Friday afternoon, Sunny walked into the coffeehouse with her small bag and was happy to find it just the way she'd left it except for a vase of roses on the counter that were a little droopy and wilted. Poppy greeted her the way she always did when she walked in—with her paws on Sunny's chest and a lick on her chin. Yazmina and Halajan were probably taking their afternoon rest time together, as they'd been doing for the past week or two. But one thing was unusual. Bashir Hadi seemed angry.

'Welcome back,' he said curtly. His back was to her. He was polishing the coffeemaker, turning its copper from a pockmarked brown to a shiny orange.

'Hello to you, too, Bashir Hadi. How are you? Your family? All is well, I hope.' She nodded toward the vase. 'Pretty flowers.'

'Sure, we're all fine here. Why even ask? Nothing much matters.'

What the hell was up with him? she thought. But she said, 'What is it, Bashir Hadi? Come on. Something's bothering you.'

He finally looked up from his work and said, 'It's good you're back. You—' But he stopped himself.

'Bashir Hadi?' She looked at him imploringly.

'You left for your trip with Tommy and then guess what happened?'

'Don't tell me another bomb?' she said, quickly

looking around the coffeehouse. 'Or that a pipe burst or the roof—'

'No!'

Then Halajan walked in and asked, 'So did you tell her that Jack was here?'

'You mean he's back? He's here in Kabul?' Her eyes lit up, and she breathed out hard.

Bashir Hadi shook his head from side to side. 'He walked in only an hour after you left.' He watched Sunny's face fall. And he pointed to the flowers. 'They were beautiful when he brought them.'

Halajan started to say something, but Sunny didn't hear it. She'd already grabbed her stuff and was running to her room.

*   *   *

She took her cellphone from around her neck and dialed his number.

'Is that you?' It was his deep, masculine voice.

'It's me,' she said.

'How're the doves?'

'Lovely, you wouldn't believe what—I'll tell you when I see you.'

'Send me a postcard.' He was about to hang up.

'Come over.'

'Yeah, maybe, when you get back, *if* you get back.'

'I'm back already, here at the coffeehouse.'

There was silence.

'Jack! You can't blame me for going. You were gone. And hardly a word the entire time! Tommy came home and—'

'Hardly a word, if I remember right. He was

never very articulate, that guy.'

Sunny had to agree. 'So come on over. I came back without even knowing you were here. And we didn't sleep together, if that's what you're worried about.'

'You think I'd worry about that? I never did see what you saw in Tommy. I mean, he's a good-looking guy, but not much in the brains department.'

'All right, you. You don't have to go insulting my choices, okay? And what about you and Pamela, anyway?'

'It's over. "We've grown apart" were her exact words. Like a scene out of a movie. "We've grown apart," can you believe it? She's gotten used to me being gone, and now, with Charlie going to college, she wants out. At least my kid still calls me "Dad."'

'Jack, I'm sorry.'

'I can't blame her,' he said. 'I feel the same way.'

There was a long, silent pause. And then Sunny asked, 'So, tell me. You didn't sleep with your wife?'

'Funny, and this may be the first time in history that a man is proud to say this to the woman he loves: I promise I didn't sleep with my wife once. I'm on my way.'

And she, the woman he loved, waited for Jack to come home.

CHAPTER TWENTY-SEVEN

Isabel took Candace to the Pul-e Charkhi prison east of downtown Kabul. It was even more shocking for her on this second visit, perhaps because sharing it made it more real than it had seemed the first time. There were some faces she hadn't remembered seeing, but there in the fifth cell, locked behind the blue bars with a dozen other women, was the one who haunted Isabel, the one who spoke English and pulled on her *kameez* and begged her for help.

This time, Isabel was able to steal a minute to talk to the woman while Candace chatted with the guard. Isabel squatted low so that she was face-to-face with her. She looked younger than she'd remembered.

'What's your name?' asked Isabel.

'Jamila,' she answered.

'Jamila, how are you doing? Are they treating you all right? Do you have enough to eat?'

She glanced quickly at the guard to be sure she wasn't listening.

'They treat us like animals—only goats are fed more than we are and have a choice between grasses on the hillside or leftovers. We eat only leftovers.'

A voice behind her said, 'The grasses would be better!'

And all the women laughed just enough to get the attention of the guard, who said nothing but glared at them. But then Candace said something to her, and the guard turned her attention back to her.

'Can you help us?'

'That's why we've returned. To help get you out.'

'I cannot go without my sisters. Please help them, too.' And she gestured to all the women in the cell. 'And their children, who must stay with them

251

wherever they are.'

'I don't know when or how many, but we'll try.'

'Otherwise, they will sell me as a slave for—' But she stopped herself, the color in her cheeks rising. 'For men.'

'What are you saying? The prison will sell you?'

'Yes, they send the young ones like me to the Gulf, or worse yet, we stay in Afghanistan, for the pleasure of men.'

'How do you know this?'

'Because they took my friend Haliya, whom they traded for money outside of Kabul, but she ran away. She'd overheard them talking when she pretended to be sleeping in the back of the van. When they caught her, they beat her, destroyed her face, and threw her away like garbage. The police picked her up and brought her back and she told us what she'd heard.'

'Is Haliya here now?'

'Yes, in the corner there. I'll get her.'

Jamila brought over a woman whose face was covered with a scarf. She held it close to her, allowing only one eye to be seen.

Jamila whispered something in her ear. Haliya looked at her, and Jamila nodded. Then Haliya removed the scarf from her face.

Isabel's stomach turned. Haliya's face had been hideously disfigured. One eye was gone, the skin on that side of her face bunched and ribbed like a sock that had fallen around an ankle. The corner of her mouth blended into her cheek, leaving a gaping hole in the side of her mouth.

'Because she ran away, they did this to her, they threw acid on her, saying, "Now you're too ugly for anyone." They are worse than dogs, these things

252

that would call themselves men.'

Isabel looked at Haliya, trying to keep her eyes on her so as not to make her feel ashamed that she couldn't be looked at. But she couldn't help but feel relieved when Haliya covered her face again.

'Can you help us? Will you?' pleaded Jamila.

'We will try.'

'Is this your friend?' She pointed to Candace, who by now was at Isabel's side, having so charmed the guard that she'd backed off and was standing in the doorway.

Isabel looked up at her and felt strongly that, yes, she was her friend, even with their differences. It was Candace who'd encouraged her to come, to help. It was Candace who believed in her. 'Yes,' she said, 'and my partner. We work together.'

Candace put a steady hand on the woman's shoulder. 'We will be back for you. Don't be afraid.'

'Please don't go. Take us with you!'

'It's not as easy as that. But we will be back,' Candace said, not taking her eyes off the woman. 'I promise you that.'

*   *   *

Wakil made the arrangements for a car to drive them to his valley. Candace had called him to let him know that she was coming with a friend, a journalist for the BBC who wanted to write a story about his school. (At least the BBC part was true.) She had a feeling he'd be pleased to get the media coverage, and she was right. In return, she hoped to enlist his help for the women in the prison. She thought that with his contacts he'd be able to get the necessary food and supplies, and then bribe their way through the gauntlet of officials and guards. In the meantime she could focus on raising enough money and finding a place to shelter them once she got them out.

He was there waiting for them, wearing his best *shalwaar kameez,* Pashtun vest, and expensive silk turban when they pulled up. His beard was neatly trimmed, he was as tall and fit as ever, and he looked strikingly handsome. Candace felt the hollowness of yearning in her chest. It had been over a month since they'd been intimate, but sex with Wakil wasn't something she'd ever forget. He greeted her in his usual publicly stolid fashion, with a small bow and a cool smile, and when he was introduced to Isabel, he smiled broadly and became expansive as he talked about his achievements. Candace was both proud to be a part of what was going on here and hurt that he didn't appreciate her anymore beyond her ability to bring in money. But she did her duty and brought up the rear as Wakil took them on a tour. As he talked, Isabel taped him with her recorder and stopped to take photographs. Candace couldn't wait to hear what Isabel had to say.

The clinic was even more impressive than the last time she was there. It was clean, well staffed, brightly lit, and amply supplied. There were more doctors now because Candace had raised extra funds from private donors and had loosened up some American money from health organizations.

The school was another thing altogether. It was afternoon, so the girls had gone home and the boys were studying. Before they entered, Wakil asked Isabel to turn off her tape recorder so she wouldn't inadvertently interrupt the boys' studies. She was to stop taking pictures so as not to cause a distraction. Candace noticed Isabel frown, unhappy with the restrictions but polite enough to adhere to them. She watched Isabel jot down some notes, her eyes narrowed with suspicion. Then she looked out at the serious young faces in the room, and she made some notes again. Candace had a feeling that Isabel was going to be critical of the school, probably accuse it of being too serious, overly disciplined. The boys were studying the Koran, sitting on their knees on carpets, swaying forward and back as they read along with the teacher at the front of the room.

There was one boy, who couldn't have been more than fourteen years old, following her with his eyes. He smiled thinly at her, and she smiled back. And then his smile disappeared and all that was left were his dull, dark eyes, a bitter look on his face.

When she mentioned him to Wakil later, he responded, 'You'd look like that, too, if your entire family was killed by an American bomb dropped on your village. These are all sad boys. They are lost and we provide a home for them.'

*   *   *

During the tour of the grounds, Isabel whispered to Candace, 'It's a little quiet here, no? For all these kids? Very disciplined.'

'Wakil's a serious guy. He's intent on teaching these kids something so that they'll have more of a future than selling some rugs in the market with a made in china label on them.'

'Well then, he's doing a good job.'

What Isabel didn't mention was the notion that

255

was gnawing at her insides. She'd seen reports on similar places in Pakistan. Schools, madrassas, that were covers for terrorist training. The school had an extremely rigid feel to it: no talking, all prayer, nothing childlike about these children. Could it be a training ground for the boys? That there were girl students here felt disingenuous. She'd have to do some research when they got back to Kabul. She'd have to find out more about Wakil and his pursuits. He seemed too slick to be in this for the kids alone.

*　　　*　　　*

Candace finally got Wakil alone, in his office, while one of his assistants continued to show Isabel around the compound. Candace locked the door from the inside and said, 'When will I see you again?' She walked up to him, daringly close. She could feel the warmth emanating from his body.

'Soon, my love, soon. I've been unable to get away. But do you see how much we've accomplished here?' He took a strand of her hair between his index and middle fingers.

She took that as an invitation and stood on her tiptoes and whispered into his ear. 'When soon? Will you come to Kabul? Wakil,' she said, her lips fluttering against his skin, 'it's been too long. What about us? Can I stay here with you?'

He lifted her chin and kissed her softly, his full mouth lightly on hers. 'My dear Candace, nothing has happened, only that critical things have taken precedence. I will come to Kabul very, very soon—to see you.' He kissed her again, more firmly this time. 'And also, because our resources are running low and we need to invest in some major supplies, such as computers and better Internet.' He took her in his arms and kissed her hard and passionately. 'Will you help me?'

'I was just going to ask you the very same thing,' she said before feeling his tongue in her mouth and his arms circling her and then one hand on her breast and then down her side to her legs, and then between them. Her knees weakened, and she let her hand roam until she felt his hardness and there, against the wall of his office in the school he'd built from nothing, Candace made love to Wakil with the hope that this meant he did truly love her, knowing all the while he didn't.

*   *   *

When Wakil escorted the two women to their car, he was formal and distant, as if the last hour they'd spent together hadn't happened. Candace knew he had to keep up appearances, but sometimes, just sometimes, a smile or a knowing look would be nice.

As they approached their car, she noticed another parked on the other side of the building. Two men were getting in the front, and a third turned their way. It was that same sullen, dull-eyed boy she'd seen earlier. Wakil waved to him and turned to her and Isabel and said, 'Excuse me one moment, please,' and walked over to him. They spoke, the boy nodded, he got into the car, and it sped off.

Candace turned to Isabel, who was watching as well. It was nothing, a word, a good-bye. She hoped hers with Wakil would be warmer, that for her he would say something to remember. But as he walked back their way, stiffly, his chin high, his expression blank, she knew she was going to be disappointed. She'd keep helping him—how could she turn her back on the children?—but she was going to shoot herself if she ever, ever again expected more from him than a periodic smile and a roll in the hay.

CHAPTER TWENTY-EIGHT

The bottle of scotch was heavy on Isabel's lap as her car made its way through the city to the home of the Last Jew of Kabul. She knew to take a gift, and since it was Friday night, the beginning of the Jewish Sabbath, this was the most appropriate one she could imagine. Since she was a little girl, she'd watched her father have a shot every Friday night. It was the end of the workweek, he'd said. Time to relax. Jewish Brits were more assimilated than most, probably as a defense against the prevailing anti-Semitism. She grew up knowing she was Jewish but never observing much tradition other than her father's weekly shot of scotch. It was a huge hypocrisy, she felt, given that her mother's family had been mostly wiped out in the Holocaust.

The irony to Isabel was that so much of what made her who she was—being Jewish, having been raped, being a journalist—was undercover. But after meeting Jamila, and hearing from Sunny about the Last Jew, Isabel realized undercover was overselfish. People took moral stands every day: The Last Jew against religious persecution, and Jamila against sexual persecution. Isabel felt she was headed toward a stand of her own.

His home was located on Flower Street, adjacent to the old graywhite synagogue, now cracked and in decay, looking more like an old house than a place of worship. It had been very difficult to find. But finally, the car pulled up, and she told the driver to wait for her. Then she ascended the stairs to the second floor, which led to a dark hallway and his door. She knocked. A balding, stout man wearing glasses and a woven yarmulke opened it and said, 'Come in.'

She held out her hand, which he took firmly in his. 'This is for you,' she said, after introducing herself. She handed him the bottle in the thin plastic bag. His shoes were worn, his shirt so thin at the elbows that she could see through it, and his pants were fraying at the ankles.

He took it, opened the bag, and nodded. 'Want a shot?' He smiled. He went to the back to his tiny kitchen and brought out two glasses.

His name was Zablon Simintov. His small room with its red threadbare carpet contained only a *toshak,* a low table with a pile of old Jewish prayer books, a *bokhari* to ward off the winter chills, and a small table with a couple of white plastic chairs. They sat and Isabel asked him about the things that were burdening her. When Sunny first told her about him, she'd Googled him and there'd been many stories. But no one had asked the questions she was most interested in, or if they had, he hadn't answered. So she asked them now.

'Your wife and daughter are in Israel. Your business has been destroyed. You are alone. Why are you still here?'

The forty-five-year-old former carpet trader

259

smiled and said, 'Stop or you'll make me depressed!' and he sucked back another shot of scotch.

For eight hundred years, he said, Afghanistan had had a vibrant Jewish community, which shrank after 1948, when many families left for Israel, and then again in 1979 after the Soviet invasion. And now Simintov was alone, his wife and daughter having moved to Israel in 2001, and his best friend and worst enemy, Ishaq Levin, with whom he shared the synagogue, having died a few years before. He'd been jailed and beaten several times by the Taliban, who ransacked the synagogue and carried off its four-hundred-year-old handwritten Torah scroll. Simintov blamed the loss of the Torah on Levin, who'd told the Taliban that it was worth millions. That was the two men's falling-out. Now Simintov was on a mission.

'I stayed to find the Torah. To save the synagogue.'

'But how do you live? The Taliban stole your carpets and everything you—'

'Everything I owned of value. My entire business. So can you help me?' He put out his hand as if begging.

She laughed uncomfortably.

'I'm not kidding. I rely on the kindness of strangers,' he said with a twinkle in his eye.

'But wait, Mr Simintov. How do you propose finding the Torah? And don't you think the same guys who destroyed the giant Buddha statues probably destroyed your Torah, too?'

'Not if they thought it was valuable. There's some guy being held in Guantanamo who knows exactly where it is. We just have to ask him.' He

260

smiled, knowing how foolish he sounded.

Isabel looked at him and wondered if he was insane or just a little crazy.

And then he said, 'Don't you see? If I leave, there are no Jews left in all of Afghanistan. And Hitler and Osama bin Laden and every other madman bent on the decimation of an entire people will have won. "If I am not for myself, who will be for me? And if not now, when?" as the saying goes. If I leave, the crazies win.'

They drank to that, and Isabel realized there was crazy and then there was crazy, and Simintov's brand wasn't so bad. She gave him a hundred American dollars, kissed him on the cheek, and promised him she'd come back to visit before leaving Kabul.

On the way home the driver took a circuitous route to avoid the police checkpoints because of the traffic. Sitting in the back of the car, Isabel leaned her face on her hand and looked out the window. And then she did something that hadn't happened to her in months, maybe years. Isabel let herself cry. She wasn't sure why or what had moved her so, but she had a feeling that, as darkness fell across the city, she was crying for Simintov, living lonely and apart from his family, who'd locked himself in his own prison of sorts—his stubborn defense of his heritage—alone in the synagogue. She cried for Jamila living in squalor in the prison, for Jamila's friend imprisoned by the violence to her horrible face, and in frustration because the only way to be sure that Jamila would not be killed would be to get her out of the country, and that was an almost impossible task. She cried for Layla, who could at this moment be sitting in a similar prison if she

261

hadn't already been sold to someone as his third wife. She cried for herself, for in her freedom she, too, was behind bars—the bars that blocked her from feeling connected to her family, from finding love, from facing her painful past.

*   *   *

Ahmet couldn't stand it any longer, so he walked stealthily upstairs to his mother's apartment and slipped inside, knowing that she was in the coffeehouse getting it ready for the dinner hour. What was she thinking, this mother of his? She'd always been a rebel, with her smoking, her jean skirt under her dress, and, of course, her unique way of seeing the world. (And, though she tried to hide it, he knew she'd cut her hair, having seen her more than once smoking in the back courtyard without a scarf on her head.) On the one hand he was proud that she was so intelligent and had her own mind. On the other, he was angry that she had no respect for tradition, no worries that she'd shame the family by her actions, or more to the point, that she'd shame *him* most, since he was the man of the house. And after all the sacrifices he made for her, staying with her, watching over her, protecting her.

He knew the importance of carrying on the traditions of one's people. That's why he was waiting for his mother to choose a bride for him. Though, given her rejection of such 'nonsense rules,' as she called them, he might be waiting forever. The front room was neat, but he checked under the *toshak*s and in the drawers of her small cabinet, where he found nothing.

And besides, he thought, there was Yazmina.

A widow, yes, but those eyes made him forgive all that had gone on with her before. But is forgiveness enough? he wondered.

In the sleeping room, there was one *toshak* covered in pillows and blankets. There was also a cabinet for his mother's clothes. He opened it, his hand first touching the exterior wood, engraved with a traditional Islamic design, which he had loved to follow with his fingers when he was a young child. He knew that inside were three drawers with blue ceramic pulls. And he knew that in one was the mosaic box that his father had bought when Ahmet was born, an offering to her of thanks for bearing him a son.

But the box was empty except for a beaded necklace with an amulet and a few wrist bangles and earrings.

Where was the letter? He turned to look out her window from which he could see over the walls and out into Kabul. Where would his mother hide a letter from a man whom she hardly knew? A man whose reputation was in question? He replayed the meeting he'd witnessed in his mind: the quick walk through the marketplace until she reached his shop. Him standing outside, waiting for her. Him slipping his hand into his pocket and pulling out a note. Then her pulling her hand from her coat, taking it, her fingers lightly touching his, and putting it in her pocket.

He went through every article of clothing, careful to put each one back exactly as he'd found it. Nothing. Frustrated, he decided to look through everything one last time to be sure he hadn't missed something. He methodically opened one drawer and then closed it, moving one by one. When he

263

arrived at the third drawer, he found he couldn't close it all the way. He put his hand in the back to clear what was blocking it, pulling out a stack of letters, and then another, and then another. And the next drawer and the next, in the back, more letters. They'd been stacked neatly, until his slamming the drawers had caused a stack to fall over. The letters were tied, and there were many more than he'd ever expected.

Ahmet untied them and began to read.

My dearest Halajan,

Today is a day of mourning, declared by Karzai, the hypocrite, for the forty Pashtun killed at the wedding up in the Uruzgan province. The Americans raid the hiding places of the Taliban and in so doing, kill many innocents, celebrating love and family. You tell me, please, my Halajan, why the Helmand River survives but all those lives are taken.

And yet today, life goes on in Kabul. I ate my bread and tea for breakfast, some sweet oranges with seeds for lunch and my beloved eggplant, and tonight I wish I were eating with you. Here is life as Rashif sees it: We eat breakfast, we get bombed, and if we're lucky we survive to look into the eyes of loved ones. My children loved ones are far away. My heart loved one is a mile away and yet a lifetime. One day, Halajan, one day . . .

They were sometimes serious and sometimes nothing, simple stories of what happened on a given day, where the tailor went, what he saw. A fat old man needed a new *kameez*. His grown son asked for some money. A family of birds built a nest in a tree in his backyard. Some refugees greeted him with *chai* when he delivered ten new *shalwaar kameez*es to their tents outside Kabul. They were full of details, and some even made him chuckle from the truths of an observant eye.

This man, this stranger to his family, this *modernist* had been writing his mother letters for several years, going against every teaching, threatening their position in the world and their place in the afterlife. Everything Rashif represented went against Islam and therefore, everything Ahmet believed. Without the proper introductions, without Ahmet's agreement—for he was the authority of his mother's house—there could be no letters, no communication whatsoever! If anyone were to find out, his mother would be called a whore and he an infidel. Women were sent to prison—or worse—for smaller offenses than this. Wasn't a woman stoned to death just recently for leaving a husband who had beaten her? This man, this Rashif the tailor, deserved punishment. How dare he violate his mother like this? He was godless and he could ruin her.

But what bad thing did his mother really do? Receive some letters that she couldn't even read?

And was Rashif really so bad? Helping the Afghans who could not help themselves? He worked hard; he was thoughtful, if not religious enough for Ahmet's taste.

And then Ahmet realized something far more illuminating than finding these letters: He was arguing with himself about the right and wrong of his mother's liaison with Rashif. He was truly a mix of his mother's son, a child of the Koran, and an

Afghan. His heart saw gray when his brain saw only black and white.

But a man does not go unpunished for such a violation. Ahmet knew what had to be done. He put the letters back very carefully in their neat stacks and tucked them in the back of their drawers.

But one he kept for himself. It wasn't a recent one, but one from the middle of a stack, one that wouldn't be missed. He folded it in half and put it deep into the pocket of his pants.

*　　　*　　　*

Halajan made her way on the bus, across the dry riverbed on foot, and into the Mondai-e. Something made this trip, on this day of this week, more urgent than ever before. Her concern about Ahmet seeing the letter on the floor or Yazmina and her pregnancy or that stupid old Candace talking about love and men or Sunny having taken that stupid trip to Mazar-e Sharif with Tommy . . . something. She walked as fast as her two spindly legs would carry her, looking down at the rough ground, careful not to turn an ankle, until she got to Rashif's shop.

She entered. He stood. He walked to her, and, alone in the shop, he took her hands in his and put his forehead against hers. She backed away, looked around to be sure no one was watching. She couldn't help but smile.

'You,' he said.

'Yes,' she answered, 'me.'

'I can't wait much longer. I'm tired of these stupid letters.'

'You don't look tired,' she said, smiling. 'You look like a boy.'

But he did not return her warmth. He was impatient. 'No more letters. I want you, your inane son, and your life with mine.'

She looked at him closely, wondering if he knew, wondering if she'd read the wrong Rumi poem that day, and said, 'Do you have a letter for me or not? Maybe, *Inshallah,* if Allah smiles on you, I will write you back.'

'The day you write me back is the day everyone leaves Afghanistan—the Americans, the Pakistanis, the Russians, everyone—except us Afghans.' He sounded bitter.

'Okay, that is a challenge that I accept. Now give me the letter.'

'Here it is. Read it.'

'How can I? I must go.'

'Why will you not read it in front of me? Go on, read it!'

He knew and he was angry. 'Then I will read it to you.' He tried to grab it from her hand, but she stuck it deep into her pocket.

Read it to her! Blood rushed to her face and she feared he'd notice her excitement. To actually hear him read a letter! She swallowed to contain herself. 'It's too late.'

'Do you think I need the letter itself to know what it says?'

Halajan knew this was improper, but her feet were glued to the floor, as if they were weighted by her love. She could not walk away from Rashif.

He recited the letter:

'Dear Halajan, On Christmas Eve I visited you in your place of work. And look: We survived! Ahmet didn't hurt me, of course he would never hurt you, and lightning from the heavens did not strike. There

267

*are no rules to keep us apart. I will win your son over.
You shall see. And he will be my friend, like a son.*

'I wish I'd said something funny in there, but I
did not.'

'It's good,' said Halajan. 'Keep reading, or
reciting, or whatever it is you're doing.'

'And do you know why, Hala, that this is so?'

And now, Rashif whispered, his tone softening,
his voice like the sweet music of a summer's night:

*'Because when two people are meant to be together,
it is as if their souls are entwined like the roots of an
elm, needing each other for support, helping the other
to find water under the soil.*

'A little corny, right? When I write it, the words
sound like magic. When I recite it, they sound silly.'

Halajan's heart went out to him. 'Go on. Your
words are good.' She wanted to kick herself. *Good?
Stop saying good! Say good-bye!*

He continued. *'I have made a decision. This is the
year we will happen. This is the year we will begin our
lives as one. Good night, my Hala. Yours, Rashif.'*

Rashif put his hands together and bent his head
as if in prayer. He stood that way for what felt like
minutes and then he looked up, directly at Halajan,
and said, 'All these years, and you have never read
one, have you?'

She could feel all the blood in her body rush to
her face, where it burned through her cheeks like
wildfire. She turned toward the door.

'You knew,' she said, her back to him.

'Not long,' he answered.

'I was ashamed.'

'I know.'

'But I have found someone to read them to me,
and we're almost caught up.'

268

'I am so pleased,' he said. 'Yazmina?'

She heard his footsteps behind her, felt his breath on her neck. She locked her knees so they would not buckle under her.

'Yes, and she will teach me, too. You will see. I will write back.'

'And I will be here, waiting.'

CHAPTER TWENTY-NINE

. . . and so I said to the boy, why do you steal? You know it is wrong. No matter how hungry you are, no matter how the pain gnaws at your insides, there is no acceptable human reason to steal. Only the rat in the gutter, who cannot reason, steals when he is hungry. And then, my dear, do you know what this wise old man did to teach this boy a lesson? I handed him some afghanis—enough to buy a week of food. I've gotten soft in my old age . . .

Yazmina was reading Rashif's newest letter to Halajan when Ahmet stormed in.

'Did you ever hear of knocking?' asked Halajan, as she and Yazmina tried in vain to gather the letters and hide them under their clothing.

'You!' he yelled at Yazmina. 'You are involved in this?'

Yazmina's green eyes widened. 'I am only reading her a shopping list.'

Ahmet laughed with anger. 'A shopping list? Are these the words of a shopping list?' He grabbed the letter from her and started to read it.

269

'Ahmet!' yelled Halajan. 'I am your mother. You bring disrespect into my home.'

'You both bring shame upon this family,' he answered. 'Your actions are outside the law of Muhammad. You must stop with these letters now!' His bellowing shook the thin windows.

'Shame can only be brought by the man who allows himself to be shamed,' said Halajan.

She tried to take the letter back from him. But he held it, and then tore it in two, and then again and again. Then he threw it on the floor and spit on it. His face was red with anger.

'You will destroy everything we have worked hard for. If anyone else found out, we would be—'

But Yazmina groaned loudly, and then again, grabbing her stomach and breaking out in a terrible sweat.

Ahmet stood still, his eyes popping out of his head, his brows furrowed in concern and confusion.

Halajan went to Yazmina, sat behind her, and held her head against her chest, wiping her sweaty face with her dress. 'It is time.' To Ahmet she said, 'Go get Sunny. We need hot water.'

Yazmina moaned in pain, her green eyes dull, unfocused.

He stood there frozen. 'What is happening? Is Yazmina all right? We should get her to a hospital!'

'Don't ask, just go!' Halajan yelled, thinking that for once it was to their benefit that her Afghan son was as ignorant as other Afghan men. To the Afghan man, there is sex and then there is a baby. 'Get Sunny!'

He turned and slammed the door behind him, his footsteps loud on the stairway.

When he was gone, Yazmina said, 'I am wet.'

270

Halajan looked under Yazmina's *chaderi* and saw that her water had broken. The baby was coming now.

In seconds Ahmet returned with Sunny, who knelt down next to Yazmina and asked, putting a hand on her cheek, 'What is it? Is she sick?'

'Not really,' said Halajan. Then she looked up at Ahmet and said, 'You need to leave. This is a woman's affair.'

Ahmet didn't know what to think. But facing Yazmina's pain and possible illness, he knew he couldn't just leave her. 'What is it? Will she be all right?'

'You have to leave, Ahmet. You haven't always listened to your mother, but now you must.'

And Yazmina screamed in pain.

'This is what I need from you.' And, though it had been almost twenty years since she'd practiced, all the years of midwifery came back to her. 'I need towels and hot water, I need the shears Sunny uses to cut her hair, and—'

'Shears? You will not cut my Yazmina's hair!'

When he said that, Yazmina stopped moaning, and all eyes were on Ahmet.

'No, I will not hurt her, nor will I cut her hair. But if you want to help, then get out of here and help!'

And he ran out the door. Yazmina looked at Halajan. And Halajan said, 'And why shouldn't he love you? How could he help himself?'

And then Halajan took off Yazmina's heavy *chaderi*, and she and Sunny were wide-eyed with how large Yazmina had become since they last saw her.

'Halajan, the hospital.'

271

'We cannot. They will—'

There was a knock on the door. It was Ahmet, this time knowing he should give the women time to prepare. They covered Yazmina and told him to enter. He was carrying towels, a steaming teapot of water, and the other supplies his mother had asked for.

'And now, Ahmet, you must stand guard outside and not let anyone in,' said Halajan. When he was gone, she said, 'Now, no more talk. We have a baby to bring safely into the world.'

*　　　*　　　*

Ahmet was sick with worry. What illness could possibly possess Yazmina, making her so suddenly, so violently ill? As he stood outside at the top of the stairway looking east, he could see the reflections of the setting sun in the windows of Kabul and the glow on the mountains beyond. What beauty would allow another to suffer so? he wondered. The world was not always a fair place.

And then he heard her scream. It was as loud and as blood chilling as the scream of that soldier whose leg was torn off right in front of his eyes in last year's suicide bombing on Chicken Street. But those screams stopped when the soldier lost consciousness. Yazmina's continued for an hour or more, but in his frustration over his powerlessness, he lost count. All he knew was that she didn't deserve the pain she was in.

He almost opened the door several times. But it was only when he heard another scream, which at first sounded like the cat out his back window, the one that cried in the night, that he finally couldn't stop himself. He opened the door and then he saw it: his mother handing Sunny a baby, covered in blood and thick fluids, and Yazmina, finally lying quiet, exhausted, her face covered in sweat, her hair damp with it.

'Wha—?' he began.

'Come in and keep quiet,' interrupted his mother with a harsh whisper. 'You'll disturb the baby.'

*   *   *

Just as Yazmina had known, her baby was a girl. Halajan's experience came back to her, and both baby and mother were well. Sunny washed the baby, wrapped her in one of Halajan's chadors, and laid her on Yazmina's chest so she could hold her.

The baby's tiny head was covered with wispy black hair. Her eyes were closed, but Yazmina knew they were Najam's eyes.

Only Ahmet couldn't understand what he was seeing. 'But how?' he demanded. 'You have no husband! Who is the father? Who did this to you?' His head was spinning, he felt as if he were in someone else's body, and he couldn't believe the words coming from his mouth. 'Whose baby is this?' he bellowed.

'This is *my* baby,' answered Yazmina. 'My Najama. Daughter of my dead husband.'

'*Your* baby? You disgust me. You are a dirty *kafir*! Like the foreigners in the coffeehouse who bed down with anyone, like animals.' He felt as if his whole world was collapsing. Not just the traditions forsaken, not just her betrayal, but his dreams of love, his hope for a future, his heart itself, all were shattered.

273

Halajan stood up, put her hands on her hips, and faced her son. 'Najama is *my* baby,' she said.

Sunny looked at her and understood. She stood, too, and faced Ahmet and said, 'She is my baby, too.'

Ahmet looked at them, thought about how he'd be seen in the coffeehouse, how weak and not in control of his own home, and he spit out these words: 'Then you're all the same, all *fahesha*. And you will pay for your willful ways.'

*   *   *

'Now do you see what I meant when I said that you cannot keep this baby?' Halajan asked Yazmina after Ahmet left, slamming the door behind him. 'It's dangerous, not only for the baby, but for you.

'Now, Sunny, you see why she had to hide it,' she explained. 'A woman without a husband, who is with child, is nothing. Or less than nothing.'

'Now what do we do?' asked Yazmina, stroking Najama's head. 'You gave me a bed and a roof and a purpose. Now it's not only me. It is too much. Please, Miss Sunny, I beg you. Do not fire me. I am so happy here. I work hard, I—'

'I would never fire you, Yazmina. You are part of our coffeehouse family—my family. And your baby, well . . .' She laughed. 'I don't love all babies, to be honest, but I will love yours.' She was lying, a little. But look at what happened with Poppy. She couldn't imagine life in Kabul without that mangy mutt, as Jack called her.

'Now we have something to celebrate.'

'No, Sunny,' warned Halajan, 'this is not a happy occasion. Don't you see that this birth, with no

274

father—'

'But there *was* a father,' Sunny said.

'—with no *living* father, could mean the death of Yazmina and of us all? What is Bashir Hadi to say? And we heard Ahmet. We bring shame on their heads. To have a baby means you have to have made the baby, and with no husband—'

'But I did have a husband—'

'But nobody knows if he is really the father. And it doesn't really matter. He's not here. For all concerned, there is no father. Yazmina's life will be in danger. She will be seen as impure, or as a woman who makes money from men, and she works in the coffeehouse with *khaareji*, foreign men, so people will think it is a *khaareji*'s baby, so no *khaareji* who speaks to her will be safe. They'll think she is selling more than coffee, and you know the power men have in Kabul.

'Do you see, Sunny, that this is why a pregnant woman in Afghanistan does not discuss her condition? She barely acknowledges it. Do you not see? It's very embarrassing to discuss it because it is admitting that you did the thing that got you pregnant in the first place. Those things are not discussed in our world. I know that's difficult for a *khaareji* like you to understand—'

'Like me?' Sunny was surprised at Halajan's use of that term, usually used only to insult or demean. 'But I thought we were friends, and friends help one another.'

Halajan answered, 'We are friends. But there will always be the distance of oceans, customs, and history between us. Besides, you're the boss.' She smiled.

'Really? I thought *you* were the boss.' She smiled

back.

The baby let out a cry.

'She is hungry,' Halajan said. 'It's time to learn to feed her.' But what Halajan really wanted to say was, *Don't let yourself love this baby, because soon, when she is strong enough, she will be gone. So don't let yourself love.*

*　　　*　　　*

Ahmet answered the muezzin's call and went to the mosque for the evening prayer. He usually prayed on the small rug in his own home, but tonight he felt he needed the mosque and his community around him, as did others, apparently. It was very crowded. He greeted the familiar faces and wished his father were there with him. Attending prayer at the mosque made him think of ancient traditions and family, of fathers and sons, of loyalty and responsibility to the faith. He knelt on his prayer rug facing east and put his nose to the floor in front of him and begged God to reveal the truth and show him the way. How does one love God, he wondered, and love a woman? A woman with a baby? A baby who's not your own? How do the teachings deal with such issues? He knew the Koran to be a book of patience and wisdom, of love and kindness, and not the book of violence and retribution that some had attributed to it. He knew Muhammad married many widows with children and that loving Yazmina and her baby would be a righteous thing to do—if it was true that she really was a widow.

And yet. Had he been a man for whom crying came easily he would surely be crying now, in frustration, in sadness, in pain.

There were expectations. There were ways a woman was supposed to behave in Kabul and ways a man was supposed to react. There were obligations to fulfill and lessons to be learned. The Koran wasn't always explicit about what to do under which circumstances. Sometimes it was vague and up to interpretation.

And yet.

The one thing he knew that was very clear, with not an iota of ambivalence, was that love was the highest form of being. This was one thing the teachings and his mother had in common: their respect for love. And the basis for love was individual feeling. Again, his mother's teaching: You must be true to yourself, even if it goes against the grain of what is expected. Just as Muhammad proved, just as he taught.

If only he had the—what did the Americans call it?—the *balls* to do it, to allow himself to love. And what about his mother? He felt the letter in his pocket. Could he allow her to love as well?

CHAPTER THIRTY

All of a sudden it seemed as if everything in Sunny's life had changed. She felt like an adolescent kid again, who awakens one day to find herself in a new body with no idea who she is or what she will become. Sunny had inherited a dog, a baby, an old boyfriend back from the dead, a new love with an old friend, and a booming business at the coffeehouse. Her life was in flux; she didn't know what she wanted and felt that everything was happening *to* her, instead of *because of* her.

The mural remained unfinished, and whenever Sunny looked out her front windows, she felt a guilty tug in her stomach. It simply looked terrible, and empty. Sunny had thought she'd enjoy it. It was something she could do alone, outside in the early spring sunshine, under the budding trees, the paintbrushes and paints hers to choose, her vision of the wall hers alone. To be alone was what she needed when the baby cried, when Halajan made her snarky observations, when Tommy encroached on her physical space. The only time she didn't want to be alone was when Jack was around, which wasn't often because of the increased need for his expertise. He was gone again and had been for weeks. Three American aid workers had been kidnapped in Kandahar, and he had been sent to negotiate their release.

His work was something they didn't discuss in detail. She could accuse him of being secretive, or at minimum, unforthcoming, but it was her fault as well. She didn't want to know. Though the real truth was that she *did* know.

When she'd asked for his help finding Layla, he'd been very clear about how dangerous a mission it would be, how difficult, virtually impossible.

'The villages in Nuristan are run by drug lords and warlords,' he explained. 'There are no laws, Sunny, except those imposed by them. There are no real roads or village markers. There's almost no cellphone reception and no email connections up there in the mountains. One doesn't go there. It's rugged, rough, and restricted territory. Finding one young girl whose uncle owes money to the drug lords or warlords—and then getting her safely to

Kabul with no further repercussions—will be as difficult and dangerous as climbing Mount Everest.'

'But what about Yazmina? It's her sister. What do I tell her? That there's no way?'

She remembered how he looked then. The pain on his face, as he shook his head. He'd try, he said, to contact people he knew up there, military guys, shooters. If there was a way, he'd find it. But she shouldn't be too hopeful. Somehow, she understood then, how different a man he was from Tommy, who said he couldn't do it either, but his were selfish reasons, not the reasons of someone who cared about someone he didn't even know.

So, how could she not know how dangerous it was? She knew it as if it were she out there herself, in the rugged wasteland of the treacherous south, where the Taliban slept in caves, their vast stores of weapons hidden in underground shelters they'd built into the rocky earth.

The night before he'd left for this latest job, Sunny and Jack had gone to the roof after dinner and looked out over Kabul. The night was black, but the sky was starry, like a protective blanket over them.

'I leave tomorrow. I could be gone longer this time.'

'I'll be here when you get back.'

'If it gets bad here, which it's going to, you'll have to make a decision.'

'About what? About leaving Kabul?'

'Americans will be targets. It'll be very dangerous here for you. And it's not far off. You can feel the dangers growing in Kabul every day. We've been lucky so far.'

'What about you?'

279

'For me, too. And I want to be with you.'

'So you're saying we just pack up and leave our lives here and go back to the States?'

'An argument can be made for leaving Afghanistan to the Afghans. We treat them like idiots. And you know, and I know, that Halajan, Yazmina, Bashir Hadi, even Ahmet are not idiots. We Americans infantilize everyone not like us. Make them into babies like Najama.'

Sunny loved this thoughtful, intelligent man. But she didn't believe he could stop doing his work, ever. Not to save his own life, and certainly not for her. Nor would she ask him to.

'But right now, it's you, me, and the stars.' He pulled her to him and kissed her hard on the mouth, feeling her open for him, feeling her arms around him, feeling her body against his.

They made love that night in her room with all the abandon of young people not yet disappointed or embittered or weakened by life. They made love as if it could be their last time.

And the next morning, Jack said, 'I'll be back as soon as I can, and then we'll figure out what's next. I'm sick and tired of being away from you.'

Then her cellphone rang, rattling from its perch on the low table.

'Wait,' she said, 'let me get rid of this.' She picked up the phone and flipped it open. It was Tommy.

She looked at Jack. *Shit, not now*, she thought.

'So answer it,' Jack said.

'No, they can call back.' But she looked like she was hiding something, she knew.

Jack scrutinized her, squinting. 'It's Tommy, isn't it?' He waited for a response and when there was none, he said, 'It's not over, is it?'

'It's over, Jack. How can you ask me that? Now, with everything?'

'Does *he* know it's over? Maybe you need to let him in on it.'

'I know.' She shook her head. She didn't know what was holding her back. Breaking Tommy's heart? He didn't have such a big heart to break.

'I have to go,' said Jack. 'You know'—and he let out a small chuckle—'what's the thing with him? So he's young and good-looking.'

'It's not that,' she said.

'So what is it?' He was angry.

'It's nothing. Time, I guess. History. Waiting for so long and then here he is.

He shrugged. 'This is bullshit. I gotta go.'

'But now there's you.' She went to him and kissed him hard. 'I love you,' she said.

'Yeah, okay,' he answered.

'Just come back in one piece. Okay? And alive would be good. It's a small request. I don't ask for much. Just you.'

CHAPTER THIRTY-ONE

'More tea?' Yazmina asked Candace and Isabel, who were chatting and eating candied almonds, figs, and dates. The baby was swaddled to her chest with a long piece of fabric wrapped around her waist and the ends tied behind her neck. The baby cooed and gurgled.

Bashir Hadi, from his perch on the other side of the counter, smiled with every little sound from the baby. His was a father's heart.

'Let me take a look at her,' Candace said, standing. 'May I?'

Yazmina tilted her body forward so that the baby's face was visible.

'She really is beautiful,' said Candace, as she stroked the baby's cheek, gently, tentatively, with one finger. 'Look, Is, she really is something.'

Isabel took a sip of tea and said, 'I'm sure she is, but I'm not a baby kind of girl. Never have been.'

Candace just hummed to the baby, and when she looked up, she blinked back some tears. 'I'm a fool.' She laughed. 'She's just so pretty and I have a feeling'—she sighed loudly—'that it's too late for me.' She shook her head and sat down.

Isabel put her hand on Candace's and said, 'Nothing's too late for you. I know this to be true. If anybody can make things happen, it's you, my friend.'

'Yes, me, the oldest mother in the world!'

'You're not too old.'

'Just too single.'

They were talking so fast in English that Yazmina couldn't follow. But she saw the sadness in Candace's eyes and so she figured now was as good a time as any. 'Now that you are back, I have something for you. Do you have a moment? Please, come with me,' she said, gesturing to the back door.

'You mean the dress? It's ready? Please!'

'Yes, it is ready. I so hope that you will like it.'

And the two women walked to the rear of the restaurant, out the back door, and down the hallway to Yazmina's room.

*　　　*　　　*

Isabel took advantage of being alone with Sunny for the first time since her return and said to her in a whisper, 'I have to talk to you.'

Sunny sat down at the table. 'What is it?'

'Candace. And Wakil. She took me to his compound. It's very impressive. But I got a feeling that, well, it's a weird place.'

'Wakil's a weird guy. He's got a pole up his—'

'No, there's something else.'

'Okay, what? You have good instincts about this stuff. Come on, what're you thinking?'

'It was the boys. All young. All very serious. Praying and studying the Koran all day. Lots of money there.'

'And . . .?'

'I'm wondering if the orphanage, the school . . . I wonder if it's a cover. I mean, what happens to the older boys? I'm thinking'—and she looked over her shoulder to be sure Candace wasn't approaching—'that it could be a school for—'

'You mean they're training *terrorists*?' Sunny shook her head, disbelieving.

'It's all about the money. Listen'—Isabel put her hands on the table and stretched forward toward Sunny—'I don't want Candace to know anything until I know for certain, but I'm going to follow Wakil and his money and see where it leads. There was this one boy—'

'You should tell her your concerns, Isabel. Better you tell her yourself than she learn you've been snooping—'

And then Candace appeared at the table, with Yazmina standing behind her. 'Behold the goddess,' Candace said.

Candace was wearing a dress that could've been featured in the pages of *Vogue* by a bold new designer who used Eastern and Western elements as well as modern and old. It was body conscious but draped with fabric as if it had been created by an artist. Yazmina had given the fabric texture where there was none, had created soft gathers and constructed a neckline with a large but soft poet collar that was fresh and yet modest. It fit Candace perfectly and she looked beautiful. The golds lit her face; the purples and blues highlighted her eyes. The dress itself seemed to glow from within.

As she modeled the dress, another customer came over to admire it and asked Yazmina if she'd make her one. Before Yazmina could agree, Candace negotiated the price, excluding the cost of the fabric and any other supplies, and took into her account Yazmina's new baby, her creative brilliance, and the quality of her dresses. Yazmina stood wide-eyed, probably unable to fathom, Isabel figured, the amount of money she'd receive for doing something she loved, that moved her, and that she'd dreamed of.

It was exactly what Candace was good at. Raising money for other people's dreams.

*   *   *

Later, when the coffeehouse was closed, Sunny said to Candace, 'You did a wonderful thing for Yazmina.'

'It's Yazmina who has the talent. Look at this. She's a genius.' She stood and walked three steps, turned, and walked back, like a runway model.

In some ways, Sunny thought, Candace is like

284

a young girl, naive and easily hurt. It was going to be terrible for her if what Isabel said was true. She worried for Candace's safety and knew she had to say something, but she'd have to do it very carefully. 'But you have the business talent. Look what you did for Wakil.'

'Sunny,' Isabel said, putting a hand on her arm.

'Yes, but then, he did something for me, too.' Candace smiled and raised her brows, suggestively. Then she looked back and forth at her two friends and asked, 'What?'

'So you two are still together?'

She felt defensive, and so was not completely honest with her response. 'Not together together, but he did tell me that I am his soul mate. And we each get what we need from the other. Yes, I have been put on the back burner while he attends to more important things, but . . . What's this about, you two? He's got much more important things than me. Men like Wakil—'

'So, what do you think he's doing at the school? Educating the boys for what? College?'

'Sunny!' Isabel said.

'I think it's important that she knows you're concerned.'

Candace shook her head, narrowed her eyes. 'What's going on? Has Isabel been talking to you?' She looked at Isabel. 'I guess it's the cynical journalist in you. Totally suspicious and unable to see the goodness in people. Just because he is Pashtun doesn't make him a Talib.'

'What if I can prove it?'

'Prove what?' But she knew what Isabel was talking about. She got up and pushed her chair up to the table in anger. She gathered her clothes, her

285

bag, and said, 'You know, you're a bitch. A sad, lonely woman who wants to hurt others the way you've been hurt. Not everybody is miserable like you. Not every man is bad like the ones who've hurt you. But I guess you feel better if you think you're not alone. You just want me to be hurt like you were so you have a partner. Funny'—and she laughed through her nose—'I thought we were partners already. But it's not enough for you to help women—you have to drag them down to your level. So, yeah, go prove it.'

She looked at Sunny then. 'You, too. You're both bitches. And I'm through with you.'

And she walked out wearing Yazmina's stunning creation, knowing that something about what Isabel suspected rang true and dug into her heart like a knife.

CHAPTER THIRTY-TWO

The ball thumped against the wall and Poppy caught it in her teeth. Then she loped over to Ahmet, her tail wagging, dropped it at his boots, and he'd pick it up and throw it at the wall again. They'd done it dozens of times when Tommy walked in through the gate. He gave a small wave to Ahmet and entered the coffeehouse.

Sunny was talking to some customers, but that didn't stop Tommy from walking right up to her and kissing her on the cheek. He said, 'So, hey, babe.'

Sunny knew right then it was going to be a day of breakups. It wasn't only because he called her

286

'babe' (even though it made her cringe and she'd asked him repeatedly not to), but because she knew she had to end it finally, once and for all. She was going to say what needed to be said, what she hadn't been able to bring herself to say. Besides, Jack was due back any day, she hoped, and it was important that she be able to tell him it was over and done.

'Tommy, I have to talk to you,' she said. 'Come with me.'

Out in the courtyard, Ahmet and Poppy were into their game. It was warm and the sky was gray and heavy with clouds. The plants were lush and full.

'Ahmet, would you please take Poppy for a walk?'

He sneered at the dog and said, 'You mean, will she walk me? That's what she does. She's definitely the master of this house.' He got her leash from the wall hook and said, 'Come, Poppy, please take me out.'

She turned to Tommy and said, 'We need to talk.'

'Hey, I like what you're doing with the mural,' he said, turning his back to her to admire her work.

She moved in front of him, her back to the toucan and turtle. 'Tommy, look at me,' she pleaded, her voice softening. 'I loved you. I waited for you a long time. A very long time. But now . . . I'm sorry.'

'That's because I wasn't here. Now I'm here and'—he put his hands on Sunny's waist—'you know you'll end it with him sooner or later. And I'll be here waiting.'

'No, Tommy.' She pulled away and looked at the

287

mural—of a jungle, for God's sake, ridiculous!—
and then back at him and said, 'I love him. I hope it
never ends. And that's what I wanted to say to you.
You and I . . . it's over, Tom. Maybe if you hadn't
gone, hadn't been away—but who knows? I think
I've loved Jack all along.'

'If I'd known that taking that job was going to do
this to us—'

'You would've taken it anyway.'

He let out a small laugh. 'Yeah, maybe you're
right. But I want you to know one thing.' He took
her face in his hands. 'I'll always love you.' And
he pulled her to him and he kissed her, hard and
passionately, the way a last kiss should be.

*   *   *

Jack pulled up at the gate, parked his motorbike,
and walked into the courtyard, greeting Ahmet in
the usual way, inquiring about his mother and his
sister in Germany.

Ahmet was still playing fetch with Poppy. A red
ball was in her teeth.

'Hey, Poppy, how are you? Good to see you, girl.
Where's your mom?' He scruffed Poppy's hair.

'Well, I'm thirsty,' he said to Ahmet. 'Want a
Coke?'

'No, thank you. I'm working here, teaching this
old dog some new tricks.'

Jack laughed, thinking he'd never heard Ahmet
make a joke before. He opened the coffeehouse
door and felt so glad to be back. Glad to be alive.
Just damn glad, for crying out loud. This last
mission had been one more kidnapping, one more
senseless death. It was a bad one, and he'd decided

it was going to be his last.

'How are you, Yazmina? Your baby is well?' he asked in Dari when he saw Yazmina cleaning the counter.

'She is the light of my life,' she said as she opened a Coke and brought it to the table. 'And she seems to enjoy the rhythm of this place. She sleeps through the noisy mealtimes when I need to work and then she cries in hunger when it is my rest time. She's a very generous spirit. I only wish Layla was here to see her.'

'We haven't been able to locate her yet. I'm sorry, Yazmina.'

'You were looking?' she asked. 'I wasn't sure.'

'We are looking but haven't found her yet. She could still be at home. We just don't know.'

She shook her head and her eyes filled with tears. 'The men who took me promised to come back for her before the snows melted. And *Nowruz* is almost here.' For Persians, *Nowruz* was the first day of spring, the day when Afghans removed their woodstoves until the following autumn. For Yazmina, it was the day the roads would open, whether there was snow or not.

'We are still working on it, I promise,' Jack said, trying to reassure her.

'They may have taken her already,' she continued, turning away. Then she said, 'Everything is two things. Do you know what I mean, Mr Jack? I am happy with my Najama, and I mourn my Layla.'

'I know,' he answered. 'Life is like that.' He thought for a moment of the end of his marriage and the beginning of his life with Sunny. But then he looked at Yazmina and realized he had to do something more to help her. He sure didn't want to take on something as dangerous as this himself. *Shit,* he thought, *there's got to be someone else. Anyone else.*

'And Layla is only twelve,' Yazmina said.

'I'll keep trying. But I can't promise anything,' Jack said. He had a couple of contacts up there, paid shooters, searching for her uncle's house, somewhere in a mountainous crevice, or watching out for a girl, some brown-haired girl, in the company of men, but it was like asking someone to find a tourist in Times Square. There were hundreds of lone houses in that vicinity and even more Laylas all through Afghanistan. Young girls used as payola. He knew to go in and get Yazmina's sister would mean to hire at least four, maybe five more guys (expensive, but hey, what's money for, anyway?), to pay triple to some cowboy with a helicopter to fly them in (that wouldn't be hard), and then find Layla (which mountain, which hillside with goats, which little house with a fence and green gate, among the hundreds up there?), and then take her with the warlord and his fucking henchmen on their trail all the way back to Kabul, where they'd turn up one night with Uzis and a knife to cut his throat, unless Jack killed them first. The only thing Jack could do to prevent that would be to give the uncle three times the money he owed on his debt. Only then would the bad guys be happy.

'*Tashakur,* thank you,' Yazmina said, lowering her head. 'I would be in your debt.'

'You don't owe me anything.'

'I do. May Allah hear your prayers.'

He took a swig of Coke and heard footsteps from the courtyard. He turned and saw Tommy walking in with Sunny, his arm around her waist. They were

290

laughing, looking like damn lovebirds.

'Jack!' Sunny said, with a stunning smile. 'You're—'

But he was already up, heading to the front door. On his way out he turned to Yazmina and said, 'I'll find your Layla. Don't you worry.'

He heard Sunny's voice behind him, heard her footsteps, but he refused to look at her. He waved good-bye to Ahmet and Poppy, and made it out to the street and onto his motorbike before she could reach him. It's a good thing, he was thinking, as he pulled away with a roar of the engine. He was so angry, so outside of his normal parameters of emotion, he didn't know what he would've done or said if she'd caught up with him.

*   *   *

Sunny ran into the road, yelling for Jack as his motorbike sped off. She was breathing heavily when she got back into the coffeehouse, where Yazmina was explaining everything to Tommy.

Tommy looked up at Sunny and said, 'It's very dangerous, what Jack's going to do. More than any hostage negotiation. Money owed to a drug lord is money owed. And if a girl's been used as payment, there's only one way to get her back. And that's something you don't want to know about.'

'Tommy,' Sunny said, sitting down next to him. 'I've never asked you for anything. But you have to do this for me. You have to help him. Don't let him go up to Nuristan alone. Not like this, not without . . .' Her eyes filled with tears. If she had to get on her hands and knees she would. It wasn't that she didn't think Jack was capable, but that he'd flung

291

himself into a suicide mission because he'd read her smile all wrong.

*   *   *

After Jack didn't return her dozens of calls, Sunny went to the supply room, took out the bucket of old leftover paint used for inside the coffeehouse, brought it to the front courtyard, looked at her dirty wall, which was a complete mess, after stupid attempt on top of stupid attempt, opened the can, and threw the paint on the mural. Again and again.

When Bashir Hadi saw what she was doing, he ran out. 'Stop, please, Miss Sunny! Stop!'

But she ignored him. Only when the can was empty did she stop. The paint was dripping down the wall, and she put her two hands right into it and began to move the paint, like a child at nursery school, to spread the paint everywhere, her tears coming, then, and she turned to him, wiped the hair that had fallen into her face with her upper arm, and said, 'Help me.'

He went back into the café, silently. And she watched him, the backs of her hands on her hips. She'd already gotten paint on her jeans, so a little more wasn't going to hurt.

He returned with two rollers, handed Sunny one, and with the other began to spread the wet paint over the charcoal mistakes. Sunny wasn't satisfied until every inch was covered.

When it was finished, Bashir Hadi asked her, 'Why? It could've been a beautiful thing.'

'It was a stupid idea. A jungle in Kabul?'

'Are you joking with me? It's a jungle out there! A whole lot of monkeys in Kabul!'

292

Sunny laughed a little through her tears but turned to Bashir Hadi and said, 'You tell me, Bashir Hadi, what is all this?' She flailed her arms. 'It's not fair. I'm sick of it. And now Jack's heart is broken. How is that fair? How is that right? There should be some correlation between being good and having a good life.'

'Life isn't like that. Is that why you cry, Miss Sunny?'

'Why do I cry? Why, you ask?' she yelled, flinging her arms wide and feeling completely out of control, as all her anger and sadness and frustration spilled out. 'Life here is horrible. It's wonderful. It's dangerous. It's home. I hate it. My loved ones are here. My family. And yet, it's probably time to go. I love Jack. I hate him.'

'But your house has not burned down,' Bashir Hadi replied. He turned around to face the wall and said, with a lowered voice, 'I am sorry, Miss Sunny, I apologize, it's just—'

'What do you mean, "burned down"? What is it, Bashir Hadi?' She softened her voice. 'Say what's on your mind.'

'All I mean to say is that your house, it stands. Look at this. Look at what you have.' He gestured to the coffeehouse. 'In Afghanistan, you cry when your house burns down with everything and everyone in it.'

'So you think because you have lived through such terrible troubles that you get to determine when I can cry? Your life, Bashir Hadi, hasn't been so bad either.'

'Do you know one thing about me?' he asked. When she didn't answer, he continued, 'Do you? Tell me.' He crossed his arms, waiting.

'I know your lovely wife, Sharifa, and your two children, who are beautiful and good students and—'

'Do you know my son has trouble learning to read? That he sees a special doctor and much of my salary goes to that? Do you know that my wife's mother is ill and will probably die before Ramadan?'

Sunny shook her head and said, 'I didn't know. I'm sorry, I guess I thought if anything was wrong, you'd tell me.'

'Am I crying because I have difficult things happening to my family? They are *alive*. And so I am celebrating.' He kicked a stone into the wall. 'The only thing that makes the Afghan cry is war and hunger and losing an arm in a blast, and . . . people who think only about themselves. I am sorry, Miss Sunny, to talk to you this way. But there is a wise old Western saying that sums it all up: Shit happens. Excuse me, you are the boss, after all, but you Americans, I hear you talk in the coffeehouse every day and every night, revealing your personal problems. You expect so much, you feel that you deserve good things to come your way, and yet you understand so little. Afghanistan is hard and not only hard for you foreigners. You can leave and get a job and see a doctor and go to college and buy whatever you want. We are trapped here always. You whine and moan over little things, and we're the ones who have to clean up after you.'

She was shocked at the depth of his feeling. 'I'm sorry, Bashir Hadi. I didn't realize. I'm such an idiot. I hadn't wanted to intrude in your life. You are a very private man, and I have much respect for you.'

'None of that matters. What I'm talking about is that Jack will come back. Alive and well. But don't you see? Your tears aren't for a philosophical principle of who is deserving or what is just, but because of your own heart.'

'But Jack thought . . . and it wasn't what he thought.'

'It doesn't matter what he thought. He'll be back. What would he do without . . . his crispy potatoes every morning?'

He smiled, and Sunny laughed again, then moved as close as she could to him while still keeping an appropriate physical distance. 'You are my friend. And I care about you. Maybe you need to get a little more American in you and talk more about things you think about. The more you say, the more I know. Now tell me more about your son. Does he see a doctor at the German clinic?'

Sunny sat in one of the patio chairs and pulled one out for Bashir Hadi. Eventually he sat, but only after he said, 'You will paint a mural on the wall, right? We can't have it looking like this. Easter will be here soon, and we had a pact: The wall will be finished by Easter.'

CHAPTER THIRTY-THREE

Ahmet had arranged in advance for Khalid to work as *chokidor* at the coffeehouse for the morning. He said his morning prayers on the small rug in his room and drove Sunny's car to the road across the river from the Mondai-e to the tailor's shop behind the red and white Coca-Cola umbrella. The letter from Rashif to his mother felt as heavy as a stone in his pants pocket and weighed on him with its complete repudiation of acceptable behavior. The knife he carried weighed even more.

When he got there, he went inside, closing the thin door behind him. Rashif was wearing reading glasses and was bent over a small sewing table with a lone lightbulb hanging over it. Surrounding him were vests and pants, jackets and dresses, hanging above from wire hangers. The whirr of the sewing machine prevented him from hearing the door open and close, and by the time he looked up, Ahmet was looming over him.

'*Salaam alaikum,*' said Rashif kindly, as he stood. 'You surprised me.' He removed his glasses, which hung on a black cord around his neck.

'*Wa alaikum as-salaam,*' replied Ahmet, politely, but his hands were clenched, perspiring.

'And how may I help you?' asked Rashif. 'You have something to be altered?'

'I have this.' He put his hand into his pocket, took out the letter, and hammered it onto the table with his fist.

'My letter,' Rashif said calmly. 'Where did you find that? Wait—I know you,' he said, smiling. 'Sometimes when I sew, it takes my eyes some time to refocus. You are Ahmet. I am so pleased to see you.' And he started to hug him, but Ahmet pulled away with such a violent force that he pushed Rashif into the table, almost toppling it over.

'You have shamed my family, sir.'

Rashif's shoulders sank and he shook his head. 'Young man, how can my letter shame you?'

'You have made my mother unclean! I am not the son of a whore.' He moved his vest aside to show the knife hanging from his belt.

'You come to kill? Why? Where is it written that such a letter is wrong? There is no husband here. There is no wife. Yes, they'd be dishonored if there were, because adultery is forbidden. But here both husband and wife are long dead. How can a simple letter between a widow and widower bring shame?'

'It is not one letter. It is years of letters! It is the words of a husband to a wife.'

'Did you read them, Ahmet? Now, that would be wrong.'

'I read only one or two,' Ahmet lied. 'To protect our family. This is my mother you have destroyed. My family!' He laughed. 'And here is the irony: My mother cannot even read.'

Rashif sat. 'I know she does not. I think I've known for some time but only recently have I known for sure. But that is exactly what love is. To write, unread. To travel far each week to receive that which is unattainable. Muhammad knew the truth about love. It doesn't come often. And there is no reason when it comes to love—pretty or not, young or old—so go figure.'

'Do not talk to me of love!' Ahmet bellowed. But he thought of Yazmina and how his feelings for her could not be explained. Then he remembered his duty. 'This isn't a girl. It's my mother. An old woman!'

'And I am an old man.'

'Who has no respect for the traditions. Who has a history of laughing at tradition and aligning yourself with the West. You bring shame into our house. I have come for one reason only,' Ahmet said, now taking out his knife, clenching it in his hand.

297

'Killing me for no reason will only bring more shame. The West, you say?' He stood, his brow furrowed, his temper clearly rising. 'Helping our own countrymen to find their lives again when they return to Motherland Afghanistan? That is a bad thing? Under whose eyes? Allah's? Show me in the Koran where it speaks so! And your mother? It is known that Muhammad married women whose husbands had died!' He stopped, drew in a deep breath, and sat once more.

'Then there is only one other thing to do,' Ahmet said, his knife pointed at Rashif. 'You will marry her.'

Rashif smiled at first, and then stopped. He lowered his head respectfully and said, 'I know I must pay for my transgressions. I will make restitution. I will marry Halajan, your mother.'

'And you will pray to Allah for forgiveness.'

'Yes, I will pray.'

Ahmet felt lightheaded, as if the rage and self-righteousness that had lifted from his body made him like a feather in the wind. He put the knife back in its sheath and leaned against the wall.

'Will you sit?' Rashif asked. 'We can discuss the details of the marriage agreement. I will pour us some tea.'

Ahmet sat and Rashif went to his back room, where he had a sink and a hot plate, and prepared the *chai*.

Carrying a small tray with a teapot and two cups, Rashif said, 'You are a good son, Ahmet, to protect your mother so. But what about your own happiness?'

'Me? I eat, I pray. I am happy.'

'But what about a wife? Will you marry one day?'

298

Ahmet sipped from his cup and then put it down with a sigh. It was a long time before he spoke. 'There is one,' he confessed. It was odd how he could say such things to Rashif, as if he was already family. 'She has eyes like the forest in springtime.'

Rashif nodded. 'Remember that life is short and full of surprises. If you wait too long, opportunities fade like the setting sun.'

'She still mourns her dead husband.'

'Here is something I've learned, if I may offer it to you. What is in our hearts is never a one-way street. Only as children when we're too young to understand the signs do we love unrequitedly. If you love, it's because you feel its power reflected back on you.'

'She has a baby who she says is her dead husband's. She has a baby!' he yelled, slamming a fist onto the table.

'That only proves she was a good, loving wife. And that she is a loving mother.'

'If only there was no baby,' Ahmet said, barely hearing what Rashif was saying.

'You know what Muhammad would say. She deserves to be loved. Baby or not.'

Ahmet sipped his tea, feeling very uneasy about more mentions of love. Men he knew would never talk this way. Maybe it was Rashif's age, or his life experience, but there was something about him that made it almost acceptable to discuss such things aloud.

'The baby is a fact. She must be accepted,' said Rashif.

'That might prove impossible,' Ahmet said stiffly.

'I know you would never hurt the baby.'

'Of course not,' said Ahmet dismissively.

299

'Or try to give it away.'

Ahmet was unable to respond to this.

So Rashif said, 'Sometimes another power can take control of a man's will and darken him with terrible thoughts that lead to terrible deeds.'

'What do you mean by that? That I do not have full control over my deeds?'

'No, only that sometimes a man needs all the help he can get in order to keep him righteous in the eyes of God.'

The two men sat silent for a while. Ahmet looked up at Rashif and saw concern etched on his face.

Finally Rashif spoke. 'A thought occurs to me. Love makes all things possible. So, should you ever need someone to act as your father's proxy, since he is no longer alive, to ask a woman of your mother's choosing to marry you, I could be that man.'

Ahmet put the notion, with Rashif's letter, in his pocket for safekeeping. He repeated, 'If there was no baby . . . But when you speak of this to my mother—and I know you will—reassure her that I would never hurt the baby.'

When he got back to the coffeehouse, Sunny was working at the counter, Bashir Hadi was in the kitchen, and Yazmina was sweeping the floors, the baby attached to her chest with the long scarf.

'Hello, Yazmina,' he said softly, standing several arm lengths away.

'Ahmet, good day,' she answered, without looking directly at him. The baby cooed. Yazmina leaned her broom against the wall and moved aside the fabric of her sling to see her baby's face. She smiled.

Ahmet actually liked the baby. He liked her smell, the little gurgles she made, but most of all he liked her reflection in Yazmina's eyes. Never had a baby been so loved, he was certain of that. He only wished her eyes would look at him with a portion of that love.

And then Yazmina looked up at him. She smiled, her eyes glistening like stones in a river. He smiled back and fought the desire that surged through him to take her in his arms and hold her that way forever.

Could Rashif be correct, Ahmet wondered, that if he felt that way about her, perhaps she felt the same about him? That love made the impossible possible? One day soon, maybe, *Inshallah,* with Muhammad's help, he would find the strength to test that theory.

CHAPTER THIRTY-FOUR

'I know you're still upset, but we promised we'd try,' implored Isabel, sitting with Candace in the back of a black SUV. 'You can be angry at me, but don't take it out on those women.' They were on their way to a fund-raising meeting with representatives from American women's aid groups.

'Well, it's not as if any of this is rocket science,' Candace replied.

'But the bureaucracy, the red tape—'

'What red tape? All you need is cash and you can accomplish anything in Afghanistan.'

'I'm not so sure. There are extreme attitudes to contend with.'

'Money talks. You'll see.'

'So we're still partners. Not just this meeting—'

'On one condition: Unless you have real, hard proof, you keep your suspicions about Wakil to yourself.'

'Understood.'

Candace looked out the window and saw two boys running with kites trailing behind them, held aloft by the wind. One turned and ran backward as he pulled on the kite's string, and she wanted to scream out to him to watch his footing, don't trip in the gutter, but, as if he'd heard her, he turned around and caught himself in time.

She put a hand to her cheek, turned back to Isabel, and said, 'But if you find anything real, which you won't, you tell me.'

'It's a deal.'

'Okay then. Let's do this meeting. You do your job—have all the information including the number of women behind bars, the so-called crimes they committed, the conditions, et cetera—and I'll do mine.'

Isabel put a hand on Candace's arm. 'We can do this.'

*   *   *

Days had passed and there wasn't a word from Tommy or Jack. Sunny knew they'd left together, because Tommy had called her one last time before leaving Kabul to let her know they were on their way to the north. She wouldn't be able to call them again, nor could they call her, because they'd be using untraceable phones. Sunny was beside herself with worry, but there was nothing she could do. They were completely on their own, without the support of an agency or even anyone else who might

302

know where they were.

She kept busy in the coffeehouse, which was bringing in excellent business. From early morning to late at night the place seemed to buzz with activity. But her friends were elsewhere: Candace and Isabel were attending daily meetings.

Sunny was lonely. The coffeehouse was filled with people and yet *her* people were gone. And for the first time in her years in Kabul, she felt uneasy. The police and military on the streets seemed to have doubled in recent weeks, as if something was coming, something furious and uncontrollable. The *wop-wop-wop* of helicopters washed the skies, along with the muezzin's calls. The increase of people at the coffeehouse was good for business but bad for its implication: People had stopped going to many restaurants and clubs and were going only to places authorized as safe, as if they were all waiting for the next shoe to drop.

News reports were bleak. There was a sense of impending trouble, and no wall, no matter how high, and no windows, no matter how strong, were any match for what might come.

She was on the roof after the breakfast crowd left, while Yazmina and Bashir Hadi were making the place ready for lunch. She was sitting on the bench, looking out over her troubled city, missing Jack, her skin tingling with memories of his touch, his mere presence. A flock of birds flew by in that miracle V formation, their wings fluttering hard and their bodies black against the vibrant blue sky, and just for a moment, she was up there with them. She, too, was flying over Kabul, watching it change and its people be moved by the whims of power— like a tree in the wind. And she remembered the

303

other time when she felt so overtaken by a place, a moment. It was at Mazar-e Sharif.

Then she saw the birds swoop down and disappear from sight. She could still hear their calls, as if they were right outside. She ran downstairs and into the courtyard, the warbles and calls loud and crackling. The few trees were rustling with life; their leaves seemed to be lusher, deeper, thicker.

She saw again the large plaza at the mosque covered with doves and the women in the white burqas, and she turned, got her paints, and began to mix the colors herself. There was no compromising. She finally saw the mural in her mind and knew she wouldn't be satisfied until she got the colors just right, even if she had to re-create them on her palette. This time she didn't need charcoal or sketching. This time she'd begin with brushes and paint. She spent hours experimenting until she was satisfied. Nothing was perfect. But she was in Kabul, after all, and not in Jonesboro at the Country Roads Mall with a Home Depot and Michaels, the craft store that was crowded with the scrapbook-crazed. She had to make do with what she had. *Indigenous*—was that the word Isabel had used?

Finally she dipped her brush into the paint of her palette. She put the brush to the wall, the paint to the rough surface. Yes, she thought, after a few strokes, taking a step back. It was, indeed, the most beautiful blue.

*   *   *

It took little time for Candace and Isabel to raise enough money to bribe the prison warden for

Jamila and her friends' freedom. But that was just a start. They'd have to find places to house them, money to feed them, medical care, schools for their children, and, of course, security so that they'd be safe from family members who wanted them dead because of the shame they had brought upon them.

First Jamila, and then, hopefully, Candace and Isabel would be in the position to help more women across the country. With the support of various international women's aid groups, they intended to create a shelter system for women to prevent them from being incarcerated, and a safe haven for those once out.

But Isabel knew, from her years in Africa and the Gulf, that bribing a warden was one thing; dealing with hundreds of years of repressive attitudes was another.

Protecting Jamila, who had escaped from the men who'd been pimping her, often several times a day, for pennies to any man who could pay, wouldn't be easy. The men who'd bought her when she'd been sold to repay a debt would want the return on their investment and would be after her to put her back to work as a prostitute. Or they'd simply kill her. Isabel knew she'd have to get her out of the country to keep her alive.

At the prison, Isabel admired Candace's deft way with the warden and the guards, and soon they were in the women's building, walking its long, dank hall toward Jamila's cell. When they got there, the women were huddled in the far corner; one child was lying across his mother's lap, asleep. Candace and Isabel looked for a familiar face but couldn't find one until Haliya came forward, her head and face fully covered with a large scarf as always.

She approached the blue bars and put her hand around one, her fingernails blackened from dirt, and whispered in broken English, 'Jamila is gone. They took her.'

'What do you mean? To another cell?' asked Isabel, in her broken Dari. And in that way, the women were able to make themselves understood.

'No, they took her away.'

'Who did? Where?'

'The guards came with the men. Jamila cried, so I think she knew that they meant to finish what they'd started. To take her to Bahrain, Dubai, or Qatar to work for them.'

'Jesus. Those motherfu—' Candace started to say but stopped herself, her teeth clenched, her jaw tight.

'The Gulf area,' Isabel said, knowing what this meant. 'When was this?'

'Two days ago, more or less.'

'Let's go,' said Isabel, patting Candace's shoulder with the back of her hand.

'Will you try to find her?' asked Haliya.

'Yes,' answered Candace. 'We will.'

But Isabel knew it would be impossible. The Gulf was like quicksand where women sank, suffocated, and died beneath the sexual morass of being bought and sold against their will. There was no way they would ever find Jamila in the Gulf, where she'd be put to work as a sex slave for local laborers. She was gone. The thought made Isabel sick.

All she could do was hope, even pray, that the Gulf wasn't Layla's fate as well.

It would be days before Candace would accept the fact that there was nothing they could do. But during that time, they made arrangements,

306

with the magic of bribery, the way all things were accomplished in Afghanistan, to get Haliya and the others released.

* * *

The black car was met by two security guards with machine guns over their shoulders at the gate of the Serena Hotel. One guard said something to the driver, who rolled down the windows so they could search the inside of the car. The guards leaned their heads in, first examining the front seat, and then the back, where the women sat cross-legged. The guard commanded the driver to open the trunk and the hood. Then they checked underneath the car with a mirror on a long handle, and only then, apparently satisfied, waved the car through. The driveway was long and U-shaped and made of a light-gray stone. In the center of the drive was a thick carpet of grass surrounded by small flowers, and sitting in the middle, a large marble fountain with water spouting twenty feet into the air before cascading down a sculpture of a large fish.

Isabel watched from her rear window and seethed with anger. Here the Afghan government provided police, here they provided security and protection, because here were Westerners, here was money, here was political power. In the prison, they provided nothing to their own people, to women and children who barely had enough bread and water to survive. They provided no clothes or schooling or beds, and only threadbare blankets to withstand the cold. She shook her head and pounded her fist on the car door's handle.

'We're almost there,' said Candace, gently

patting Isabel's hand.

Isabel looked at her and breathed out, wondering if she, too, was raging. 'Can you believe this place?' she asked.

'What did you expect?' answered Candace. 'This ain't no democracy. Come on, you've seen this before a thousand times.'

'And it always gets to me. But more here than anywhere.'

'That's because you're in it now. You've drunk the Kool-Aid.'

Isabel raised her brows and said, 'Indeed I have, haven't I.'

'And I'm proud of you,' Candace said.

'The last time someone said that to me, it was my own mother.'

She thought back to her home in London, the house where she grew up, going to her school with only British girls, the 'Pakis' going to their schools, the blacks going to their schools, the neighborhoods divided by history, color, and language. And then she remembered something her mother had told her before she died. 'You will find that thing that makes you unafraid to die. That important thing that makes your life of value.' All these years, Isabel thought that being a journalist was the thing of value that she was bringing to the party. Now she knew there was more. Now she knew that a person had to act, to be truly engaged, in order to make a real difference. *Mum,* Isabel thought, *it's taken me eons to understand. But now I do.*

At the front, the women got out and walked up the few steps to the atrium leading to the hand-carved wooden doors. Isabel led the way and said, 'Here's good,' at a sofa that looked out from

308

the wall of windows onto a tree-filled courtyard.

The women sat, Isabel on the sofa that faced the entrance and Candace adjacent to her in a low armchair covered in a woven fabric with a geometric design. The lobby had the same maroon and orange Afghan colors of the warden's rooms in the prison, Isabel noticed. The minute they sat, they were approached by a young man in a freshly pressed, crisp *shalwaar kameez* and embroidered vest, and asked if they wanted something to drink. Something about him looks familiar, she thought.

Candace ordered tea, but Isabel was distracted. The waiter repeated the question.

'Yes, yes, tea for me, too, please,' Isabel answered. She still couldn't place him.

They waited quietly for their guests to arrive.

The waiter returned with small plates of *kish mish*. As he stood, he looked directly at Isabel before walking away. A shiver ran through her. She'd seen those eyes before and figured they were the eyes of so many Afghans or other people living in third world countries who worked in places like this, serving wealthy Westerners. But there was something about this particular man. She knew for sure that she'd seen him before.

She watched him pause in the doorway, behind Candace, and perhaps it was the angle and the distance, but she remembered where she'd seen him before. It was at Wakil's school, the same young man who'd driven off in the car after talking to Wakil.

She stood up, unsure why, on instinct.

At that moment he shouted in Dari, 'Death to the Western oppressors! *Allah akbar!*' a phrase she'd heard before in many languages all around the world.

Isabel cried out, 'Oh my God. We have to—'

And then he put his hand in his vest.

She threw herself on Candace.

The force of the explosion shattered walls and windows. She lost all hearing, pain shot through her neck, and blood gushed into her mouth. She coughed and screamed, she thought, and fought for air. But little came. *Wakil,* she tried to whisper to Candace, who was underneath her. *Wakil!* Then she saw her mother, sitting on her bed reading to her. She could smell her perfume, feel the silk of her blouse, feel her hand stroking her hair. And then she saw Jamila's face, her dark eyes pleading for help. *Jamila,* she thought, *Jamila.* There was so much left to do! Layla! She told herself not to panic. There was so much left to do. She thought she heard someone say her name. Then she closed her eyes.

*　　*　　*

Sunny painted the entire background of the mural the color of the Afghan sky that day in Mazar-e Sharif when the sun was high and reflected in the blue and gold tiles of the mosque. She used the same roller that she and Bashir Hadi had used to whitewash the old mural. She could feel the weight of the paint in her shoulder as her arm dipped and then rolled up and down again and again. She stood on a wooden box from the storage room so she could reach the top of the wall.

Once the background was done, she began to use smaller brushes to get the images just right. White was easy, but the off-white and shadows, the gold of the roof in the sunlight, took time, was harder to achieve.

But the doves came, the doves and the women who looked like doves, a few larger, closer, many smaller in the distance, the mural emulating the courtyard she experienced that day at Mazar-e Sharif.

She was in the midst of painting her sixth dove, getting its neck right. This wasn't a photograph, of course, so there was room for artistic license, but they had to look like the beautiful doves she remembered. She had dipped her smaller brush into the white circle of paint on her palette, and was reaching for the wall when the earth rumbled and she heard something that sounded like distant thunder. It sent a current of fear through her as if she'd been struck by a bolt of lightning.

But not one window was shattered. The wall stood, but a car alarm went off, and then another. Birds flew from the trees and over the roof, and the sky blackened with soot. When she ran into the coffeehouse to check the radio for news, it was as silent as a church, though it was filled with customers who were frozen with fear. She turned on the radio and quickly learned there had been a suicide bombing inside the Serena Hotel, followed seconds later by another near the U.S. Embassy and another at the circle less than a mile from the coffee shop. Soon, the customers returned to their conversations, now in hushed voices of concern, and Sunny hoped with every ounce of her being that her friends were safe.

CHAPTER THIRTY-FIVE

Sunny sat at Candace's bedside at the emergency hospital, holding her hand, waiting for her to regain consciousness. She'd just come out of surgery for her leg, which was broken in seven places and required two pins. Her face and arms were covered in scratches; her head required fifty-seven stitches. Had the wooden shard hit her any lower, she might've been killed. But as it was, she'd be fine soon enough, the doctor had told Sunny.

It wasn't long before her eyelids fluttered open.

'Sunny.' She smiled, squeezing her hand. 'Am I glad to see you.'

'You, too.'

'Everything hurts.'

'You're going to be fine. Just no high heels for a few months.'

Candace tried to raise her head to look down at her body but couldn't.

'The doctor said he'd be here soon to explain everything. So just relax.'

'It was terrible. The explosion . . . wait, how's Isabel? Where—'

'Candace,' Sunny began, and then stopped. She looked away.

'Was she hurt? She threw herself on me. She must've seen it coming, and she threw herself right on top of me. I thought I heard her try to tell me . . .'

'Candace,' Sunny said again, and then, she couldn't help it and she began to cry.

'Sunny, what is it? Tell me.'

'She's gone. We've lost our girl.'

'Oh, God,' cried Candace. 'Oh, no.'

Isabel was dead. She'd acted as a blanket for Candace, protecting her from the worst of the broken windows and falling beams, while taking their deathly impact herself.

As Sunny held Candace, they both cried.

'She saved my life.'

Sunny squeezed Candace's hand.

'She was one brave and stupid Brit.'

Sunny laughed a little.

Candace continued, 'I hate her for doing that. Her life was so much more . . . much more . . . than mine.'

'How can you say that?' Sunny said. 'You—'

'We were sitting three feet away from each other!' Candace interrupted, shaking her head. 'One dies, the other breaks her fucking leg?' She began to cry again, this time uncontrollably.

'There is no making sense of it. There are no rules and no reason.' Tears streamed down Sunny's cheeks as she remembered a tornado that came through their town when she was a kid. It decimated an entire neighborhood, but every so often, it would jump a house, leaving it intact, while destroying the house next door and every other house on the street. What luck is that? What luck kills one friend when the other requires a few bandages and a cast for eight weeks?

Candace must've been thinking the same thing because she said, 'But she threw herself on me.'

'I know.'

'It should've been me. Her life was so—'

'It should've been neither of you. Or any of the others.'

313

'But Isabel! She was the one who got me . . . who tried to warn me . . . about Wakil.' She looked away in tears.

Sunny recalled what Bashir Hadi said to her in anger that day, and she said it to Candace. 'But you were helping her, too. Who's good and who's bad, who's to judge? Nobody can, so there is no justice when it comes to what happens in life.'

'Please,' said Candace, 'spare me the pep talk.'

Sunny squeezed her hand again, pleased that she was her old self.

'What I'm trying to say,' Candace continued, 'is that Isabel tried to tell me about Wakil and though I had a gut feeling she might be right, I didn't listen. But when I saw that waiter, the one with the bomb, I recognized him immediately from Wakil's school. I was about to say something, but then . . .'

Sunny put her hand on Candace's face and wiped her tears with her thumb. She whispered, 'There was nothing you could've done.'

'He couldn't have known we'd be at that hotel on that day, could he? It was just our dumb luck, right? You think Wakil meant . . .?'

'No, there's no way.'

'As soon as I'm out of here, I'm going to the embassy.' Candace looked up at Sunny with a fierce gaze. 'It's one thing to steal my money. It's another to steal my friend.'

'Not the embassy. They won't do a damned thing. I have a better idea. Remember that night we drank a little too much and talked about our pasts?'

'You mean with men? I think I know where you're going with this. Isabel's army guy.'

'Exactly.'

'I know he'll follow up on Wakil once he hears

314

about Isabel,' Sunny said. 'If only I could remember his name.'

'Stewart,' Candace said. 'General Stewart. Stationed in the south somewhere.' Then she smiled sweetly and started to cry again. 'Isabel would be glad to know that *shagging* a general had a higher purpose.'

Sunny laughed. 'General Stewart, you may have been a *wanker,* but your past is coming back to haunt you. You have no idea.'

CHAPTER THIRTY-SIX

It was early morning and the emotional residue from the bombings lay over the café like a thick black coat of soot. Bashir Hadi silently prepared the coffeemaker and Sunny sat on a stool at the counter, signing the papers and making the final arrangements for shipping Isabel's body to London. It was overwhelming, but she knew that Isabel would want to be buried with her parents. Sunny still couldn't believe she was gone, that Isabel, with her prickly nature and her mushy interior, with her *fags* and her *mobile* and her *mad lovely* self, wouldn't walk into the café, nudging Sunny to laugh and think. She slammed her hand down hard on the counter. She immediately turned to Bashir Hadi, who had turned to her. They nodded and went back to their tasks.

She opened her computer, hoping for an email from Jack but knowing better. Where he was there were no computers, and besides, she couldn't be sure he was even still alive. There'd been no contact from Tommy or Jack since the day they left.

The quiet was broken when Yazmina ran into the coffeehouse screaming.

'My baby! Najama! She is gone!'

Sunny and Bashir Hadi ran to her.

'What do you mean, gone?' Bashhir Hadi asked.

'She is not in her bed. She is not in my room.' The fear on her face was etched as deep as the dry gorge of the Kabul River. She began to choke on her sobs.

Sunny put her hand on her arm to soothe her. 'Did you see someone come into your room? Last night? This morning?'

'No, I saw no one.'

Then Sunny asked, 'Did you leave the baby alone in your room even for a moment?'

And Yazmina looked up and said, 'Yes. This morning, while I was in the *tashnab*. But who would've—?' And then she stopped and looked at them, her eyes wide. She knew the answer to her own question. 'Ahmet,' she said, and she sank to the floor sobbing.

'But why would he do that?' Bashir Hadi asked.

'He threatened us the day the baby was born. He was so angry.'

'I'm sorry, but I don't see Ahmet stealing your baby. He loves her. He loves you.'

Yazmina's eyes lowered in embarrassment when she heard his words.

'But she's shamed him. He is not a man like you, Bashir Hadi,' Sunny said. 'We don't have time to argue. He could be selling the baby as we speak!'

'Please, wait a minute. Let's think. Someone has taken the baby, but I just don't think—'

'Well, I'm going out with Poppy in the car to

316

try to track him down. Where would he have taken her? What would he do with her? You don't think—'

'No, I don't. Not for one minute. Ahmet may be stubborn and old in his thinking, but I . . . And where's Halajan? I wonder—'

And Sunny suddenly realized what he meant and she ran out the door and up the stairs to Halajan's apartment and banged on her door. She could hear Bashir Hadi's voice yelling to her. When no one answered, she ran back down into the coffeehouse.

There was Ahmet, helping Yazmina up and into a chair.

'It's my mother,' he said, 'I'm sure of it.'

And Sunny replayed their conversations and Halajan's words about Yazmina's life being in danger, about her being perceived as a *fahesha* in the eyes of the Afghans, promising to do whatever it would take to save Yazmina's life. And giving the baby to a hospital when the baby was strong enough to be separated from her mother, in about a month or two, Halajan had said. Sunny realized then that it was six weeks to the day that Najama was born. And the bombings must've made Halajan's fears for Yazmina living on the street even greater. She could almost hear her thoughts: The baby would make Yazmina a pariah in the eyes of her son. He would throw them out on the street, and with no protection, a bombing, like the recent ones, would surely kill them both.

'I know where she might be,' she said. 'Bashir Hadi, please hold down the fort. Yazmina and Ahmet, let's go.' And she grabbed her bag, threw on her chador, and ran out with Poppy following behind.

*   *   *

They left Poppy to guard the car while they were in the hospital. Sure enough, the receptionist said an old woman had come in an hour before with a baby she'd found in the street, she'd said. She'd taken it to the maternity ward, where a doctor would check on the status of the baby's health.

The three of them ran down the dark hallway and made the first left as they were told. And there, in the blue-walled waiting room, was Halajan, rocking Najama in her arms and singing to her softly under a lone dim lightbulb. Halajan was crying, her tears landing softly on the baby's blanket.

'Halajan,' Sunny said. She let out a sigh that was as big as the breath she'd been holding for the past half hour.

'I thought you loved the baby!' cried Yazmina. 'Why now? I thought we had made a good life.'

The old woman in the tattered brown clothes stood and screamed, 'You will not hurt her! Do not come closer!'

She was looking directly at Ahmet, accusation exuding from every pore of her body. She held the baby close. 'Don't you see? He will hurt her. He will sell her or kill her! Rashif told me what you said, Ahmet. He didn't believe you would harm the baby, but then the bombs happened and showed me again that belief in goodness is stupid. I cannot take any chances.'

Ahmet collapsed into a chair. 'I did say words to Rashif that were in my heart, but I thought he knew they were only words. I never would . . . never!'

318

'He didn't think you would. He only told me so that I might protect you, my son.' Halajan looked then at Yazmina, the corners of her mouth turning down, her eyes filling with tears. 'Even if Ahmet has no ill intentions for the baby, you are not safe. As long as you hide in the coffeehouse, you might be. But if you venture outside, Yazmina, they will kill you. And I couldn't bear that. I love you and I love Najama. I don't know what I'd do if—'

'You can't give away her baby, Mother. That will kill her, too,' Ahmet pleaded gently. He stood up and walked to her slowly. She turned away, but then he put a hand on her shoulder. 'Mother, Najama must be with her mother.'

Halajan looked into his eyes, as if trying to read what was behind them.

Ahmet reached out slowly and gently took the baby from his mother. He cradled her in his arms while looking lovingly into her face.

Yazmina looked at him with grateful eyes.

'But she is like a daughter to me. Shall I lose her, too? I lose one to Germany and now lose another to our stupid way of thinking? To hands like yours, Ahmet.'

Ahmet looked as if a sword had pierced through him, body and soul. 'Mother, I would never hurt Yazmina. And I would never let anyone hurt her or the baby. This baby is like my very own.'

Sunny stood silently, hoping mother and son would figure this out. She looked at Yazmina. Her eyes were as wide as the sea, as if she couldn't believe Ahmet's appeals on her behalf.

'Besides, Mother, I have an idea that Rashif offered to propose to Yazmina. But I suppose he told you that, too.'

319

'No, my son, he didn't speak of your entire conversation, only that he was concerned for you,' said Halajan.

'Well, it's a long story, but,' he said looking at Yazmina, his face opening into a sweet smile, 'I am so shy with you. I don't know why. I've so wanted to talk to you, to tell you that . . .' He paused, looked down in thought, then directly at Sunny and said, 'You said the baby was yours. And Mother, you said the baby was yours. But the truth is'—and now he looked at Yazmina—'the baby is mine. She has always been mine since the moment you came to our coffeehouse. And if you will have me, I will be Najama's father and your husband. That is, of course, if you, Mother, agree to the match.'

Halajan sobbed, answering only with her tears.

'You're a good man, Ahmet,' Sunny said softly.

'Mother?' he asked Halajan, his eyes pleading for her approval.

Halajan stood and said, 'I have never been prouder than I am today. You have become the man I always dreamed you would be.' And she reached up to kiss him on both cheeks.

Ahmet turned to Yazmina and said, 'And you? Will you have me? I know this is very modern, to ask you like this, here, directly. But there it is.'

All eyes in the room turned to Yazmina, whose tears were streaming down her face. She looked down to her feet, then to Halajan, then to Ahmet holding her precious one so sweetly, and said, 'Some modern is good. You are a fine man, Ahmet. I never thought this day would come. I have wanted it for so long.'

'So, yes? Your answer is yes?' he said excitedly.

'Yes,' Yazmina said.

320

Then Ahmet sat, feeling slightly dizzy, on a red vinyl chair and took a deep breath in to steady himself. 'I have been arguing with myself for weeks now. It's very tiring.'

'Son,' Halajan said, 'I believe that baby is blessed with love. She changes everyone who holds her.'

Yazmina nodded with a smile.

Ahmet pulled Najama to his chest and lowered his face to her face and said, 'I will protect you and your mother always.'

Sunny opened her cellphone and said, 'Bashir Hadi, we have Najama. We're coming home.'

*　　*　　*

Later that night, once the coffeehouse was closed, Halajan was in her sleeping room, taking off her scarf, when there was a knock on her door. She put the scarf back on her head, wrapped it around her neck, and opened the door.

It was Ahmet.

'Come in,' she said, closing the door behind him.

'I have something to say to you,' he said.

He looked terribly serious, worrying Halajan that he'd changed his mind, that the traditionalist teachings had gotten the better of him.

'Rashif,' he said.

Halajan's heart dropped. She thought she would faint. She leaned on the wall, felt her body's weight against it. What had happened? What more could happen?

'You will marry him,' he said.

For once in her whole long life, she couldn't speak.

'Because,' Ahmet continued, and now he smiled

widely and without guile, 'because he loves you, and I have a strong feeling that you love him as well. And there is the matter of the letters, of course. Entirely improper.' He smiled again.

And Halajan took her son, her boy, in her arms and held him the way she had when he was too young to protest, before there were talks of love and letters and marriage.

CHAPTER THIRTY-SEVEN

Loss hit Sunny hard, but she had no time to mourn. She continued to work on the wall, which had to be completed before the wedding. Easter had come and gone, forgotten in the aftermath of Isabel's death. Now she had the wedding decorations to attend to. But tonight the coffeehouse was the site of a memorial to Isabel. Sunny thought it was ironic that in the course of two weeks, the four walls of the coffeehouse would honor the death of a cherished friend and celebrate the wedding of two others.

But that was precisely the point all along. The coffeehouse had become, to Sunny's deep pride, a place where people gathered, whether just to talk and hang out or to mark life's most important moments. She had accomplished what she'd set out to do and felt as if her work, and her life in Kabul, was complete.

*   *   *

It was only six o'clock, and though the memorial had been called for seven, the coffeehouse was

322

filled. Sunny sat with Candace and Petr, who'd crawled out from under a rock to attend. He brought some friends from L'Atmo as well, people Sunny hadn't seen in years. But instead of making her feel nostalgic for that life, they made her feel relieved to be out of it. Probably every journalist in Kabul was there, as well as embassy, UN, and NGO workers whom Isabel had befriended during the course of her work. She'd been tough, but she'd been respected. And by the coffeehouse friends, she'd been loved.

Candace invited women from RAWA, the Revolutionary Afghan Women's Association, to speak on behalf of women imprisoned for moral crimes, as Isabel would've wanted. And she was going to speak about Isabel's efforts to save Jamila.

The ceremony started with the recitation of the Jewish mourner's kaddish, led by Zablon Simintov, the Last Jew of Kabul.

'Yitgadal v'yitkadash sh'mei raba,' he began, reading from a small prayer book. 'Let us meditate on the meaning of love and loss, of life and death. The contemplation of death should plant within the soul elevation and peace. Above all, it should make us see things in their true light. Grief is a great teacher when it sends us back to serve and bless the living. Thus, even when they are gone, the departed are with us, moving us to live as they wished themselves to live.

'Our Isabel lived a life dedicated to helping others, to telling truths so that others' lives might be better. But life is finite. Like a candle, it burns; it glows with warmth and beauty. Then the flames fade, but we do not despair for we are more than a memory fading to darkness. With our lives we give life, and Isabel's life gave life to many. Let us continue her work and her love here on earth.

'*Oseh shalom bimromav, hu ya-aseh shalom,* may the Source of peace send peace to all who mourn. *Amen.*'

The room was silent. Candace and Sunny, Halajan and Yazmina, along with almost everyone else, wept for Isabel and for a brilliant life taken too soon.

Candace got up and introduced the women of RAWA, who'd brought literature about women behind bars, or stoned or killed for making their own decisions in personal matters. Then Candace talked about Isabel's passionate desire to create a network of safe houses for women once they were able to get them released from prison, and for those women running away from untenable circumstances.

Sunny watched her from the back of the room and felt as if a star had been born. Out of the horror of Isabel's death, which could've been meaningless, came Candace, a true force of nature, whose actions could change many lives. Sunny was so proud of her then. But it had always been within Candace. She'd just needed to find the right cause.

At the end of the evening, after people signed up to help with Candace's safe house effort, and almost everyone had left, including Halajan, Yazmina, and the baby, who'd gone to bed, as well as Bashir Hadi, who'd gone home, Sunny sat with Candace, drinking scotch that Petr had brought in honor of Isabel's memory. They clinked glasses and then said the Jewish salute of '*L'chaim!*'

They decided that Candace should spend the night, on this night when neither woman could bear

324

being alone. They'd been cut down by one, making the two of them even more critical in the enduring relationship. So Sunny tucked Candace into one of the *toshaks* that lined her walls, kissed her on both cheeks, and said, 'Good night, dear friend.'

And then Sunny was alone in the coffeehouse. With thoughts of the countless coffeehouse nights, of Jack in her arms, and the beautiful tribute paid to Isabel, she went outside, lit some kerosene lanterns, and began to paint. Only when she'd finished the final feather on her last dove did she put her brush down and look up at the night sky. It was filled with stars. Sunny felt a profound sense of powerlessness—that she, like every other being on the planet, was at the mercy of the gods.

And then Sunny, who never prayed but who felt its power during the service for Isabel, prayed to whichever God might be listening—whether Jewish or Muslim or her own Christian—for Jack's return.

CHAPTER THIRTY-EIGHT

The wedding was to take place the next night, before the onset of Ramadan. Yazmina had made her own wedding dress, and Rashif had sewn a special matrimonial vest, pants, and jacket for Ahmet. Bashir Hadi had planned the menu and ordered the ingredients. Sunny was in charge of decorations, and Halajan was supervising everyone. It was, after all, to be the wedding of her only son with her daughter-in-spirit.

Friends of the coffeehouse were invited by phone and email. Sunny had gone to the market

325

to purchase fabric with the traditional patterns in bright colors of pink and orange, blue and green, woven into bold prints of medallions and geometrics. When she told the shopkeeper what the fabric was for, he was delighted and handed her the business cards of florists, musicians, photographers, and an entire phalanx of specialists in Kabul's wedding industry. Bridegrooms were expected to pay, and not only for the wedding itself but for the several pre-wedding parties as well as a kind of reverse dowry—a payment to the bride's family. Middle-class families, who lived on seventy-five hundred dollars a year, often shelled out twenty grand or more for a wedding.

She'd gone to the gold market with Ahmet, where they both bought Yazmina gold jewelry as part of her dowry. Sunny was surprised to find herself taking on the role that would normally belong to the bride's mother, as if she were Yazmina's. She didn't mind it. In fact, it suited her.

Now Sunny stood on a ladder and nailed the edges of the fabric to the walls so it draped over them, much like her tents outside on the patio. The entire place looked like the interior of a grand palace. She hung lanterns and made sure that every detail was in place: the speakers and microphone were working, the toilets and sinks were clear, the floors were spotless, the dishes and glasses were sparkling.

Then her cellphone rang, buzzing against her chest where it hung, as usual, on a silk cord around her neck.

'Sunny, is that you?' It was a terrible connection.

'Tommy! Where are you? How's Jack? Is he—'

And then she was cut off and the connection was

gone. She tried calling him once, twice, ten times, but couldn't get through.

She clasped her phone tightly and prayed they were coming home. She prayed they finally had found Layla and that she was fine, and they were fine, and they were all coming home.

And maybe they hadn't and they weren't. But it had been three weeks, so why not now? The wedding was tomorrow. She let herself think foolishly then, to believe like a little girl, that because the day was special, other good things could happen. That the world was like that—things happen in multiples. Isabel is killed. And conversely, Ahmet and Yazmina get married, and Jack comes home with Layla.

You're a fool, she said to herself. Yeah, and so what of it? As Halajan said to her, since we're all fools, why not dance? She could believe if she wanted to. And she wanted to.

*　　　*　　　*

Halajan put twelve small candles on every little table and lined the counter and the window ledges with them as well. Candles would be everywhere, letting off the flickering light of new life. Her son was to be married tomorrow. The loyal son who stayed by her side all his young life instead of making a new life somewhere else. The traditional son, who surprised her with his open heart.

People, even those closest to you, are surprising. The strength of Yazmina, the gentle spirit of Ahmet, the persistence of Rashif, the vulnerability of Sunny. Nobody is everything that they seem. Least of all her.

She was gaining a daughter and a granddaughter tomorrow. She couldn't be happier. But she'd also learned a lesson. She, who loved her son, had taken him for granted. So as pleased and proud as she was by his forgiving nature and his ability to change, she was going to cry tomorrow like a river rushing from the Hindu Kush in springtime. Not out of sadness but out of appreciation for her wealth of love. She was going to cry and surprise everybody. She reminded herself to bring plenty of tissues to the ceremony to wipe away her tears.

And the other good part of all this? Rashif and she would have a future together. It was only a matter of time until she'd be decorating her own wedding with the light of many candles.

She pulled Rashif's most recent letter from her apron pocket and opened it. But she didn't have to. She'd memorized it from Yazmina's voice.

Dearest Beloved, my Halajan,

Your son, Ahmet, is to be married and I am honored that I'll be at his side to give him away as if he were my own son. I am so pleased he has forgiven me for telling you that one part of our conversation, for I was worried I might have lost him for good. Custom has it that I am to bestow upon him my hopes for his life with his new family. But, as usual, I find myself thinking of you.

This is what I wish for you, dear Halajan. I wish for you to continue to live as you have all these years, fearlessly, with passion, with big dreams, with caring and kindness, with your strong opinions, and with your arms outstretched. There's just one other thing I wish for you, and that is to live a life of love with me.

This is my very last letter to you.

Yours,

Rashif

She folded it carefully, put it back in her pocket, and let out a deep sigh. Funny, after all the years of letters, the one thing she'd always wished for, she'd gotten. The writer himself.

*   *   *

Bashir Hadi had already polished the coffeemaker, marinated the meat for the kabobs, and now had time to decorate the car. Everything else was under control.

The boy who delivered the bread every day was delivering it tomorrow as well. Bashir Hadi and Sunny would go early to get the sweets from the bakery. Candied almonds and figs, pistachio cookies, baklava, and honey cakes, raisins, and dates were being prepared. On the way, they'd stop on Chicken Street and pick up an entire carton of boxes of chocolates from Belgium.

As for music, he'd arranged for his wife's brother and cousin to play the harmonium and tabla, the goat-skinned drums. The classical musical duo were famous in Kabul and known to make parties last into the early morning because of their brilliant beat-dancing music, for which Afghanistan was known.

And he'd hired the best restaurant in Kabul, as Halajan had instructed, to make the food. But who knew better how to make good kabobs? He couldn't trust anyone else to pick out the perfect young sheep, cut the meat correctly, and prepare the marinade. He'd just finished, and the meat was soaking in the marinade in the refrigerator overnight so that it would be tender and delicious tomorrow.

He wiped his forehead with the back of his hand and leaned, exhausted, against the counter. His wedding hadn't been like this one at all. It had been almost twenty years ago, when he was only seventeen, his wife a mere fifteen. He'd never met her or even seen her before the wedding. She'd been chosen by his parents, and that was that. He smiled to himself with the memory of that first meeting, as he walked to the stage to assume his seat next to hers. She was completely covered in a large scarf, but when the traditional cloth was put over them so that he might see her with the use of a mirror, she pulled off the scarf and he gasped loudly. Everyone broke into applause upon hearing him. For they already knew what he learned right then: His bride was a beauty, and not merely for the distance between her eyes or because they were as black as night but because those eyes held the warmth and sparkle of Kabul's stars. They were kind, and they looked at him with love.

His was a successful marriage; others weren't always. But he knew why his had been so happy. Had he been allowed to see, to get to know, to touch his wife before the wedding, she was the woman he'd have chosen himself.

*   *   *

The last time Ahmet was at Rashif's tailor shop he'd been pointing a knife at the old man. Now he was standing in front of a mirror, trying on a brand-new suit that Rashif had made for him. He smiled at the irony of the situation, and Rashif, who stood behind him, smiled back, probably thinking the very same thing. Ahmet's pants were perfectly tailored, as were the matching vest and jacket. The white shirt was crisp but needed a slight adjustment in its sleeve length. Rashif helped him out of the jacket and vest, hanging them carefully, while Ahmet took off the shirt and handed it to Rashif. He sat at his sewing table, put on his reading glasses, and hunched over the machine.

Ahmet stood shirtless in front of the mirror, looking at himself. His shoulders were broad, his chest was taut, his arms muscled, his stomach firm. His was a body formed from years and years of holding that rifle, carting boxes for Sunny or his mother, moving equipment in the coffeehouse. But he liked what he saw. He imagined the wedding night, with Yazmina, lying alone on the new *toshak*s his mother had made them for the occasion. Yazmina's hands, right here, on his heart, which he covered now with his own. His hand on her hair, down her back, touching for the first time, her beautiful skin, all the while his eyes on those dazzling green eyes of hers . . .

'Dreaming of your wedding night?'

Ahmet jumped slightly, embarrassed. He looked at Rashif, who smiled.

Ahmet blushed and dropped his hand. 'No, I wasn't.'

'We all do,' Rashif said. 'Dream on, Ahmet. I'll have this ready for you soon.'

Did Rashif mean he dreams of Ahmet's mother? What a thought! But love, Ahmet now knew, was a powerful thing. And even his mother and Rashif deserved theirs for each other.

* * *

331

Rashif watched Ahmet with a smile, his eyes crinkling at the corners. He'd never seen the boy so nervous. Ahmet, always the serious *chokidor,* with his strict and narrow interpretations of the Koran that made him seem so young.

Look what love does, Rashif thought, as he pulled Ahmet's sleeve down to be sure it fit properly at his wrist. It turned a serious boy into a generous man. This was the real Islam, the Islam of love, not hate. Muhammad would be proud, he thought.

Of course, he didn't have to look farther than his own face to see the effects of love. He himself had never looked so good. He looked at himself in the mirror. He was short, even compared to Ahmet, his hair was now gray, what was left of it, and his shoulders a little stooped. Yet he couldn't wipe his own grin off his face without Muhammad's help, and he certainly wasn't going to ask him to do it. He'd loved Halajan for so long—forty years? more?—that to have lived long enough to be able to spend his life with her, instead of just thinking about her, made him feel young and spry and, he thought, looking at his stubborn smile, just a little silly.

At the wedding tomorrow night, which was to be mixed, men and women together but on opposite sides of the room, in honor of the modern ways that Halajan was so passionate about, he would be able to be in the same room with her for hours, to enjoy the party with her and watch her dance.

*   *   *

Candace vowed to herself to put Wakil behind bars forever. In the weeks since Isabel's death, Sunny had found Isabel's general, and Wakil had been arrested because of information Candace had provided to the authorities. But she knew all he had to do was pay some bribes and he'd be out. Then he'd find another lonely woman to take advantage of. And if he ever found out that it was Candace who betrayed him, he'd have her killed. So it was time to let go of Wakil in every way. She had to put her energies into something positive, instead of obsessing about his punishment. Let the military do that. She had so much to do in Kabul, and all the time in the world to do it.

She looked out the window of the small boardinghouse where she was renting a room. It had a lovely view of a dirt-filled, scrappy yard and a wall. What a comedown from the days at the Serena Hotel, or at Wakil's mansion, which it made her shudder to think about, or in Boston on Beacon Hill. And yet, she felt more at peace and more focused, and simply more comfortable in her own skin than she'd ever felt before. She just didn't want to spend the money she raised on a fancy place when she was going to need it for bribes, safe houses, food, and support for the women she was able to get out of prison.

But she had a wedding to go to tomorrow. She leaned her crutches against the wall, pulled off her T-shirt, and stepped carefully out of her baggy pants—the only kind that fit over her cast. She took the dress that was hanging on her door and felt the luxurious material, ran her hand across the stones, and put the fabric up to her cheek to feel its silkiness. Then she put it on and looked at herself in the mirror.

Her blond hair was perfect with the color, and her skin looked rich and smooth against it. The details of the dress were extraordinary—tucks and pleats, the collar and cuffs, the exquisite fit. Perfect in every way. So she couldn't wear her high heels. The thigh-high cast added drama of its own.

It wasn't her wedding, but the intense feeling she had that life for her was beginning anew could've convinced her that it was. But this time there was no man to lean on, to support, to help, and to forgive. This time, there was only herself.

*   *   *

Yazmina stood in her room in her wedding dress facing her mirror. She'd made it herself. She'd made Sunny's dress as well, and baby Najama's. She'd gone with Sunny to select the fabrics. But she alone had chosen them. She would wear the traditional green of Afghan brides. Sunny's dress was orange, and Najama—who was asleep on her *toshak*—was going to wear a dress of deep blue, the color of lapis.

Yazmina's dress glittered in the sunlight that streamed in through the window, and it flowed to the floor like the river near her home in the north. Thoughts of home, of her uncle and Layla, drifted through her mind the way memories do on such important occasions. If only Layla could be here for this day! If only Yazmina could know that Layla was alive and well. But if Sunny had heard from Jack, she hadn't told Yazmina. Not one word since they left weeks before.

But her Ahmet was here. And not only in her

334

heart, but present and helpful and concerned unlike any man she'd known, except perhaps for the way Jack was with Sunny. Yazmina prayed to Allah that Jack would return for her, for no one deserved more happiness than Sunny, for it was she who'd saved Yazmina, who'd given her a home, a new family, and life itself.

And now she was to be married. The dress fit perfectly, but was her heart as well suited for what was about to take place? She knew the answer. Ahmet was not just handsome and gentle. He had changed for her. He allowed himself to open the walls that bound him. He wanted to marry her and to be Najama's father. He was well aware that he would never replace Najam in her heart but that he would open another room of her heart to love.

CHAPTER THIRTY-NINE

The night before the wedding, Sunny and Halajan threw a *Takht e khina,* a traditional Henna Party. It was like an American shower, except that in Afghanistan, the female friends and family of the bride gathered not only to eat and drink but to have a henna master apply the exquisitely patterned dye on the bride's hands and arms and on her palms and the bottoms of her feet.

Sunny hired a henna expert from the same salon where she, Yazmina, and Halajan were going tomorrow to have Yazmina's hair and makeup done. Everyone—Candace, Halajan, Sunny, and Yazmina—came to Halajan's wearing their most dressy, sparkling outfits. Candace wore her cast as if it were the latest accessory, Sunny, a traditional Afghan party dress in a vivid green that made her hair and complexion radiant, Yazmina, an outfit she made herself with pants and a long fitted top that was at once traditional yet chic, and Halajan, a rhinestone-studded dress that definitely made the statement Mother of the Groom.

The henna was brought in on a tray by Ahmet, and then put in a basket decorated with flowers and candles. Ahmet then took a little of the henna and tried to put it in Yazmina's hand, but Yazmina kept her hand closed, as was the tradition. Only when Ahmet opened her hand by force could the party begin. With much cheering, the bride and groom went at it, Yazmina proving to be a strong and worthy opponent.

The women's laughter was so infectious that Yazmina laughed, too, and she released her clenched fist. Ahmet put henna onto her palm. Then, because the party was for women only, he left. The rest of the henna was then distributed among the other unmarried women.

As the henna woman worked on an intricate pattern on Yazmina's arm, Halajan once again surprised everyone and brought out the tabla, two drums covered with beads and shells on their sides, the tops made of goatskin. She began to play and sing. At first the younger women just stared at her and then applauded Halajan's musical ability. But, as the beat got a little faster, they got up and danced. The beat got even faster, Halajan's hands working as if she did this every day with the strength of a twenty-year-old. And the women spun and dipped, raised their hands over their heads, and twirled like whirling dervishes. They took

336

hands and danced in a circle, and then alone, and then together again.

They rested for a drink—the wine Candace brought for the foreigners and Coke for the Afghans—or a piece of cake. They toasted Isabel more times than they could count. They made Yazmina laugh with embarrassment when they teased her about the wedding night, and she reminded them that she'd been married before and had a daughter, so she knew very well what would happen. But then Halajan would begin again and they were up and dancing. The night flew by, with the friends laughing, dancing, and singing until the sun lightened the sky in the east.

*   *   *

Inside the Humaira Aria Salon, the walls were painted a gaudy pink and covered with posters of Bollywood stars wearing the most opulent dresses and overdone makeup. Children were running around, music was playing, and it was noisy and lively. Yazmina seemed very excited. She looked through all the photos and magazines, carefully reviewing the hairstyles and makeup until she was so confused that she allowed the girls to decide for her.

While Yazmina's and Halajan's hair was being washed, one of the salon women sat next to Sunny, who was waiting patiently, reading a magazine.

'Come, now, it's your turn,' she said. 'What would you like to do with your hair? And you could use a bit of eyebrow threading,' she said, running a finger along Sunny's brow.

'Oh, no, no,' answered Sunny. 'Not for me, thank

you. Yazmina is getting married tonight. I'm just her friend.'

'And so why not? You are going to the wedding, are you not? Come on, let's beautify you as well. Besima, come! What shall we do with this one?'

The two women were speaking Dari so quickly that Sunny had trouble understanding it all, but they were saying something about her brows and her wavy hair, and then about purple eye powder, and she thought she even heard them mention rhinestones or glitter on her forehead.

'Wait a minute,' said Sunny. 'Okay for a little makeup and maybe blow out my hair. But that's it.'

'Yes, of course, come,' said the first woman, who led her into a back room with sinks, where Yazmina and Halajan were getting up and where Sunny was, apparently, sitting down.

'This is wonderful, Miss Sunny. Thank you so much!' said Yazmina, her hair tied up in a towel on her head. 'Thank you again and again!' And she was led out.

Five hours later, Sunny looked at herself in the mirror and damn if her forehead wasn't lined with a row of rhinestones that spanned from one side to the other. Her hair was even thicker than usual because they'd added a fall that only resembled her real hair's color and texture. It was in curls down her back with tendrils at the side. Her makeup was piled on bright and thick, her cheeks pink, her eyelids purple, her mouth a deep red, and her fake eyelashes so heavy she had trouble keeping them open. She looked like a drag queen, she thought. And her brows hurt like hell from the threading, where they yanked out a few hairs at a time using a thread and a fast, jerky motion.

'Beautiful!' they all agreed.

'Miss Sunny,' Yazmina said with a little laugh, 'you certainly don't look like yourself.'

'You've become a white dove!' Halajan teased.

Sunny looked in the mirror and thought, *I wish Jack was here for this. But then I'd never be able to live this down.*

*   *   *

Prayers are sometimes answered when and how they are least expected.

When the women were ready to leave the salon, dressed in their wedding clothes, Yazmina was covered with a veil so that no one could see her face. Ahmet met them inside and led Yazmina outside, where the wedding car was waiting for them. Sunny laughed so hard, she thought she'd glued her eyelashes together. It was her car, but it had been decorated with plastic flowers and ribbons. It was so gaudy and ridiculous, it was almost beautiful. She knew it was Bashir Hadi's work, for he'd bought the ribbon when they were shopping together, saying it was for a school project for his kids.

A video photographer was filming the whole scene, including Sunny in her embarrassing makeup. But she figured, what the hell, it wasn't her day. It was Yazmina's and she'd be a willing participant.

They got into the car. Sunny sat with Yazmina and Halajan in the back. A driver was at the wheel and Ahmet climbed in front next to him. As the car made its way to the coffeehouse, the driver kept looking at her from his rearview mirror. Sunny couldn't really see him because of her heavy lids and the angle.

But then he said, 'So you're a female impersonating a female impersonator?'

It was Jack.

'I hate you!' she screamed with a smile so wide she was afraid she'd messed up her makeup.

His response, which he mouthed very clearly into the rearview mirror, was: 'I hate you, too.'

But she wouldn't let herself cry because it would ruin her makeup, and more importantly, this was Yazmina's day.

'Mr Jack,' Yazmina said, leaning forward, holding on to the front seat. 'Layla, did you find her? Is she here?'

Sunny searched for his eyes in the rearview mirror but couldn't see them. He only said in Dari, 'I'll explain everything, Yazmina, when we get back.'

Yazmina slumped back in her seat. Sunny took her hand and held it for the entire ride.

*   *   *

When they arrived at the coffeehouse they thought they'd come to a palace. A row of women on the right and a row of men on the left greeted them at the gate, as a friend of Ahmet's held the Koran over the bride's and groom's heads.

But before the wedding party could begin, the religious ceremony was to take place in Halajan's house. Sunny hung back to say to Jack, 'You're here.'

'I am,' he said.

'You clean up well,' Sunny whispered as they

340

climbed the stairs. Jack looked so handsome in his suit. 'No Layla?'

But before he had time to answer, they heard a voice behind them. 'Yazmina! Yazmina!' And there was Layla running to her sister from the coffeehouse.

Yazmina ran down the stairs. When she reached Layla, she lifted her veil and folded it back over her head. Then the two young women wrapped their arms around each other and held firmly that way for a long time, both girls crying. Yazmina put both hands on Layla's face and kissed one cheek and then the other. She had the same sun-kissed complexion, waist-long braid, and magnificent green eyes of her sister. And then she kissed her again and again. Until Layla laughed and said, 'Stop, you'll ruin your makeup.'

'But you're as tall as a tree!'

'You've been gone a long time.' She looked down. 'I thought you were dead. I've spent all these months sad because of losing you, praying you were well and that I'd find you again.'

'But what about you?'

'Uncle tried his hardest to keep me with him, but the men—'

Yazmina lifted her face by her chin. 'Never mind that. You're here with me now and you will have your life back.'

'I thought my life was over,' Layla cried. 'But Mr Jack . . . I don't know what he did, but he got me just in time.'

Sunny squeezed Jack's hand.

Yazmina let go of Layla for a minute to turn to Jack and say, 'This is the best gift I could ever receive on my wedding day. Thank you.' She bowed

341

her head, the tears coming again. 'May Allah bless you, Mr Jack. Thank you for bringing my Layla home to me.'

'Don't cry!' said Layla. 'Your kohl will run down your cheeks.'

Jack nodded to let her know he accepted her blessing. Then he turned to Sunny and was about to say something when she interrupted.

'What about Tommy?' she whispered. 'Did he come back with you?' But before he could answer, she added, 'Not that I care, it's just—'

'It's okay. He explained it all to me. And he's fine. Good thing he came along, too. He's fearless, that guy. But he won't be back. He took another job. I don't get it. If I had to choose between you and all the money in the—'

'And the adventure—'

'You *are* an adventure,' he whispered.

CHAPTER FORTY

Only the family—which in this case extended to close friends—attended the religious ceremony, the *khutba nikah*, the marriage speech and the signing of the contract. A mullah from Ahmet's mosque had come to officiate.

Rashif stood by Ahmet's side, like the father he was to become. Rashif hugged him, gave him the three cheek kisses, and whispered into his ear, 'I am as proud of you today as if you were from my own blood.'

Ahmet looked at the older man with gratitude. Rashif was giving him away today, and it was he, in his little tailor shop, who first spoke the words to Ahmet that brought him to this glorious day in the first place.

The wedding contract specified nothing about the number of goats or money or anything material, for Yazmina had no parent or guardian. Sunny acted on her behalf, and agreed that the words Ahmet was going to say to Yazmina were binding enough.

'I will love and honor you as long as you live,' Ahmet said. 'And I will love Najama as my own daughter. Both of you for all the days of life. Your concerns are my own under the light and wisdom of Muhammad.'

Yazmina answered, 'And I will love you and honor you all the days of my life, in the light and wisdom of Muhammad.' She said it two more times, as was the tradition.

Their palms were then dipped in henna and held together as a reminder of the ancient times when the bride's and groom's palms were cut so that they'd be joined in blood.

By seven, the sun had just dipped behind the hills in the west. The sky was washed with lavender and pink, and the light was soft. It was time for the wedding party to begin. The family and friends walked together down the stairs to the coffeehouse, with the new bride and groom following behind.

*　　*　　*

A car pulled up to the gate, its horn blaring. Everyone who was waiting to greet the bride and groom at the front door rushed to the gate. There, getting out of a big black SUV, was Candace.

343

'Sunny!' she yelled.

Sunny and Jack pushed their way to the front of the crowd.

'What's so important?' asked Sunny. 'We've got a party to go to—and you do, too!'

'Seriously, you've got to see this,' Candace pleaded. She opened the door of the SUV and gestured inside.

Sunny and Jack bent forward to get a look inside.

'Excellent gift,' said Jack with a big laugh.

Then Candace told them the story. Earlier that afternoon while Sunny, Yazmina, and Halajan were at the salon, Candace had called her driver and told him she needed a wedding gift. She said she wanted something traditional and was willing to pay good money for it. Could he pick it up for her on his way over to get her for the wedding? She needed the time to get ready.

He knew just what to get, he told her.

Then, around six-thirty, he picked her up at the boardinghouse.

'And there it was,' Candace said.

'And here it is,' said Jack, reaching in and pulling on a rope. Out came a big, hairy sheep, its neck wrapped in a red ribbon.

'You see?' said Candace. 'A living, breathing, hairy as an unshorn sheep, sheep! It shed on my dress. I have hair all over me.' She brushed at herself while balancing on her crutches.

'Thank you very much, Miss Candace,' said Yazmina, with a small bow of her head.

'This was our number one wish,' added Ahmet, 'to have our very own sheep. What we will do with it, I have no idea!'

The crowd wailed with laughter and applause.

344

Bashir Hadi came forward. 'I'll tie it up out back,' he said.

Then they all went inside, first the bride and groom, and then Sunny, who walked slowly with Candace. *This woman,* Sunny thought, *she is something.*

The coffeehouse had been transformed. It buzzed with excitement, color, and light: the walls of boldly patterned fabric, hundreds of candles glowing, lanterns ablaze, roses in vases on every table, on the counter, and in hand-blown glass containers that hung by metal chains from the ceiling, their scent rich in the air. Rose petals were strewn on the floor leading from the door, where the bride and groom were ushered in by two people holding the Koran over their heads. They were taken to the two large thronelike chairs at the far end of the room, where they would sit like king and queen during the course of the party.

Bashir Hadi acted as MC and organizer, telling everyone where to go and what to do. As people arrived, he had them line up to greet the bride and groom, women on the right and men on the left. He motioned for the band to start, and traditional Afghan wedding music wafted out onto the street, carried by the rhythmic beat of the tabla.

Ahmet and Yazmina were put under a large, lavishly decorated shawl, where Yazmina would take off the scarf from around her face and Ahmet would look at her fully, and they would see each other for the first time as husband and wife in a mirror that Ahmet held. Layla walked to the throne, carrying the Koran in a basket, and Ahmet took it to read a prayer to his new bride.

Under the shawl, with the diffused light casting a soft glow on her face, Yazmina looked like an angel from God, thought Ahmet. She took off her veil. Her hair was filled with glitter. Ahmet reached out a hand to touch her face but lowered it before he did. She put her hand on his.

He held the mirror, as was the tradition, and saw her face reflected in it. Then he looked straight at her. She was his wife. All his years at study and prayer, all his time spent standing at the gate, protecting his mother and the coffeehouse. Allah had heard his prayers, finally, but only when he opened his mind as wide as his heart did he listen.

'I love you,' he whispered to Yazmina.

'I love you, Ahmet,' she whispered back.

*   *   *

Once out from under the shawl, they walked around the hall as a couple, with a friend of Ahmet's holding the Koran over their heads, as if they were being blessed by Muhammad himself.

Dancing began, and though it was a mixed wedding, with men and women in one room, men and women did not touch or dance together. It was enough for Ahmet to explain to his friends from the mosque that the mixed wedding was necessary because both he and Yazmina were friends with Sunny, Candace, and Bashir Hadi. And besides, his mother wouldn't have had it any other way. But he could never begin to explain mixed dancing.

So the men held hands over their heads and the women held hands near their hips and danced without intermingling. But there was no wall separating them, no cloth or sheer curtain.

When the party was over, Candace, Rashif, Halajan, and Bashir Hadi accompanied Yazmina to her new home in Halajan's house. Bashir Hadi offered to sacrifice the sheep Candace had brought, as was the ancient custom, but everybody protested with a loud, 'No, thank you very much!'

At the doorway, Halajan handed Yazmina a hammer and a nail, which Yazmina pounded into the door's frame. It was said that the bride who did this would stay at her husband's home forever. Then, the women escorted Yazmina into her new bedroom, kissed her cheeks three times, and held her close and said good night.

Finally, Ahmet and Yazmina were alone together for the very first time.

*   *   *

As they said good night, under the moon on the coffeehouse patio, Halajan said to Rashif, 'One thing before you go.'

'What more is there on this glorious night?' Rashif said. 'The only night I will be happier is the night you and I are married ourselves.'

But Halajan put her right hand up the sleeve of her left and pulled out a folded piece of paper. She handed it to Rashif.

He looked into her eyes, disbelieving. Slowly he unfolded the paper, again and then again and once more until it was opened. He looked down at it and then up into Halajan's face, his eyes filling with tears.

She smiled. 'My writing is like a chicken's scrawl.'

'It is like a work of art,' he said, and he read aloud, pausing here and there when his throat became too full to go on.

My dearest Rashif,

Today my son, Ahmet, and Yazmina have wed. Soon it will be our turn. We won't need letters then. Funny, because now, finally, I am reading. We begin our life together laughing, as it should be.

Yours,

Halajan

He looked around, saw they were alone, and kissed her then, for the very first time, under the acacia tree.

CHAPTER FORTY-ONE

This was to be their last Wednesday night together in the coffeehouse. They closed for the afternoon and nobody was allowed to enter except Candace, Jack, and Bashir Hadi, Halajan and Rashif, Yazmina and Ahmet, Layla and baby Najama, and, of course, Poppy. Good-byes were going to be said and promises made to stay in touch forever.

Tomorrow it was Sunny's turn. She was leaving Kabul. She set a long table outside in front of her mural and planned a delicious menu, to be cooked and served by the staff of Rumi, her favorite restaurant in Kabul. She had invited everyone with a letter or email so that they'd understand that even her Afghan friends were expected as her guests, not as employees or servants, to sit at her table and eat her meal, so that she could say good-bye.

She'd given the coffeehouse to Halajan, Ahmet,

348

and Yazmina to own and run with Bashir Hadi as a partner with the family. But Yazmina was going to be very busy working as a designer and dressmaker for Rashif's shop, which would be the first unisex tailor shop in Kabul—with separate entrances and changing rooms for the men and women, of course.

So the daily job of cleaning would be Layla's, who was going to live in Ahmet's old room in Halajan's house. And Ahmet and Yazmina were taking Sunny's rooms for their family. Poppy would protect them all.

Candace was staying in Kabul to continue the work she and Isabel had started on behalf of women convicted of 'moral crimes.' She regarded the American government's warnings to evacuate Kabul as premature and unnecessary, and she vowed to stay until her work was done.

And Jack was going back to America to live near his son, who was going to college in Ann Arbor. He had an interview with an NGO there that needed a security director for its international operations. He could work right out of the Ann Arbor office. He felt strongly that the American presence in Afghanistan was only adding fuel to a volatile fire.

Sunny stood, waiting for her guests to arrive, surveying the coffeehouse that had been her home for over six years. She put her hands on her hips and breathed in deeply, her chest expanding, and then let it out. She'd accomplished much—the floors, the generators, the roof—and yet nothing at all. It was only a coffeehouse, after all. It wasn't a school, or an NGO, or an organization to help women or children. It was just a place for people to come and hang out.

The door swung open and Ahmet entered,

349

holding the door open for Yazmina, who carried the baby in a sling, and Layla following behind. Sunny greeted them and led them to the table, which sat under the trees that twinkled with the tiny lights Sunny had woven up their trunks and through their branches. Flickering candles and fresh flowers decorated the length of the table. Sunny served Cokes and tea.

Then Jack came through the door with Bashir Hadi, followed by Halajan and Rashif.

Jack first said his hellos to everyone individually, walking around the table, speaking in the native tongue of each person, shaking hands, kissing cheeks three times. Sunny watched him, her chest filling with love and pride. He looked up, their eyes met, and Sunny felt for a moment like a character in a romantic movie. *You idiot,* she said to herself, *don't get all sentimental.*

And then Candace blew in as if powered by the winds from the Hindu Kush, looking more beautiful than Sunny had ever seen her. It wasn't her clothes, or her hair, or her bangles and bling; it was that she was *happy.* Sunny knew that her work and her independence were fulfilling to her. Who knew what the future held—how long she'd want to stay, whether she'd become lonely or if she'd meet someone who loved her the way she deserved to be loved. For now, she was content.

Sunny was overcome with emotion as she sat next to Jack, among all her friends laughing and drinking, while the crew served the food they'd cooked in what was her kitchen for this one last night. She thought back to kissing Jack in the closet, laughing with Bashir Hadi, seeing Petr slink in with Isabel, hating, then loving Candace. She

350

thought of the Indian doctor's speech. Of Malalai Joya. Of bringing Yazmina here, of Ahmet falling in love with her. Of his discovering the relationship between Rashif and Halajan. Of Tommy leaving, then returning and, finally, leaving. Of knowing Jack for so many years before she realized she was in love with him.

Of the damn wall that she'd finally finished painting in time for a wedding. This place, this nothing of a coffeehouse had had miracles happen in it. It had been a home away from home for many people. Most of all for herself.

She'd changed here. Her entire life had changed here.

She raised her glass and said, 'To friends. To living a life of love and good health. To a safe Kabul forever! *Salaamat!* To peace!'

And everyone answered with shouts of *'Inshallah! Inshallah! Salaamat!'* God willing. To peace.

Her last night in Kabul. Early in the morning she would be leaving with the one thing she could never leave behind. She and Jack were headed for a new life together in Ann Arbor, Michigan, in the United States of America. She reached down under the table and took his hand; he looked at her and squeezed it. She smiled at him widely and fully, with the unself-consciousness of love.

Behind him was her mural. This she was proud of. Gray doves filled a stone courtyard under a blue sky. But every seventh one was white. Because each of her friends in Kabul was a seventh dove, the one with the spirit that rose to the heavens.

ACKNOWLEDGMENTS

I am a storyteller first, a writer only later. These stories could not have been transformed into a novel without the help of some of the world's greatest editors, first among them the amazing Leslie Schnur, who not only helped me shape my ideas into the novel they became, but who also always spoke the truth. Working with her has been the best education I could have wished for in fiction writing. Her gifts and wisdom are on every page. More than just an editor, she has become a valued friend. I also owe a great debt to the fine editors at Random House. Caitlin Alexander and Jane von Mehren made me go deeper and work harder than I ever thought possible. I owe you both so much, along with the wonderful publicity, marketing, and sales departments of Random House, who have always supported my work so wholeheartedly.

As a hairdresser and coffeehouse owner, I had the opportunity to hear everyone's stories, one of the great privileges of these occupations, and I am pleased now to present a few of my own stories to readers. While this book is fiction, many of the characters were inspired by the wonderful people I met during my expat life in Kabul, behind both the coffee bar and the beauty chair.

None of this would have been possible without my two favorite people in the world: Marly Rusoff, my wonderful agent, and her amazing, funny, and sweet husband, Michael (Mihai) Radulescu. Marly, you stood by me and held me up when I couldn't do it myself. You always believed in me and helped me understand that anything is possible. Michael, you are one of the few people I know who would travel to the end of the earth to help me, even offer to risk your life for me. This will never be forgotten.

I would like to thank my daughter-in-law, Tannaz Ghanei, who not only is a great wife to my son Zach but also a wonderful woman who gave me a window into much of the Persian culture and its beautiful lifestyle.

I will never forget the time my sweet friend and muse Karen Kinne from Holland, Michigan, helped me birth the idea of this book over a bottle of wine and a pizza. Thank you, Karen, for being a lifelong friend. May there be many more pizzas and wine in our future.

Heidi Kingstone, what can I say? You are a great inspiration for this book. I love your style, laugh, and humor. You are a beautiful woman inside and out. Thank you for being a true friend and for saving my life in Afghanistan.

Daniel Cooney and Mireille Ferrari Cooney, your friendship has meant so much to me over the years, both in Kabul and in the States. I am proud to be Auntie Debbie to your sweet Maia. Thank you for advising me on subjects that went well beyond my experience in Afghanistan. I am truly grateful that our paths crossed.

Lindy Walser, you have been such a strong advocate for the women of Afghanistan. Thank you for all your effort with Oasis Rescue. Your compassion is extraordinary, as are you.

Chris Gara, it was you who gave the Cabul Coffee House in Afghanistan its true colors. I drew upon the works of art that you painted in the courtyard and on the walls of the coffeehouse for

354

this novel. Thank you so much for your endless devotion to making the world a more beautiful place through your art.

Edie Kausch, thanks for being my first friend in California, but more important, a friend for life.

Bill Kish, thank you for the great times we had at the Cabul Coffee House. I loved your stories and the knowledge you shared with me about the Nooristan area. I gleaned so much from you then and now. I always looked forward to seeing you walk through that coffeehouse door. Thank you for always being only an email away.

To Betsy Beamon, one of the bravest expat women in Afghanistan, you are an inspiration not just to me but to the world. I am so proud to have you as my friend. Thank you for letting me bounce ideas off you while I was writing and for sharing your rich knowledge about the traditions and culture of the wonderful country of Afghanistan.

Polly, you listened to me complain, laugh, and cry. You sat on my lap as I told story after story while working on the book. You never had a negative thing to say . . . well, maybe just a little meow now and again.

Last, I feel a great debt of gratitude to so many of the fine men and women of Afghanistan, who have struggled so long and endured so much. May peace soon be yours.

HIRST.

(Z)